Acclaim for Suzanne Adair

Paper Woman
winner of the Patrick D. Smith Literature Award

"...a swashbuckling good mystery yarn!"
–The Wilmington Star-News

The Blacksmith's Daughter
"Adair holds the reader enthralled with constant action, spine-tingling suspense, and superb characterization."
–Midwest Book Review

Camp Follower
nominated for the Daphne du Maurier Award and the Sir Walter Raleigh Award

"Adair wrote another superb story."
–Armchair Interviews

Regulated for Murder
"Best of 2011," Suspense Magazine

"Driven by a desire to see justice done, no matter what guise it must take, [Michael Stoddard] is both sympathetic and interesting."
–Motherlode

Books by Suzanne Adair

Mysteries of the American Revolution
Paper Woman
The Blacksmith's Daughter
Camp Follower

Michael Stoddard American Revolution Thrillers
Regulated for Murder

Camp Follower

Suzanne Adair

A Mystery of the American Revolution

ISBN: 978-1470017804

eBook Conversion December 2009

Excerpt of *Regulated for Murder* © 2011 by Suzanne Williams

Map of Helen's Journey © 2008 by John Robertson

Cover design by Karen Lowe

Acknowledgements

I receive help from wonderful and unique people while conducting research for novels and editing my manuscripts. Here are a few who assisted me with *Camp Follower*:

Mary Buckham and her January 2007 online course on "The Hero's Journey"

The Guppies October 2005 "Chocolate Challenge"

The 33rd Light Company of Foot, especially Ernie and Linda Stewart

Carl Barnett

Lonnie Cruse

Bonnie Bajorek Daneker

Marg Baskin

Howard Burnham

Larry Cywin

Mike Everette

Jack E. Fryar, Jr.

Nolin and Neil Jones

Rhonda Lane

John Robertson

John Truelove

Dr. Alan D. Watson

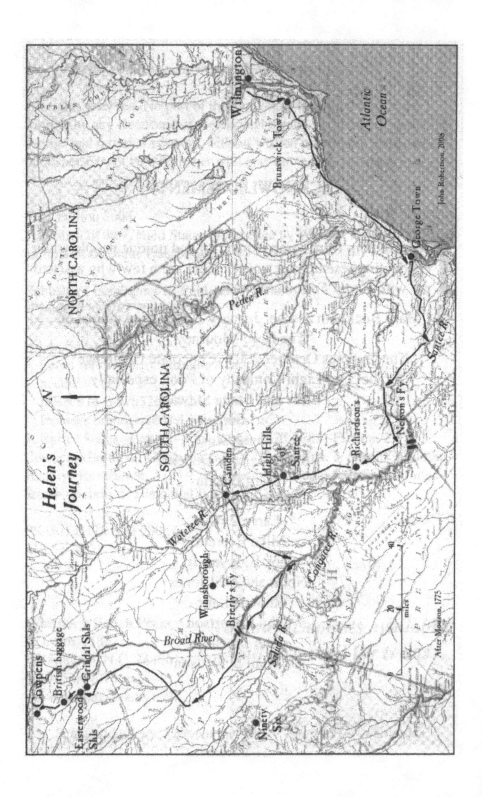

Helen's Journey

N

NORTH CAROLINA

SOUTH CAROLINA

Atlantic Ocean

Wilmington

Brunswick Town

George Town

Santee R.

Pedee R.

Nelson's Fy

Richardson's

High Hills of Santee

Camden

Wateree R.

Congaree R.

Winnsborough

Brierly's Fy

Broad River

Saluda R.

Ninety Six

Cowpens

British baggage

Easterwoods Shls

Grindal Shls

John Robertson 2016

After Mouzon 1775

0   20   40
miles

Chapter One

Wiltshire, England–1768

NELL CLENCHED HER petticoat and followed the maid down the oak stair at Redthorne Manor. Her burgundy silk gown whispered elegance. Since she'd been a little girl, she'd dreamed of wearing just such a lady's gown. A mirror in the maid's attic bedroom had implied a magical transformation with the borrowed clothing.

But apprehension agitated her pulse and yanked her attention off the luxurious brush of silk upon skin. Procured to be the wife of a merchant: Nell entertained no hopes for a better lot in life. Earlier that year, another girl her age was sold to a bordello to ease her father's debts. A second girl, indentured as a servant in London, had brought her widowed mother a healthy purse. In the village, Nell's future meant more thrashings from drunken parents and marriage to a local lout.

She murmured pleas for succor from the Great Lady and the Lord of the Wild Beasts. The maid threw a backward glance at her. Annoyance soured her appealing features. "Hurry up, you."

At the foot of the stairs, Nell stumbled and righted herself. Three centuries of nobility smirked disdain from portraits on the walls. She caught up with the maid, each breath sliced into gasps by stays laced tight to swell her bosom. Thoughts leapt and tangled in her head.

Nose in the air, the maid opened the parlor doors. "In there."

Two men in their early thirties turned from the fireplace to regard her: Lord Ratchingham's youngest son, Dick Clancy, and a shorter, rounder fellow with brown eyes and a powdered wig. Their leers flushed Nell's veins with panic, fired her instinct to flee. The maid shoved her farther inside. "Get on with you!" Then she closed the four of them into the parlor, curtsied to the men, and assumed her post on a stool near the doors, leaving Nell standing.

Tow-headed Clancy approached, and his leer sprouted teeth. "She cleaned up well, Annie. Another shilling for your efforts."

The maid caught the coin flipped her way. "Happy to be of assistance, sir."

He grasped Nell's chin and tilted her head higher. "Seventeen years old. I fancy 'em your age. Little girls are a waste of my time." He released her and trailed fingers across her left breast, and she flinched. "Now, now, don't you worry. If Silas Chiswell doesn't want you, you shan't go to waste." Her pulse beat staccato revulsion. "But I believe you'll dazzle Chiswell. Here, say good morning to Mr. Tobias Treadaway, the procurer for this arrangement."

She shrank at his approach, at the memory of a darkened tool shed, and batted back the six-year-old nightmare. After today, maybe she'd never see Treadaway again. No telling what else he procured, besides young women.

He showed no sign of recognizing her. "What's your name, wench?"

"N-Nell Grey."

Treadaway coughed. "Nell Grey? Sounds like a horse's name. That won't do. I shall change it to something striking, cultivated. Let me think. Nell is derivative of Helen, isn't it? Helen. Hmm. Rare, but I rather like it. Helen of Troy and so forth. Very well, your name is Helen from this point forward. Understand?"

They were changing her name? She glanced from Treadaway to Clancy. They expected compliance. Her confusion was immaterial. She blinked back tears and nodded.

Beneath his wig, Treadaway's dark eyebrows met in scrutiny. Clancy laughed. "Very well, she isn't quite the blonde you requested. More like honey, but still lovely, what hey? I like honey-colored hair on a pretty woman."

"I've seen her somewhere before."

Apprehension curdled in her gut. Treadaway recognized her.

"Of course you've seen her before, covered with a commoner's filth and hardly worth notice. This is Chiswell's first look at her, though. He'll find her irresistible. Smile, Helen." When her lips were slow to comply, Clancy gripped her upper arm, hauled her toward him, and snarled. "Smile, damn you. Don't ruin this by sulking."

Nell — no, she was *Helen* now — grunted in pain. Clancy's thumb dug into a weal her mother had made with a leather belt. She forced a smile to her lips. More tears stung her eyes. In the world of procurement, a wife wasn't so very different from a servant. Or a prostitute.

"Look there, Treadaway. She has all her teeth, and they're white. What do you say?"

The procurer walked away to pace near the front window. "She carries herself like a commoner."

Clancy shoved her away and whirled on Treadaway. "I gave those drunken parents of hers six pounds to pay off their debts, and I'll be compensated for it, by god. Show her to Chiswell. Let him make up his own mind. If you back out on me, I shall see to it that you never again use Redthorne for your client meetings while my father is away." Harsh laughter erupted from him. "Besides, after Chiswell finds out how my stepmother educated her, he'll buy, oh, yes. A common wench who reads, writes, and ciphers! You want polish, I give you polish!"

Carriage axles squeaked from the direction of the front driveway. Treadaway ceased pacing and lifted the heavy velvet drape aside a few inches to peer out the window. Then he allowed the drape to fall back into place. "My client has arrived."

Clancy clapped his hands once. "Excellent."

Treadaway massaged his temple. "You don't see the enormity of the problem. Chiswell's mother, Agatha, expects the daughter of a merchant when he arrives with his bride in Boston."

Boston, in the North American colonies? Her lot couldn't be better in America. The land was full of savages who scalped women and skewered babies on branches.

Clancy sneered. "I'd like to see *you* find a merchant's nubile get on such short notice."

"You want a commission, Clancy? Sit beside your friend the maid and follow her example of silence. I shall manage this muddle, although I doubt it's salvageable." He strode over, grasped Helen's forearm, and towed her to a plush chair in a shadowy corner. "Sit. Straighten your back. Fold hands in your lap. That's it. Keep your chin up. Good. You can be trained."

A wife was expected to be trained, obedient. Still, desolation bruised her soul, just as each inhalation aggravated a bruise on her ribs, delivered two days before during her father's tirade over how long she took to scrub their cottage steps. She made her breaths shallow to compensate and remembered how her parents bartered her price up with a lie that a small landowner like them planned to wed her. Then they'd lunged for the money like feral dogs after a pig.

Foisted off on a Colonial merchant to a land of bloodthirsty Indians, famine, and plague. Anxiety ground at her gut.

The procurer assessed her. "I know I've seen you around somewhere, girl." The leer returned to his mouth, and his fingers tickled her chin.

She jerked her face from his touch. *Girl.* The tool shed. Bound wrists. Nauseated, she slammed the memories away with greater resolve. Forget. Must forget.

Treadaway strutted for the parlor doors and conversed with the butler in the doorway. Then he shook hands with two well-dressed men and led them into the parlor. Faux-joviality creased his face. "Brandy for either of you gentlemen?"

"I'll take a brandy," said one. From halfway across the room, he stank of spirits, and Helen implored the gods that he not be her future husband. His bloodshot brown eyes, sallow complexion, and disheveled graying hair — it all repulsed her. She'd seen plenty of the pain that drove people to drink that way. Being drunk gave them an excuse to visit their agony on others.

She glanced at the second fellow. No gray streaked his brown hair, caught back neatly with a silk ribbon. Except for crows' feet at his eyes, his handsome face was devoid of wrinkles. He might have been any age between thirty and sixty. Serenity suffused him, absent from the demeanors of the other men in the room. Absent from most men she knew, in fact.

She bit her lip. Which man was Chiswell? Who was the other fellow?

Treadaway handed a half-glass of brandy to the man who'd requested it. Then he aimed a polite smile at the drunk's companion. "A brandy for you, too, Mr. Quill?"

Quill. Then the sot must be her future husband, Chiswell. Helen's spirits plummeted further.

"Not this morning, thank you." Quill inclined his head to Treadaway.

She regarded the first man, who belted down brandy as if it were tea and deposited the glass beside a crystal decanter. He looked to be in his early forties but was probably younger. Excessive consumption of spirits aged people. More revulsion rolled through her.

Treadaway continued to address Quill. "Well, then, why don't you make yourself comfortable in the library while Mr. Chiswell and I transact our business here?"

Chiswell cut the air with his hand. "Jonathan stays. He'd be bored in Ratchingham's library. His family imported silk and porcelain from China, and he's traveled the world collecting books. South America, Africa, Asia."

Dazed, Helen studied Quill again. Jonathan Quill. Who was this man to travel the world collecting books? Then she spied the clench of frustration in Treadaway's jaw and grasped reality. The procurer might have played up her physical attributes to pass her off on Chiswell, but Quill, with the wisdom of the world, wouldn't be duped. The deal would collapse. Worse than marrying a drunk, she'd become the sport of Treadaway and Clancy. Dread danced specks through her vision.

"All right, where is she, Treadaway? I rose an hour early this morning to squeeze in this meeting. I'm a busy man. I won't be kept waiting."

Treadaway gestured to her. "I present Miss Helen Grey. Miss Grey, Mr. Silas Chiswell."

She gawped at the fine Persian carpet beneath her slippers, appalled by heat and brutishness in Chiswell's eyes. A chuckle like a bear's growl issued from him. "Bloody hell, you found a docile one. Is that why you thrust her back in the shadows, like a harem wife?"

Treadaway's obsequious tone brandished renewed enthusiasm. "I complied with your wishes. She's the eldest daughter of a merchant who died earlier this year, leaving the widow in debt. If she's what you fancy, she can easily become *your* harem wife."

"Heh heh heh. Harem wife. She literate?"

Treadaway placed an opened Bible in her lap and pointed out a verse. "Read it."

Her hands shaky, Helen cleared her throat. "'Who can find a virtuous woman? For her price is far above rubies.'" Odd. She'd read that very passage years ago in the parlor, for the vicar.

Chiswell strode forward, snatched the book away, flipped to another section, and handed it back to her. "Miss Grey, read that passage so I know Treadaway hasn't made you memorize verses to simulate reading."

A reasonable request, considering the reputation of men like Treadaway. But Chiswell, perhaps aroused by the idea of bedding his own harem wife, had selected the sensuous Song of Solomon. Helen's ears burned with modesty as she read. "'O my dove, that art in the clefts of the rock, in the secret places of the stairs, let me see thy countenance, let me hear thy voice; for sweet is thy voice, and thy countenance is comely.'"

Over Chiswell's shoulder, Quill watched her. His blue eyes resonated with neither heat nor brutishness. Seldom did she encounter a man not ruled by lust. Some of her jitters calmed. What would it be like to travel the world, as he had done? Her hands stopped shaking.

Treadaway yanked the Bible away. "Yes, yes, arise my love. Song of Solomon segues nicely into a discussion of her physical attributes. Stand, Miss Grey, and turn slowly for Mr. Chiswell."

Humiliation flushed Helen's face. Was this what captured Africans felt like, forced to strut upon the auction block? Chiswell's leer cavorted from her bosom to her slender waist. The only difference between him and the local louts was that Chiswell had money.

But Quill's mouth tightened, and she realized that he'd noticed the way she clambered to her feet like a commoner. In haste, she straightened her back, as Treadaway had instructed.

The procurer beamed. "Smile, Miss Grey. She has excellent teeth, does she not?" Chiswell licked his lips. "And teeth being an indicator of overall health, I venture to say that if you apply yourself to task, within a year, you'll have that heir your mother has been nagging you about."

Without taking his eyes off her, Quill said, "The plantation, Silas."

"Eh? Oh, yes. Treadaway, I told you I need a wife who can help manage the books for my turpentine plantation in North Carolina. Computational skills."

Treadaway cocked an eyebrow at her. "Miss Grey, what is seventeen multiplied by six?"

She pondered a second. "One hundred and two."

Chiswell grinned. Quill pursed his lips and said, "Twenty-three multiplied by fourteen."

She pondered several seconds longer. "Three hundred twenty-two."

Chiswell's grin enlarged. "God's foot, she's docile, comely, *and* intelligent."

Quill said to Treadaway, "Allow Mr. Chiswell and me five minutes complete privacy with the young woman."

"Of course." Treadaway signaled the maid and Clancy, and the three left the parlor.

Chiswell slapped his knee. "By god, this timid creature is perfect, Jonathan. I shall purchase her and marry her, and Mother will finally cease badgering me."

Alarmed that she'd slumped without realizing it, Helen straightened her back. Quill marked her posture correction again. "Miss Grey, what is the capitol of China?"

World geography hadn't been a topic the vicar taught her. She stared at Quill. He intended to prove her a fraud. If Chiswell failed to purchase her — her heart stammered several beats. Would life with the merchant be an improvement over her current situation? Perhaps she could dance around facts. "I-I'm nervous and cannot seem to recall, sir. Bombay?"

"Bombay is in India. François-André Danican Philidor is a French composer of opera and comedies. For what other discipline is he famed?"

An opera composer? The only tunes she knew were folk ballads. It dawned on her that there was much more to education that reading, writing, and ciphering. Exploring the breadth of the world, for example. What *was* it like to travel?

Quill cleared his throat. He expected an answer. Her palms sweated. "Um, he studies the stars?"

"Chess, Miss Grey. Philidor is a chess master."

With ease, he'd exposed her lack. Despair clogged her soul.

"Bah, Jonathan, only a chess devotee like you would give a damn about Philidor."

"Miss Grey isn't who Treadaway claims she is, the daughter of a merchant."

"So what? She's not a whore, either."

"No, but basic education cannot hide common birth. Your mother will never accept her."

"Damnation, I'll have no part of marrying a Boston merchant's daughter as strong-willed as Mother. This wench will do as she's told, and I'll go on living my life the way I want to live it."

"Marry a commoner like her, and Agatha Chiswell cuts you from her will. You know that."

The two men squared off in what looked like a well-worn argumentative rut. Ignored, Helen fought with tears and whispered invocations to her gods.

The merchant's expression grew sly. "I've a thought. Let's transform Miss Grey into a gentlewoman."

"What nonsense are you babbling?"

"Use the Atlantic crossing to teach her how to walk and talk. Shakespeare, Haydn, Plato. Unload what's in that brain of yours. I'll pay you one hundred pounds if my mother accepts her."

One hundred pounds? Clancy had doled out a mere six pounds, yet Chiswell was willing to pay many times more for her, educated. Did the worth of a person so increase with learning? And what did money mean to these men?

Quill drew back in indignation. "By god, I don't need your money."

Another grin consumed Chiswell's face. "I know that. But you do need challenges." He pivoted Quill to face her. "And there's one colossal challenge for you."

Suspicion eased from Quill's face. "What do you know about America, my dear?"

She shivered. "Indians and Frenchman with tomahawks. Yellow jack and malaria. Tropical storms that destroy towns. Not enough food or clothing."

Chiswell snorted. "Where the devil did she hear that balderdash?"

"Probably from Wiltshire's soldiers who returned from the French War." Quill sighed. "You poor child. You must be frightened out of your wits."

Helen bit her trembling lower lip. If she wept before the men, they might think her silly.

Quill's tone mellowed. "Miss Grey, America is what you describe, but new settlers arrive there every day. Why? Opportunities can be found in America where they've vanished elsewhere."

In curiosity, her gaze reached for his. Years earlier, at a Beltane feast, a village elder had told her that everyone she met was her teacher. What would Quill teach her to increase her worth more than sixteen times? Until that moment, she hadn't much considered the procurement as an opportunity.

Quill smiled gently. "Your mother isn't really widowed, is she, my dear?"

Instinct prompted her to trust him. "No, sir."

He nodded, as if he'd seen through Treadaway's lie. "Do you want to leave England?"

Why, no one had ever asked what she wanted! She stared at him, stunned.

"Yes. Yes, sir."

His expression grown pensive, Quill crossed his arms. "Silas, you realize that many commoners practice the ancient faith, older than what those Druids parade about Avebury and Stonehenge."

Chiswell's lip curled. "Bah, pagan rubbish. We'll end that with a proper wedding in the Anglican Church. She'll be an Anglican wife." He glared at her. "You understand me?"

They were replacing her gods? They'd already replaced her name. Was that the price she paid for increasing her worth, for *opportunity*? Anxiety bounded into her confusion, and she trembled again. If she didn't comply with his terms, Chiswell would terminate the transaction. "Yes, sir."

"Splendid. Ratchingham's brandy is excellent. Time for another. Where's my host?" The merchant headed for the doors.

Quill studied her, the electric blue of his eyes keen, as if he'd detected something in her that everyone else had missed. Terrified of what was to come, Helen Grey, soon to be Helen Chiswell, an Anglican wife, turned away. When she glimpsed her reflection in a vase on a nearby table, she didn't recognize herself at all.

Chapter Two

Wilmington, North Carolina–1780

AT MARKET AND Fifth streets, the fishy fog off the Cape Fear River thinned to divulge Helen's destination: the brick manor home of publisher Phineas Badley. She shivered at the chilly caress of November mist beneath her wool cloak and petticoat, admitted herself past the iron gate, and strode up the walkway. Whatever "plum" Badley planned for her, she had to accept the assignment.

The creditor who held her mortgage had sold it. Transfer costs would be dumped on her unless she employed an attorney, and she couldn't afford one. Uneasiness gnawed her stomach. She squashed it down and raised her chin.

No sooner did she gain the front porch than the bewigged butler, Charles, whisked the door open and gestured her into a paneled foyer. "Good to see you again, madam."

She knew he meant it. "Thank you." Warmth enveloped her when he shut out the fog, and her mood lifted a bit at the scents of orange and cinnamon. But closer scrutiny revealed fatigue beneath Charles's eyes and sunken cheeks. He'd never looked haggard in *her* employ. If only she hadn't had to let him go. Guilt and concern nudged her. From her first day in Wilmington, Charles had been considerate of her. "How are you?" He assisted her out of her cloak, his face trapped in shadow. Mystified, she lowered her voice. "Is all well?"

He opened his mouth to speak but paused when a maidservant entered the foyer to dust the dark, walnut banister. "Not to worry, madam. Mr. Badley will join you presently in the parlor."

Without another word, he led her upstairs and closed her within the parlor, alone. Ticking from the clock on the mantle and sighs from wood burning in the fireplace cozied the room. She ambled past two overstuffed couches and a table. Pensive, she gazed out the window at an afternoon sky the hue of pewter.

Ever since the rebels chased Governor Martin from North Carolina five years before, Badley had steered his magazine's content to the bland middle ground. Otherwise, his Loyalist press would have been shut down. Perhaps he'd have her cover Mrs. Page's supper with the vicar. The old lady had a penchant for entertaining town peacocks she knew. Or the publisher might desire an article on Mr. Flynn's portrait sitting. The visiting artist had painted prominent area residents including her neighbor, William Hooper, and others from the Congressional Committee of Safety. Committee of Safety. Bah.

A bequest from Helen's late husband's estate subsidized production of *Badley's Review*, so the publisher possessed funds to dispatch his journalists after sensational leads. She wrote about tea parties and edited the men's stories. Women didn't cover events that convulsed the colonies: riots, battles, protests. Meetings of those rebel popinjays on the Committee of Safety.

She turned her back on the window and yawned. A self-inspection in the mirror above the fireplace sent her rearranging her lace tucker to ensure modesty. She could do nothing about the smudges of sleeplessness beneath her eyes, but at least the walk had raised healthy color in her cheeks and a sapphire sparkle to her eyes.

Badley's tread thudded the stairs. He flung open the door, face corpulent, wig freshly powdered. "Mrs. Chiswell, good of you to take tea with us. Do sit down." He waved her to the couch nearest the fire, lace on his cuffs aflutter, and waddled for the opposite couch.

Us? Who else was invited to tea? Helen eyed the open door and lowered herself to the cushion, her back straight.

The other couch groaned when Badley deposited his rump on it, and she caught a whiff of herbal poultice from his gouty knee. He tugged at his embroidered silk waistcoat to relieve stress his girth imposed on the buttons. "I've a splendid opportunity to offer you. Since the gentleman who'll join us shortly has already been briefed, I shall apprise you while we start on tea."

Maidservants entered the parlor with a steaming kettle and china tea service for three. After hot water was poured into the teapot, the maids closed the door behind their exit. Badley, humming "The Death of General Wolfe," spooned real tea leaves — not a colonial concoction of tree bark and weeds — from a canister into the pot, stirred the infusion with a silver spoon, and draped a little quilt over the pot to keep it warm. A sealed note lay atop a cloth on the tray, but he made no move to retrieve it. "I've noticed how wasted your talent is, writing about Wilmington society."

She sat still and said nothing. Disgust coiled her neck. Badley's circuitous approach implied her new assignment was sheer ennui.

He drummed plump fingers on his thighs, covered in buff-colored breeches of fine wool. "My magazine has attracted the attention of an editor at the *London Chronicle*."

Ah, the gentleman invited to tea must be the editor. Perhaps he traveled with a wealthy mother who required a widowed companion in Wilmington. While keeping the dowager company, Helen would interview her and pen the family history. There'd be money in it for her. Not likely enough money for an attorney, but the publisher's assignments remained her primary source of income.

Unless, of course, she encouraged the lust of several merchants. She allowed herself a second or two to imagine sloppy kisses, flabby buttocks, and rank breath — just long enough for stomach acid to sour the back of her throat. Then she dismissed the thought.

"Your skills convey professionalism upon the *Review*. I've made certain the editor knows it."

She studied him, her doubts plowing a chasm of mistrust. Generosity was out of character for Badley. A hefty purse must await him for his effort. Or perhaps an elixir more alluring than money.

He blotted his forehead with a perfumed handkerchief, the diamond in his ring prisming light. "Dreadful business, Major André's execution last month. And Major Ferguson's slaughter at King's Mountain — they say he had two-dozen balls in him before he dropped. Then those rebel barbarians desecrated his body. We must seek out stories that yield a positive picture of His Majesty's efficacy at managing the rabble here.

"London is enamored of that dashing colonel of the Legion, Banastre Tarleton. Young fellow, all of twenty-six." Badley peeked at the tea. "The Earl Cornwallis's favorite. He showed Buford for a fool in the Waxhaws and ran Sumter off half-naked after Camden, what hey?"

Get to the point, Badley, she thought, weary, tense. More to the point, where would she find enough money for an attorney?

"Londoners want a candid portrait of the Lion of the Waxhaws. How do his men express loyalty to him and convivial spirits after a victory? With what terror do rebels cower at the approach of the Green Dragoons?" Badley winked at her. "Do the ladies swoon over him?"

Gods, how she wished she'd never taken that devil Prescott's advice about mortgaging her house. The mortgage had seemed a reasonable idea back then. She'd run out of slaves, servants, property, employees and investments to sell or divest while paying off Silas's gambling debts.

Badley winked again. "London wants to know what it's like to ride with the Legion. So the editor is experimenting with a new format, a features magazine. I've been asked to send a journalist out with the Legion for a few weeks."

Without a doubt, one of the men had a gripping assignment awaiting him. Then she would have editing dilemmas for weeks. No wonder Badley wooed her on the idea first over tea. But surely he was proceeding in a naïve manner. "Come now. The colonel won't give Warwick, Sellers, or Ricks a *candid* view of his unit. Your man will get what Tarleton wants him to see — Odysseus, Alexander — if he isn't accidentally killed."

On the verge of response, Badley plucked the note off the tray and broke the seal. Helen watched his mouth tighten with disappointment as he scanned the scrawled message. "Bother." He tossed the note into the fire, oriented his attention on her, and simpered. "Why let Tarleton know he has a reporter in his midst?"

"Faugh. Don't insult his intelligence by attempting to pass your man off as a recruit, sir. Warwick would soil his breeches and weep for his mother at a hint of battle. Sellers would pilfer the rum —"

"I'm delighted to hear you concur with my assessment of the lads." He stirred the tea and poured some through a strainer into a cup. The aroma beckoned to her, and the dark amber color seduced. "Few are better suited for the assignment than *you*."

She blinked at him. "Excuse me, sir, I misunderstood —"

"*You* for the assignment. You heard correctly. *You*." He extended the cup to her and pushed the creamer and sugar bowl toward her.

Astonishment clobbered her. Then she noticed his coy smile. A wave, half relief and half-disappointment, wiped out the shock. She accepted the tea, poured in enough milk to lighten the amber, and sipped. "You've quite a sense of humor, sir."

"I'm not jesting, madam."

She drank more tea. "Mmm, divine. Do you fancy to pass me off as a re-cruit, then? Or perhaps a slattern?"

His smile enlarged. "The sister of an officer. A gentlewoman." He poured tea for himself.

As she watched him hack the head of a cone of sugar into the teacup and top off the cup with milk, it occurred to her that he might *not* be jesting. Her stomach flip-flopped, mostly with thrill. But exactly what sort of assignment did Badley offer her? "A gentlewoman accompanying a kinsman officer on campaign cannot project anything less than aristocracy."

He slurped tea. "You'll need your own tent and food supply, at least two men to set up camp and transport your property, an appropriate wardrobe, a woman to help you dress — your Enid Jones would be an excellent choice for that."

Heavens, Badley *was* offering her the assignment — a *man's* challenge. She mustn't let him know how thrill peppered her spine. "Tarleton has no time for such fluff." She set down her cup. "The key to his success has always been the mobility of the Green Horse."

"Quite. But the baggage with the 'fluff' eventually catches up. You'll land an adequate enough story traveling with the sutlers, artisans, servants, wives and brats — and yes, the slatterns. And the best part is that the *Chronicle* is funding the experiment."

"*All* of it?"

"Yes, plus a salary for you amounting to twice your daily rate."

Her stare narrowed. The scheme had the appeal of a perfumed, jeweled courtier whose teeth proved rotten. Badley had something afoot, but for the time, buoyed by excitement, she slammed the door on her instincts. Good gods, she'd landed a goliath of a *feature*. "What of this officer? Even if he agrees to pass me off as his sister and deceive Tarleton, you cannot expect a provincial to bear enough cultural resemblance to me and be credible as my brother."

The eerie humor on Badley's face chilled her worse than any fog.

His plump forefinger stroked the third teacup. "Alas, he was unable to at-tend today. King's business, his note said.

"The gentleman is a regular in the Seventeenth Light Dragoons. He helps train Legion recruits at combat and horsemanship. In his mid-twenties, aris-tocracy, perfect age to pass for your little brother." Badley leaned forward in conspiracy. "He's from Wiltshire."

Wiltshire. Redthorne. The procurement. Silas Chiswell. Her pulse hopped in chaos, just as it had done more than twelve years past, the morning she'd been sold — as if she'd been transported back to that parlor. Flustered to find her professional composure wobbly in Badley's company, she made for the window and stared out at his garden.

In his mid-twenties, aristocracy, perfect age to pass for your little brother. Now, there was an intriguing puzzle. Lord Ratchingham's youngest son was in his forties, too old to portray her little brother. Did she *know* this fellow from twelve years ago, before he was an officer, before he was even a man? She faced the publisher, her expression stone. "What is the officer's name?"

He'd risen also, gloating. "Great Zeus, I've piqued your interest in the assignment! I shall invite him to tea on the morrow at three. Return then and meet the fellow. Agreed?"

A fabulous feature she'd landed, yes, but every nerve in her body warned of murkiness in Badley's motivation. Long ago, she'd made it a personal rule to neither accept nor reject an offer from him up front. It prevented his knowing exactly how to manipulate her.

But how he'd fired her curiosity. With Wilmington under control of the rebels, by necessity, the redcoat would disguise himself as a civilian — just as the unfortunate Major John André had done before his capture by Continentals. Either the officer from Wiltshire was quite courageous to duplicate the deceit that had earned André execution, or he was quite mad. Either way, she must meet him.

She pursed her lips at Badley. "Agreed."

Chapter Three

IN THE FOYER, Badley wished her a good day and toddled for his study. Charles bustled forward with Helen's cloak. "Madam, I —" He cut himself off, and Helen realized that Badley stood near the door of his study examining a portrait of some corpulent, lace-endowed ancestor. Charles coughed. "Er — your permission to call upon Mrs. Jones on the morrow, the eighteenth, at one o'clock in the afternoon."

Her preoccupation over the new assignment rifted. Charles Landon knew he didn't need her permission to call upon Enid. He had something to say to Helen, and he didn't want Badley's household privy to it.

What troubled Charles that he couldn't speak of it before Badley? His sunken eyes shot concern through her heart. She cared about him the way she'd have cared about an uncle, if she'd ever known one who didn't stink of rum or beat her. "Enid will be delighted."

Relief sagged his shoulders. He bowed and opened the front door for her. A second later, the publisher entered the study and grunted at someone waiting. "You're early, old boy." Before he shut himself inside, Helen glimpsed his visitor and gritted her teeth. She wasted no time letting the dreary afternoon reclaim her.

No mistaking Badley's pear-shaped guest: Maximus Prescott, her former attorney, the devil himself. As long as she worked for Badley, she'd encounter Prescott. For nine years, she'd suspected the two had swindled Silas's money from her, leaving her near destitution with the meager dower she'd scraped from the estate settlement. Alas, the legal system offered scant justice to poor widows. And she'd no energy to fritter away on what she couldn't change.

She proceeded home on Market Street, the pulse of Wilmington all around her — laughter from a tavern, the drill of militia, a barrel's rumble on a wharf. A wagon of spars and yards creaked past, its driver a huddle of greatcoat in the mist, the fragrance of new-hewn lumber trailing. Chickens and goats scattered

before the wagon, and a scrawny cur chased it, his bark swallowed in fog.
Mist clung to her eyelashes and drifted a film onto her cheeks. She ignored
the weather, her thoughts again shuffling. What was she to make of the assignment dangled before her nose? How easily she could be killed in the backcountry following Tarleton's dragoons. The challenges, the dangers. Dared
she venture into a domain almost exclusively masculine? What different kind
of story would a woman's voice tell of war?

But her instincts vibrated at the memory of Badley's smug expression. The
officer from Wiltshire was in on the dangerous ploy with him. Why wasn't he
a guest in the publisher's home?

Near her brick house on Second Street, the fishy odor of the fog blended
with the bitter and sweet smells of turpentine, tar, pitch, and lumber. Enid
had a fire built in the parlor and took Helen's cloak. "Some wine for you by the
fire, mistress. You mustn't catch cold."

Helen headed for her chair and a mug of mulled, cheap wine made palat-
able with spices. Enid tucked a quilt over her lap and presented her with two
letters. The commissioned embroidery piece due on the morrow — a petticoat
hem — hung on a stand nearby, but she deferred embroidering until she'd read
the day's post.

Afterwards, she slapped the letters on the table and swigged wine, irked. No
employment was available with the publishers she'd queried in Williamsburg
and Charles Town. She'd received a similar response days earlier, from a
publisher in Savannah. If she wanted to sever the degenerate umbilicus that
bound her to Badley, she must query publishers in Boston, Philadelphia, and
New York for employment.

Of course, with a feature about the Legion to her credit, she'd have far more
to bargain with.

"Everything all right, mistress?" From the parlor doorway, Enid's Welsh
accent was audible, harbinger that she'd picked up on the tone of Helen's
thoughts.

Enid Jones had stayed by her side when she sold the plantation and later,
the carriage, horses, furniture, and most of her jewelry and wardrobe, then terminated employment of the townhouse servants, including Charles. No point
in troubling Enid. Grafting a smile of confidence to her lips, Helen swiveled to
one asset she'd refused to give up. "Quite."

Enid's plain features brightened. "Good." She straightened her apron.
"How is Charles?"

What the devil was bothering Charles? Helen maintained her smile despite
her unease. "He asked to call upon you on the morrow at one."

"Well, now. Right good of him." The Welshwoman glanced away to hide
the gleam in her dark eyes. Her accent had subsided. She and Charles, both
in their late forties, had lost spouses to malaria. In October, they'd strolled the
autumn fair arm-in-arm. "I shall heat soup for supper, then." Her footsteps
faded toward the rear of the house.

Helen took up needle and embroidery thread to her client's petticoat hem
but paused to regard the room: a chair, couch, table, and mantle clock. All
other furnishing had been sold. Much of the empty space was occupied by her
watercolors and sketches of Wiltshire and the Salisbury Plain. The parlor had
begun to resemble an artist's gallery. She'd considered hosting a show, selling

her artwork, and making money off the rebels, but few of them had more than two pence to rub together.

At dusk, the embroidery finished, she and Enid drew drapes throughout the house, secured the doors, and ate pork and barley soup in the dining room. Upstairs, heat from the first floor warmed the bedrooms. Enid assisted Helen out of her gown, petticoat, and stays and into an old wool shift. While the Welshwoman banked the fire in the parlor below and made a final round of doors and windows downstairs, Helen washed her face and hands and cleaned her teeth. She crawled into the bed she'd seldom shared with her husband, read Homer a few minutes, and blew out the candle.

She'd been asleep but a few hours when Enid awakened her, a hand on her shoulder. "Sorry to startle you, mistress." The lines on the housekeeper's face softened. "He's here, waiting in the parlor. We chatted a bit while he had some bread, cheese, and wine, and —"

"*Who* is here?" Helen struggled up on her elbows, still negotiating the sleep-to-wake transition.

Enid's expression grew tender. "That dear, sweet Mr. St. James."

Helen's heart skipped a beat. Then she rolled out of bed, shoved her feet in slippers, and draped a shawl about her shoulders. On her way to the stairs, she took Enid's candle.

Upon her entrance to the parlor, tall, dark-haired David St. James straightened from inspecting a watercolor and bowed. In the seconds that she set down her candle and crossed the floor to him, she noticed that he'd grown hollow-eyed and lankier in the six months since his last visit. But it didn't stop her from embracing him.

The warmth of his hands wandered from the shawl over the small of her back to her shoulders, and he separated from her just far enough to grasp her hands in his and kiss them as he always did when he first greeted her. Along the way, his fingers roamed her wrists, assessing in the silence and semi-darkness her own loss of weight. When he took her face in his hands and kissed her lips, the half-year separation diminished.

A few minutes later, Enid buzzed in with wine and a steaming bowl of soup. "Is that for me?" David disentangled from cuddling Helen on the couch. "Enid, you're too kind, but I cannot stay."

"Pish-posh." She set the bowl on the table and spread a cloth napkin in his lap. "From the looks of it, you seldom slow down enough to enjoy a decent meal."

"Oww!" He rubbed his bicep playfully where she pinched it.

"I hope you've the sense not to be living on brandy at them card tables. There's your spoon. Eat." The housekeeper bustled out.

His familiar jaunty smile in place, he eyed Helen, jest parting his lips. She imitated Enid's scowl. "No talk. Eat!"

He saluted and obeyed, and she studied him, puzzled by his worn appearance. As always, he was well-groomed and clothed — fine wool for his mauve coat and matching waistcoat, silk for his shirt and stockings, a silk ribbon pulling back his long hair. His cocked hat, held in her hands, was so new that the label was legible on the inside — a prestigious hatter in New York. Whatever trials David endured hadn't affected his purse, or his appetite.

Still, he looked like a hunted man. Was someone after him? An irate debtor from the card tables who didn't understand that David loved reading the cards far more than winning the money? Or perhaps some wealthy widow's jealous beau?

The spoon clacked in the empty bowl. He wiped his mouth, swigged wine and winced at the poor quality — David the wine connoisseur — tossed the napkin beside the bowl on the table, and called his thanks to Enid over his shoulder. Gaiety departed, and his voice lowered. "For my safety, I'd decided earlier to pass through Wilmington without visiting you."

"Your *safety*?" Why did David believe his safety was compromised?

He nodded. "But I spotted Charles at White's Tavern, drunk."

Memory whispered the butler's need to speak with her in private. Premonition zinged through her. "That doesn't sound like him."

"Not at all. He waved me over. I ordered us a round. He muttered, 'You realize they'll kill Madam if they find it.' Before I could question him, the front door opened, and in trotted my family's hellhound. I exited through the back door, hoping to gods he didn't see me."

David pushed up from the couch and paced. "'They'll kill Madam if they find it.' Any idea what Charles was talking about?"

For my safety, David said. His agitation, so haunting and uncharacteristic, spilled onto her and gurgled around in her stomach. She shook her head. "I think he plans to talk to me on the morrow."

"Is someone trying to kill you for money?"

She swallowed. "What a futile gesture that would be."

"Sweetheart, this feeling has niggled me for years, but tonight I cannot shake it." He pinned her gaze with his. "You're in danger here." His expression tightened. "Prescott is up to something."

The old wound in her heart ached. She clenched his hat, relaxed her fingers. "Of all people, he should know there's no more money."

"Damned right, after wringing your estate of every last penny and throwing you the husk. And the worm bloody well better keep his hands off you." David paced more and brooded. "I've never seen Charles drunk. I had to make certain you were well."

He hadn't yet explained why he felt Wilmington was dangerous for him. What — who — was "my family's hellhound?" Knowing David, he might not tell her straight out. She brushed lint from his hat and kept her tone light. "Where have you wandered since May?"

"Havana."

"Cuba?" She stifled a laugh and sobered. His expression told her he wasn't joking.

"My sister and I chased Father there, hoping to talk sense into him. He'd operated a spy ring out of our family home in Georgia, printed sedition on his press. The old man sailed to Havana to negotiate a deal between the Continentals and the Spaniards. There it all exploded."

"Gods," she whispered in horror. "Was he executed for treason?"

"Oh, no. The redcoats bungled his capture. He escaped. Major Ferguson nabbed him as a spy last month on King's Mountain. He was behind British lines, a noose draped round his neck, when the rebels opened fire on Ferguson. Somehow his fellow rebels didn't slaughter him. I hear he's found his way to Dan Morgan's camp. Huzzah for the old man!"

Helen had never met Will St. James, but every step his son David paced in her parlor snagged her heart with sorrow. Her lips fumbled for words. "How it must break your heart to know your father's in danger, but he isn't your responsibility. You must let him go."

He stopped pacing and faced her. Firelight carved the haunted shadows of a prey animal into his handsome face. "When I went to Havana, I was judged by the company I kept."

Her stomach burned, and her eyes widened. "Oh, no. The king's soldiers are hunting *you*." After tracking him half a year, after the stinging defeat at King's Mountain and unrelenting attacks from backcountry rebels, the British Army wasn't amenable to straightening out such a mix-up. With time and money invested in David, the Army wanted his hanged corpse swaying in the wind, his face purple and tongue protruding.

At least with the Committee of Safety in Wilmington, the redcoats couldn't just storm through the city and arrest David — Helen caught herself. David's pursuit had followed him into the tavern that evening. Good heavens. *Another* British agent wandering Wilmington in civilian clothing. Dozens of them could be slinking around town, each dressed as a civilian and thumbing his nose at the rebel government.

"Yes, they're hunting me. My hellhound is a redcoat, Lieutenant Fairfax. You see why it's prudent for me to make this visit short."

Her blood heated. Scant tenderness had she received in her life, and David had provided most of it. She stood and stamped her foot. "You're exhausted. Stay here and rest a day. Everyone knows Enid and I are Loyalists. This is the last place a rebel spy would hide."

"This fiend, this parasite never gives up on a scent. He tracked us to Havana."

"So he's a prideful, pompous ass, eager for promotion —"

"No, you haven't understood me!" David's expression went rigid. "He tried to violate my sister in East Florida —"

"Oh, David, come now —"

"— and he shot a friend, someone I've known my entire life, in cold blood in Havana. Gods, Helen, listen to me, please believe me!"

Still carrying his hat, she went to him and gripped his hand in hers, hoping to convey calm and safety, despite the alarm spiking her heart. True, the British Army had its bad material — rank and file who plundered, raped, and murdered. But never had she heard of a regular officer of His Majesty who'd committed the vile acts of which David had spoken. Rules of war: commissioned officers were of a different cut than the men, supposedly even within the Continental Army. Were solid proof of such a crazed officer's activities leaked to the rebels' propaganda machine, any pretense of civility and protocol between the rebel and Crown forces would evaporate.

Her heart sank. Weeks on the run had unhinged David. "Darling, I'm listening. You know I'm here for you. You're safe. I've no traffic with rebels. Your 'hellhound' cannot intrude in *my* house with the Committee standing in his way. Stay here tonight. Tomorrow night, too. You look like a wraith, for heaven's sake."

His gray-eyed gaze bored into her before his shoulders relaxed. "I don't want to cause you more trouble, but I'm so damned tired."

"Of course you are. Can you find safety outside of Wilmington?"

"Yes, with my sister."

"Back home, in Alton? Aren't they looking for you in Georgia?"

"No, Sophie, the other sister, the one who went to Cuba with me. She's hiding among the Cherokee in western South Carolina. Her daughter, Betsy, too." Pride firmed his mouth "I shall be a great-uncle before Yule."

Helen warmed to his joy. "You must be among family when your niece delivers." How did it feel to belong to a family whose members sheltered each other? How did it feel to share in the joy of marriages and births? Charles knew, as did Enid and David. "We shall see you rested and fed, and after a few days set you back upon the road. Where's your gelding?"

"In your stable."

She tossed her head. "I sold my team years ago. If someone snoops, it will be obvious that I've a visitor. Enid shall sneak him into Mr. Morris's stable and at first light board him in a public stable."

"That's far too much effort on your part."

"Hush." In light of her persuasion, she sensed resistance ebbing from him. Good. He sounded irrational, and she couldn't envision his success at finding safety until he'd rested and recovered enough clarity to not regard his pursuit in supernatural terms. She suspected that he'd projected fears for his own safety onto her, although concern did twinge her over the thought of Charles, inebriated and out late at night. "See here, it's almost midnight, and you look ready to drop. Let's get you up to bed. Enid will have the guest room prepared in five minutes."

"Guest room?" He reeled her against him, his humor returning and impish. "I'm not *that* tired." A knife-edge appeared in his smile. "Have you a lover upstairs abed waiting for you, cranky from the time you've spent down here with me?"

Odd. Had David grown jealous? The only other man who spent the night under her roof was Jonathan Quill, and he slept in her guest bedroom when he visited. David knew that. She dropped David's hat on his head and adopted a gruff tone. "If you share my bed, you must stay a second night so you can catch up on your sleep."

"So you can deprive me of a second night's sleep, eh?" He kissed the palm of her hand. "Madam, I agree to your terms."

Her hand in his, she guided him toward the door. At the easel with her latest watercolor, he paused and pushed back the cloth. "Yes," she said in response to his grin, "More of my 'rocks.'" She stored most of the paintings upstairs, out of sight. Standing stones, barrows, and sacred wells and their link to her religion made certain devout Anglicans in Wilmington frown. In her memory, she heard Silas's reprobation: *pagan rubbish.*

"So this is Midsummer dawn at Stonehenge, eh?" David smirked. "Where are those druids?"

"Bickering over whose belt has the finer gemstones, which foods to serve at feast, and what ceremonial practices are appropriate."

"Alas, O noble druidism. Once a priesthood that shocked Caesar with human sacrifice, now but a playground for the aristocracy." He winked at her. "Reminds me of the Congress and Parliament."

Chapter Four

DAVID'S TONGUE TRACED the curve of her shoulder blade, inviting Helen back from the precipice of sleep. Curled against him in bed, she smiled through near-darkness and murmured, "Sleep, dear, or you shall require a *third* night's rest before you leave."

"An appealing thought." His fingers tickled her shoulder and roved down to stroke her breast. "But you haven't answered my question. Why have you lost weight?"

She yawned out a half-truth. "Oh, sometimes I have so much business that I forget to eat."

He rolled her onto her back, light from the single candle etching his frown. "Helen, stop toying with me. You and Enid have forgone meals. You haven't enough money."

"Don't let's quarrel about this again."

"People need help from others every now and then. Why won't you let me help you get through a tight time?"

She bristled. Never again was a man going to purchase her.

"I'm not asking you to cease writing and respond to my whims. No, you have this inane notion that you should be able to do it all yourself —"

"— I *should* be able to do it all myself!"

"Since *when*? Let me confess a little secret. Do you know why Prescott waived the final fifteen pounds of your legal fees? It wasn't out of the goodness of his heart. It was because I paid him off, and I told him to lie about it. So you see, you haven't done it all yourself."

Indignation churned her gut. She shoved herself up and glared at him. "I cannot believe you paid off my debt without telling me."

"Once, I was dazzled by how well you held your head up and fought. Lately I'm alarmed. If you don't learn when to take, when to bend a little, when you don't need to keep fighting, you're going to destroy yourself. Much as the way my father is destroying himself."

She swung out of bed, stomped to the window, cracked it open, and glowered out at night. Tears pressured her eyes, but she squeezed them back. Beneath her outrage crawled the fear of her own vulnerability. Her naked skin chilled.

"Helen, Badley's using your pride, throwing you bones, confident you'll take them. He could be feeding you from a richer plate."

Years of insipid assignments. Of course Badley used her pride. But pride wasn't all he counted on when he dangled the Legion project before her. What was his motive for offering it? Her voice emerged dull. "He's asked me to ride with the British Legion, write a feature about the unit."

David laughed. "Yes, he does have a wicked sense of humor. Oh, bugger Badley. What news from other publishers?"

Her heart submerged in dismay. David didn't believe her about the assignment. Or perhaps he didn't believe her capable of handling it. "Rejection."

The bedroom grew too quiet. Wax sizzled on the candlewick. From the corner of her eye, she saw him shift to the edge of the bed, posture contrite. "Sweetheart, you're still in this house with memories of Silas, still drinking from Badley's cup. You need a fresh perspective of your options. Come away with me for awhile to South Carolina."

Other widows from New York to Augusta welcomed David's visits, but she was certain he hadn't made his offer to them. They couldn't claim an acquaintance with him that extended back more than a decade into a past tapestried in skeins of delight and devastation. "What would I do among your kin?"

"Do? I wouldn't ask you to *do* anything."

Whatever response she'd expected from him, that wasn't it. Her teeth chattered, and not from the brisk night air. "The law is hunting you, David."

He emitted a sardonic laugh. "Is that an excuse? How unlike you."

At thirty-one, David was very different from the man she'd met eleven years earlier. He'd learned when to walk away from card tables, rivals, even love. As certain as she knew the sun would rise in a few hours, she was certain that declining his offer meant she'd never see him again. Fear of more loss clenched her throat.

He stood and went to her, offering the warmth of his embrace from behind, his voice tranquil and kind. "There is so much more out there for you, waiting. Experiences to be had, life to be lived, gifts to receive, people who will embrace you, rejoice with you, help you fill that emptiness, that hunger, if only —" His voice faltered around sentiments he'd always stumbled over expressing. "If only you'll accept it and — and — oh, gods, Helen." He turned her around to face him and grasped her shoulders. "Do you want me to marry you? Is that it? I would do it, if that's what you want."

Anxiety supplanted her astonishment at the torment knotting his expression: as if he were a fly thrashing in a spider's web. Was that a metaphor she wanted for marriage?

Panic swept away the torment, and his expression settled into ambivalence, confusion. He stepped back, as if to ward off his own proposal. "Even if that's not what you wish, consider coming with me to South Carolina anyway."

The bedroom grew quiet. She heard herself gulp.

The batter of someone's fist upon the front door of her house yanked a gasp from her. David recoiled and snarled at the closed bedroom door. "Bloody hell, that son of a whore has found me!"

Wham, wham, wham! Neighborhood dogs began barking.

David snatched his shirt and shrugged into it, so she fumbled for her shift, her heart jumpy with distress and bewilderment. Just outside her bedroom door, Enid grumbled, clomped downstairs to investigate. "Son of a whore!" muttered David. "Damn the stinking son of a whore!" Crouching, he hopped into a stocking, almost unbalanced.

Helen jammed feet into slippers and threw on a bed gown. "Stay here and keep quiet."

"The hell I will!" David tugged the other stocking over his knee and grabbed a garter.

"Listen to me, and don't act the fool. I shall manage this." She jerked open the bedroom door and slammed it shut on her exit.

Trudging back up the stairs toward her, a candle illuminating her way, Enid layered contempt in her tone. "Mistress, George Gaynes is on the front step with committeemen. Says he must talk with you right this moment."

"Blast that strutting parrot!" Helen rapped once on her bedroom door. "Rebels from the Committee, David. Stay put while I rid us of them."

Enid scowled. "Those jackals shall wake the neighbors."

"Give me your candle." Helen stomped downstairs with it, Enid padding after.

By the time she reached the front door, every dog on the street had an opinion of the ruckus. Neighbors' servants cursed the commotion. A dog yelped, encouraged to shut up by a thrown object or kick across the ribs. Light from lanterns outside bobbed on draperies like St. Elmo's Fire. "Open in the name of the North Carolina Committee of Safety!" bellowed the voice of George Gaynes, the Committee's most loud-mouthed deputy.

Helen delivered her tone icy. "For what purpose do you disturb our sleep?"

"We've tracked a spy to your house and require admission to assure your safety."

"We harbor no spies on this property. Away with you, and next time verify the address of your spy's lair so you don't awaken decent citizens!"

Enid drew back from where she'd peeked between front drapes. "I count over a dozen men out there."

"Mrs. Chiswell, if you don't open this door, I'll see that you and your servant spend the morrow in jail for obstructing justice. We got scant patience in Wilmington for the bloody King's Friends, we do."

The inflexible element in his tone was distinct. The two women regarded each other. Enid licked her lips. "Do as he orders, mistress, so we'll be rid of them."

Helen glanced upstairs, knowing she'd have to keep them from her bedroom. With a nod for Enid, she handed over the candle, pulled back the bar, and opened the front door.

Lanterns scattered and bounced shadow off the men's surging entrance. They possessed the foyer with the clatter of muskets and the smells of black powder, alcohol, and masculinity. Most were pups younger than age twenty. The door banged shut.

Gaynes, stocky and swarthy, clumped over to Helen, preceded by a blast of poor hygiene. A sneer rippled his mouth and fanned ale fumes in her face. "I knew it, you bloody Tory wench, pretending to comply with us while you've harbored a spy for General Cornwallis!"

Fear clutched her throat at the malevolence pulsating from Gaynes and men around him, and she barely stopped herself from backing away. "How dare you barge in my house in the middle of the night?" Despite her effort, her voice quavered.

"No need to terrify the lady, Mr. Gaynes." A man of medium height, in his mid-twenties, stepped parallel to the committeeman, his tone and expression dispassionate. "I'm certain she doesn't require the use of a heavy hand to allow us a look around."

Still shaking, she regarded him. His suit, of the quality and workmanship that George Gaynes couldn't afford on a year's pay, was tailored with precision to his solid build. Education and culture oozed from him. He carried himself with the excruciating posture she'd observed in military officers — as out of place in Wilmington as a tiara of emeralds on a two-shilling whore. Her pulse whammed her throat. Who was he? Where had he come from? And his accent: Carolina gentry?

Gaynes transferred his sneer to him. "Oh, right, this is *your* show tonight. But if your way don't work, we'll try my way." He glared back at Helen. "Forgive my manners, Mrs. Chiswell. This fellow, Mr. Black, is a special agent who's come straight from General Washington on the trail of a dangerous Tory spy. If you cooperate, he and his lads will have your house searched and be gone in five minutes." Gaynes grinned. "But I'd really rather you didn't cooperate with him so my lads and I can have some fun. Now, what's it going to be?"

Helen stared from the inferno in Gaynes's face to the frostbite in Black's and swallowed. "I've no spies harbored under this roof, Mr. Black, but if you insist upon a search, make haste."

With a curt nod, Black faced Gaynes. "Wait with your men outside while we search."

The committeeman scowled. "Aw, no, we finish this job together."

"We've already had this discussion. My team and I have received special training from French investigators in search and apprehension techniques. Your presence will impede our efforts. We require your cooperation for success. Wait outside."

Anxiety jangled Helen's instincts. Faint, almost imperceptible undercurrents wove through Black's accent, belying him as Carolina gentry. He wasn't who he professed to be.

Gaynes growled but backed down, pummeled into submission by inhuman chill in the other man's eyes. "French investigators. Huh." The committeeman stumped for the door. "Come on, lads."

As soon as Gaynes and six men had exited, Black directed an expression of stone upon the remaining men and said quietly, "You five, search the grounds out back including the kitchen and stable. Morton, you search the study. Farmer, the dining room. When you two are finished, search the remainder of the ground floor."

"Sir." They clomped off. Outside, dogs barked and servants cursed.

The Carolina accent had vanished. In its place was an accent every bit as English as Helen's accent. Shock slammed her. Mr. Black was most certainly David's family hellhound, Lieutenant Fairfax. What a brazen, perilous act of impersonation he'd undertaken.

Chapter Five

HELEN COULDN'T EXPOSE Fairfax. Gaynes wouldn't admit being duped, and Fairfax knew that the only way she'd have knowledge of him was through recent contact with David.

"Mr. Black, you lied to the Committee. You're as English as I am."

Fairfax didn't even look at her. "McPherson, escort the ladies to the parlor and keep them out of the way. Parker, upstairs with me. We have him at last, like a fox in a den."

Horror cut Helen. Fairfax would succeed in his ploy, apprehend David, and haul him off to the gallows. "I forbid you to enter our bedrooms! Mrs. Jones and I are decent widows and will not be treated like slatterns!"

The lieutenant took the stairs two at a time, his man following. Enid tramped for the parlor, muttering in Welsh, outraged. McPherson wrapped a hand about Helen's upper arm. "This way, madam."

She pivoted and kicked his shin, startling him enough to wrench loose. Halfway up the stairs, she heard bedroom doors whammed open. She'd failed to protect David.

Heart in her throat, she gained the second floor and skidded to a stop before her bedroom. Inside were Parker and Lieutenant Fairfax, each with a lantern. David was nowhere in sight.

Fairfax turned from the window to her, lantern light tossing russet highlights through his hair and gouging darkness in his face. "You appear as surprised as I at not finding him here." Without unpinning his stare from her, he rapped the frame of the wide-open window behind him with his knuckles. "Next time, I shall remember his climbing skills, useful in eluding husbands."

Dogs redoubled barking efforts in response to the men combing Helen's yard. She reassembled her glare and steadied her pulse. Wherever David was, thank heaven he hadn't been apprehended. "How dare you insult my honor and presume I entertain men in here?"

Fairfax held up his thumb and forefinger and rubbed a bit of fabric between them. "Was it you or your servant who tore this piece of mauve wool from a garment upon the sash?"

She gaped, then closed her mouth. "I've no idea what you're talking about."

Parker, several inches taller than his commanding officer, advanced on her. "Sir, shall I escort her to the parlor?" Devonshire farm-boy stock, from his accent.

"Unnecessary. She's quite helpful." He strode to the headboard of the bed, and she caught her breath when he plucked David's hat off the post. "Her personal fashion tastes are unique, wouldn't you agree, Parker?"

Parker stretched his lips over a smile. A front tooth was missing. Helen doubted he'd lost it while milking a cow in Devon.

"Inspect the other bedrooms again."

"Sir." Parker saluted and stomped past Helen for Enid's room.

"That hat belonged to my dead husband."

"Of course it did." Fairfax peered at the label. "Mr. Chiswell had exquisite taste. Sutton and Miles — out of Boston or New York? When was the last time you saw David St. James?"

She tilted her nose up. "I don't recognize that name." Outside, neighbors' servants had regressed to the point of offering each other vulgar suggestions about how to silence the dogs. The outrage had gone on long enough. "Your spy isn't here. Leave my house." He sallied past her with the hat. She grabbed for it, incensed when he tucked it beneath his arm and trotted downstairs holding his lantern high. "Give me the hat, you cad!" Fuming, she trailed after him.

On the ground floor, she heard soldiers report that they hadn't found David. Parker thumped downstairs and confirmed the quarry absent from the second floor. By then, she knew better than to rejoice.

David may have escaped, but Cerberus patrolled her house, the consolation prize of a fashionable hat secure beneath his paw. The concerns David had expressed earlier about Lieutenant Fairfax no longer seemed irrational.

Leaving men in the foyer, Fairfax strode into the parlor, where several candles had been lit, and signaled McPherson to join those outside, giving him his lantern in passing. Helen entered the parlor in time to see Enid rise from the couch where she'd been guarded, her lips pinched with ire. Fairfax bowed. "Ladies, His Majesty appreciates your cooperation."

Enid jutted her jaw. "And where is your spy?"

"Alas, Fate has granted him a few more hours' freedom."

"For naught you disturbed my mistress's sleep."

Helen caught Enid's eye and shook her head, wary of five hundred years of Welsh resentment she heard smoldering in her servant's voice, wanting only to be rid of the men.

"Regrettable, but necessary. As loyal subjects, you understand."

"Aye, we do —" Enid's upper lip curled. "— *Saesneg.*"

English. Dismay and fear plowed through Helen, and her gaze riveted to the lieutenant. Did he understand Welsh and the insult Enid had delivered?

He slammed a stare harsher than sleet at the servant, flogging defiance in her posture into submission within seconds. "Tongues less insolent than yours have been cut from their owners' mouths. The only king in the civilized world is named *George*, not Llewellyn."

Pivoting to leave, he clipped the edge of the easel. Down it clattered. Before Helen could rush forward and rescue her watercolor, Fairfax had snagged it off the floor. She sucked in a breath of consternation, again hearing Silas's disapproval in her memory. If the soldiers had recognized the shrines to the gods she and Enid set up in the back yard, she hoped they wouldn't make a fuss.

She bit her lip, picked up the easel, and reassembled it, her back to Fairfax. Then, she stiffened, hands atremble, skin prickling. He lowered the watercolor into place on the easel from behind her, so close she could hear his breathing, sense it against her neck. Derision drenched his murmur: "You omitted the druids."

Gooseflesh possessed her arms and neck. Feeling him shove something upon the crown of her head, she winced but remained motionless, her back to him. Even when he swaggered out to rejoin the soldiers in the foyer, she stared at dawn without druids on the Salisbury Plain. Her front door crashed open. Clattering and shuffling, the men headed from the house, banging the door shut after them, renewing the interest of dogs on Second Street. "Mr. Gaynes," said Fairfax, faux-Carolina accent revived, "our spy isn't here. Has he another petticoat to hide beneath in town?" Men's voices faded, and oppressive silence seized the house.

Dazed, Helen snaked her fingers up. David's hat rested atop her head.

In a blur of fury, Enid shoved a front window drape aside. "Bastards, all of you!" She shook her fist at the darkened street. "Not a decent *Cymro* among you!"

Helen strode forward, yanked her away from the window, and shook her by the shoulders. "Have you lost your wits? You might have been flogged for your insolence!" Enid's expression yielded to shock and dread. "Give me your word this instant that I needn't worry about you brandishing your — your *opinions* again."

Devotion displaced defiance in her eyes. Enid nodded. "You have my word." Her gaze lodged on the hat perched on Helen's head, and her expression became forlorn. "Did Mr. David escape?"

Helen tossed his hat onto the couch. "Get your cloak and clogs. We shall check Morris's."

The barking of dogs had subsided. Reluctant to stir things up, wary that soldiers might lurk in hopes of catching David, the women waited several minutes before they slipped from the rear of the house and sneaked across the yard for the neighbor's property.

The door of his stable was ajar, and Helen smelled horse and fresh dirt on the night wind. She nudged the door open six inches with her clog. A horse within roused. In case David was holed up inside, ready to clobber anyone who entered, she hummed a few bars from one of their favorite tunes, "Over the Hills and Far Away." But only the horse responded, a sleepy snort.

Dried grass beneath the housekeeper's clogs rustled. "He's gone, mistress. The only horse inside is Mr. Morris's."

Helen's sigh blended relief with melancholy. David had gone without even a goodbye. She might never see him again. Head bowed, she toed the stable door shut.

"The King's men are crazy to pose as rebels. Mr. David's no spy." Enid's hand sought hers in the darkness, a fleeting comfort. "Soon as it's light, I shall put out some bread in the garden. Rhiannon will watch over him."

Helen plodded back to the house, Enid following in silence. Rhiannon. What special magic could a Welsh mare goddess conjure in defense against a fiend?

***

Her bedroom was icy cold, the window left wide open. She closed the window, dressed, ordered Enid to brew coffee, and descended to the study. She'd write overdue letters to avoid feeling the space left empty in her heart by David's departure.

The study was as frigid as her bedroom, the window jimmied open. A soldier inspecting the yard must have forced reentry to the house that way. Annoyed at his insensitivity, she shoved the window shut. Then she realized she'd need a carpenter to repair it because of the way it had been forced, and she cursed the soldiers aloud.

Dried mud and grass boot prints extended from the window. She followed the trail, arrived at shelves holding her ledger and legal documents, and quivered with resentment until a survey assured her that nothing was missing or seemed out of place. Even the case holding Silas's dueling pistols on the top shelf appeared undisturbed. Misbegotten mongrels, nosing in her possessions.

Enid announced coffee but scowled at the mess on the floor. Helen retreated to the dining room while the servant swept out her study. Night held the sky, and she pondered over her coffee.

If she sold her house and moved to a smaller dwelling, the money she cleared from the sale plus her dower should enable her to live with less struggle. But more than six years of war had ensured that a healthy market for house sales didn't exist in the colonies. Wilmington, prosperous due to the naval stores industry, suffered the indignity of being governed by a rebel minority while occupied mostly by Loyalists and neutrals, a condition that depressed the sales of houses.

If she managed to sell her house, would the money allow her to support herself and Enid the rest of their lives? She gnawed her knuckle. Keep going. Was that the culmination of her life, then, to keep going, to merely exist?

She peered out the window. Fog from the previous day had rolled off, leaving a clear sky. She needed a fresh perspective. Realizing that she'd echoed David, she swallowed at the lump in her throat. Where was he — safely upon the road and well south of Wilmington? Would she ever have the satisfaction of knowing?

***

In the solitude of her back yard, Helen faced east, waiting while the sky paled. She breathed into her belly as much as her stays allowed, and exhaled it in slow rhythm. Every morning since Silas's death, she'd reached for the old faith. Like the tide, her breath wove in and out, in and out. Awareness of cold dawn dusting her cheeks faded. The tide of breath became all.

Her chin level, she spread her arms, lifted them at her sides halfway, and bent them, palms forward and faced toward the east, her shoulders flung back. In the dawn place, she opened her heart and sought clarity. Those moments, the rhythm of the earth poured inside her. Birds sang from within her soul.

Later that morning, she delivered the embroidered petticoat to her client, wife of a Loyalist merchant. "How lovely, Mrs. Chiswell! Such a unique blend of colors and even stitching. I shall look divine in this. Here. Another shilling for you. I cannot wait to show the ladies. You know the vicar's wife is interested in your embroidery?" The client peered at her. "We haven't seen you at church lately."

"Enid and I have had colds." Helen faked a cough and tried not to imagine one of her watercolors hanging in the woman's parlor.

"There's a vile cold going round. Do take care of yourself. I hope we see you at the service on the morrow."

It was probably time to make another appearance in church. Helen smiled noncommittally, curtsied, and headed back home in the Indian summer sunshine.

The Anglican Church was the religious institution of choice for affluent merchants, artisans, politicians, and military officers: all aspirants within King George's empire. In the colonies, one found many flavors of Christian fervor, not to mention Judaism, Unitarianism, Rationalism, Naturalism, and even Atheism. No one in Wilmington expected the decent widow of a wealthy merchant to practice an ancient pagan faith. That was for the lower classes. Hence Helen's pre-dawn practice and disguised shrine in the back yard.

At least David didn't harass her about covertly observing the rituals of rustics. He never set foot inside church except for baptisms, funerals, and weddings.

Weddings.

Do you want me to marry you? I would do it, if that's what you want. Disbelief and loss raked her heart. More than a decade they'd known each other, yet he'd flung a marriage proposal at her as if he'd received an ultimatum.

She dodged a crucial question awhile before it cornered her. Did she want to marry David St. James? Her heart didn't leap for matrimony.

She arrived home just before one beneath a cloud of pensiveness, unable to fathom Enid's chipper mood. Then she remembered that Charles was due to visit and hurried through a cup of coffee. One o'clock came and went. Charles was running late. Unable to bear another second of Enid dusting the parlor, tidying pillows, and, in general, fidgeting like a smitten fifteen-year-old, Helen donned her straw hat and retreated to the garden to read.

Later, a subdued Enid meandered out to deliver the day's post, one letter. Helen squinted up at her. "Did Charles come by?"

"No, mistress. It's going on two o'clock."

Hair tingled on the back of Helen's neck. Charles was punctual. For Enid's sake, she withheld concern from her expression and voice. "He must have been sidetracked with some odious chore Badley inflicted upon him. Not to worry. I'm sure he'll make it up to you. Speaking of Badley, I must return for tea at three today."

"Ah. Will you be wanting to change?"

"Yes. The rose silk and garnets just as soon as I have a look at today's post."

"Very good, mistress." Enid retreated into the house.

Helen broke the seal on the letter. An introduction from the new holder of her mortgage announced that her next payment was due in two weeks. The amount was twenty percent higher than her current payment. Her mouth went dry. *Twenty percent.*

In her study, she opened the ledger of household income and expenses. For a quarter hour, she calculated and projected in attempt to make ends meet, factoring in that twenty percent increase. Then she slumped in the chair, her earlier euphoria about the assignment stomped out by reality in her ledger, replaced with the queasy sensation of being backed into a corner.

At most, she could find an extra five percent. She'd have to negotiate with Badley that afternoon for an advance to cover either the twenty percent or an attorney's retainer.

The assignment with the Legion had arrived just in time.

Chapter Six

AT THREE, HELEN stepped onto Badley's porch and whipped open her fan. Flushed from the walk, tendrils of hair escaping her mobcap, she longed to cool down. When Charles didn't open the door, she rapped on it, shaded her eyes, and peered through a window.

A maidservant bustled to the door. "Afternoon, madam. Here to meet Mr. Badley for tea?" She drew a breath, as if she'd been running. "He's —"

"Upstairs in the parlor, I know. Where's Charles?"

The woman opened the door wider for Helen. "I don't know. No one knows. He stepped out for a pint last night. Said he was going to White's. No one's seen him since."

Helen's jaw dangled, and concern bored her stomach. She envisioned Charles drowning in the Cape Fear River, pushed there after a footpad robbed him. "Why, that's contemptible! Hasn't anyone been out to look for him?" She whisked off her straw hat.

The maidservant shrugged. "Shall I show you to the parlor?"

"I know the way."

"Yes, madam." With a bobbed curtsy, the young woman sprinted for the rear of the house.

Irked that the servant hadn't offered to take her hat, flabbergasted over Charles's disappearance and the maid's lack of concern, Helen took a few deep breaths and climbed the stairs at leisure. No sense in compounding her agitation. There was nothing she could do for Charles at the moment. On the way up, she fanned herself. Her lips and cheeks became rosy when she sweated, and she was in no mood to tolerate Badley's gawking at her invigorated condition.

Outside the open parlor doors, he awaited her with a nervous smile that converted to unabashed ogling. "Delighted you could make it today, Mrs. Chiswell, and I must say, you look splendid."

She drew level with him at the top of the stairs, her head held high. "Where is Charles? A maidservant says he has been missing for twelve hours."

"Yes, I have Fergus and Abraham looking for him, and I've notified authorities that he's missing, if you can call them authorities on anything except rebel idiocy." He slipped the hat from her fingers and steered her for the parlor. "But this moment, we must straighten out a misunderstanding between you and the gentleman in our assignment."

"What are you talking about? I haven't met —" The man gazing out the window on the other side of the parlor turned to regard her. Disbelief and rage boiled up Helen's neck like a blast of steam and torqued her lips into a snarl. "*You!*" She shook off Badley's hand.

"Delighted to meet you again, Mrs. Chiswell." Lieutenant Fairfax bowed his head, unflustered. "As Mr. Badley commented, you look splendid."

She spun about to find the publisher braced against the closed door with the look of a child caught sneaking sweets. "Phineas Badley, at one-thirty this morning, that lout and his ruffians woke us and the entire neighborhood. He impersonated an agent from George Washington, enlisted the help of the Committee, accused me of harboring a spy, and searched my house. One-thirty in the morning!"

"Er, yes, so he informed me."

Oh, gods, of course the assignment had seemed too good to be true. Knowing what she knew of Fairfax, she wouldn't accept it on the terms Badley had offered. She'd have to find another way to handle the mortgage dilemma. Disappointment scalded her throat.

No. She wouldn't give up the feature to Warwick, Sellers, or Ricks. If she put her house up for sale that day, she wouldn't realize profit from the sale in time to make the new mortgage payment.

Was there an option she wasn't seeing? Options. Opportunities. Twelve years earlier, on a brig bound for America, Jonathan had insisted that she focus less on having opportunities than *seeing* them. She flung back her shoulders with dignity. If Badley wanted her for the job, he'd work it out. "Mr. Badley, I will not participate in an assignment with Lieutenant Fairfax on the terms you specified yesterday. If you want me for the feature, you must provide acceptable options."

"Let us not be rash. As I've said, it was a misunderstanding. He wishes to apologize. At least listen to him."

Helen scrutinized Badley's face. Men like Fairfax didn't apologize unless it provided a means to an end. He and Badley sought some outcome together.

How important was the outcome to Fairfax? The thought that she might witness some groveling amused her. "Apologize?" She pivoted and loaded venom into her smile. "Fancy that! Mr. Badley believes you've an apology for me."

He stood at attention. "My intelligence sources were ill-informed about the spy. I apologize for causing you discomfort early this morning."

By daylight streaming in through the windows, she received her first good look at him. It reinforced her earlier impression of education and aristocracy. He was also handsome, but no emotion moved in his face to encourage interaction with him, and he invested no contrition in his apology. She felt her ire swell. Did he fancy her a lamebrain? Who in hell did he think he was?

Badley shifted from one foot to the other. "Er, Mr. Fairfax, who is this fellow you've mistaken for a rebel spy?"

"His name is David St. James."

"David St. James, a *rebel*?" Badley squinted at Fairfax. "Oh, come now, sir. I know the rebels in this city — in much of the Carolinas, too. St. James is a gambler, an adventurer, and a bit of a ladies' man, but he's no rebel spy."

"As I said, my intelligence sources were ill-informed."

After what David told her the night before, Fairfax's statement registered as absurd to Helen. He baited a trap for David with the shammed apology. And there was something weirdly familiar about Fairfax. His accent confirmed him as a native of the Salisbury Plain, and from his acerbic comment about druids, he must share her disdain for what had become diversion and recreation for the aristocracy.

When she sailed for America, he'd have been no more than thirteen or fourteen. Did she have a more personal remembrance of him from her childhood in Wiltshire? Was he Lord Ratchingham's bastard son, perhaps?

However arrogant he was, he wasn't stupid. How many convolutions of the truth would he employ to get what he wanted? And was David all he wanted? "Exactly what made you decide you were wrong about the spy?"

"I discovered my intelligence sources were ill-informed." Still at attention, still no emotion.

A circular argument that gave nothing away. Helen grew edgy, realizing she wasn't in as much control of the scene as she'd imagined a minute before.

"There! You see? An apology." Beaming, Badley reopened the door, called for tea, and escorted Helen to a couch. "Let us all enjoy tea and discuss this glorious opportunity."

Back to the "glorious opportunity." Her instincts reminded her that both the assignment and Fairfax were dangerous. What feature was worth spending weeks with him underfoot? How important was it to Badley that *she* be the reporter on assignment, not one of the men? And why?

The lieutenant shifted to stand before the couch opposite hers. Helen, also standing, held his gaze while the maids arranged the tea service, left the parlor, and closed the door. "Mr. Badley, I haven't yet heard Mr. Fairfax account for why he's agreed to deceive Colonel Tarleton: participate in your scheme to plant a journalist among the Green Dragoons."

Irritation rippled Fairfax's expression. "How is that deception?"

"The colonel has an image to maintain. Journalists report facts."

The irritation flared. "The *facts* are that Colonel Tarleton is one of the finest officers His Majesty has in the field: a brilliant tactician, revered by his men, fearless in battle, ruthless with rebels. But he has no patience for journalists he perceives as meddlers, distractions, reporters from magazines with no solid political connection." Non-emotion reclaimed the annoyance on his face. "Many officers envious of his talents seek to downplay his merits and brake his advancement. He must receive the credit he deserves."

An ambitious junior officer was wise to swath himself in stardust from the tail of a rising comet. From what she'd heard of Tarleton, she wondered how he managed all the lap dogs — not that the colonel himself didn't practice his own version of lap-doggery. It *was* what made the British Army so interesting.

Badley applauded. "Lovely. Let's have tea."

The electricity of sparring crackled the air between Fairfax and her. Weeks

in his company could be horrendous for any reporter. And she had that mortgage to pay. Could she push Badley far enough to make the stress and menace
worth her while? "Mr. Badley, if you really want me on this assignment with
him, I require an aggravation fee."

Badley floundered his way back up from the couch when he realized she
hadn't assumed her seat. "Aggravation fee?" He frowned. "What do you mean
by that?"

"I want double the rate you quoted me yesterday."

"*What*?" Badley's frown contorted, and his face reddened.

Fairfax's eyebrow cocked, and his lips parted. Badley's indignation entertained him. Not two but *three* agendas scuffled for dominance in the parlor
that moment.

Badley swabbed his sweaty face, handkerchief flapping the air. "That
wasn't what the editor and I agreed!"

Four times her daily rate was probably what papers like the *Chronicle* paid
their first-year reporters. She let out a slow breath, feeling her way with caution, an acrobat balanced over a pit. "And I require an advance of fifty percent."

"Advance?"

"You'll find a way to make it happen. I'm worth it."

While the publisher's face ruddied further, Fairfax restrained a sneer. It
would seem he shared her opinion of Phineas Badley.

Badley worked his mouth, pig-eyes mean. "Madam, if I accommodate such
a change, the delay to rewrite your contract will certainly be more than Mr.
Fairfax's schedule can allow."

Fairfax bared his teeth, but Helen wasn't sure whether he meant the gesture as a smile. "By all means, sir, do not deny her ample compensation on my
account. I shall adapt to the delay. I shouldn't think rewriting the contract
would take more than a day."

She nearly exploded with dark humor: Badley backed into a corner. For
him to even consider such a rate meant that he was desperate for her to accept
the assignment. What in blazes was he up to? By then, her curiosity far ex-
ceeded her instincts. She simply had to know what was driving the publisher,
but she wasn't going to uncover the whole story unless she officially accepted
the assignment. Fair enough. "Prescott won't mind rewriting. Attorneys do it
all the time, and he seems to enjoy it more than most."

"I'd insist that you cover Enid's expenses from your salary," growled Badley.

Helen shrugged, nonchalant. "Oh, before I forget, what did you say was the
name of the editor at the *Chronicle*, the one who founded the new magazine?"

"That's entirely superfluous information for you."

She glowered a bluff back at him. "I don't have time for this nonsense.
Good day."

"Samuel Kerr!" Badley barked.

"And how did you and Mr. Fairfax become associated in pursuit of such a
righteous cause?"

"A mutual acquaintance. Lieutenant Adam Neville."

Adam Neville: no doubt she'd hear the name again. "Yes, tea sounds de-
lightful, Mr. Badley. Thank you for inviting me." And she lowered herself to
the cushion with grace.

Chapter Seven

BY THE TIME the affair concluded, she felt a migraine in her left temple: less from Badley's jabber and Fairfax's observations of their interaction than from the suspicion that somewhere during the afternoon, she'd sold her soul to the devil. As if to assuage her uneasiness over her capitulation, Badley had handed her the advance she demanded — more than enough for her to hire an attorney — and notes to mantua-makers and a shoemaker in town with whom he'd contracted. Her appointments with them on the morrow guaranteed her a wardrobe for the assignment equal in stylishness to that which she'd sold to help pay off Silas's debts. Most women would be giddy with delight. Instead, Helen had a headache.

What happened to David? Had he escaped Wilmington? Would she ever see him again?

Half a block from Badley's house, faux-Carolina accent honeyed the air behind her. "Dear sister, hold up so we might chat."

Over her shoulder, she spotted Fairfax on horseback, trotting to overtake her, every movement that of a gentleman planter, five men on horseback accompanying him. She continued walking, and he caught up with her afoot. At a discreet distance, his men followed, still mounted, his horse in tow. She said, "Major André took acting lessons from the wrong coxcomb."

"Thank you, madam." The Carolina honey fled his voice, and a faint smile on his lips didn't carry to his eyes, the color of green quartz. "You intrigue me. You identified me by name and rank in the parlor this afternoon before Badley had even introduced us."

Her skin crawled. "What are you talking about?"

"He introduced us after we'd sat for tea, but just a few minutes earlier, you'd said to him, 'Mr. Badley, I will not participate in an assignment with *Lieutenant Fairfax* on the terms you specified yesterday.'"

Anxiety drove a flush into her cheeks. Gods, she'd slipped, and Fairfax had picked up on it. How could she prevent herself from blundering like that again? She scowled, building bluster. "Badley told me your name yesterday while he and I were having tea."

"Good of you to clarify that." He affected a disarming shrug, his eyes cold. "I presumed David St. James warned you about me during his visit early this morning."

"I've already said —"

"— you don't know him, oh, that's right. Well, then, why not save us some time and tell me what old Badley is up to?"

She stared ahead, tried to calm her pulse. "Is old Badley up to something?"

"The *London Chronicle* has no editor named Samuel Kerr."

Eyes widened with surprise, she swiveled her head to look at him. "Are you certain of that, Mr. Fairfax?"

"Dunstan. Dunstan Fairfax. Yes, I'm as certain of it as I am that Sutton and Miles haven't been in business above five years."

She frowned at him. "Sutton and Miles? Who are they?"

"The makers of that fashionable hat adorning your bedpost."

Heat snaked up her neck. She jerked back around and again focused ahead. *He never gives up on a scent*, David had said. Embarrassment became wariness. Her head throbbed.

"Since the *Chronicle* doesn't employ Samuel Kerr, Mr. Badley lied to you and is up to something. Since Silas Chiswell died nine years ago — suicide, wasn't it, tragic, my stepfather was also a suicide — that gentleman's hat couldn't have been Mr. Chiswell's, and you lied to me. I've serious doubts about exposing Colonel Tarleton to such a formidable pack of liars."

Of course he hadn't ceased hunting David St. James. She glared at him. "By all means, poke your snout into Badley's affairs and dig up filth about him. It appears that's the only way you'll be satisfied as to my innocence."

Mockery hovered on Fairfax's mouth. "No love lost between you and Badley. How long have you danced this minuet — nine years?"

She sighed and faced him. He stopped walking, expectation supplanting the sarcasm on his face. The men halted the horses. She lowered her voice. "Cease snooping into my life."

"I cannot help myself. As I said, you intrigue me." He flashed his teeth.

She felt a sneer curl her lips. "Oh, poppycock."

"And there's something tantalizingly familiar about you."

Oh, no, he recognized her from Wiltshire. Dread pressed her chest. "Why not be helpful instead of boorish and repair the damage your man did to my study window?"

"Damage?" Fairfax sounded puzzled.

Ire added to the weight on her chest. "Your man forced the window open from the outside during the search this morning. He broke the latch and tracked mud on the floor." Exasperated, she flung up her hands. "Don't you see? I cannot secure my own home until a carpenter repairs the damage. You and your ruffians are responsible."

A furrow appeared between Fairfax's eyebrows. At that moment, she realized she'd told him unexpected information; his man hadn't admitted an act of vandalism. Fairfax didn't know *everything*. Some of the tightness in her chest eased.

After a sideways glance at his men, he returned a thoughtful expression to her and fished around in his purse. "Madam, my sincere apologies. I was unaware. Allow me to compensate you." He held out a sovereign. "Please inform me if you require more."

"Thank you. Good day." Snatching the coin, she strode down Market Street, relieved that he didn't follow.

Concerned over David, baffled how to break the news to Enid that she'd be spending weeks in the company of Fairfax, Helen arrived home to a quiet house. Presuming Enid had stepped out to market, she mounted the stairs to her bedroom and hid her new cache, including Fairfax's sovereign, in several wall panels that Silas designed. When she glanced out the window, she spotted Enid kneeling in the garden, her shoulders slumped. Was she weeping?

She hurried downstairs and out the back door. The servant lifted a grief-blotched face, and the realization that she was sitting before her shrine to her most beloved goddess, Rhiannon, shot dread through Helen. Ah, no. "Enid, whatever is wrong?"

Enid wrung her hands. "Charles has been murdered." Welsh accent wrapped her tongue.

"Murdered?" Helen's knees gave way, and she sank beside Enid. Peculiar noises issued from the back of her throat, as if her larynx had been paralyzed, and the garden tinted gray. It couldn't be true.

Enid snuffled. "Someone shot him in the head. The Morrises' washer-woman, Molly, came by a quarter hour ago to say they'd found his body at the wharf."

Charles had been the closest person to a caring parent Helen had known. Through her mind flashed images of him as she'd last seen him, pale and worried. And the butler's final words, conveyed by David. *They'll kill Madam if they find it.*

Loss and horror compressed her lungs. She gripped Enid's quivering shoulder. "I'm so sorry! I know how much you loved him, and — and — who would do such a thing to a good, kind man like Charles?" But the Welshwoman was beyond consolation.

Releasing her shoulder, Helen stood and steadied herself. Her knees still shook. "I'm going to the wharf. Perhaps an investigator from the Committee can tell me more. I shall return before dark." With an hour of daylight left, and the wharves just a few blocks away, she needn't worry about being out after sunset. Enid's weak nod communicated that she'd understood.

Cloak draped over her shoulders, Helen let herself out the front door. As usual, the docks were so cluttered with stacks of lumber and barrels of naval stores that she had to thread her way around the goods. Men from a boat unloaded crates of live chickens, contributing blown feathers and the sharp stink of chicken turds to the smells of tar manufacture, tobacco smoke, and unwashed humans.

In the lengthening shadows, onlookers had gathered before a warehouse near the intersection of Dock and Front Streets. Deputies from the Committee blocked the doorway. The press of spectators kept Helen on the periphery of the crowd, but comments she heard from the curious, the nosy, and the tragedy leeches made her thankful she couldn't move closer, where she might draw attention to herself.

"When did *he* kill hisself?"

"He didn't kill hisself. Someone shot 'im. Early today, after midnight, I heard 'em say."

"Weren't 'e Chiswell's butler years ago?"

"Ya, an' Chiswell shot hisself in the head."

"Shot hisself, my arse! We know better, don't we, lads?"

Stomach knotting, Helen kept to the shadows. Deputies made way in the crowd for the egress of two men, between them a stretcher bearing a man's supine, sheet-covered body. Waving off queries from onlookers, George Gaynes followed them out, caught up, and led the procession — to a surgeon's office where there'd be an autopsy, Helen knew, shaken. She'd seen it all before.

Her gaze followed them back nine years, when she'd watched Silas's covered body removed from another warehouse on a stretcher. At her left on that day stood Charles, and at her right was Jonathan Quill: the Seconds. At the funeral, Charles had again stood on her left, and Jonathan on her right. Beneath the mottle of bruises on her ribs and abdomen, hidden from the world by a polonaise gown, her early miscarriage gathered momentum. Ashes to ashes, dust to dust.

She blinked, jolted to the present by grief for Charles, an intensified headache, and the eerie coincidences. Had anyone yet informed Hannah, Charles's newlywed daughter? It was too late in the day for her to walk to Hannah's house — probably for the best. If she paid her respects on the morrow, she'd be less visible. The last thing she wanted was for residents of Wilmington to string together coincidences, dredge up the business of Silas's death, and connect it to Charles's.

Chapter Eight

"THE FUNERAL IS Monday morning, the twentieth." On the couch beside Enid, Helen released the housekeeper's hand and massaged her own brow with a sigh. "In the morning, we shall visit Mistress Hannah. Let us rest tonight. We've slept little."

"You've a headache." The Welshwoman rose. "Wait right there. I've just the thing for you. A boy delivered it while you were at the wharf." She bustled from the parlor.

Helen rested her head in her hand. When would she tell Enid about the assignment? She had to do it soon. Badley had paid the mantua-makers and shoemaker to expedite their work, tipped them a prodigious amount to fit her for a wardrobe at ten the next morning, Sunday. But informing Enid was the easy part. How in the world would she negotiate a truce for *weeks* between her and Fairfax?

Enid returned, and Helen studied the label on a bottle of wine she held for inspection. Not for several years had she been able to afford such an Italian red. Mystified, she searched the servant's face. "You said a delivery boy brought it, but who sent it?"

A wise smile curved Enid's lips. She handed her a card withdrawn from her pocket.

An audacious, masculine hand had scrawled the letter "D" on the card. No other message. Helen cupped the card in her palm, deep relief piercing some of her grief over Charles. Amused, embarrassed, she recalled David's grimace when he sipped her wine. "Open the wine. You shall share it."

As soon as Enid left the parlor again, Helen pressed the card to her bosom a moment before tossing it into the fire. Audacious. She hoped David hadn't compromised his escape and was at least thirty miles south of Wilmington, enjoying brandy at an obscure inn that hadn't seen traffic with soldiers in a long while.

After drinking a goblet of wine, Enid secured the house and retired to bed. Helen nibbled bread and cheese, drank wine, and brooded. By three-quarters of the way into the bottle, the Italian red had swelled to a delectable, sensuous experience that blunted the edge on grief, fear, and loss.

Like a paramour, she thought later, sitting on the side of her bed and staring drunkenly at the empty bottle on the nightstand. No, not quite like a paramour. The wine was more like a temple priestess of ancient Babylon, condemned by the Biblical prophet Hosea, worshipped and delighted in by warriors who returned from battle. A snort of irony escaped her, and she traced the bottle's label with her fingertip. Fancy that. She was a warrior, and her temple priestess was a bottle of wine.

At dawn Sunday morning, she was awake. Silas had trodden over her dreams, the ball from his dueling pistol embedded above his right eyebrow and dribbling blood and brains. He pursued her down Market Street, swinging at her with his riding crop, second to his fists as the preferred tool for discipline. She'd shaken herself awake when Charles — a ball from a dueling pistol embedded above his eyebrow, too — joined them.

Her skull felt stuffed with goose down, the migraine unabated. And, of course, anguish took pleasure in her company, undeterred by wine. She hadn't expected grief to vanish. At least she hadn't laced the wine with laudanum. For her, that would have induced worse than nightmares: hallucinations and visions most unholy.

She sought the dawn place after she'd dressed, almost too distracted to lose herself in earth's wisdom. At the back door, Enid awaited her, eyelids swollen and red. "I've porridge and coffee ready, mistress." Her tone lacked spunk, and her dark gray jacket and petticoat leached color from her face.

"I shall breakfast in the study. Jonathan must be notified of Charles's death." A memory from the Atlantic crossing surfaced: Silas drunk in their cabin, she and Jonathan exploring predawn star clusters up on deck with his spyglass. How pleasant his company, compared to that of Silas. Her throat tightened. Aware of Enid's astute expression, she cleared her throat. "If Jonathan is in residence at his estate, you know he'll attend the funeral." But he was likely elsewhere than his estate half a day south of Wilmington. Africa. India. China.

At seven o'clock, a letter to her former teacher composed, she found dawn's light through the study window blocked. Startled, she looked up from her desk. Fairfax fingered the window frame at the spot where one of his men had jimmied it open early the previous morning. Indignation frosted her expression. She stood, fists balled.

He spotted her, removed his hat, and bowed. "Good morning."

From his lack of emotion, he might have addressed a farm animal. She compressed her lips. "How dare you peep in on me like that? Remove yourself from my property this instant."

Enid huffed into the study and glowered. "What's *he* doing out there?"

"Mrs. Chiswell, as you and Mrs. Jones are decent widows, do allow me an audience lest neighbors presume me a loiterer."

Welsh accent ground from between Enid's clenched teeth. "Heigh, where's my pitchfork?"

Helen gripped the housekeeper's upper arm to restrain her from storming out to the shed and making good on her threat. "Meet me in the parlor straight away, Mr. Fairfax. You've five minutes for your audience. After that, Mrs.

Jones and I shall leave on errands, at which time we expect you to depart the property."

"Thank you, dear sister." He bowed again and headed around front.

"'Dear sister'?" Enid looked to be tonguing rancid pork.

"Admit him to the parlor — quickly, so we're rid of him."

Enid curtsied and bustled out. Helen allowed herself several deep breaths to order her thoughts, straighten the desk, and cover Jonathan's letter. From the foyer window, she saw men standing on her front walkway. Enid had made herself invisible.

In the parlor, Fairfax examined her latest watercolor, hat beneath his arm. "Midsummer dawn. I can almost feel dew evaporate and hear sparrows sing." He indicated her other paintings. "You've an excellent hand at landscapes. A baronet over in Avebury would pay well for your work." Filing away the potential business lead in silence, Helen strode forward and seized the canvas from him. He watched her stash it in a corner facing the wall. An unsettling radiance glittered in his eyes. "I've never met an Anglican gentlewoman who painted sites of the old gods."

She grew uneasy with the conversation thread. Fairfax fished for something from her past. With her station in Wilmington society as a middle-class, virtuous widow, she'd plenty of past to be uneasy about. "My husband was a *deacon* in the Anglican Church."

"Of course he was. Remember the old days, in the sixties, before the druids barged in and tried to regulate our celebrations? I wonder how many colonists would chuck the Christian gods and frolic with the rest of us if they could sample a truly invigorating Beltane."

She gaped. Fairfax was no Anglican.

The glitter in his eyes became incandescent, imbuing him with angelic beauty. "Ah ha. You remember Beltane."

No one forgot Beltane. She swallowed. The weird familiarity in his features struck her anew. She must know him from her childhood, although, dismayed, she couldn't yet place him in her memories. Perhaps if she hadn't tried so hard to forget what came before Silas Chiswell —"Mr. Fairfax, you're here to discuss my broken window."

"Quite. I questioned the men under my command and am satisfied that none is responsible for your broken window latch."

She scowled. "I catch you snooping around my house, and that's all you have to say? Do you expect me to believe you or your men? I think you've used the incident and this jabber about my watercolors as a flimsy excuse to gain access to the interior of my house during the day so you can search again for your alleged rebel spy.

"Perhaps I hid him in a wall compartment or beneath floorboards, eh?" She swept her arm outward. "Do search the house again and satisfy yourself that I'm not entertaining men here. Then leave my property."

He studied her, the unearthly glow in his eyes unabated. "What time did you and Mrs. Jones repair to bed two nights ago?"

"Nine o'clock, if it's any business of yours."

"Helpful information. The drizzle two days ago moistened the turf enough outside your study window to capture boot prints of your intruder. He was approximately five feet four inches in height, slightly overweight, favoring his left leg, and wearing a dark blue wool coat." He shook his head. "Doesn't match the description of any of my men.

From the way the wood is splintered on the outside, the intruder used a metal bar to force the window." Fairfax retrieved a kerchief from his waistcoat pocket and unfolded it. "He crawled inside your study some time between nine o'clock and midnight and snagged fibers of his coat on the wood. See here." He extended the opened handkerchief to her.

She inched forward, skeptical, for a look. Sure enough, a few dark fibers of wool resided there. He'd also found wool fibers from David's coat snagged on her window frame upstairs. Grudging respect for Fairfax's investigative abilities stirred within her.

He folded up and replaced the kerchief. "You mentioned that the intruder tracked mud on the floor. Any idea where he was headed?"

"The shelves where I store the household legal documents."

"Were any records stolen?" She shook her head. "If he'd carried a lantern, perusing certain crucial records, rather than stealing them, may have been his intent."

More disquiet built within her. Charles's final words haunted her memory. *They'll kill Madam if they find it.*

"I presume Mrs. Jones cleaned the floor yesterday? A pity. Obliteration of evidence. Since my five minutes have expired, and you aren't predisposed to a search of your study for additional evidence, I've no more to say on the matter."

"If it sheds light on the intrusion, for heaven's sake, please do search the study. Right this way."

Enid withdrew into gloom near the stairs as Helen and Fairfax crossed the foyer. That moment, eavesdropping was the least of the Welshwoman's faults. The look on her face earlier — Helen pursed her lips. Time for an earnest reprimand of her servant. A sweep of her hand encompassed the study interior. "You may conduct your investigation, Mr. Fairfax. I shan't be long."

"Five minutes, I take it?"

She contained a smile and walked from the study back into the foyer. Enid tried to scurry away. Helen caught up with her in the dining room and shut both of them within. "Enid, what did we discuss early yesterday morning?"

"Mistress, something's wrong inside that *Saesneg's* head."

As if Helen didn't already suspect it. She wagged a finger at her servant. "Answer my question. What did we discuss?"

The older woman pouted. "My opinions."

"You let your opinions show. You gave me your word that you wouldn't do so again."

"But he's —"

"Your *word*." Helen clenched her fists. "You've broken it."

Enid's face blotched while she grappled with what Helen was sure was the need to protect her mistress and the desire to prove her intentions honorable. Helen's heart ached. If only she hadn't had to accept that assignment with the Legion. Enid bobbed her head, and Helen heard tears in her voice. "I've disappointed you, mistress. What would you have me do?"

Helen made her tone gruff. "Walk in the back yard for five minutes. Cool your head."

The Welshwoman curtsied and departed. Alone in the dining room, Helen leaned against the table and released a sigh.

With delight, Enid would have poked Fairfax full of holes with the pitchfork had Helen not stopped her. Time to face the truth. If Helen didn't leave her in Wilmington during the assignment, Enid and Fairfax would throttle each other. Besides, Badley had twice indicated that he expected Enid to go along — perhaps he even counted on it — a sure sign that she needed the vigilant Enid at home as her eyes and ears. Perhaps if she presented it that way, the housekeeper might comprehend her crucial role in Helen's absence and not feel cast aside.

But if Enid didn't travel with her, who would serve as Helen's maid during the trip?

For the moment, she shoved aside the complications of the assignment, of a mood to see what evidence Fairfax had dug up in her study. Upon her return, he showed her more dark blue wool fibers and strands of mouse-brown hair that had escaped Enid's feather duster on an inside slat of the window frame. The intruder didn't realize the ways his identity had been marked.

Stimulated at the possibility of catching the brute from the evidence he'd left behind, she said, "What will you do with this?"

Mockery cocked his eyebrow. "Nothing was stolen, and only the window was vandalized. Do you intend to file a complaint with the rebels about the incident?"

She opened her mouth to respond but stopped herself. The intrusion had occurred almost atop Gaynes's intrusion. If she reported the incident to him, he'd consider her daft, at best.

"I shall keep the evidence for now. Mr. Gaynes doesn't appear to have been blessed with surplus intelligence." He retrieved his hat from atop the letter on her desk. "Without a more compelling case, your complaint will likely serve only to aggravate him."

Frustration soared through her, not unlike the way she felt whenever the weather delivered a springtime tease just before a winter blast. Instinct whispered that the man who'd broken her window had committed crimes against her in addition to vandalism and entry. How was she to discover more? "If this intruder wasn't one of your men or Gaynes's, aren't you curious why he broke into my house?"

"I don't have jurisdiction." Sarcasm stamped his face. "I'm curious about something else, though. Did you enjoy the vintage?"

She stared at him, lost. "Vintage?"

"The Italian red. Any woman of quality would appreciate it." He sneered full out at the shock in her face. "As I see you did. True, it was ungentlemanly and covert of me to sign the card with just my initial, but who locally might you have mistaken me for, also bearing a first name beginning with the letter 'D?' Hmm. Daniel? Donald?" He paused for effect. "*David.*" The sneer exploded into wicked laughter, and he headed for the door. "Good day, dear sister."

The door closed on his exit. She grimaced and massaged her pounding temple, gaze drawn to the desk. Sunday. No post. She must find a special courier for Jonathan's letter — wait, she'd covered it! She rushed over. Fairfax had placed it in the open, advertisement that he'd inspected it while she disciplined Enid.

And David hadn't sent her the wine. She'd been bolstered by false hope that he'd escaped and she could expect to hear from him again. In reality, she'd accepted a luxury from Fairfax — taken it to bed with her, in fact. She winced at the metaphor. Hardly a gift. He'd expect payment.

Chapter Nine

"PAPA WAS SO happy for us." Her blue eyes teary, Hannah Landon Pearson gazed without seeing the autumn flowers in her back yard. At vigil beside her on the bench, Enid covered her hand with her own. Hannah focused her imploring on Enid. "What shall I do without him? What shall *we* do?" They embraced.

Their lament lumped in Helen's throat. Atop her pain and loss, fatigue fueled the pounding in her head. She'd started her menses that morning, an event that seldom coincided with gaiety.

Who would murder a good man like Charles? *They'll kill Madam if they find it.* Charles died because he knew something, or at least someone thought he knew something, about her.

Roger, a yellow-haired, big-boned Saxon like his bride, escorted Helen to a nearby bench. "Have a seat, madam. Grief won't be rushed." He flopped down beside her, a pucker of sadness on his young brow.

"Thank you for sending your apprentice as courier."

"Let's hope the Professor is home to receive your letter." He sighed. "Charles was such a kind fellow. I feel as if I've lost my own pa." Roger glanced at his wife. "And I'd do anything to see her joyful."

"She will be again someday." Helen forced her lips to approximate a smile because Roger needed support. "She'll have you to thank. Charles told me what a wonderful husband you are."

He licked his lips. "I wonder, after the funeral, Hannah might enjoy leaving Wilmington for awhile. She mentioned traveling so she didn't have to look at the same people and be reminded of her pa."

"A break from routine might help her. But wouldn't your locksmithing business suffer in your absence?"

"My journeyman and apprentice can hold it for a time."

Helen rotated her neck to ponder the women on the other bench. "How was Charles's mood this past week?"

"Amiable, as always."

"When did you last see him?"

Roger chuckled. "Three days ago. You sound like an investigator." His humor faded. "I should warn you, you'll get a visit from them. They asked us a number of questions. About you. About Mr. Chiswell. They pressed us for a motive you might have to kill Charles."

"I? Kill Charles? Why do they think I did it?"

Roger lowered his voice. "The Committee of Safety is nervous at the helm of Wilmington, what with Cornwallis close at hand and most of the town loyal or neutral." His larynx bobbed in a swallow. "Rebels want to put a head on a post so they can feel powerful."

Her head.

"That Committee's full of suckling calves. Accusing a widow of murder makes them feel like bulls. Every committeeman would soil his breeches if Tarleton's men came to town. Now, *there* are some professionals for you. Finest unit under the Earl's command." Roger's blue eyes radiated pride. "Ah, what I'd give to meet Tarleton, shake his hand. I fancied riding with them, doing my part to protect the land from insurgents." Resolution on his face transformed to complacency. "I gave up the dream when Hannah said she'd marry me."

Helen looked from Roger to Enid. In contrast to the housekeeper, Roger just might put up with Fairfax. If she convinced Roger to accompany her on the trip, if he convinced Hannah to come along and serve as her maid, if she found a man willing to help Roger —"Lady" Chiswell's retinue would be complete. The thought calmed some chaos in her immediate future.

"Roger," she said. "I've a business proposition for you and Hannah."

***

The sparkle of interest in Roger's eye when she described the assignment heartened her. She sent the housekeeper home ahead of her and proceeded to the clothing shops, where she was flattered among bolts of fine silk, wool, and linen. In addition to six beautiful gowns, the wardrobe included a heavyweight cloak plus two petticoats and simple, short jackets for travel over more rugged terrain, where wearing gowns of a gentlewoman was impractical. Noontime, she left the shops entranced and floated home.

It took turning the corner onto Second Street at noon and the sight of Fairfax's men outside her home to dent her mood. She couldn't imagine him the harbinger of good news. Her gait faltered. Then the mental image of Enid and Fairfax alone somewhere together on the property inspired her to resume a hasty pace, if only to avert disaster.

Fairfax emerged from the side yard and overtook her at the front door. "Greetings, madam. I only just arrived."

She opened the door. "State the nature of your business."

"With whom do you prefer to discuss Charles Landon's murder, me or investigators from the Committee?"

"I prefer to discuss it with no one."

"Since the Committee will shortly pay you a visit, you'd best select your poison in haste."

In the doorway, she met his gaze. "They won't visit on Sunday. Good day."

She shut the door in his face, untied the ribbons of her straw hat, and removed it.

At the end of her exhale, Fairfax's voice penetrated the door. "They skipped church, just for you. Fortunately, you've the broken window as evidence in your behalf. It may be enough to exonerate you and calm a mob that intends to hang you on circumstantial evidence."

Enid appeared and gave the door a tight nod. "He arrived a couple minutes before you did, seemed miffed that I wouldn't let him wait for you in the parlor."

Resigned, Helen stepped back from the door. "Show him in." Turning on her heel, she strode in and tossed her hat on the couch.

The servant made as if to clear her throat, but in a more uncouth manner, and yanked open the door. "Mistress will see you now."

While examining another embroidery project, Helen heard Fairfax enter and Enid shut the front door behind him. She kept her face averted. "Brevity, sir."

He stepped into the parlor. "Five minutes, yes, I know. What was the nature of your relationship with Mr. Landon?"

"He was the butler here, before my husband died."

"How satisfied were you with his work?"

"Very much so. He is — was efficient, courteous, and kind to visitors and the household. I cared for his well-being. He was a good man. Loyal. Devoted."

"Ah. Then he was someone who would 'stand by you.'"

Fairfax loaded the phrase with double meaning. In a manner of speaking, Charles had stood by her when he'd acted as David's Second. She kept her voice neutral. "Yes."

"Would Mr. Landon have stood by Mr. Chiswell, too?"

No, Jonathan Quill had accepted *that* task. Apprehension flooded her. Fairfax's fishing into the past had grown on-target, productive. He mustn't have the truth confirmed about Silas's death. Dueling had been just as illegal in 1771 as it was in the present. She flicked lint off the fabric. "As my husband has been dead for nine years, your question is immaterial in the investigation of Charles's death."

"I suspect not. If Mr. Landon was indispensable, why was he no longer under you employ?"

She nibbled her lower lip. "After my husband died, I could no longer afford him."

"So Badley got him instead. Fascinating how his financial star has risen as yours set." Black humor slathered Fairfax's tone. "What do you know of Badley's association with Lieutenant Adam Neville?"

"The mutual acquaintance that introduced you to Mr. Badley? I've never met him."

"He's riding with the Legion on detached duty from Thomas Brown's Rangers. Perhaps you encountered him late last year or early this year when you and Badley met to discuss an assignment? Mid-twenties, dark hair and eyes, an inch or so taller than I am, lean build."

Peculiar, Fairfax's line of question. She wondered what role Lieutenant Neville played in the assignment. "I've never encountered Mr. Neville. Nor have I heard Badley speak of him."

"I see." Disappointment submerged the humor in Fairfax's voice. "And when was the last time you saw Charles Landon?"

"About three o'clock in the afternoon, two days ago."

"And his mood?"

"Preoccupied, worried. He intended to call upon Enid here yesterday at one o'clock. I felt he wished to speak with me, too."

"He never kept that appointment because he'd been dead about twelve hours by then. Where were you between eleven two nights ago and one-thirty the following morning?"

"In my bed sleeping."

"You've a witness to that?"

"Enid."

"Your servant was abed with you, awake, watching over you during that entire time?"

She allowed a silence to pass before she finally faced him. "Enid was asleep in her bedroom, and I was asleep in mine."

"I'm afraid your word won't be enough. The testimony of the gentleman who shared your bed that night is your immutable alibi that you weren't down at the wharf shooting Mr. Landon in the head." Fairfax's gaze held hers pinioned. "The gentleman's name, please."

Exhaustion and horror hiked the pulse in Helen's throat. Unable to extricate her gaze from his, she felt the pressure his will exerted on hers, ensorceling it in ice.

At a rap on the front door, Enid sprang to open it from her eavesdropping position in the foyer. George Gaynes stalked in without invitation, followed by committeemen and hangers-on. Fairfax stepped aside, ignored, as they and their zeal filled the parlor and formed a semicircle around Helen, backing her toward the fireplace.

Victory stretched Gaynes's lips. "Mrs. Chiswell, we're here to question you about the murder of Charles Landon." No "good afternoon," from Gaynes, and no "excuse the interruption." "And we've evidence to implicate you."

Chapter Ten

"EVIDENCE?" DESPITE JITTERS, Helen squared her shoulders. "I didn't kill him!" Many of the men she didn't recognize. In the eyes of none did she see leniency. Gaynes had rum on his breath. No doubt others had fortified their courage likewise. She flicked a glance at Fairfax. He yawned. No help there. "How dare you swagger into my house and accuse me of murder? On *Sunday*!"

"Murderers hold no day of the week sacred."

She glared at Gaynes. "Get out, all of you!"

"Let's see how high and mighty she feels sitting in a jail cell," said one man.

"And I wager she was his mistress and didn't want it known that she serviced the servants."

"Lads, let us have clarity here." Gaynes simpered, and the mob took its cue from him. "Madam, you look a bit pale. Sit down. Please, give the lady room." He sprawled in her chair.

She sat on the couch. Palms on his knees, the investigator leaned toward her. "Mrs. Chiswell, where were you two nights ago between eleven and one-thirty?"

"Abed, asleep."

"And I shall witness to it." Enid waved from the foyer. "Mistress and I were both abed asleep in our rooms that night."

Gaynes's grin revealed brown teeth to Helen. "You cannot be a witness for each other if you were both asleep. We've a murder to solve, and with the evidence we've collected, you're a top suspect."

"That's the second time you've mentioned evidence. What evidence?"

Gaynes snickered. "Nine years ago, the surgeon who autopsied your husband after he — er — shot himself removed and kept the ball. Yesterday, the surgeon removed a ball from Mr. Landon's head. It was the right size for Mr. Chiswell's dueling pistols, so he compared it with the first ball." Gaynes beamed at her. "They appear to have been fired from the same pistol."

Men grumbled and nodded, satisfied of her involvement in the crime to some extent. Gaynes held up his hand to calm the buzz.

She realized her hands had clenched and tried to relax them. The throb in her head increased in tempo. "Mr. Gaynes, no one can match a ball to any firearm with absolute certainty."

"True. The surgeon suggested that we examine the pistols, make some shots with them, and recover, study, and compare the balls. Have your servant fetch the pistols."

Helen signaled Enid, who returned to the parlor with the case of dueling pistols from the top shelf of the study. Enid handed the case to Gaynes, who opened it in his lap. Curiosity lit his face. "Madam, where is the second pistol?"

"Whatever do you mean?" Helen rose.

He stood and turned the case toward her. "If these were a pair, one is missing. Where is it?"

She gaped at the empty space in the case. "I don't know!"

"She's lying!"

"She shot Landon with the pistol and hid it!"

Gaynes tossed the case upon the couch and growled. "You murdered Charles Landon."

"No, no, absolutely not, I —" The semicircle tightened, and the grumble of men elevated in volume. Truth slammed her then. Panicked, she spread her hands. "There was an intruder in my study two nights ago!"

"Intruder? Likely story!"

"What did I tell you, fellows? In cold blood, she shot Landon."

"Lads, I insist that you lower your voices." Gaynes timed his imploring to incite rather than calm the mob.

Helen staggered to the opposite end of the couch. That no one seemed eager just yet to clap her in irons was small comfort. Too many men present volunteered scenarios of how she might have lured Charles to the warehouse at midnight and blown his brains out with the pistol. Motives were ventured and details were imagined, waxing more grotesque with each moment.

Her knees knocked. She crept around the men until she stood beside a granite-faced Fairfax and whispered, "Tell them what your investigation uncovered about the forced study window."

Arms crossed over his chest, he ignored her to maintain scrutiny of Gaynes's mob.

She squeezed her fists but sustained the whisper. "Ye gods, will you stand aside and allow me to be jailed, or perhaps hanged? I'm innocent! You know I didn't murder Charles!"

"Lads," said Gaynes, "nothing is settled. We've further questions of Mrs. Chiswell."

Helen stared at the impassive man beside her. "Have you no honor?" She recognized his price, then, felt her heart rent by a decision she never dreamed she'd face: to sell out. Everyone did have a price at which they might be bought. A piece of her soul withered, and an acid taste formed in her mouth. She felt like vomiting.

"Damn you!" she said instead, just loud enough for him to hear. "My guest two nights ago was, indeed, David St. James."

A glacial smile slipped over Fairfax's mouth before receding into granite.

The Carolina gentry accent rang out. "No one heard the lady! A burglar stole the pistol!"

The hubbub in the parlor dwindled, and the mob oriented on Fairfax, of a mind to string *someone* up. From the toxicity of their expressions, Helen doubted that hovering near a "special agent" who'd usurped Committee authority aided her cause. She inched away from him.

Gaynes frowned. "Where'd you come from of a sudden, and who made you her advocate?"

Fairfax sprang away from the wall toward the cluster of men, his expression frigid. As one, they shuffled backward half a step. "Do you plan to solve Charles Landon's murder, or will you play at investigation the way you play at the government of this town?"

"Why that son of a —"

"Quiet." Gaynes pushed his way into the forefront and sneered. "Special Agent Black. Why do I get the impression that you have knowledge of a related crime?"

"Mr. Gaynes, I've examined the scene of the burglary, in Mrs. Chiswell's study. Two nights ago, before midnight, a man broke in and stole the other dueling pistol. He left behind boot prints and textile and hair evidence."

Several rebels' jaws hung slack. Gaynes stared in disbelief.

"Your suspect is about five feet four inches in height and has brown hair. He's plump, limps on his left leg, and wears a dark blue coat."

Gaynes scratched the back of his neck. "How do you know?"

"His name is Arthur Sims. He lives in a hovel near the wharf. Here is the direction." Fairfax extended a folded paper. "Lack of steady employment suggests he was ripe to be hired for burglary."

Helen couldn't stop herself from gaping at Fairfax. If his information about this suspect was accurate, then his talent at investigation was preternatural. Sweat trickled down her back, and she shivered.

Gaynes retrieved the paper. "Just *how* did you figure all this?"

"I spotted Mr. Landon in White's Tavern two nights ago, before he was murdered. After an analysis of evidence in Mrs. Chiswell's study, I returned to the tavern with an adequate description of the burglar. The tavern owner recognized Mr. Sims and confirmed that she'd seen Mr. Landon and Mr. Sims in conversation just after midnight. In fact, they left the tavern together.

"Since you aren't adverse to working on Sunday, apprehend the suspect today and recover the pistol. Interrogate him to reveal who hired him and why his employer was motivated to frame Mrs. Chiswell."

A man bellowed, "Don't tell us how to do our job, you bastard!"

"Then do your job. I've completed ninety-five percent of the investigation. A halfwit committeeman could close the case from here."

"Stay where you are, Dan." Gaynes, aware that his fellow deputy prepared to lunge across the parlor at Fairfax, sniffed. "Show me this broken window."

Fairfax gestured, palm up, toward the foyer. "This way to the study. Since the room is small, I suggest you bring only one attendant, Mr. Gaynes, and instruct the others to leave the house."

At Gaynes's orders, men muttered, filed past Fairfax on their way out. Most eyed the lieutenant as if he were a coiled rattlesnake.

Her blood emptied of frenzy, Helen attempted to breathe calmness and experimented with the sensation of catastrophe averted. But calm eluded her, and her head still pounded. She didn't feel protected. From where she stood, she could see the case with one pistol resting on the couch, the absence of the second pistol a damning piece of circumstantial evidence. Lieutenant Fairfax had enough evidence to arrest her. Why had she placed her salvation in his hands?

Chapter Eleven

HELEN CLOSED THE pistol case and handed it to Enid. "Put this back." Enid glanced at the door to the study, and Helen, certain her housekeeper again fancied use of the pitchfork, felt her patience fray. "Give Mr. Fairfax no trouble in there."

Enid studied her face, an uneasy marriage of skepticism and chagrin roving her expression. "He defended you, as if he'd some honor in him."

Honor. Hypocrisy embittered Helen's heart. She wasn't the person she'd thought herself to be and hoped Enid possessed the judgment to not regard Fairfax as a hero.

The reproving edge melted off Enid's frown. "He *saved* you."

"Damnation." Helen left the parlor and rushed out the back door, just reaching the vault in time to puke. Despite the heat, the flies, and the stink, she remained inside with the door closed a few minutes after the heaves subsided. Anger denied her the relief of tears, and she was angry with just about everyone: herself, Badley, Prescott, Silas, David, Arthur Sims, Fairfax, Enid. Charles, too. She pounded the wall with her fist.

Self-pity exhausted, she stumbled out, dizzy and sweaty, at the same time Enid emerged from the house. The servant rushed forward and caught her about the waist. "This has been too trying for you. Lean on me, now. Upstairs you go, and let's get you to bed."

Helen might have shrugged off the housekeeper and lurched up to bed by herself, allowing Enid space for her own grief. But all she wanted that moment was freedom from the fiery spear in her temple. Enid whisked her past the study, where Gaynes and Fairfax discussed evidence, and upstairs to the bedroom, where she stripped Helen down to her shift and tucked her into bed. "I shall be back with chamomile tea after those men leave." Enid supported her shoulders and pressed a goblet to her lips. "Drink this. All of it."

Parched, Helen gulped the water. Near the bottom of the goblet, a faint aftertaste registered on her tongue. Laudanum. Knowing her sensitivity to the poppy, Enid hadn't added much.

Her tone gruff yet gentle, the servant eased her back onto the pillows. "You sleep a few hours."

Already the headache thrashed her with less ferocity. Enid drew the drapes, and as she let herself out, Helen heard the committeeman and Fairfax in the foyer. Gaynes, grudging and subdued, said, "How long you been piecing together evidence this way?"

"When I was a boy..." The bedroom door closed on Fairfax's response.

The poppy cradled Helen, cushioned the throb in her head, eased her passage into slumber she'd craved. *When I was a boy*, she thought with curiosity. Then sleep swallowed her.

***

Night had fallen. Feet on the floor, Helen realized she'd been sitting on the edge of the bed several minutes, traveling from the sleepy haze of narcotic to a wakefulness that was, at last, headache free. Enid puttered about the floor below. Helen imagined smelling a multi-course meal: roasted chicken, buttered rice and squash, an apple tart, fine wine. For almost a year, she hadn't had the money to afford it. She shook off the fantasy. In another minute, she'd awaken enough to realize she was ravenous and thirsty. She'd make do with soup, bread, and coffee. But first she had to remember her dream.

Except, she recognized as she came more fully awake, it wasn't a dream. It was a memory from almost two decades past, when she'd been about eleven years old. With a frown, she rose from bed, padded to the window, and pushed back the drapes, allowing cool night air in.

Relax, she told herself, relax, and it will return.

***

His expression a prune of piety, Vicar Hopkins paced before village children in the parlor at Redthorne Manor and tapped the palm of his hand with his cane. He seemed jumpy that morning, more eager than usual to apply the cane and remind a distracted student how fortunate he or she was to belong to the special group that received the educational largesse of Lord Ratchingham's second wife.

She finished the final algebra problem on her arithmetic slate, as usual well ahead of the others, stood, and approached Hopkins, gaze lowered. "Master, I have completed the assignment and beg your leave to visit the vault."

The vicar snatched the slate from her and inspected it. "How can a girl be more intelligent in mathematics than boys in this class?"

She didn't answer. No answer was expected of her.

"Go on, then, and no dawdling. I expect you to read Proverbs 31 from the tenth verse to the end. 'Who can find a virtuous woman? For her price is far above rubies.' In one quarter hour, you will tell me the proper applications of mathematics for a virtuous woman."

"Yes, Master." She curtsied. "Thank you."

Outside the parlor, she noticed two chambermaids and the butler snooping through study doors left ajar. "Lud," whispered the butler, "this is going t' be rich." Curious, she joined them without a second thought for the vicar's cane. They allowed her to crouch at their feet.

Inside, Ratchingham paced the furniture-crowded study. Bewilderment and worry trampled his amiable expression. *Too many adults were edgy that morning.* Dick Clancy posed behind the desk, a smile to sour milk upon his lips. A boy stood beside the desk, as motionless as death, head bowed, fine wool breeches, waistcoat and coat impeccable, silk stockings without wrinkle.

She stared at the boy and summoned recognition. *Stepson. Yes, that was it.* Twice, at a distance, she'd seen Lady Ratchingham's only child by her first marriage. He wasn't very old, not more than seven.

Ratchingham halted, almost blocking the boy from view, and faced his stepson. "Tell me the truth. Did you mutilate those frogs?"

Sunlight warmed russet highlights through the boy's brownish hair when he raised his head, but his eyes stared past the man and through the wall like chips of ice. "No, sir."

"Did you place the carcasses where Vicar Hopkins could step on them this morning?"

"No, sir. I was in my chamber studying mathematics this morning."

"Lying scoundrel," whispered the butler. "I saw him do it."

Exasperation flooded Ratchingham's voice. "For god's sake, we've a witness. Jedediah says he saw you drop them in the vicar's path just before eight."

An emotionless void occupied the boy's face. "The blacksmith's son and the dairyman's son resemble me in stature from a distance. And the butler has cataracts."

"You little shit," muttered Jedediah the butler. "I'll get you for this."

"Lad, I want you to be happy. Is there anything you lack?"

Something moved in the arctic wasteland of the boy's eyes: hatred. "No, sir."

Ratchingham gestured in futility. "We've not yet discussed this man-to-man, but what would you like to do when you grow up? I've the means to help you on your way. What is it you dream of doing when you're older? Law? Medicine? Banking, perhaps?"

The boy's response was prompt. "I should like to be an officer in His Majesty's army. Sir."

Clancy's smirk vanished. His face screwed up in disbelief, and he jiggled a finger in his ear.

"A military officer!" Ratchingham clapped his hands once. "Excellent career choice, lad. I shall be delighted to fund your commission. Let's talk about this again soon." He patted the boy on the shoulder. "Back to your science lesson. Remind Master Gerald that I'll have no more of that business of dissecting frogs."

***

The breeze wafted in through the window, stroking Helen's face, but she ignored it. *When I was a boy.*

Lord Ratchingham's stepson was Dunstan Fairfax. She shuddered, repulsed. It was all wrong. The eyes of a seven-year-old boy shouldn't harbor such malice. Even street urchins — impoverished, hungry, cold — didn't possess that level of loathing. Why was Fairfax that way?

Jonathan might remember more. A peculiar emptiness panged her soul.

Back in April, he'd mentioned an upcoming trip to England. She missed their spirited academic and philosophical conversations. She missed *him*. She should have contacted him after David's visit in May.

David. She hung her head. By then, she'd have to be a fool to believe she'd ever see him again. She told herself that she must let him go, but her heart tangled resolve. Grief, guilt, and confusion moistened her eyes. Why had she always been so stubborn over David? Why had her heart skirted love with him instead of embracing it?

A hot tear tracked down her cheek. She sagged against the windowsill in relief when another tear followed. Thank all the gods she could weep after all.

"You're up! Ah, that's good to see." Candle in hand, Enid pushed the door open further and entered. "How do you feel?"

Blast. Enid's timing couldn't have been worse. Helen thrust back her tears. Under no circumstances must she let Enid know that David wouldn't return. Enid adored him every bit as much as she adored Jonathan. "I'm much better." A smile trembled on her lips. She wiped her cheek with the back of her hand. "I hope the Committee apprehended that rogue, Arthur Sims."

"Not yet, mistress." Lips tightened over a reprove, Enid set the candle down on the nightstand. "Those deputies have a bit to learn about catching criminals. By the bye, Mr. Badley has the revised contract available and requests that you sign it. And the mantua-makers and shoemaker request a visit."

Even by candlelight, Helen read judiciousness flitting about Enid's eyes. Where had her mistress come by the money to purchase a wardrobe? She *must* explain the assignment to her that night, but not on an empty stomach. "I've worked up quite an appetite."

"Supper awaits you downstairs as soon as you've dressed."

"Dressed?" She eyed Enid. "I don't plan to leave home tonight, and I don't expect visitors."

The servant gnawed her lower lip. "He said the two of you had a conversation to finish and that he'd arrive at eight-thirty. Forty-five minutes from now, that is."

Fairfax. He expected her to reveal David's destination in exchange for rescuing her from the Committee. Helen expelled a deep breath. Sleep had helped her recover clarity. Time to put the handsome, macabre Lieutenant Fairfax in his place, or he'd dance her like a poppet before she completed her obligation with the Legion.

"We'd finished that conversation. Obviously I need to remind him. Fetch water for the washbasin, and help me dress."

Chapter Twelve

THE SILVER AND china had been sold years before, but Enid rounded up serving dishes to accommodate the feast that awaited Helen in the dining room. Speechless, she studied the label of another bottle of exquisite Italian wine by candlelight. Her initial reaction, to donate the meal to the destitute, was tempered by Enid's famished but patient expression. She anticipated a full belly. Helen would have to absorb the expense, cover it with more money from Badley's advance.

At eight-thirty, Fairfax and his men returned. Enid admitted the lieutenant to the foyer, where Helen waited. Then she retreated to the dining room to clear the table.

Helen curtsied, and Fairfax bowed, his gaze slithering the length of her. "Madam, repose has done you well."

"Thank you. The meal was a considerate gesture. Enid has been too busy to go to market." She extended a small purse to him, and he closed his hand over it in perplexity. "This more than covers tonight's meal as well as the wine you had delivered yesterday. Since it was the odious Mr. Sims and not one of your men who broke my window, I'm also returning the sovereign you gave me for that."

"Nonsense. Take it. It's yours." He tried to hand her the purse.

"Good night, Mr. Fairfax." She curtsied again and opened the door.

Again, his gaze glided over her. "*Mr. Fairfax.*" He lowered the purse and pushed the door closed. "We must discuss this formality between siblings."

As in the morning, she felt the force of his will grope for her, seeking to choke her, and she clenched her jaw against it. "We shall cross the formality bridge when the time arrives."

"Speaking of uncrossed bridges, our conversation this morning was interrupted by rebels."

"I'd naught left to contribute. Let me press straight to the point. David St. James didn't tell me his destination."

"I find that difficult to believe."

"For my safety, he insisted on not revealing his destination. Almost his first words when he arrived were that you were hunting him."

"You've been his paramour for a decade. Of course he told you where —" Fairfax fingered the pendant of one of her earrings, caressing her neck in transit. "Extraordinary garnets. Are they American?"

Slivers of unease worked up her spine. She pushed his hand away and slathered her voice with acid. "He called you a 'fiend.'"

"Trite, but affectionate." He grinned.

"If he considered me in danger from a 'fiend,' why would he imperil me further with knowledge of his own itinerary?"

In the half-light of the foyer, his grin vanished, replaced by a stare as harsh as January ice on the sandstone sentinels of Stonehenge. "He sought his sister and niece, yes? They're hiding with the Cherokee."

She felt as if the breath froze in her lungs. "A wretched break for you, if so. Indians don't betray their allies."

"True. I wonder what would entice him to emerge from safety?"

She tossed her head to disguise the shaft of cold through her heart. "Don't waste your time baiting a trap with me. I'm one of many women in David's life." But David hadn't proposed marriage to any of them. Across a decade, the suspicion had grown in her soul that David was waiting. Waiting for *her*.

That angelic luminance consumed his face. "You've the distinction of being the only woman for whom he's *murdered*."

Her throat parched. Her pulse jumped. Never mind that David had demanded the duel after Silas had beaten her and she'd miscarried. Dueling was criminal.

"You're withholding valuable information. In the name of His Majesty, I invite you to reconsider."

Indeed, she was reconsidering, estimating how much she'd have to pay Badley to withdraw from the assignment. Close to a year in wages. Although she hadn't yet signed the contract, Badley could file suit through Prescott for breach of verbal contract. He'd take her house. She'd be ruined.

And less than an hour ago, she'd presumed to put Fairfax in his place.

Seconds passed while he waited. She slouched to project defeat and stared at the floor. "He didn't want anyone to track him to his sister, so he was to visit a widow near Charlotte Town."

She gasped in shock when he gripped her upper arm, wheeled her into the parlor, and pushed her into her chair. He leaned over and braced both hands on the arms of the chair, so close she tasted the musky heat of his body. "St. James women cannot lie with conviction."

"Damn you, David didn't say where he was going! Arrest and execute me, yes! We must maintain order in our colonies. What finer evidence of order may we present the rebels than the dangling corpse of a widow whom we deem uncooperative in an investigation?"

Fairfax straightened, tucked the purse beneath his arm, and applauded. The face of Adonis, the physique of Odysseus, and not a drop of humanity inhabiting those eyes. Ye gods, he *was* a fiend. Helen shuddered.

His bearing aloof, he dropped the purse into her lap and seated himself on the couch. "Keep the money. A reversal of fortune is wretched for a gentlewoman. I can think of few more barbaric places for it to happen than these colonies."

Her tone curdled. "And now you expect me to sell my soul to you for food and wine, or because you did what a decent human would have done by explaining the burglary to that mob."

"I don't expect you to *sell* your soul to me at all."

Unmistakable, his emphasis on the word "sell." The seven-year-old boy with eyes of malice flashed teeth at her. Through the morass of fear and fatigue, outrage over his arrogance clambered up inside her. David had arrived on her doorstep haunted and hunted. How many people — women, in particular — had Fairfax browbeat into betraying David? Was anyone capable of getting the upper hand on the lieutenant?

But had anyone who'd crossed paths with Fairfax known a little of his history?

She tilted her head and hoped it looked imperious. "Are you quite certain you don't need this money more than I?"

A gust of amusement left him. "Your means are clearly strained. You need the money." He stood.

She rose without losing eye contact. "Ah. Then you *were* successful at wresting a piece of fortune from Lord Ratchingham. I congratulate you." Jingling coins in the purse, she sashayed for the foyer.

At the front door, hairs on the back of her neck polarized. He'd navigated around the couch toward her: wary, a predator surprised by a foreigner in his domain, trying to ascertain the other's strengths and weaknesses. She squashed down horror and pressed her lips together to give him the impression of disdain. The man before her seldom met his match in cunning. If she didn't tread with prudence, he'd make financial ruin by Badley seem a tender mercy.

In the foyer, he regarded her, self-assurance subdued. "You know the Clancys."

Had she knocked the dark prince onto his bum? If so, it was too soon to celebrate, and perilous to relax her guard. She rolled her eyes. "Everyone in Wiltshire knows them."

"I recognize you, but I cannot recall having you presented to me."

Any respect he had for her derived in part from his belief that she'd been born into the aristocracy. She'd lose that advantage if he discovered her birth circumstances. "Why should I have been presented to *you* when wealthy, old Silas Chiswell was waiting for me?" She dosed her laughter with mockery and yanked open the front door. "Good night, sir."

***

After he exited, she lowered the bar across the door. The scuff and shuffle of the men's departure did little to ease her frayed nerves.

Enid approached, jaw and shoulders set with determination, face calm. "Mistress, I've cleared the table and put away the food." Mindful of the servant-employer relationship, she made no demands, but Helen heard her unspoken question: *And isn't there something you need to tell me?*

Helen nodded for the parlor. When both women were seated, she let out a heavy breath and explained to Enid that the mortgage transfer had necessitated her accepting the assignment with the Legion. Rugged approval seeped into Enid's face. Helen had never felt less worthy of her servant's devotion and stood to stoke the fire in the fireplace. "I've concerns about the safety of our home in my absence. That rascal, Arthur Sims, is still loose. If those deputies don't apprehend him, he might burgle us again. And Mr. Badley, through slips of the tongue, has indicated that he expects you to join me on the road, leave the house unguarded.

"Therefore I think it unwise to take you with me." She set down the poker, faced Enid, and registered the dismay and bewilderment swelling her expression. "I need someone here to keep an eye on my property, someone whom I can trust implicitly. I prefer that you, with your sharp eyes and ears, remain behind in Wilmington."

The housekeeper sprang up from the couch. "You cannot manage by yourself among soldiers. It's improper, unsafe, impractical!"

"I don't intend to go alone. I hope the Pearsons will join me."

Welsh accent trickled into Enid's voice. "No doubt they'd serve you well, but surely after all the years we've been together —"

"To obtain as candid a portrait as possible of Tarleton, I must pose as the widowed sister of one of the regular officers in the Seventeenth Light Dragoons."

"Ach, Rhiannon, spare us! That *Saesneg!*" Her tongue tangled in accent, Enid lifted hands to her face. "I don't trust him! *Lloerig*, not well in the head. Without conscience. Can you not see it in his eyes?"

Helen steadied her chin. "I see it."

"I implore you, don't go with *him*."

Helen wondered whether she'd sleep that night, unassisted by laudanum. "Unfortunately he and the assignment go together. The advance I've received has helped me with the new debt. I might put the house up for sale, but what if it doesn't sell for months?" She paused and studied Enid. "Or I might release you from my service."

Face drawn in misery, Enid lowered her hands and hung her head. "Don't send me away from you." Her lower lip trembled.

"Then help me here, at home."

The servant nodded, beyond speech, her cheeks blotched with unshed tears.

Helen lay awake long into the night. She'd never found it wise to dismiss her instincts, and her instincts were sending up an awful ruckus. She may have flummoxed Fairfax by springing Ratchingham's name on him, but he wouldn't stay stumped for long. Many weeks in his company stretched before her. She had no doubt he would adapt with alacrity to the task of convincing her to surrender her soul to him.

Chapter Thirteen

"SIGN HERE." THE arthritis-knobby forefinger of Maximus Prescott stabbed the bottom of the document's third page before scooting the inkwell closer across the surface of the desk.

"Not before I read the entire contract again."

"No need. I corrected all five mistakes. Simply sign the document where indicated."

"Leave me." When he didn't budge, Helen pushed up from the cushioned chair in Badley's study, her glare fixed on the attorney. The powdery pallor of his wig emphasized the seethe in his dark eyes. Why did Prescott hate her so? She chilled her tone. "If *this* version also contains errors from your incompetence, I shall refuse the project."

He stomped for the door and slammed it behind him.

Unnerved, angry, Helen resumed her seat, inhaled three times to clear her mind, and read the contract aloud. Twenty minutes later, she set the document on the desk and reached for pen and ink, disappointed that all was in order and Prescott hadn't left her an exit. Having failed in the previous draft to obtain her agreement on unfavorable conditions, he knew better than to sneak in more "errors."

Although Badley had agreed to pay her four times her daily rate and fund two men to maintain the horses, equipment, and camp, he refused to fund a female attendant, presuming Helen to take Enid. He and Enid knew where they stood with each other. As Badley would discover, the joke was on him. Enid wasn't leaving Wilmington. Still, Helen found her sense of selling her soul to the devil deepened, rather than eased.

Since Tarleton's parties were the stuff of legend, the contract called for a report on Yule spent with the British Legion. Other than that, she must record her adventures daily for the duration of the journey and make effort to contact Badley at least fortnightly. Posts were often lost to rebel interference, and delayed by inclement weather and poor roads, so she must create copies of everything she sent him, as well as her journal entries. Badley couldn't require her to engage in battle — but she knew an account of a skirmish would titillate Londoners.

After signing the contract, she left the study. From the stables at the rear of Badley's house, men already loaded the wagon that would be her "home away from home" for more than two months. She observed them a few minutes before walking to the mantua-makers' and shoemaker's shops. All three shop owners' eyes were bloodshot, as were those of their employees. From the clutter of fabric, leather, and sewing implements that had possessed the shops overnight, Helen realized no one had slept much. Still, they greeted her with smiles, eager to gauge the fit of her partially completed wardrobe. Some of their enthusiasm transferred to her.

Wrapped in her cloak, she scurried back for Second Street. Fog besieged the town again, inauspicious weather for a funeral, and the air stank of dead fish and tar. Charles's service started in half an hour, and she and Enid barely had time to bustle to the churchyard together.

On Second, she stopped mulling over the retainer she'd given the Pearsons' attorney first thing in the morning to resolve her mortgage muddle, and she squinted through fog at a large, dark blob in the street ahead. The mass resolved itself into a fine new post chaise and four horses parked before her house. Who was her visitor? The driver's greatcoat and cocked hat looked to be of quality. He tipped his hat to her when she passed.

Enid, a bloom on her cheeks, opened the door before Helen reached the step. "Welcome home, mistress." She reached for Helen's cloak and lowered her voice. "While you were out, you'd a visitor from New Berne, name of Layman, come on behalf of a Widow Hanley."

Hanley. The name seemed familiar, but Helen couldn't place it just then. Still in the doorway, she glanced again at the post chaise.

"Layman was on horseback and said he'd return mid-afternoon." Enid grinned with pleasure. "The Professor awaits you in the parlor."

Further thoughts of the mysterious Layman and Widow Hanley from New Berne scampered from Helen's head as she rushed past Enid. Jonathan Quill looked up from an examination of her watercolor and smiled. "Good morning, my dear. Lovely new landscape you've painted. I presume your omission of druids was intentional?"

Emotion tumbled through her, gratitude the foremost. "Oh, Jonathan."

He deposited the painting on the couch and met her with outstretched arms and his familiar scent of the exotic East. "Shh," he whispered into her hair. "I'm here now. I owe all of you at least that much — you, Enid, Charles." He grasped her shoulders, set her back from him, and appraised her with pleasure, as always. But this time, sobriety and sadness laced the pleasure. "What devilry in Wilmington. Poor Charles. Tell me they've caught his murderer."

"Alas, no." She glanced him over, too, and studied his face. The crow's feet around his clear, blue eyes were no more advanced than when she'd seen him in April, nor was the gray dusting the hair at his temples. Time didn't mark its passage on Jonathan's serene countenance or his lithe, medium stature. He must have been at least forty years old when she set foot in Boston twelve years earlier; yet he was as supple and fit that moment as a twenty-year-old.

"Well. A knave cannot catch a knave." Jonathan sniffed. "Lurid, the ineptitude of these committeemen with the law."

He didn't know half of the story. "We *must* talk."

"I surmised as much." He checked the time on a gold watch drawn from the pocket of his embroidered silk waistcoat. "Do allow me to provide our transportation to Charles's funeral."

***

Two sextons' shovels scraped in unison, and damp clods of dirt thumped the wooden lid of Charles's coffin six feet below sight. Halfway around the grave from Helen, Roger enfolded Hannah in his arms. To Helen's immediate left, slow tears tracked Enid's face, lifted to the misty, gray sky. Grateful for the solid presence of Jonathan on her right, but aching with the women's distress and her own, Helen blotted tears from her eyes with a handkerchief. Several paces back from the graveside, George Gaynes and two deputies whispered between themselves and directed scowls at her.

"...through Jesus Christ, to whom be glory for ever and ever." The vicar spread his arms to congregants at the graveside, his black frock flapping like the wings of a buzzard.

People muttered, "Amen," and withdrew. The vicar and several congregants escorted the Pearsons over to a small reception behind the church.

Helen signed for Enid to join the bereaved. She intended to mosey that way herself when she felt more like eating. With Jonathan her silent companion, she walked among headstones until she found that of Silas. Then she stood at the foot of the grave to contemplate the metaphor of its autumn-brown grass.

When she stirred to rejoin the Pearsons, Charles's graveside had gained a familiar visitor, his gentleman's cocked hat upon his head. Jonathan regarded him. "Curious. That fellow over there reminds me of a peer who died twenty-three years ago near Avebury."

Helen's skin crawled. "Was the peer's name Fairfax?"

The electricity of astonishment sparked Jonathan's eyes. "Why, yes, Timothy Fairfax."

Helen nodded toward Fairfax, who was studying Charles's grave. "I believe he's the son of your acquaintance. His name is Dunstan Fairfax."

"The fellow you wrote me about." Jonathan grunted. "An officer out of uniform — and after what happened to John André."

For André, civilian clothing had been a disguise allowing him to attempt a desperate mission behind enemy lines. For Fairfax, Helen knew it was a prop in a perverse game he played.

Jonathan squinted at Fairfax. Helen could almost see twenty-year-old memories roam his face. "Fairfax's widow, Jane, remarried. I recall it."

"She wed Lord Ratchingham."

"Henry Clancy, yes." He turned back to her, one eyebrow hiked. Sanguinity emptied from his tone. "Ratchingham hanged himself seven or eight years ago. Did you know that?"

How tragic, my stepfather was also a suicide. Fairfax's words returned to Helen, and she nodded. "Let me introduce you. I suspect you'll find it quite interesting."

Jonathan strolled her over, their footsteps muted in the fog-drenched grass. His back to them, Fairfax scrutinized the crowd at the reception, where Gaynes and his cohorts glowered at him and stuffed their faces with food. He turned to face Helen and Jonathan with detachment. "Madam."

Conscious of the Committee's proximity, she kept her voice low. "How considerate of you to pay your respects to Mr. Landon, sir."

His gaze hopped from her to Jonathan and assessed his carriage, the quality of his suit, and the ease with which her hand nestled in his elbow. "Mr. Landon was law abiding." He tilted his head toward Gaynes. "Were *I* officially the investigator, the perpetrator would have been apprehended long ago."

Jonathan also kept his voice low, so the Committee wouldn't overhear. "How now, sir, Mr. Gaynes over there is one of North Carolina's finest examples of Yankee Doodle law enforcement."

Fairfax's lips twitched. "I haven't yet the pleasure of your acquaintance."

"Jonathan Quill, at your service."

Helen noted Jonathan's special smile, reserved for occasions that required rather than merited cordiality. Fairfax's expression remained bland, but she knew he'd placed Jonathan's name and relationship with her from his snoop into the contents of her letter the previous day.

"Dunstan Fairfax, sir." He nodded toward the committeemen, who watched them. "Also known as Mr. Black, special agent for General Washington. Your accent — Wiltshire?"

"Yes. I had the acquaintance of your father, a good man. I also had the acquaintance of your stepfather, Lord Ratchingham."

"I see." The gaze of glacial green shifted to Helen. "Clearly your friendship with Mrs. Chiswell extends back decades. May I presume a business connection with her family?"

He leaned into the silence that followed, and Helen's stomach tensed again at the predator grope of his will for hers. Jonathan patted her hand on his arm, alerting her that she'd clutched him, and while she eased tension from her fingers, he said in a breezy voice, "I defer to the lady for a history of our familial connections." Thrust and parry.

"Of course." Unsmiling, Fairfax continued to flog her with his stare. "Madam, Mr. Badley informed me the contract is signed and in order. We've mapped out the route. Do me the honor of dining with me this evening, and I shall present you the itinerary."

Sensing the myriad questions Fairfax's announcement aroused in Jonathan, Helen drew a steady breath. "My good friend Jonathan is only just arrived this morning from his estate on the Lower Cape Fear. We plan to dine together tonight, catch up on family news."

Jonathan patted her hand again, his tone chipper. "My dear, clearly you've pressing business matters to discuss with Mr. Fairfax. I've no objection to sharing you with him over supper."

Parlor games. So long had it been since she'd played them that she'd lost a good deal of nimbleness for the sport. She may as well roll with it. "How considerate of you, Jonathan. Now, then, Mr. Fairfax, how does seven o'clock tonight suit?" The idea that he'd eat leftovers from the meal he'd purchased the previous night amused her.

"Very well, madam."

A smirk caught Jonathan's lip. "I look forward to hearing rollicking stories of your adventures with your wild Clancy stepbrothers."

The seven-year-old swung loose in Fairfax's eyes before he seized and submerged the beast. Helen's breath caught in her throat. She must warn Jonathan. Needling Fairfax was like yanking the tail of a famished tiger.

"I shall endeavor not to disappoint. Madam. Sir." He pivoted and headed from the churchyard toward his men waiting in clear view on the street. Helen, eyeing the track his shoes made in the wet lawn, fancied she heard grass sizzle.

Jonathan sighed. "Helen, what in Hades have you fallen into?"

"Mrs. Chiswell! Mrs. Chiswell!" Hannah, her face splotched from tears, strode to them from the reception. Roger and Enid trailed after, concern and grief congesting their expressions.

Remorse wrung Helen's heart. Preoccupied with her own affairs, she hadn't tended the bereaved. She caught Hannah's cold hands in hers. "Oh, Hannah, do forgive me for not joining the reception sooner —"

"Bah, never you mind that." The blonde planted her feet and jutted her jaw but quieted her voice, conscious of committeemen nearby. "Roger told me of your project. Papa's in the ground now. I'm ready to leave whenever you are, proud to help you on your assignment with Colonel Tarleton for that new magazine in London. Just let me out of this town for awhile."

Well, that just about covered everything, didn't it? Between Fairfax and Hannah, Jonathan should be able to summon the grand picture of her adventure into Hades long ere they'd have a chance that afternoon to talk in private about it. She squeezed Hannah's hands. "Thank you, dear." Roger caressed his wife's shoulder from behind and nodded approval. Helen said, "I thank both of you. Join us for supper tonight at seven. We shall discuss our route." Releasing Hannah, she turned to Jonathan.

He propped a fist on his hip. "You weren't jesting earlier when you said we must talk."

Chapter Fourteen

HELEN BADE THE Pearsons good night, dropped the bar on the front door, and returned to the parlor. The clock chimed ten. She stifled a yawn, eager for bed after the awkward supper.

At Badley's insistence, the route to the Crown's backcountry base of Camden, South Carolina zigzagged through the Santee, realm of rebel-lord Francis Marion, and farther north, where rebel Thomas Sumter reigned. Fairfax had explained the risks to the publisher, but Badley was keen to thrust his journalist in the path of potential opportunities for interviews.

Helen couldn't envision either rebel chief pausing reconnaissance of the backcountry to chat with a journalist. If the rebels discovered she was a Loyalist, she'd never leave the swamps alive. Fairfax agreed. As a counter-measure, everyone in their party would don the garb of backwoods dwellers before their arrival in the Santee, to help them blend in with residents. Some of Helen's misgivings about their route eased. Still, Marion and Sumter had spies.

The departure awaited only Helen's wardrobe, complete by Wednesday, and a man to assist Roger. But Hannah's worn expression concerned Helen. She wondered whether the younger woman was up for the journey, whether she'd be better off spending the immediate weeks after her father's death at home.

She regarded Jonathan, who stared into the unlit parlor fireplace. His reserve throughout supper and physical distance from others afterwards reinforced for her how confounded he was by the venture. Never had she seen him so preoccupied. She said, "It's late for you to drive back. Stay here tonight. Enid can ready your room in a moment and prepare a pallet for your man."

"You're most obliging." He bowed his head. "I shall stay, then, and if the night isn't too damp, stroll in the back yard while my room is prepared."

In response to his request for her company, Helen preceded him, pausing at the dining room to request that Enid prepare accommodations for their guests. In the middle of the back yard, Jonathan inhaled and took his time releasing the breath, as if the atmosphere of the parlor were noxious. Helen waited while he repeated the exercise. Never would Jonathan be rushed into conversation.

Uneasiness groped at her throat. Jonathan disapproved of the project. She hoped he wouldn't try to talk Badley out of it. While never close friends, he and Badley were cordial. If anyone could change Badley's mind, it would be Jonathan, but that must involve Jonathan's offer to compensate Badley for his losses.

"My dear, David St. James would be perfect for your second man on this expedition." A half-laugh of denial escaped her, and she faced him. He meandered over, his scrutiny of her expression keen in the semi-night conferred by lamplight from neighbors' yards, and fog. "Why not?" His tone firmed. "Have you two quarreled again?"

She wondered why Jonathan was so strong an advocate of her relationship with David. At times, he almost seemed to shove David at her. "Yes, we did, three nights ago." Exasperation vented through his nostrils, so she summarized what had happened between David and Fairfax.

"Good gods, Helen." Astuteness seized Jonathan's expression. "And your rationale for accepting the assignment with the Legion?"

She lifted her chin. "I'm bored writing about Wilmington society."

Motionless as a sculpture from an ancient temple, he studied her. "The Chinese believe that everyone who enters your life is your teacher with a lesson for you. Should you fail to learn the lesson the first time —"

"The universe will provide me a more potent teacher the next time, and stronger and stronger teachers, until I've finally learned the lesson."

"Jolly! You remember!" He grimaced. "Now, what lesson does the universe intend you to learn with Mr. Fairfax as your teacher?"

As if his rebuke had delivered a physical slap, she recoiled and touched her face. "Really, Jonathan, you've never toyed with me in such a manner."

"You've never toyed with yourself in such a manner. Something catastrophic influenced you to accept the assignment. Your quarrel with David — no, you've more sense than to make decisions with your heart. And I'm certain you've more courage than to run away from the Committee's bluster over Charles's murder." Enlightenment flooded his face. "Only one topic backs you into a corner. This is about money, isn't it? You accepted that wretched assignment for *money.*"

She stalked away. Jonathan could speak of money with contempt. Not for a day in his life had he worried about it. Her transformation during the Atlantic crossing had drawn upon all the alchemy in his repertoire, but Silas's monetary reward had been immaterial. Jonathan's true "payment" had arrived when Agatha Chiswell approved of Helen after spending less than an hour in her company.

"This is a once-in-a-lifetime opportunity for me to write more than society drivel. Badley's paying me four times my daily rate."

"Yes, this *is* about money." Jonathan overtook her, yanked her around to him. "You hit a financial snag. David offered help. You declined. That's what your quarrel with him was about."

"I suppose now I shall hear *your* offer of financial help?"

"No, my dear. You would despise me for it. You've made your aversion to being purchased quite clear. Help me comprehend how Phineas succeeded where all men since Silas have failed."

While Helen worked her mouth for a retort, she almost missed Jonathan's glance to her left. He shoved her away with a shout. A flash lit the night, the report of a pistol thundered in her ear, and she smelled the sulfurous heat of a ball singing air that separated them.

Before she could gasp, before the first neighborhood dog had responded, Jonathan vaulted in pursuit of the assailant over the low hedge between her property and Mr. Morris's.

***

Gaynes completed a lap of investigator-strut before the fireplace. "You're certain you didn't see enough to corroborate Mr. Quill's description?"

Helen wondered when she'd get a good night's sleep again. Unable to sit, she fidgeted in the doorway near two deputies who leaned against the parlor doorjambs. They stank of ale. "The pistol flash startled me. By the time I recovered my bearings, Jonathan had given chase, and the assailant was well away."

Gaynes grunted. "Mighty detailed, your description of him, Mr. Quill. Five feet four inches tall, plump, limping on the left leg, wearing a dark coat. To be sure, he sounds like Landon's killer and our fugitive. If I were you, Mrs. Chiswell, I'd sleep with the doors barred and windows locked."

The latch on the study window wasn't yet repaired, thanks to her recent distractions. Indignation seared her weariness. The Committee's priority had always been clear: protecting Whigs in the community. Gaynes implied that she must provide her own defense against Wilmington's criminals.

He waved a battered, cocked hat at Jonathan. "Too bad he escaped, but at least you recovered his hat."

Also posed near the fireplace, Jonathan squared off with Gaynes, dignified despite hedge-stains and a tear on one stocking and a pocket flap dangling from his coat. "Arthur Sims remains at liberty with murderous intent and a stolen pistol. Apprehending him is the responsibility of the Committee of Safety. You'd best do so soon, lest he attempt another murder, and you find yourself replaced as deputy."

Gaynes's eyes bugged. He swelled his chest and jutted his jaw. "Are you threatening me, Mr. Professor?"

Jonathan studied him, his tone calm. "Did you understand nothing of what I said?"

"I got ears, don't I? And with those ears, I heard you browbeat me to find Sims."

"I've heard that Special Agent Black handed you a number of excellent leads on Sims. Exactly what progress have you made toward finding this killer and closing the case?"

"I ain't required to give you any details, but we're making plenty of progress. Rooting out criminals ain't like hanging laundry. There's skill to it, like — like baking bread."

Helen repressed a sigh. Heaven help them. Gaynes had learned crime solving from a baker.

"Well, then," said Jonathan, "I trust you won't leave the majority of those

Wilmington loaves in the oven too long, simply because they're loyal to the king or neutral."

Fury flared in Gaynes's eyes. "Tory dung!" Like a bear, he swung a fist out at Jonathan.

Reverberations of Gaynes's bulk sprawling to the floor between the couch and fireplace echoed through the house for several seconds. Helen blinked. Jonathan had stepped aside with the reflexes of a deer and allowed Gaynes's momentum to pitch him forward onto the floor.

The deputies in the doorway guffawed. Enid and Jonathan's driver, Peter, ran in from the kitchen to investigate the clamor.

Jonathan took a step toward the fallen man in concern. "Are you injured, sir?"

With an oath, Gaynes lumbered to his feet, straightened his clothing, and snatched his hat and Sims's from the floor. "We're competent at catching criminals." He scowled his deputies into silence and stomped for the door. "Tories — always trying to order how we conduct our business."

Helen and the two servants stepped aside to allow the investigators egress. Enid secured the front door behind them. The clock struck eleven.

Helen turned to Jonathan. Fear for his safety climbed atop fear for her well-being. "I dread the thought that this scoundrel who stole Silas's pistol may return to complete his work on me and murder you by accident."

"Complete twaddle, my dear." From the easy smile on Jonathan's face, they might just have finished a stroll in a meadow. "He hasn't the gall to repeat an attempt tonight."

"How can you be certain?"

"Mr. Sims made his intentions clear. He aimed the pistol at me. *I'm* his target, not you."

Chapter Fifteen

HELEN LAY AWAKE long into the night, despite the safeguard of the driver, Peter, on a pallet in the study below, a loaded pistol beside him, and pots and pans piled upon the desk at the broken window to raise a clamor at any intruder's entrance. Arthur Sims had murdered Charles and tried to kill Jonathan. Charles and Jonathan had been Seconds in that duel. Someone wanted revenge.

Perhaps the Chiswells figured out that Silas hadn't committed suicide. If so, David was the crown jewel on that assassination list. Such a list might include her name.

But — *They'll kill Madam if they find it.* What had Charles meant? Who were "they," and what was "it?" Why wait nine years to serve revenge? Or did revenge provide too convenient a motive for murder?

As she drifted toward sleep, a random thought tugged her back to partial wakefulness. A man named Layman, sent by Widow Hanley out of New Berne, had arrived to speak with her that morning. Hadn't Enid said he'd return mid-afternoon? Hanley. New Berne. Something familiar about that combination, but she couldn't quite recall. Perhaps she'd remember in the morning.

***

Between the stable and house, mist hugged earth and warped into wraith-melody the driver's merry whistle while he fed the horses. Helen heard Peter's tune, disembodied and eldritch, as she descended the stairs. It sent a shiver from the soles of her feet to her scalp, gifted upon her another memory, from the weeks prior to the procurement, when whispers circulated among servants at Redthorne. Carcasses of small animals turned up in conspicuous places about the property once a month or so: mutilated rabbits, squirrels, and rats. Christian servants murmured of devilry. The other servants murmured of old gods who walked the land eons before Roman soldiers. Lord Ratchingham seemed oblivious.

What had Jedediah the butler thought of all that? With a start, she remembered that he hadn't been the butler at Redthorne her final years in the village, but she couldn't recall what had happened to him. Odd. Perhaps Jonathan knew.

She eased open the back door. Jonathan parted mist in the yard, at one with the filmy, damp cloud, earth scents, and bird-warble, movements of his early morning dance a silent, silky ritual. She'd first seen him perform the dawn dance on the deck of the brig to America. *China*, he'd told her, when she'd asked where he learned the dance.

Beside her, Enid watched him, no stranger to the movements. "Look at that. Just like a swooping hawk," she whispered.

Indeed, each motion called to mind swaying of plants or lithe activity of wild creatures. Comprehension hit Helen that moment; his remarkable ability to avoid Gaynes's assault the previous night was an application of his dance. Thoughtful, she withdrew into the house.

Enid shut the back door and followed her into the study. "Mistress, I've coffee set out in the dining room. Shall I make toast?"

Chagrin tugged Helen. The pantry was almost empty. Little could she offer her guest and friend to break his fast, but at the very least, she wouldn't insult him by serving cold toast. "Allow Jonathan to settle in with his first cup of coffee before you toast bread."

Enid bobbed a curtsy and left Helen in the quiet of the study. Her gaze roved over the dueling pistol case, ledgers, and storage boxes, and her random thought from bedtime solidified to carve out direction. Letters. Perhaps a clue waited in Silas's old letters.

She dragged the box to the window, providing her enough light to read, and pulled up her chair. Meticulous and exacting, Silas had filed correspondences in reverse chronological order. With but the faintest idea for what she searched, Helen began in the mid-1750s, when Silas was around twenty years old.

After a few minutes, she could hardly stomach more. "Sowing wild oats" didn't begin to describe the debaucheries staining her husband's early manhood, detailed to extreme in missives from rakes who'd shared his adventures. Season after season, inheritances burning holes in their pockets, they flocked from surrounding counties with as much purpose as the hadji that gathered en route to Mecca — except that their sacristy destinations were London hells.

No normal married man would keep reminders of such depravity. With a shudder, Helen imagined Silas rereading his treasures late at night, long after she'd fallen asleep alone, and easing his arousal with his own hand. Maybe he'd planted the testaments for her to stumble upon after his death: his final mockery of her from beyond the grave.

The rakes became fewer and farther between in the 1760s. Those who persevered in acquaintance commiserated with Silas over pressures exerted by stodgy families upon fun loving fellows who showed no signs of settling down in their thirties. Assume a prominent role in family business, patriarchs and matriarchs nagged. Marry and beget children. How stifling.

From the sympathy he'd received from friends, Silas must have complained often about the company of businessmen thrust upon him by his parents — advisers like Jonathan who embodied responsibility. One of the last acts of his father before dying in 1767 was to order Silas's journey to visit a business partner in North Carolina and study, firsthand, the Chiswell family's naval stores trade.

Helen stared at a letter from 1767, its writer Isaiah Hanley of New Berne.

Unsure of the value of her find, she extracted Hanley's letters from the box and skimmed them. Early on, he acknowledged that Silas barely tolerated his input and regarded him as some sort of restrictive outgrowth of the Chiswell patriarch. That changed in 1769, after Hanley suffered a series of strokes. He required a secretary for dictation. By 1770, he'd lost the ability to speak. From the warmth of the secretary's responses, however, Silas had finally recognized a friend in Isaiah Hanley. Alas, too late for either man.

The final letter, penned by Hanley's widow, announced her husband's death. Helen remembered Silas receiving it in the summer of 1771, just a few months before the duel. He'd flown into a grief-fueled rage, slapped several servants around, including Enid, drunk himself into a stupor, and vomited all over his bedroom. Summer days when the weather was hot and humid, she imagined she smelled vomit in that bedroom still, even though it no longer contained a stick of furniture and had been scoured from floor to ceiling.

Why had the widow of Isaiah Hanley attempted to contact the widow of Silas Chiswell in 1780, nine years later?

Helen scrutinized each letter for a clue. In 1770, the secretary had scribbled a peculiar postscript: "If perjury is still a fear, we shall keep it safe for you."

It. That peculiar pronoun again. Cold air scraped Helen's neck, and she pulled her lace tucker closer about her throat. In the darkness of a far corner, greenish phosphorescence crouched, and she heard a whisper: "They'll kill Madam if they find it."

With a gasp, she stood and spilled Hanley's letters onto the floor. "What is *it*, Charles?" she demanded of the dark corner, although the glow had vanished. "Tell me!"

"Good morning, my dear." Stockings and coat pocket mended by Enid, Jonathan strolled in and drew up short when he spied the letters on the floor. "Allow me to help you tidy up. I thought I heard you conversing with someone."

She gulped. "Jonathan, did Silas confide in you fears of perjury back in 1770?"

"Perjury?" He knelt and collected letters. "Not that I recall, but by 1770, our relationship was much strained by the melancholia induced from his use of spirits. I was quite surprised when he ask me to be his Second." He stood and handed her the letters. "Here you are. Reading over some correspondence to Silas, eh? What have you found? Did someone commit perjury against him?"

"I'm not sure. These are from Isaiah Hanley."

"Ah, yes, Hanley. A wise man."

"His widow sent a fellow named Layman with a message for me. He arrived from New Berne while I was out yesterday morning. According to Enid, he was supposed to return later."

"Don't fret. He'll turn up. The Hanleys hire responsible servants. In the mean time, Enid sent me to fetch you for breakfast."

Minutes later, while she and Jonathan dispatched toast slathered with blackberry jam, a knock sounded at the front door. Enid bustled past the dining room to answer the door. Then she poked her head in to them, expression dour. "Mr. Gaynes and some men to see you, mistress."

Chair legs squawked in Helen's haste to rise and blot her fingers clean on a napkin. "They've caught Arthur Sims?"

"I don't think so. Molly, Mr. Morris's laundress, is with them. It smells of more trouble. Shall I admit them to the parlor?"

"No." With Jonathan at her heels, Helen swept from the dining room, pulled the front door open, and looked from the pale face of Molly to the blood-shot scowls of Gaynes and several deputies. "You have news for me? Make haste. My breakfast grows cold."

Gaynes jerked his head at Molly without taking his eyes off Helen. "Tell her."

Blonde Molly chewed her lower lip. "I don't want to cause you more trouble, Mrs. Chiswell. I was one of the early ones to market this morning, see. I f-found a dead man, and recognized him. I w— wasn't snooping yesterday morning, honest, when I overheard him talking with Enid at your front door. I heard him say he was sent out of New Berne, c-come to talk with you."

Shock swirled through Helen. Light-headed, she pressed her hands to her cheeks. Layman, Widow Hanley's messenger, dead before he could deliver information from his mistress.

Murdered, perhaps, to prevent his doing so?

Gaynes's lip twitched at Molly. "Run along back to Mr. Morris. We know where to find you if we have more questions." The girl scurried off after a curtsy.

"How was he murdered?" To Helen, her own voice sounded distant, dreamy.

"Shot in the head. Surgeon's autopsying him, but let's you and me wager he finds it was a *pistol* ball, same as what killed Landon." He sneered. "Don't know what your plans are for the near future, but the Committee of Safety insists that you not leave town until we capture Arthur Sims."

Chapter Sixteen

PETER CLOSED THE front door and took Helen's hat and cloak. A burst of carpentry from the study subsided. "Where's Enid, Peter?"

"Still at market, madam."

Helen peeped in on the carpenter. He spied her and tugged the brim of his hat in deference. Jonathan had tipped him to have the window installed, functional, and lockable by nightfall.

At her entrance to the parlor, Jonathan rose from the couch and bowed. Peter closed his master and Helen in, blocking some of the carpentry noise. Helen motioned Jonathan to sit and took her chair. "Stymied in his pet project by a pack of rebels: I thought Badley would die of apoplexy when I told him Gaynes had ordered me to remain in town. I spared him the detail that Gaynes dispatched a deputy to New Berne to question Mrs. Hanley."

Jonathan crossed his legs. "Probably a wise idea. Besides, those four days round-trip to New Berne give you more time to locate and hire an intelligent, competent fellow to assist the Pearsons. What progress has been made on your wardrobe?"

Jonathan seemed to have accepted her assignment overnight. "All ready on the morrow."

His jaw dropped open. "No wonder Phineas is distressed. That Samuel Kerr fellow must have paid him quite an incentive."

"Remember, according to Mr. Fairfax, there is no editor by that name on the *Chronicle*."

"Consider Kerr a third party, then, employed by someone with another agenda."

She cocked an eyebrow. "Such as?"

"So many agendas to chose from. Hmm, how about Banastre Tarleton's eye on Parliament?"

Helen felt a sharp edge emerge on her smile. "My stars! Have I been planted in the Legion to pass along muck about Tarleton so his opponents can foul his budding political career?"

Jonathan shrugged. "It's a common procedure in journalism. I presume you know your fate if you're implicated in such a scheme?"

She slapped her knee and laughed. "Badley, that scoundrel! I always suspected he wanted to be rid of me. Well, not this time. Let someone else sully Tarleton's reputation. It won't be me."

Jonathan's smile at her pluck submerged into sobriety. "Don't allow the first probable agenda to blind you. Other players inhabit the stage. Mr. Fairfax, for example."

"Mr. Fairfax?" Helen grinned. "An intriguing variation."

Jonathan strolled to a window, hands clasped behind him. Daylight from an overcast sky paled his skin. "'What may man within him hide, though angel on the outward side.'"

"William Shakespeare." Her grin faded. "Angel on the outward side" certainly described Fairfax.

"Excellent recall. I've been reminiscing. Ratchingham purchased a cornet's commission for his stepson but then hanged himself two days before Mr. Fairfax left for America. If I remember correctly, Lady Ratchingham had died in childbirth the previous month."

Fairfax's mother had been in her early forties when she died: in a high-risk, late pregnancy. Recalling Fairfax's air of omniscience when he'd caught up with her on the street the previous afternoon, Helen realized he'd baited her about Silas's death, as if he were already certain it wasn't suicide.

That was when he'd mentioned his stepfather's suicide.

Chills crept up her arms. Had Fairfax blamed Lord Ratchingham for his mother's death and taken a hand in his stepfather's death? Did someone in Wiltshire — one of the Clancy brothers, perhaps — now want evidence unearthed against Fairfax?

Why not save us all some time and tell me what old Badley is up to?

Jonathan's voice softened. "There are ways a man might hang another, make it appear suicide."

More chills quivered her. "Why speak of this?"

"You've plans to spend time with Mr. Fairfax." He turned to her, his expression inscrutable. "You must find a reliable man to help you, someone to assist the Pearsons."

"Roger inquired of his contacts. Perhaps he shall have luck today."

"Luck is often created. *You* inquire of all your business contacts, including the clothiers."

She fidgeted. "I'd planned to help you examine the letters for clues on that business of perjury."

"Thus far, I've found nothing to substantiate Silas's fears, but I shall continue reading."

"I also planned to study records of Silas's debts and claims from his creditors for discrepancies."

Jonathan indicated a bound record book on the table. "I shall assist you at that. Run along."

She glanced at the clock. "And I've a meeting here with Mr. Fairfax at noon."

A sharkish grin spread Jonathan's lips. He strolled over and helped her stand. "Not to worry. When he arrives, I shall make profuse apologies for your inattendance and act as host until your return. Now go out and thrash the brush until you find a man to help Roger and Hannah." He strode to the doors and flung them open. "Peter, fetch the lady's cloak and hat!"

★★★

An embroidery client's seventeen-year-old son had lost work in timber less than a week earlier, but hardworking, reliable fellows such as he didn't go unemployed for long. As Helen and the lady were talking, the lad jogged back home with a happy smile to inform his mother that he'd taken a job unloading turpentine and rosin barrels poled down the Cape Fear by rafters.

By mid-afternoon, Helen had chased three more leads to oblivion. Frustrated at the unavailability of reliable help, she purchased a hat and placed it on Badley's tab before heading home. The new hat upon her head, she executed a slow pirouette for Jonathan. "Do you like it?"

"Lovely." The word barely escaped a stiff upper lip.

"You're quite the moody one this afternoon."

His nose twitched. "Mr. Fairfax checkmated me twice, rot him. I've never seen such audacious moves with rooks and knights."

Helen couldn't suppress a laugh. Never had she thought Jonathan would meet his match at chess.

His upper lip curled. "And that fellow can really dance."

"You *danced* with Mr. Fairfax?"

"Dash it all, Helen, not literally. No, he danced all around details of his upbringing at Redthorne while trying to squeeze me for information about your background. And he sniffed a good bit around the murders of Charles and Mr. Layman."

She replaced her hat in its package, uneasy. "He'd love to uncover the truth about my common birth." The clock struck four. They sat. "Where is he now?"

"Ill humored by your absence, returning on the morrow at noon."

"Well, thank you for pulling the hound off me for awhile."

"Don't mention it. You're the one privileged to spend so much time in his company." Pensive, he regarded her. "He wanted to see more of your watercolors. I said I didn't know where you stored them."

She expelled a breath. "Good. He follows the old ways."

Jonathan slapped his forehead. "I should have guessed. Another scion from the Ratchingham druid brood."

"No. The *old* ways."

"Oh." The pensiveness in his eyes deepened. "Let us hope he doesn't remember details from Beltane '67. May Queen isn't usually the sort of honor conferred upon a gentlewoman."

Beltane '67. Sixteen years old. Flowers twined in her loose hair and circled her wrists and neck. The scent of crushed petals ascended to the heavens from her Queen's litter. When her bearers lifted her high, a great cheer rose from the men, women, and children assembled on the plain. Amidst a torrent of flower petals, she was conveyed to the Maypole. Wood smoke from bonfires, the air heavy with wine and laughter, drums throbbing and pipes screeling, an enormous moon in full sail come unpinned from cloud tatters and agleam on hundreds of sweaty breasts and buttocks...

"Helen, what luck have you in finding a man to assist Roger?"

She cleared her throat, propelled forward in time more than thirteen years by Jonathan's question. "Ah. None. What luck have you on the issue of perjury?"

"None."

They sighed in unison.

"Jonathan, perhaps there was no perjury. Perhaps Silas's mind manufactured it."

"Yes." He frowned. "His mind was so clouded by drink that he grew distrustful of everyone. He had delusions that all his chums like Phineas conspired against him."

"He mistrusted you, too." She watched Jonathan look away to hide the score of disappointment in his expression. Sorrow pinched her heart. "No one cared for his company. He drank, grew isolated and suspicious, drank more, became more isolated, suspicious."

They fell silent. Helen could envision Silas's concerns a product of his ravaged mind only, not of reality. But Isaiah Hanley's secretary had suggested that Silas send him something tangible for safekeeping, and Charles had suspected something hidden and tangible connected with her as incriminatory to a third party, and Widow Hanley had attempted to contact her. To be sure, it was a great puzzle that had yielded too few pieces thus far.

Jonathan agreed to remain for supper — beefsteaks that he'd purchased — and spend another night as Helen's guest. Even with the window in the study repaired and a cheery fire in the parlor fireplace, Helen couldn't shake a sense of doom. The household retired to bed before nine.

At midnight, they were awakened by a pounding on the front door reminiscent of the Committee's spy hunt several nights earlier. Flanked by Enid, Jonathan, and Peter, Helen opened the door to deputies with lit torches, the scowl of George Gaynes at their forefront.

The committeeman looked her over once, his expression the wary regard of a man with a troublesome tooth for a surgeon's tongs. Then he flicked his gaze to the three faces around her. "Where have you been for the past six hours, Mrs. Chiswell?"

Ire stung her voice. "Right here in my house."

"You have witnesses, I presume."

"I'm a witness." Jonathan's tone was dry. Enid and Peter joined him.

With a growl, Gaynes thrashed around the contents of his tote sack, yanked out a dueling pistol, and suspended it by its barrel. "Is this your husband's?"

She stared at it, astonished. "Yes, it is! Where did you find it?"

"In Arthur Sims's house, beside his body. Apparently he shot himself in the head with it sometime in the past six hours. Another suicide. Fancy that. We'll be keeping the pistol awhile for evidence, but it looks as though you're free to go about your business. Pleasant dreams tonight."

Chapter Seventeen

"SO, THE COWARD took his own life. Too bad he didn't hang for murdering Papa." Hannah kneaded her lower back and shot Helen a glance. "Are your gowns finished yet?"

"This afternoon."

She stopped rubbing her back, surprised. "Huzzah! We're off first thing on the morrow!"

"Only if I can find a man to help Roger."

"Pshaw. I'm able to do a man's work and a good shot with a musket. Between the Pearsons, you'll be well cared for. Let's be off."

Sadness sifted into Helen's heart. How splendid if adventure was all one needed to swallow the portion that grief flung out. "Jonathan advised me to find a second man, and I've learned not to ignore his advice. I'd like you to ponder the possibility that Sims didn't kill himself yesterday but was killed by the person who hired him to murder your father."

"Serves him right, the scum."

"What if Sims was killed to keep him silent?" From Hannah's stare, Helen had piqued her interest. "Whoever hired Sims suspected your father had knowledge that could undo him. Perhaps one night when Mr. Chiswell allowed your father to pull the bottle from his hands and help him to bed, he spoke of someone who'd wronged him. Charles might have hinted of confidences."

Hannah's stare drifted over Helen's shoulder. She shook her head. "Nothing comes to mind this moment."

"Of course not. Knowing your father, any reference he made would have been subtle. Think on it. Let it come to you when it's ready." If Charles had confided in Hannah, it might take the distraction of travel and adventure to bring it to the surface.

***

Behind the closed door of the study, Jonathan shoved the record book back on its shelf. "I found no discrepancies in the accounting. There were no anomalous debt amounts, such as for a series of blackmail payments. You clearly documented the payment for each debt with its corresponding date." He shook his head. "I see no evidence of perjury here."

She indicated the box of letters. "What of his correspondence?"

"Nothing there except —" Jonathan's face pinched with disgust. "— vulgar reminiscences from his youth not fit for a lady's eyes. I suggest that you burn the whole box."

Admiration for Jonathan rushed through Helen. David would have suggested the same. True gentlemen. "And the letters to Isaiah Hanley?"

"Nothing in any other letter gave weight to that peculiar postscript. Helen, if the murders of Charles, Mr. Layman, and Arthur Sims are somehow related to actions of your late husband, I don't see clues here. For now, move on to more pressing matters. What information did Hannah offer about Charles?"

"None. I followed your suggestion and asked her not to dwell upon our theory. Perhaps something will come to her."

"Has Roger found a second man yet?"

"No."

Arms crossed over his chest, he walked to the window and stared out. "You won't find him this late. The trip is perilous, demanding an elevated standard of fitness and intelligence of your attendants that excludes the majority of candidates. It also excludes any candidate who is even marginally sympathetic to the rebel cause." He faced her, arms at his side, his blue eyes electric. "If you are to be guaranteed any reasonable level of security and safety, you must have a second man. I see no option but to accompany you myself."

She snickered. "Now, now. December and January can be bitter out of doors."

"I'm aware of that." His jaw was set.

Disbelief speared her. "You're *serious* about this? Wouldn't you rather sit by your fire?"

"Why ask me such an absurd question? Do I look like a doddering old man?"

"Doddering? Surely not."

"It's settled, then. Peter and I shall ride home and pack. Meet me at my estate on the morrow. Plan to spend the first night there."

"*Nothing* is settled, Jonathan. You mustn't risk your life on this assignment."

Enid knocked on the study door. "Mistress, Mr. Fairfax has just arrived for your noon meeting. I've admitted him to the parlor."

"Yes, thank you, Enid." Fairfax. Perhaps Jonathan's inclusion in the party was judicious. Still, for him to endanger his life — she lowered her voice and met the level gaze of her former teacher. "I've never disputed your wisdom."

"Trust me to guard my own back."

Her shoulders dropped in acquiescence. "I presume you won't object to packing away the gentleman's clothing while we travel through the Santee?"

"Not at all."

Her lips kinked with irony. "Care to leave your chessboard behind?"

Mock-indignation bit his expression. "Do you fancy me a coward? Of course I shall bring it!"

***

From Fairfax's poise upon receiving news of Jonathan's inclusion in the party, he'd anticipated it as the move of a well-bred lady and widow. Helen concluded the meeting and sent the lieutenant on his way, saw Jonathan off by half past twelve and brought Enid to the merchants' shops, where all her clothing had assumed final shape overnight: a gentlewoman's winter travel wardrobe that dazzled Enid and drove back Helen's misgivings. With the gowns bundled away home between Enid and one of the apprentices, she hurried on to the office of her attorney, humming despite the overcast. The message he'd sent her earlier that day said he had good news. Never had she the luxury of arriving at a lawyer's office for good news.

Attorney Chapman ushered her in, seated her with his blue eyes a-twinkle, and offered coffee, which she declined. Then he took a seat across from her and crossed one bony knee over the other. "All is very well, Mrs. Chiswell. Your monthly mortgage payments won't change, and you've nothing to be alarmed about."

Relief punctured some of the foreboding she'd acquired that morning, and she expelled a sigh. "Excellent work, sir. Then you've settled with my new creditor over my monthly payment?"

He nodded. "Wise of you to hire me to investigate the matter. Deceit is more common than you'd imagine, and good folks are often swindled by these creditor frauds."

Helen frowned at him. "Creditor frauds?"

"Your original creditor never sold the mortgage to another party. In fact, he has no idea who this third party might be and is indignant to have his good name sullied for this operation. We initiated an investigation to discover who might actually come round to pick up payments delivered to the addressee indicated on the letter, but thus far, we haven't caught anyone.

"So congratulate yourself on being shrewd enough to not send money to this third party. Someone was most definitely trying to swindle you."

Helen gulped. The relief she'd experienced earlier evaporated, leaving her the sensation of having passed beneath a spillage of rank water.

The attorney registered the distress in her expression, and his tone grew soothing. "Would you care for some brandy?"

"No, thank you."

"Perhaps I should have approached the situation more delicately. Respectable widows on fixed incomes present irresistible targets for swindlers. Your creditor and I want to apprehend these scoundrels. Have you any idea who might be trying to swindle you?"

She regarded the spines of leather-bound case studies on shelves behind his desk. A pair of cold eyes haunted her memory. "Prescott."

Chapman emitted an awkward cough. "*M-Maximus* Prescott?"

She met the fledgling attorney's gaze and read terror in his face. So much for his youthful exuberance at saving Wilmington's fixed-income widows from swindle schemes. If Prescott were involved, he'd squash any meddler like a mosquito, fellow attorney or not.

"Never you mind, Mr. Chapman." She stood, as did her attorney. "I cannot thank you enough for preventing my victimization in this scheme. If ever one of my friends or neighbors needs an attorney, I shall recommend you highly."

He bowed his head, his expression stamped with the relief of a knight who learns he doesn't have to vanquish a fire-breathing dragon after all. "You're most welcome, madam."

She shivered the whole way home, less from weather than the ominous track of her thoughts. *Prescott is up to something.* Almost a week earlier, David had declared it, but she'd disregarded his idea.

Oh, the bottomless hatred in Prescott's eyes two days ago when she'd stood her ground over the contract. He knew he'd wrung her estate dry, and all she had left was her home on Second Street. Was he trying to defraud her of the house, her final material possession? If so, why? He was one of Wilmington's wealthiest residents. He didn't need the house.

Perhaps he'd leaped in over his own head in some nefarious deal and found himself the debtor to a man even more ruthless. But she didn't quite believe it.

If Prescott had masterminded the scheme, he'd intended to achieve a purpose other than quick monetary gain.

That moment, she wished herself on the other side of the world from him. The assignment with the Legion assumed even more the shape of a blessing.

Chapter Eighteen

AT SIX THURSDAY morning the twenty-third, Badley's servants arrived with the tarp-covered wagon, horse team, and additional horses, one of them a lively, saddled mare. From the window of Silas's bedroom, Helen watched Roger examine wagon and horses by torchlight and inventory the wagon's contents. His proficiency eased her pre-journey jitters.

Badley's servants were sent on their way. Enid lugged out personal gear. Flimsy, gray dawn sieved through the cloud cover. At seven, Fairfax and nine men on horseback rode up and possessed the street outside the house. Morning traffic detoured around them.

Back in her own bedroom, Helen beckoned Enid to the hidden panel in the wall. "This slides open, see? There's enough money in here to keep you through March." It was every bit of her money not required for the trip, and she hoped Enid wouldn't blow through it like a Clancy son on the eve of his majority. "I expect to return well before then, by the end of February at the latest."

"Aye, mistress." The sagacity in the housekeeper's dark eyes spanned many eons. "By the bye, I had a word with Rhiannon last night. She assures me you'll be back in good time."

Helen appreciated her servant's consideration. Danger lay ahead, she knew.

"Rhiannon thinks you'll do some singing on this quest of yours."

Helen glanced at David's hat on her bedpost and cocked an eyebrow, curious whether singing carried the same implication for the Welsh that it did for her people. They embraced. Downstairs, she donned her new cloak, gloves, and hat. Fairfax, who lingered just outside the front door, offered a civil bow and the courtesy of a lift into the saddle of the mare without any attempt at glibness.

The overcast failed to clear during the morning. Along the way, cultivated, flat fields reinforced the monotony of an autumn-denuded landscape in shades of brown and gray. Mid-day, at the end of a winding drive of rhododendron, hardwoods, and spruce pines, the impeccable lawn and two-story mansion of Jonathan Quill came into view and broke the dreariness. Helen watched Fairfax absorb details of their host's wealth and hoped he formed impressions of her far from the truth of a commoner purchased as a bride the year after she, as May Queen, had blessed the county with a fertile Beltane.

Jonathan jogged from the wide front porch out to greet them. Not the slightest bit winded from his sprint, he kissed Helen's temple. "Welcome, my dear." The luxurious, teal-colored silk of her new gown rustled, and he held her out from him, his gaze a caress. "Such color in your cheeks. The open air agrees with you. I take it your journey from Wilmington was without incident?"

The hug and compliments left her a little breathless. She nodded, non-plussed to find him dressed in plum-colored velvet, white silk, and lace. How handsome he looked.

"Mr. Fairfax, thank you for bringing my friend to me without mishap."

"Sir." It was almost the first word Fairfax had spoken all day.

"My extensive library is open for your perusal this afternoon. I trust you won't deny me another rousing game of chess?" Jonathan offered Helen his elbow.

"As you wish." A glint of ice replaced indifference in Fairfax's eyes.

"Ah, my apologies. You're also a man of action. A tour of my estate, then, and — I say, do you fence, sir?"

Ice gleamed. "Indeed."

"Splendid. Let us offer the lady entertainment this afternoon, prior to supper."

Without a shred of warmth, Fairfax grinned. "I'm at your disposal, sir."

Unease spiked Helen. She darted a look between the two men. "I shall only be 'entertained' if you gentlemen fence with the foil." In other words, if they practiced.

"Of course, my dear." Jonathan patted her hand where it rested on his elbow, not taking his eyes off the lieutenant. Five stable hands strode across the lawn toward them. "Thackery has set out beef and chicken for everyone. Allow my lads to care for the horses and baggage, and let's all take refreshment."

***

Servants had pruned hedges and bushes in the gardens covering three acres of Jonathan's property. Even with a fishpond as the centerpiece of the largest garden, there wasn't much color. When the overcast released a sprinkle, Jonathan, Helen, Fairfax, Roger, and Hannah dove into the hothouse, populated by pineapple plants and trees of citrus and banana.

Later that afternoon, Helen observed a chess game filled with more parries and feints than she'd ever seen in fencing, while both men exhibited an almost somnambulant inclination toward strategy, focus, and concentration during the fencing practice. Technically, Jonathan lost at both pursuits, but she sensed he'd held back to study his opponent. Fairfax, conscious of being revealed, resisted it and worked to draw out Jonathan. In a gruesome way, she sensed that the men enjoyed the challenge of each other's company.

After supper of roast duck, wild rice with almonds and currants, squash, and red wine, Helen strolled past the library but backtracked, alert to activity within. Fairfax, aided by ladder and lantern, browsed titles of volumes shelved floor to ceiling. He stroked the collection, a lover with too many ladies to choose from, never selecting a book. She frowned. Seldom did she search Jonathan's library more than thirty seconds before a book captured her curiosity.

The deliberate track of his search registered, then, and cold filled her arms and legs. Fairfax was mapping the large picture of where Jonathan's expertise lay. A personal library was quite a boon to a man seeking to understand a host — or enemy.

***

Footsteps in the hallway outside her door roused her from bed. She threw on her shawl, padded to the door, and opened it, but Jonathan had already vanished from the hallway. Annoyed with herself for not dressing earlier, she awakened Hannah in the adjoining room, and soon swept fully dressed from the house out onto the garden path Jonathan favored. Perhaps she'd snag him before he began his dawn dance so they could discuss the library incident.

Like scraps of indigo flannel, scud scooted across the pale sky. When Helen arrived at the lawn near the fishpond, she found Jonathan immersed in his ritual, his coat draped upon a nearby bench, the white of his shirtsleeves a beacon in the gloom. She withdrew behind a crape myrtle and waited, wrapped in her shawl to ward off nippiness. Watching his dance always filled her with peace.

Dawn engorged the east, nuzzled twilight into retreat, and suffused the garden with pink light. The air smelled raw and sharp, like the inside of a pecan shell, but with a hint of ocean. Birds landed a few feet from Jonathan and poked the grass. Squirrels and rabbits crept into the clearing and scuttled about. A buck stepped from behind an alcove of ivy, lifted his antlered head to test the breeze, and relaxed to sneak leaves from a bush. The presence of a man with whispered movements did not concern them. Time was suspended.

Of a sudden, the buck's head jerked, his haunches tensed, and he leaped away, the crash of hooves spooking the other animals. Amidst chitters and squawks of annoyance, they also cleared the lawn. Helen sighed, disappointed. Jonathan carried on, his concentration solid.

A draft of winter flowed over her neck. Her stomach growled. Thackery probably had coffee and breakfast ready in the morning room.

She turned, paused. Farther back on the path, Fairfax watched Jonathan, dawn transitioning his fine coat from black to dark brown. Curiosity on his face awakened irritation in her. She gathered her petticoat to avoid dampening it on dewy shrubs and glided up the path, where she murmured, "Let us repair inside and allow our host his privacy."

His low response halted her. "A fascinating man, Mr. Quill. Has he lived in the Japans?"

"Not to my knowledge."

"Well, then, where did he learn — *that*?" His gesture encompassed Jonathan's movements.

"The dance? In China."

"China, of course. But it's no dance. It's an ancient fighting form, a hand-to-hand combat developed to prevent a weaponless man from losing his life to a soldier."

Helen rotated a gaze of incredulity to Jonathan — who had become, for the moment, a crouching tiger — and remembered, astonished, the dexterity with which he'd bypassed George Gaynes's impulsive swing at him in her parlor. In the next second, the implication of Fairfax's knowledge struck her, and she regarded him. "Do you also know this skill?"

His focus on Jonathan didn't waver. Nor did his voice rise. "I've witnessed its demonstration. It requires years of training and practice to be rendered thus." His lips twitched. "A pity the Army isn't schooled in the technique. We'd stomp the rebels with it."

"Only if it enables men to pluck musket balls and cannonballs from midair."

"No, but it transforms hands and feet of an adept into weapons. I've seen a charge averted, an attacker knocked flat on his back, a knife kicked from the hand."

He faced her full on, then. "Our host is called 'the Professor.' Obviously a scholar, a man of wealth, a world traveler." The sweep of his arm encompassed the property. "All this land, and a library filled from floor to ceiling with wisdom of the world. But where are the grandchildren?" His smile was thin. "Where is *Mrs.* Quill?"

In truth, she wasn't sure why Jonathan's house wasn't boisterous with grandchildren. Although Jonathan had never given her substance on which to base her impression, Helen suspected "Mrs. Quill" had died decades earlier, in China. "Your inquiries tread upon personal matters."

A dismissive flick caught Fairfax's cheek. "Tempting to fancy a house of concubines in Peking who await his return, since he doesn't appear inclined toward men, boys, or beasts. The simplest explanation is that Mrs. Quill resides in Wilmington, on Second Street."

After several seconds of incomprehension, she blurted, "*I?*" and grinned. "What an absurd suggestion. Jonathan and I don't share that sort of relationship."

Incredulity bled into his tone. "You've never noticed his tender regard for you?"

"Tender regard? No, I —" She stared up at him, denial arrested in mid-sentence by his suggestion. Confusion germinated inside her. Without a doubt, Jonathan did enjoy kissing her hair, holding her hand, and embracing her.

"Ye gods." Derision drenched Fairfax's murmur. "David St. James *does* want for instruction at love, doesn't he?"

At the last second, she squashed a retort in David's defense. Fairfax's resourcefulness flabbergasted her. She'd almost spilled information about David.

"If your intention is to present a tight cover to the Legion, you've little more than two weeks to resolve Mr. Quill's role in the charade. From where I stand, he looks like your lover, not your father or a kindly uncle. I guarantee he'll look like your lover to Colonel Tarleton, too.

"Such peculiar harmonics between the two of you." Fairfax scrutinized Jonathan, whipped his stare to her, then pinned it to Jonathan again. "In some way, you are a work of art for him, like da Vinci with the Mona Lisa. No, that's not quite it. *Pygmalion.*" Fascination thawed the frigidity of his gaze. "Pygmalion and Galatea."

Panic rocketed through her blood. Her voice abandoned her.

He snaked another glance at Jonathan before evaluating her with awed leisure, a man appraising a masterful piece of artistry. "You've also little more than two weeks to accustom yourself to my name." In one step, he consumed the space between them.

She swallowed, outraged enough to not back away. With her next breath, she harnessed the cold of dawn. "Dunstan." She slathered a seductive whisper over her sneer. "*Dunstan.* Will that do for today, or shall I expedite the process of being worn down by your sincerity and charm — swoon for you this morning, crawl into your bed and await *your* tender regard tonight?"

Silent humor shook him. Again, the appraisal of her, as if she not only amused but entertained him. "How did Lady Mary Wortley Montagu put it? 'But the fruit that can fall without shaking indeed is too mellow for me.'" He stepped back, bowed, and strode up the path. A breeze of winter flung his laughter her way.

Chapter Nineteen

FROM THE PARLOR window, Helen watched Roger boost Hannah into the wagon and climb aboard. The horses looked well rested, and the soldiers in civilian clothing stamped about and conversed, eager to be on their way.

Their banter ceased at Fairfax's approach. Frowning, Helen tracked the confidence in his carriage. *David St. James does want for instruction at love, doesn't he?* Arrogant cur.

No, Fairfax was beyond arrogance. He exploited ignorance and weakness in others. She imagined that handsome face of his illuminated by a Beltane bonfire and grimaced. Surely the gods didn't wed menace with virility.

The parlor door squeaked, and she heard humor in Jonathan's voice. "There you are. I thought you'd fallen in the fishpond and was about to send Benson out with a net."

He joined her at the window, and she studied his expression. So warm, open, and embracing. How could she not have seen all that for more than a decade? She turned back to the window, slammed in the slippery whitewater of new sentiment.

"You're having second thoughts," he murmured.

"Not about the assignment."

He paused. "I saw you this morning with Mr. Fairfax."

Relieved for an escape route, she faced him. "Last night, he combed your library, examining what was there so he could —"

"— assemble a big picture of me and probe for my weaknesses. I invited him to do so." His expression serene, Jonathan took her hands in his. "Don't worry about me."

As in countless times past, his thumbs massaged her palms, but for the first time, she recognized the passion in his touch. How obtuse she'd been, never before to have noticed.

Perception deepened wrinkles at the corners of his eyes. "And?"

"Your ritual — Mr. Fairfax has witnessed the likes of it before."

Mild surprise permeated his serenity. "Does he practice the art?"

"No, but you never told me that your dance from China is a *weapon*."

"Ah, well, those who apply it foremost as a weapon have left the path of wisdom."

A half-laugh escaped her when she recalled Fairfax's desire to "stomp the rebels" by capitalizing on whatever wisdom Chinese sages had passed along to Jonathan. Intuition fueled her vision then — a petite woman nestled in the arms of a younger Jonathan, her black hair fanned upon their sleeping pallet, her luminous skin milk-white in the dusk, her almond-shaped dark eyes full with adoration and bliss while he massaged *her* palms with his thumbs. Helen gazed at her own hands, held in such tender regard within his.

"My dear, is there something else?"

How did she feel when she replaced the image of the young Chinese woman with that of herself? If only she could sort her emotions: how she felt about Jonathan as a *man*, a *lover*.

And what of David St. James?

She had just over two weeks to figure it out. Something told her it wouldn't take her that long. She'd never enjoyed ignorance.

While pasting a smile to her face, she withdrew her hands from his. "Nothing else."

***

A packed mass of crushed shell and sand, the King's Highway into South Carolina reeked of tidal debris. It stretched west-southwest, broken by causeways over creeks and rushes-choked lowland — *no* land, in Helen's opinion, one that vacillated between swamp and salt marsh. Pockets of stink hovered above causeways, decomposition's invisible kisses. Cypress, cedar, and pine trees protruded from the sloppy ground like loose teeth in swollen gums. Insects droned, and buzzards and egrets flapped about.

A northbound postal carrier hailed them on the road that afternoon. "You folks heard from down south yet? Francis Marion attacked the garrison at George Town about a week and a half ago. He got chased off, and his nephew died in the raid."

Fairfax's regard of the postal carrier was unruffled. "Why should Marion attack?"

The man shrugged. "Maybe because he was madder than a hornet with a squashed nest after what Tarleton did."

"What news of Colonel Tarleton?" Fairfax shifted forward in his saddle. Nine disguised redcoats eager for victory did the same.

"He took the torch along the Santee Road, first part of the month." The man scratched an eyebrow. "The ninth or tenth, I think. Burned rebels from their homes, middle of the night."

Fairfax thanked him for his news, and the party continued south. What the postal carrier *hadn't* said activated Helen's journalist suspicions. Tarleton chased Marion into the Santee but didn't catch him. No doubt led astray by residents, riled over his failure to capture Marion, the colonel had opted to suppress insurrection with the torch. A brutal strategy, to be sure, and futile in history as often as it was effective. Uneasiness rooted inside her when she considered the reaction of the Committee of Safety toward Wilmington's Loyalists in response to the news.

Late afternoon, west of the tributary leading to Shallot Inlet, the land offered up a dry, sandy hummock. Requiring no further endorsement of the site than charred remains of older campfires dotting the stretch, the party halted for the night. Almost faster than Helen could account for the day in her journal, Roger, Hannah, and Jonathan had the horses unhitched, unsaddled, and rubbed down.

Perched upon a stool, she dashed off a charcoal sketch of the forlorn terrain while the trio erected three tents. Then she took up a more detailed drawing of the Pearsons and Jonathan at work. By twilight, she'd captured the essence of soldiers building a campfire and tending their own horses in two more sketches. And she'd sneaked in a full-length profile of Fairfax, hands clasped behind, feet planted shoulder-width apart, scorching the road with his glare.

Jonathan knelt and examined her sketches. "Excellent work. And not a one of us held still."

She wiped charcoal off her fingertips with a rag. "Movement goes with portraiture, I'm afraid. Years from now, perhaps when I'm an old, old woman, very intelligent people just like you will have invented a device that creates instant portraits, and no one need worry again about fidgety subjects or —" She held up the rag. "— or charcoal." She sighed and rolled up the sketches. "Meanwhile, you're working. I'm just writing and sketching."

He rested his hand on the silk at her knee and whispered, "Playing the part of the gentlewoman."

Their gazes locked, and she felt it all pour into her soul: Jonathan's adoration, love, and yearning. Yes, she was his work of art, perhaps even his life's crown achievement, but was she a *woman* to him? An involuntary shiver caught her.

"Pah, how boorish of me. Night's come on, and it's grown colder." He pushed himself to his feet. "I shall fetch your cloak."

After he'd walked off, she looked at the silk of her gown where he'd laid his hand. For as long as she'd known him, he'd confined his caresses. If a man truly loved a woman, *wanted* her, wouldn't twelve years of silence and confinement make him ready to burst at the seams? Jonathan didn't look ready to explode. He looked content to pass his time with her in chaste caresses.

But David had been a mitigating factor for eleven of those twelve years. Another shiver found her, and she drew her shawl tighter. For the duel, Jonathan had agreed to be *Silas's* Second, not David's. The symbolism of his decision was clear. David was the rival.

Pricked by unease and tension, she collected her journal and sketches. As she stood, she made eye contact with Fairfax who, she realized, had observed Jonathan's caresses moments earlier. Blood-red rays of setting sunlight emphasized the sardonic twist of his lips. *Did I not tell you so this morning?* his posture asserted as he strutted for the company of his men.

***

That night, damp cold seeped upward and penetrated Helen's bones, despite a foot of space between her cot and rugs on the ground. The marsh/swamp grew boisterous with territorial rituals and predations of varmints far more antediluvian than frogs and crickets. She listened to primordial instinct and stared, wide-awake, at the canvas roof of her tent.

Creatures moaned, splashed, thrashed, and screeched the night away. Big creatures. Midnight, the ground shook near camp. A sentry shouted, "Bloody hell!" A musket discharged.

Another sentry's musket fired through the echoed report of the first. "Got it! Jove's arse, Parker, look at the *size* o' that thing!"

Helen bolted up and groped for her shawl. Parker: the Devonshire farm lad missing the front tooth, the fellow who'd helped Fairfax run David from her bedroom. Well, bless Parker's good aim with the musket in the dark, and thank the gods for the King's finest.

She heard Fairfax's unemotional growl. "Keep your voices down. Clean it up."

The tent to her right, where Jonathan slept, was quiet. She untied the top of her tent flap, poked her head out, and squinted across camp. Several men hunched over a massive blob in the sand. Fairfax strode for their tents.

"Hssst, Mrs. Chiswell!" Helen glanced to her left to spot Hannah peeking from her own tent. "What was that about?"

"The sentries shot a panther." She *presumed* it was a panther. Trappers and guides who made it to Wilmington related some fantastical tales of creatures they'd encountered in the Carolina wilds.

Hannah scrunched her face. "Roger slept through the racket."

Helen imagined his response to the horn at two in the morning for one of Tarleton's infamous surprise attacks on an enemy. Maybe if someone sounded the horn right in his ear —

Fully dressed to his shoes, Fairfax strolled past their tents, hands clasped behind. Didn't he ever sleep? "Everything is under control. Return to bed." He circled the campfire and headed for the men and the motionless thing on the ground.

Hannah stuck her tongue out after him. "'Everything is under control.' Jolly. Now I shall sleep tight indeed." With a cough of scorn, she whipped the flap of her tent closed.

***

More salt marsh than swamp claimed the scenery Saturday, and it more monotonous for the paucity of trees. To the horizon, the tideland's grass, reeds, and sedge rippled like fur on the back of a dog pestered by fleas. Turtles bobbed and flipped in the shallow water, and iridescent-winged dragonflies danced among the salt loving herbs. Helen spotted the sinuous wake of a curious alligator.

They passed ten homesteads during the day, their arrival often announced to settlers by tail wagging mongrels with salt-crusted legs. Bright-eyed children scrambled out to the road and cheered their way, and the party paused a few minutes to accept hospitality from a plump goodwife, who held out a bucket of cool, spring water and a dipper. The road bent south. By late afternoon, the air held the smell of seawater and the faint cries of gulls.

A settler invited them to pitch camp on his land. They paid him for firewood, the use of his well and pasture, and a share of fresh fish caught on Long Bay. "Menace of the Swamp Beast" consumed two pages in Helen's journal. In charcoal, she captured Parker, arms stretched wide, face animated, as he embellished his adventure of midnight musketry for the settler's family.

The bay breeze blew at night. She drifted in and out of sleep, unable to find a position in which both her nose and lower back were warm. In one dream, she and David ran barefoot across summer grass on the Salisbury Plain. Even asleep, she knew it wasn't real, and she awakened to the tickly crawl of a tear down the side of her nose. Why was it so damned cold in her cot?

She shuffled blankets and regained sleep to dream of rising from her cot a-shiver, trailing blankets over to Jonathan's tent. "Shared bodily warmth," she beseeched him with chattery teeth. His expression kind, he cuddled her and massaged her palms with his thumbs. Ah, at last — relaxed and warmed by chaste caresses. But for some reason, she shoved him over onto his back, and mounted him, and Jonathan gripped her hips. Driven to the cliff of *le petit mort* several times without release, she fought him, found her wrists bound and all control stripped from her. Her head flung back, she howled, *sang* to ride the horn of the moon. Earth-laughter boomed through her soul.

She jerked awake: half-appalled, half-aroused, wholly confused. Bound wrists?

Such peculiar dreams the cold inspired, but she needn't be cold. She'd seen extra blankets and a brazier in the wagon. Next night, she'd use them.

Chapter Twenty

THE ROAD HUGGED coastline and paralleled a swash, the thud of tide muted for highway travelers. Beyond the channel, sea oats on sandbanks billowed in the sunlight. Above sparkling water, pelicans and seagulls swooped, their shrieks high, thin. Helen tasted ocean with every breath.

Noontime, McPherson tossed a stale crust of bread to a lone seagull. From out of nowhere, the sky darkened with assault: screaming birds generous with defecation and molting feathers. Horses shied and whinnied, and soldiers cursed.

The party beat a strategic retreat southbound. The skirmish followed for ten minutes. His countenance unruffled as usual, Fairfax called a halt and walked his horse around to evaluate epaulets of mottled, pea-green slime awarded to several men and numerous white feathers clinging to hats and sweaty men and horses. A feather dislodged from the brim of his hat and drifted onto his forearm. He brushed it off. "Hereafter, *no one* feeds the seagulls. Move along."

"Tarred and Feathered" was the title of Helen's journal entry that evening.

A brazier installed in her tent fended back the cold, but she slept no better for it. Jonathan's company had become a curious exercise. Every time he touched her, her skin twitched and clicked like metal from a musket fired too often. On some level, he sensed and adapted to the change, and his caresses waned in chasteness.

Up at five-thirty, she evaluated sketches of her former teacher by candlelight, her heart atremble, territory familiar to Wiltshire girls infatuated over brawny journeymen. Infatuation: what a ridiculous state for a twenty-nine-year-old widow.

You've little more than two weeks to resolve Mr. Quill's role in the charade. Two weeks? Gods, no, she'd never endure the tension that long. She'd talk with Jonathan — but in George Town, in a civilized inn, where they'd be assured some privacy for their discussion.

***

The port of George Town, occupied by Crown forces five months earlier, bustled with commerce from the indigo and rice industries. Militiamen and redcoats shared the streets with merchants, traders, and sutlers. With such a military force in evidence, Helen doubted that Marion would threaten the town again.

The three-to-one ratio of Negroes to whites startled her, accustomed as she was to Wilmington's reduced reliance upon slavery. Silk-gowned plantation belles gabbed gaily, their accent similar to the one Fairfax faked in Wilmington, while their slaves, clad in threadbare smocks, hung their heads and waited nearby like exhausted mules.

Names of popular taverns hearkened to the area's not-so-distant pirate past. Red Anny's Attic. Caesar and Cleopatra. Blackbeard's Head. Helen grimaced at the implication of the last name, hoping the owner hadn't some-how — ye, gods — procured and displayed the severed, preserved head of some scoundrel who resembled Edward Teach.

After making certain that accommodations were ready for Helen's party at an inn of quality, Fairfax betook himself and the nine men to an Anglican church where soldiers were quartered. Roger and Jonathan stabled the horses and secured the wagon for the night, and the innkeeper's sons helped Hannah tote baggage upstairs to their suite of adjoining rooms. Helen sketched the steeple of Prince George's Church from her window and completed a journal entry. Supper that included broiled fish, fried shrimp, steamed crabs, and rice, was delivered to Helen's room. She dined with Jonathan and the Pearsons.

At eight o'clock, she closed a door leading to the Pearsons' adjoining room, lowered herself into the chair nearest Jonathan, crooked her elbow on the arm-rest, and propped her head with her hand. Eyes closed, she heard Jonathan sigh with weariness. Quiet buried the room. Such a luxurious meal after days of Spartan fare had left her head feeling as though it were stuffed with lint.

He kept his voice soft, just above a whisper. "At last, we're alone so we may talk."

Thank heavens he was going to initiate the discussion. She sat up and re-garded him.

"Have you further thoughts on who tried to swindle you over the mortgage?"

So much for amour. Helen fought a yawn. "I still think that Prescott might target me. Maybe his motive is revenge this time, not money."

Jonathan patted a yawn. "Why would he revenge himself upon you? You paid him off years ago. I cannot envision him behind simple fraud. He's far too wealthy to dabble with such amateur operations — and far too slippery."

"My thoughts, too." She felt glum.

"Much as I know you'd like to pin something illegal on Prescott and see him ruined, I'm afraid he's not your villain this time. Tally it up to the attempt of a proletarian, and congratulate yourself for not being victimized." He pushed himself up from the chair and stretched. "What time are we away on the mor-row — seven again?"

"Yes."

He leaned forward, kissed her temple, and crooked his mouth. "No doubt that bed over there will sleep warmer than your cot. Good night, my dear, and rest well." Before her fogged brain quite realized it, he'd sauntered out the door.

She stared after him, grumpy. Six days and nights, she'd reminisced about how handsome Jonathan looked when she first met him in Ratchingham's study. His warmth had bolstered her during the Atlantic crossing, when they discussed works of writers like Voltaire and painters like Michelangelo. His presence had instilled such quiet in her during the days after Silas's death.

Six days and nights, she'd twitched at his touch and tossed in her cot. By then, she knew how she felt about Jonathan as a man, a *lover*, but he'd diverted her attention with that issue of the mortgage. He never sidestepped anything he considered important. Was that it, then — he considered the tension between them a trifle? Her mouth tugged into a scowl.

At her knock, his door opened to reveal his sphinx-like expression. "I apologize for imposing upon you, Jonathan, but we do have another matter to discuss."

"Yes, I know." Clasping her hand in his, he guided her inside his room, lit by a single bedside candle. The door clicked shut, shoved with his foot, and he caught her face in his hands. Her mouth watered at the scent of his skin. "Talk, my dear," he whispered.

His lips brushed the corner of her mouth and caressed her jaw line. Her mouth sought his, tasted him. The tremble in her heart expanded, shortened her breath to gasps. His lips released hers and traveled to the pulse in her throat.

A soft moan lifted from her soul. "What a fool I've been. All these years, I never recognized how much you wanted me."

"Is this an errand of mercy?"

"No, no, not at all. You're so very desirable, and — and I see how much you love me." He laughed softly, but when he set her out from him, she realized she'd said something wrong. She snagged his hands in hers and kissed them. "You're the kindest, dearest friend I have on this earth. You've been my teacher and my advisor, and you have encouraged me."

He scrutinized her face. "But you don't love me, do you?" His breathing steadied.

"I *do* love you!" Confusion thickened her voice. "Jonathan, don't you want me?"

He groaned. "Ye gods, how can you even ask that question of me? Ah, but this isn't about me. It's about you. You and David. And you love David."

"No. He and I are finished."

Pain twisted his expression. "I've heard that before."

"But this time it's true."

"You had a quarrel about money. You misunderstood him. Won't the two of you ever listen to each other? Oh, damn it all." He pivoted and walked away from her a few feet, his back to her, his exhale sheer frustration. "I refuse to be an interim for you, Helen."

"You — you've always thrust David at me. Why? Do you think I'm infatuated with you?"

He ignored her question and seemed to ponder aloud. "Quill, *think*, man. David isn't the issue here tonight."

Her heart felt wrung and contorted. Not for the world would she have wounded Jonathan, but surely she'd just stomped all over their friendship and trust and hobbled both. She stared at his back, baffled.

"I don't understand." He wheeled back to her, frowning. "All these years, I haven't changed the way I respond to you. But the past few days — what suddenly alerted you to my sentiments?"

Her mind backtracked. "Oh, gods." Dismay and disgust shot through her, and she lifted both hands to her cheeks briefly. "*He* suggested it to me. Mr. Fairfax." She'd succumbed to his manipulation.

"Well, well." Sarcasm closed vulnerability from Jonathan's face. "It seems Niccolo Machiavelli graduated quite a Master." His expression grew pensive. "If you're to succeed in the project, you'd best understand Mr. Fairfax's motivation for wanting to control you."

"It isn't just me. He seeks to control everyone." Pity, revulsion, and fear swept through her, and she blurted, "It's the seven-year-old and his hatred." At the puzzlement that pinched Jonathan's face, she recounted her memory from nearly twenty years earlier, at Redthorne.

His face gentled. "Ah. Perceptive of you."

"'Angel on the outward side,'" she murmured.

He nodded and studied her again. "You've spent enough time in his company to guess what overall reward he expects for his efforts."

"Rank advancement."

"Of course, but think bigger."

"An award, recognition from His Majesty. A seat in Parliament."

Jonathan nodded. "Indeed, and from what I've seen, he belongs with the rest of King George's reptile collection mapping out the glorious future of Britain." More sarcasm stung his tone. "But right now, he's a junior officer on the wrong side of the Atlantic. How will he get from one point to the next?"

Helen let out a pent-up breath. "Prove himself indispensable." She pondered Fairfax's fixation on the St. James family. "Single-handedly uncover and dismantle a worldwide network of rebel spies. Make arrests. Where solid evidence is lacking, manufacture what's needed to enhance his own credibility."

"Excellent. What stands in his way?"

"The rebels?"

"Pah. Think more personally. The hate-filled seven-year-old."

She scratched her temple. "Someone with knowledge of his background, someone who suspects or has evidence that Lord Ratchingham's death wasn't suicide."

"What will he do about it?"

She considered. "He'll attempt to disarm or destroy anyone who suspects his origins."

Jonathan's expression saddened. "Now we know why you're here tonight."

She gaped at him, stunned, the taste of his kiss lingering in her mouth. Her skin twitched some more. Monstrous. Fairfax had damaged the harmony with her oldest friend. She had weeks ahead of her in the lieutenant's company. Anguished, she hung her head. "Oh, Jonathan, I'm — I'm —"

He twined one of her hands with his and tilted her chin to him, eyes kind. "I'm honored to be the dearest friend you have on this earth. But you know as well as I that you aren't finished with David."

No, she wasn't. What would the shape of "finished" look like after an entire decade?

"What concerns me more is a young woman named Helen Grey. For the sake of opportunity, she set aside her culture, her way of life. She even set aside her religion for a few years. Although I was her teacher, I don't know everything about her. That's why I suspect that while it may have been convenient for you to leave her behind in Ratchingham's parlor, you aren't finished with her." He cocked his head. "Have you asked her what she has to say about that?"

Helen — no, *Nell* — Grey. For twelve years, Nell Grey had been silent. Cold plunged through Helen, and she trembled.

Jonathan kissed her hand, led her to the door, and faced her again. "You can cast both David and Mr. Fairfax from your life if you care to do so. You can even cast me from your life. But Helen Grey walks with you the rest of your days. Have you made peace with her?"

Chapter Twenty-One

ALONE, HELEN PACED in her room, her body awakened to Jonathan and thirsting. Girlish infatuation, she told herself. By his refusal of her, he seemed to agree. Still, the foundation of admiration and respect she experienced for him felt so solid, timeless.

Between bouts of bafflement over Jonathan, she pondered the thing called love she and David had long declared for each other. Rather than mutual love, she suspected that he had given her control of his heart, and she'd held him at bay for ten years. His trapped expression their last night together added fuel to her suspicions. *I would marry you if that's what you wanted.* Didn't sound much like love to her.

What was love anyway? Could she even recognize it? Outside, the watch announced midnight. Gazing out the curtains, she finally asked herself a question she'd skirted during her pacing. What had Nell Grey to say about love?

Memory shoved her into the procurement at Redthorne. She backed from the window breathing hard, fists clenched. For several seconds, Nell Grey ignited within her, a howling titan powered by bottled-up rage and abandonment, before Helen forced her back and sat at the edge of her bed, stunned, panting. What profound shackles to carry around. Somehow she must find a way to ease the weight of them. The portmanteau of a journalist in the back-country was heavy enough.

Besides, she suspected Nell Grey had more than the procurement to howl about, and in good time, she'd hear all about it.

***

Around seven the next morning, Helen sent Hannah to track down the innkeeper and post letters to Badley and Enid. With Fairfax's strategy in mind to render their party as inconspicuous as possible, she'd packed away her silk and jewelry. Over her petticoat and jacket of homespun wool, she wore a cloak while she supervised the baggage transported downstairs, where Jonathan and

Roger waited with the wagon and horses. The foggy street writhed with activity — merchants in carriages, slaves on errands, livestock meandering, military men in threes or fours, artisans on delivery. Traffic bottlenecked around a half-dozen dismounted backwoodsmen in hunting shirts and felt hats. They and their horses took up a quarter width of street next door.

Helen glanced about. Five after seven. Where was her escort?

In her peripheral vision, a backwoodsman approached, and faux-Carolina accent groped her from the dawn. "I see you've the wagon loaded, dear sister, so let's be off."

Her double-take on Fairfax in a hunting shirt preceded her hard stare at the group of men. No Parker or McPherson. Not a man among them did she recognize. She eyed Fairfax from head to toe again and murmured, "Good heavens. What a difference."

He lowered his voice. "Legion cavalrymen over there."

Her gaze on them widened. All out of uniform, ordinary looking. Judging from the bulk packed with their bedrolls, they'd hidden away their distinctive fur helmets and tailored, green cavalry jackets. Their sabers, too.

Fairfax offered her his elbow in a stiff movement. "Allow me to introduce your escort."

The five dragoons came to attention at their approach, the regality of her carriage registering on them. They lacked some spark of bearing that she'd come to associate with British regulars. Even Parker with his gap-toothed grin possessed the spark. As proudly as the dragoons carried themselves, they were still provincials. How fortunate that Badley hadn't insisted on passing her off as the sister of one of them.

Her gaze flicked over Fairfax, and disquiet tugged at her. His carriage might mark him as a regular officer, not in the slightest a provincial. At least to her, his transformation wasn't complete. She hoped it wouldn't present a problem for their party down the road.

Their route lay west Wednesday the twenty-ninth on a well-trafficked highway, past miles of forestland denuded for the growth of rice and indigo in the rich, loamy soil of eastern South Carolina. Black gum and sweet gum trees, oak, maple, and sumac had shed their leaves for winter, enabling Helen to glimpse planters' opulent homes.

That night, she recorded her reflections of the day and sketched dragoons preparing supper. In the company of Tarleton's men, Fairfax warmed to the role of brother. And Jonathan faded into the background for his portrayal of a family servant, spending far less time in Helen's company. The isolation it imposed left hollowness in her soul.

The next day, swamp encroached with their proximity to the Santee. Helen spotted wood storks, herons, and egrets. Several times, deer leaped across the road. Once, they rode through a cloud of rank musk exuded from a black bear that had crossed the road just prior to their passage.

Tree frogs and mockingbirds sang their progress deeper into the damp tangle of cypress, pines, and pin oaks. Open stretches of water, dark with tannins and adorned with floating mats of vivid vegetation, appeared off-road. By nightfall the final day of November, civilization had petered out.

As if to counteract the absence of sophistication in a swamp singing with mosquito melody and the arias of weird night birds, Jonathan set out his chessboard after they'd finished supper. Fairfax pulled up a campstool. The prospect of sport in any form drew the interest of Campbell and Connor, two of the three dragoons not on sentry detail, as well as Hannah. The other dragoon, Davison, demonstrated musket drills for Roger.

By firelight, Helen recounted in her journal the few travelers they'd met that day and described swamp flora and fauna. In twenty minutes, she heard Fairfax murmur, "Checkmate."

Campbell, Connor, and Hannah meandered over to observe Roger at the drill. "Rest," said Davison. Roger snapped his musket from position near the outside of his right foot up and over and held it out, centered, before his torso. "Shoulder your firelock." Roger tucked the musket, rotated, against his left shoulder, the butt in the palm of his hand. His movements looked smoother than they had twenty minutes earlier. Roger enjoyed the drill. So did his dragoon teacher.

Game pieces clicked, slid together into their protective package by Jonathan. A glance over her left shoulder rewarded her with a solemn wink from him. She put away her pen and ink and closed the journal just as Fairfax straddled her bench and sat upon it.

Hands braced on his knees, he leaned toward her, unsmiling, and she, aware of the casual observation of Campbell and Connor, resisted the urge to put half a foot more distance on the bench from her "brother." His gaze strolled from her eyes to her lips, over her bosom, and into her lap, where her hands rested on the journal, before returning to her eyes. He whispered, "Congratulations. You and Mr. Quill have resolved that titillating chemistry between you to portray the unambiguous roles of widowed lady and revered servant."

"Thank you," she whispered back. Too bad whispers weren't the ideal vehicle with which to convey sarcasm. "Congratulations on your chess victory."

"He allowed me to win."

She tasted salt, musky and masculine, and swallowed. "I assure you it wasn't so."

"What are you writing?"

"Today's journal entry. What else would I write?"

His gaze stroked the journal. "Ciphered intelligence reports for rebels."

She laughed softly. His responsive grin, minus a shred of warmth, siphoned the humor from her. "You think me a spy for rebels? Why?"

He sighed with what appeared to be sincere regret, and the backs of two fingers stroked her cheek. "You abetted David St. James's escape."

She flinched from the caress. "There are dozens of *true* rebels running around out there. Fetch one of them for the feather in your cap."

"You don't trust me." The icy smile returned to his mouth. "I don't trust you."

Her pulse stammered. "If I'd grown up with the Clancys as my stepbrothers, I wouldn't trust anyone, either."

Iron control beat back the fiend that spasmed one corner of his mouth, and comprehension and fascination ripped through his gaze. "We have more in common than you're willing to admit."

Two damaged, dark stars dancing round each other in a heavens of light. Helen shrugged off the image. A gust of amusement escaped her. "And exploration of those supposed commonalities should intrigue me?"

"Why do you paint sites of the old gods? Did you lose them while you pretended to be Anglican?"

Her scalp crawled with shock. How could he know of her struggle to reclaim her religion?

Satisfaction honed his smile, as if he'd read her thoughts. "You've had no community since you left Wiltshire, have you?"

His uncanny guess rattled her. She tilted her chin up. "It's none of your business."

He chuckled. "You know where to find community." He grasped her hand and kissed her wrist. "Pleasant dreams, Helen."

***

The following day, first of December, the weather continued humid and mild, and the Santee Road wandered northwest. Helen, comfortable in the saddle of the mare, Calliope, rode among the dragoons and sneaked in the first of several questions for her report: "Why did you join the Legion?"

Surprised and pleased to have her attention, the men opened up. Four were married, three with young children. Two were farmers, two were artisans, and the fifth was a merchant. Different backgrounds, but Helen heard a united voice in their responses. There was so much at stake: property, businesses, lives of their loved ones. The settled lands belonged to them as much as to the rebels that scarred the terrain with protracted bloodshed. Thus they were challenged to end the insurrection, restore order wherever men wallowed in anarchy, and remind citizens that a power superior to partisan chieftains existed. Expecting no quarter from rebels in battle, they fought as if each moment was their last. Always.

Mid-afternoon, the party encountered a family of seven headed southeast. Horses plodded with a laden wagon, and everyone except a little girl walked. The father and boys carried muskets, and he hailed them. "What news out of George Town, friends?"

To Helen's relief, Fairfax allowed Campbell to respond in his regional accent. "All quiet on the road these past three days."

"A good thing that is. We're bone-tired of it. I'm sorry to tell you, but closer to the High Hills of Santee, your road will stink of homeless folks, burned barns, and dead stock. Last month, Tarleton came through with the torch. Then Marion followed, mopping the road with anyone gone loyal out of cowardice. Marion, he patrols the area, so watch yourself. And bugger the both of them, I say."

"Yes, we've heard about Tarleton and the torch."

"Wouldn't surprise me if he burned out a few Loyalists, too. He nearly killed Tom Sumter a few days ago." Noting their puzzled looks, he added, "News to you, eh? It happened way out on Blackstock's Hill, northwest between the Tyger and Enoree. They say the old man's arm is paralyzed from a musket ball, but he's still breathing. Don't you know, soon as he's on his feet, he'll stir up more trouble." The man spat into roadside weeds. "Blasted, mucking war."

After the family was out of earshot, the dragoons buzzed with speculation about Thomas Sumter. Their fellow Legionnaires and Tarleton had inflicted paralysis upon a great source of aggravation in the Carolinas. Huzzah for

Tarleton and the Legion!

While they advanced ideas about how to track down a crippled Sumter and finish him off, Helen glanced from Fairfax, whose cold scrutiny was for the road ahead, to Jonathan, and she paced the mare beside the wagon. "Jonathan," she said, low, "they're forgetting something."

His serene expression and soft tone hardly matched the concern in his eyes. "Marion *isn't* paralyzed, and he's out there somewhere ahead of us —" Wry humor molded his mouth. "— mopping up the road with Loyalists when it suits his mood."

Chapter Twenty-Two

THAT NIGHT, ROGER drilled with the musket, and parries and feints were executed across the chessboard. As Helen penned her journal entry, she tried not to think about residents of the Santee made homeless.

Dragoons not on sentry detail shuffled about camp, edgy and spoiling for battle. Did they ever feel remorse for their actions?

She read their responses to the day's question: "What is the most formidable characteristic of the rebels that we must overcome to end the conflict?" Perseverance, they'd agreed. If leaders like Marion and Sumter despaired, they didn't show that face to their men.

Did George the Third ponder perseverance as a force of life, or did his news arrive creamed and honeyed? Even when rhetorically asked in her head, she found the question disconcerting.

With a jolt to the bench, Fairfax sat beside her. Jonathan packed away his chessboard with a tranquil expression. Helen swiveled back around and closed her journal. "Let me guess, my brother. You won again at chess. Congratulations. How many nights of victory is that?"

He snatched the journal from her lap, wrenching a gasp from her. Perplexed, she watched him amble around the campfire with the open journal and absorb its content like a contemplative monk in an early-Church labyrinth. He progressed through entries with a reading pace faster than that of anyone she knew, including Jonathan.

When he withdrew a smoldering stick from the fire's edge and brought it to a page, she leaped to her feet. "What are you doing?" She stalked over and lunged for the journal. "How dare you burn my journal?" Perhaps imagining torched houses had gone to Fairfax's head, inspired him with the urge to emulate Tarleton and set something valuable ablaze.

"Sullivan, prevent my sister from interfering."

"Sir." The dragoon seized her upper arm and, when she'd ceased to struggle, guided her away. She blasted Fairfax with a glare.

Rather than ignite the page, he studied the effect of heat upon it and other pages using hot sticks plucked from the fire. At last, Helen realized he was looking for a cipher concealed with invisible ink and rendered legible with the application of heat. How ridiculous.

He flung a stick into the fire, closed the journal, and approached. "Thank you, Sullivan." The dragoon released her, bowed his head, and walked away. Fairfax presented the journal to her.

Straightened with dignity, she clutched the journal to her chest. "Suppression of disloyalty with the torch is an effective means of cowing insurgents. Am I officially cowed yet?"

"You sound just like one of them." He jutted his jaw ahead to where residents of the Santee had lost their homes.

"Considering that some are likely Loyalists, I'm not surprised."

"The rebels got what they deserved. Each dragoon here remembers his own home or property destroyed by partisans." He studied her face. "You're troubled because women and children were dispossessed."

"Yes, I am."

A gentle smile curved his lips. He grasped her shoulders and whispered, "You aren't the correct journalist for the project. The fairer sex does tend toward excessive sentimentality. Go home. That spitfire servant of yours will stroke your brow and remind you that you're a good writer, despite your failure."

Rage fueled by self-doubt she'd borne since the procurement seared her. Not clever enough to master poise of a well-bred lady. Not intelligent enough to maintain the turpentine plantation while Silas was gambling. Not whole enough to capture the heart of a good man. Not talented enough to write and edit for a magazine. Not thrifty enough to survive on a pittance.

We have more in common than you're willing to admit. Damn Fairfax, he *knew* her and wrung her soul at its most vulnerable spot, demanding her surrender.

She recalled his metaphor from Lady Montagu about fruit falling from the tree. He was shaking the tree.

Memory replayed the silk of Jonathan's movement when he sidestepped George Gaynes. Jonathan had deflected Gaynes, offered all that vigor back to its originator, given Gaynes the power he wanted. Power.

Her thoughts assumed cohesion, and her pulse settled into rhythm. "I shall persevere awhile longer. No doubt I shall learn something of value in the process. In the end, I just might surprise both of us."

Hair at the back of her neck stood out at the transformation of his expression — from smug assurance to wary predator, just as in her parlor, when she'd handed pressure back to him by mentioning his upbringing at Redthorne.

It hadn't taken him but a day to reevaluate her strengths and weaknesses. She expected no less of him the second time.

Emotion closed from his face, he bowed his head. "As you wish." His adaptation to the role of her kin grown smoother with each day, he escorted her to her tent and signaled for Hannah to attend her.

She lay in the cot a long while before sleep found her, the conversation with Jonathan in her back yard remembered. *What lesson does the universe intend you to learn with Mr. Fairfax as your teacher?* Whatever the lesson, she'd completed but a fragment of it.

★★★

"Large group ahead, sir." His expression grim, the forward scout, Ross, paced his mount to that of Fairfax, and dust settled around their horses. "At least thirty men riding our way."

Helen emerged from reflection. Ross didn't look pleased. Were bandits headed for their party?

"Francis Marion has found us." From his lack of emotion, Fairfax might have been offering an opinion on the placement of furniture. His gaze swept the party. "No aggression. We allow them to pass. Campbell, you're our voice again if needed."

"Sir." Campbell rode forward, and Ross fell back.

Jonathan helped Hannah off the wagon to walk beside him and left Roger to steer the wagon. The road branched. At the intersection, burned into a plank of half-rotten wood, was a sign that pointed left toward swampier ground: *Nelsons Ferry.* Campbell raised a hand to halt their progress, delay a right turn that would send them away from the ferry and swamp. Three-dozen men on horseback cantered past for Nelson's Ferry, many of them Negroes, all in brownish hunting shirts, tomahawks thrust in belts, the dull wink of musket metal across their thighs. Dust climbed at the patrol's passage. Helen fanned it away and coughed.

She and her party turned right and resumed their journey almost due north. Seconds later, more than half the men from the patrol surrounded and paced them. Uncanny how they'd slipped upon them that way, almost without warning.

A small-boned man in his mid-forties rode up and joined Campbell. Gaunt and ugly as a withered swamp root, he possessed a pair of black eyes that embodied equal parts sagacity and sorrow, and he rode with such grace that he might have been born in his saddle. Despite ungainly features, he radiated the magic of leadership. Helen flushed with fear and thrill. Badley would salivate over this story — if she lived to write it.

Campbell nodded. "Morning."

"Morning."

The dragoon glanced around to evaluate his own party's poor odds at surviving a skirmish before he returned attention to the other man and deepened his regional accent. "You fellers know these roads well?"

"We ride them all the time. Marion's the name." The man inclined his head and also sized up Helen's party, including the wagon. On the surface, they might be just another group of displaced settlers. His gaze snagged on Fairfax, who rode erect in his saddle and monitored the road ahead with the casual, bored look of a British cavalry officer.

For once, Helen wished Fairfax could read her mind. *Forget aristocracy and slump in that saddle, you dolt!*

"*Colonel* Marion? Why, I sure am pleased to meet you, sir." Campbell tipped his hat. "Zachary Downey. This here's my kin, and we're headed for kin near the High Hills. How many more days travel you reckon we got?"

"Two." Marion eyed Fairfax again, and Fairfax continued to ignore him and broadcast nobility with his posture. "I don't recollect knowing any Downeys in the High Hills."

"I 'spect not, sir. They ain't lived there above three months. We heard there's houses burned up yonder. How far north?"

"Another day."

"As far as the High Hills?"

"No, your kin are safe. Tarleton started the torch at Sumter's mills on Jack's Creek. Then he rode north to the Richardson place. Destroyed a number of homes in that area."

"He still roaming these parts?"

"No. He's gone."

"Good." Helen saw a bead of sweat roll down Campbell's face, and she gulped. The dragoon had nerves of iron to continue the charade.

Marion's head rotated on his scrawny neck, affording him another glance at Fairfax. "Next time we're in the High Hills, we'll call upon the Downeys." He tilted his hat. "Good day, sir, and luck to you on your journey."

The rumble of Marion and his men faded back south. Then Campbell blotted sweat from his face, and a snarl rippled his expression. "That old fox wasn't fooled."

"No, he wasn't," said Roger. "He's a sharp devil."

"I give him less than a day to hunt us down." Connor smirked. "But he won't return. He'll send his lackeys after us."

"In the dark. That's how he works it." His face as animated as any child's when served an apple pastry, Campbell turned to Fairfax. "What do you think, sir?"

"Let us welcome their return on behalf of Colonel Tarleton and the Legion." A chill raked Helen's spine when she recognized the hate-filled seven-year-old come out to play. By refusing to bow his shoulders, Fairfax had flaunted his birth class, made certain Marion wouldn't mistake them for Whigs, so he could lure them back.

Davison raised his musket above his head. "Huzzah!"

The responsive "Huzzah!" from the other dragoons, their faces contorted, roared to the sky.

Chapter Twenty-Three

FROM THE ROCK-STREWN darkness where they crouched, Jonathan's voice unfolded, low. "My good fellow, five nights of musket drills do not a dragoon make."

A sulk tinged Roger's voice. "'Tarleton's Quarter' is going to happen at our campsite. I'm stuck here with two women and — and —"

"And one old man." Helen heard Jonathan's humor. He shifted about, a blob by starlight. "You're the only civilian who brought a musket."

Hannah sounded grumpy. "And you're supposed to be keeping me warm." After some soft shuffling, Roger obliged. Bliss resounded in Hannah's murmur.

Cold seeped into Helen's shoes. Hopeful that the concept of shared warmth appealed to Jonathan, she looked at him. The waxing quarter moon peeked from behind a cloud and revealed the oval of his face intent upon the campsite. Dejection shivered through her.

Between winter-bare trunks of trees, the burned-down campfire flickered, rendered the site in stark shadow and orange light. Helen yearned for sleep. How long had they squatted out there in the cold behind that boulder — two hours? Whigs weren't coming to kill them. Marion had been duped. She yawned.

Jonathan brushed her arm. "Shh. Listen."

The snap of a twig about twenty-five feet to their right echoed like musket shot. To her left, Roger dislodged Hannah, replaced her with his musket.

"Shut up!" came a hoarse warning from the right. "You'll wake 'em before we kill 'em."

"They're all asleep. Nothing moving there in camp."

Helen sucked in a breath at the closer voice, fifteen feet to their left. Stealthy shapes of ten men afoot in the wood around them, muskets clenched in hand, closed on camp. The fire glow beckoned. The aroma of fried pork left on skillets hung in the air.

She, Hannah, Jonathan, and Roger squatted very still. Marion's Whigs snuck past. Their forms became silhouettes. Firelight painted them orange targets.

"Left their supper. Damn, I'm hungry."

"Give me some of that pork."

"Say, no one's here! It's a trap, lads!"

A branch behind Helen popped, and a hot body reeking of whiskey sprawled atop her, pitching her against the boulder. A second group of Whigs had followed the initial ten into camp. "Halloo, Eli, they're out here!" Jonathan hauled him off her, knocked his musket into darkness, and kicked his stomach.

Another Whig dove in. A ball from Roger's musket ripped his throat, and he collapsed and thrashed. Sulfurous black powder stench, mingled with the metallic stink of fresh blood, drenched the air.

Above the whiny ring in her ears from musket discharge, Helen heard the rumble of horses descending on camp. Whig musket-fire peppered the night, but she wasted no time speculating on the fate of militiamen afoot with discharged muskets pitted against horsed cavalry soldiers with uplifted sabers.

Alerted by movement in her peripheral vision, she flung herself into Hannah. A knife blade scraped rock beside her right ear. She rammed her elbow backward into her attacker's groin. He fell atop the man with the throat wound and sobbed.

Hannah tripped two more Whigs. Roger smacked the butt of his musket into both temples.

Stunned, shaken, her pulse at a gallop, Helen saw two Whigs leap for Jonathan. A bony thud signaled their collision with each other. Jonathan didn't occupy the spot he'd been in a second earlier.

One man lurched to his feet and slashed at Jonathan with a knife. Jonathan's foot shot out, cracked his wrist. He howled and floundered away.

A shriek of mortal terror yanked their attention to the campsite. Helen cringed and jerked her gaze away, too late. Burned into her brain was a horrific sequence of images: Fairfax raised up in the stirrups, firelight incandescent on an archangelic grimace of rapture, his saber swooping orange flame, and blood spray from a man's headless body before it crumpled.

"My g-god!" Hannah turned away, coughed, and vomited.

Jonathan spun Helen about so her back was to the campsite and gripped her to him. The stench of puke, blood, and gunpowder swirled around her. She gagged. Somehow, she retained her supper.

Horses thundered toward them: dragoons with torches beating the brush for escaped Whigs. The Whig with the broken wrist loped off faster, frantic for escape. Davison cantered past and sabered him with the fine form of a champion cricket player.

Jonathan and Roger hauled the women away from bobbing torchlight, away from five injured men who bawled for mercy and received it seconds later in the form of pistol shots to their heads.

Outside the campsite, Roger threw a blanket on the ground. The women sank onto it, wrapped their arms about each other with their backs to the metallic stench of carnage, and gaped out into night. Behind them, Jonathan and Roger dismantled tents, struck camp in preparation for two hours more travel to send them clear of Marion.

Seventeen armed men dead in less than five minutes. Phineas Badley would find the story incredible, almost beyond belief. At that moment, Helen certainly did. Instinct screamed that it wasn't the greatest shock the assignment would deliver.

***

Beyond trees that shrouded the river, the moon had set. Wrapped in a bedroll, Helen stared at the wink of stars above swaying tops of pines and the scuttle of clouds. The air smelled frosty, pine-spicy, earth-ancient. An owl hooted over the Santee.

She thanked the gods that Roger and Hannah had fallen asleep, snuggled together nearby in blankets. Not that they'd been noisy, but from Hannah's sighs and Roger's grunts, it was obvious what they'd been about. Death, flirted with hours earlier, had tagged sex to awaken for the subsequent act.

Jonathan's blanket rustled. Her skin clicked and twitched.

Snores from three of Tarleton's men proclaimed their deep, restful sleep while two others stood sentry. What did killing mean to them? Not sport. Duty, perhaps. Yes, duty. Duty, well-performed, awarded satisfaction. That's why they slept so well.

But killing wasn't duty to Fairfax. She shuddered to recall ecstasy far beyond satisfaction on his face the instant his saber sliced the Whig's neck. The paean in his expression was darkly familiar. Her mind ground away with the need to identify it, denying her sleep.

Spiritual unity. Communion. That was what she'd seen stamped on his face. "Gods!" she whispered. Killing was exaltation to Fairfax. Mouth dry, she thrust aside her blanket and sat.

"Helen?" Jonathan whispered, and he also sat.

He tried to violate my sister...he shot a friend, someone I've known my entire life, in cold blood. No, not mere killing. Before Fairfax's divinity blessed him, it demanded more than death.

There are ways a man might hang another, make it appear suicide. Such a murderer might also draw out the physical agony of his victim during a hanging, without leaving overt evidence. Helen shuddered again, hugged herself. She imagined Ratchingham choking in a noose fixed with expertise to cut off air but not snap his neck, a stool returned beneath his feet long enough for him to recover consciousness, then kicked away, over and over. And Fairfax feeding off his stepfather's terror and agony, his face illuminated by exaltation.

She drew her cloak over her clothes and slid on shoes and gloves. "Helen, wait." She walked away, knowing that Jonathan monitored her departure.

Her path intersected with Campbell's patrol. "Looking for your brother?"

She shook her head. "I need to walk. I cannot find sleep."

"I understand."

She believed he did understand. Campbell, the senior dragoon, worked well with people. Perhaps he'd had to interact with outraged and grieved civilians on occasion and explain *why.* "I shan't go farther than those pine trees over there." She pointed east.

"Very good, madam." He bowed and stepped aside.

Winter-brown grass and weeds grabbed her petticoat. Halfway to the pines, she hopped over trunks of smaller trees toppled in the same direction by a recent windstorm. She paused, kicked a fallen trunk to evict any varmints, and sat upon it.

Exaltation. Where was *her* exaltation?

Her neck craned back, she studied the empyrean. Antares, garnet heart of the scorpion, glittered. Teal trail as thin as thread, a meteor zipped across the velvet black for three seconds before it extinguished.

Elbows on her knees, she propped her head in her hands. Thoughts scattered through her mind like a child's jacks spilled upon a wooden floor. Her journal, with no entry yet for Monday the fourth of December. Badley, and what he wanted from the project, why he'd sent her into the Santee, whether he'd visited Enid in her absence. The peculiar events of her final week in Wilmington: attempted creditor fraud, and the deaths of Charles, Layman, and Sims. Jonathan's chaste caresses. David's tortured love.

Emptiness ached in her soul. Where was her exaltation?

Cold slithered her neck. She straightened and pulled the hood of her cloak over her head.

Movement in the pines drew her gaze. Fairfax strode toward camp, as full of energy as any nocturnal creature. She'd never seen him sleep. Everything about him was eldritch. Chilled, she stood.

He skipped over a downed tree and made for her, high spirits fleshing out his tone. "Helen, darling, welcome to two in the morning!" Even by starlight, preternatural beauty resonated from him. His gods had been appeased.

Her gods, too? *You know where to find community.*

Fairfax laughed when he reached her. "Let me guess. We must return to Wilmington on the morrow."

It was far too late to head back. Her voice sounded ancient, tired. "We shall continue on to my appointment with the Legion."

"Perseverance. You keep your word." His hands darted out, closed both her hands together. Heat radiating from his hands penetrated her gloves and the bones of her fingers with an almost painful jolt. "Trouble sleeping? Laudanum in wine would help."

"No, I — that combination produces visions."

"Visions? Intriguing. I wager you've lain awake wondering why we didn't take them prisoner, why we killed them —"

"*We?*" She took a deep breath and tasted a faint, new scent woven through his musk: blood. "I know why the Green Dragoons kill." Her tone remained even. "I also know why you kill."

Winter gusted over her. His fingers stroked hers. After a glance toward camp, he leaned toward her a few inches, studied her expression, and softened his tone. "Such a busy mind. Francis Marion provides quite a welcome to the Santee, doesn't he?" He tugged her closer and caught her arms. "While you're so busy philosophizing about death and killing, you'd best consider why Phineas Badley is trying to kill you. Such a charming fellow you work for."

Chapter Twenty-Four

"BADLEY — TRYING TO *kill* me?"

"He insisted that you travel into the Santee, despite my warning. To my knowledge, no journalist has ever traveled with the Legion. The chance of being killed is far greater than with a regular unit. Were I a publisher, I'd send a reporter to the Santee or riding with the Legion for two reasons. One: I was desperate for a story. Two: I wanted the journalist killed on assignment. My impression of Phineas Badley is that he isn't desperate for a story."

"See here, Badley and I never liked each other, but that's no reason for him to want me dead."

"Think base desires, darling. Comfort. Security. Money."

"*Money*? He has plenty of money."

"And a man might sleep quite well atop his mountain of coin if he were comfortable that he could hang onto it, and no one would dispute it with him. Who probated your late husband's will?"

"Maximus Prescott."

"How neatly he fits in Badley's pocket. Did you suspect nothing was amiss when the will was probated to your disfavor?"

Out of defensiveness, she firmed her jaw. "My husband never pretended affection for me. I had no reason to expect more than the dower and residence when the estate was settled."

"Who was executor for the estate?"

"Badley."

"Badley was executor. Prescott was probator. They're wealthy men, and you're a pauper, and you suspect nothing?"

Helen felt a snarl rip across her face. "What good would it do me to fight? Both are powerful men, and I have neither money nor proof that Badley misappropriated assets, or lied under oath —"

"The word you seek is *perjury*."

"*Perjury!*" Eyes wide and sightless, she stared over his shoulder. *If perjury is still a fear, we shall keep it safe for you.* Did Isaiah Hanley's widow possess documents proving that Silas had never intended to be so generous to Phineas Badley? If so, why had she come forward with them nine years after Silas's death?

Clearly, Badley had wanted her and Enid out of the house. Did he suspect that Silas had hidden a copy of Hanley's documents there? A shudder climbed through her. Enid. No!

"Perjury." Fairfax grinned. "Helen, are you very certain you know nothing of Badley's association with Adam Neville?"

Twice Fairfax had fished for information of Neville from her. The provincial lieutenant must be pivotal to Fairfax's schemes. Now she wondered if Neville were involved in the business with Badley and Isaiah Hanley's widow. She shook her head. "As I said before, I've never met him, and I've never heard Badley mention him. But see here, if Campbell spots us in such a compromising position, it'll be obvious we aren't siblings."

"From this distance, I assure you that Campbell will interpret such a compromising position as a brother comforting his sister after a frightful encounter with foes."

Their isolation registered on her, then, and she stiffened. "I want to go back. I'm sleepy."

His fingertip traced the shape of her lips. "You had no community. You lost the gods. And now you don't trust yourself. What did Chiswell do, make you give it up for marriage?"

Pagan rubbish...she'll be an Anglican wife. Her heart hammering, Helen pushed herself away from the memory, away from Fairfax. How in Hades could he read her mind?

By starlight, his eyes gleamed. "If you don't seek clarity, the manifestations of war will only confuse you more deeply."

Seconds earlier, his idea of clarity had pressed to her groin with the subtlety of a burning oak knot. Were his gods her gods? "Escort me back. I'm exhausted."

His lips pursed. "As you wish."

The sentinel awaiting their return resolved into both Campbell and Jonathan. "All quiet here, sir," said the dragoon.

Fairfax handed Helen to Jonathan, whose face held no expression. "Take my sister back to bed. Campbell's eyesight is excellent at night, but even he might miss a predator lurking in the grass."

Jonathan bowed and presented the deference of a servant, but after he and Helen had walked away, his exhale hissed. "I suppose that predator in the grass eased your mind?"

She shook off his arm and eyed him with disbelief. "You're envious."

"You're losing perspective after less than a week out here in the wild."

Acid trickled into her voice. "I had plenty of perspective in George Town. You refused me, you regret it now, and you're angry."

"I'm not angry. I'm afraid for you. I have remembered something." The way his voice softened spiked the hairs on her neck. He led her close to the pine barren where the Pearsons and three dragoons slept. They stopped walking and faced each other, and he said low, "After Silas died in '71, I returned to Wiltshire on business. I encountered Ratchingham's former butler at a tavern."

Her attention perked. "Jedediah?"

"His employment was terminated in 1766."

"He was *discharged*? I thought he was considered reliable. What were the circumstances?"

Jonathan's tone tightened. "Lady Ratchingham's jewelry turned up in his saddlebags on a day he was headed to town."

Her memory replayed the scene at the study in Redthorne: Fairfax's dismissal of Jedediah's credibility, and the butler's vow, *You little shit, I'll get you for this.* Warfare had ensued between Fairfax and Jedediah. In 1766, Fairfax had won.

"There's more." Jonathan expelled a breath. "Jedediah told me Ratchingham hired almost a completely new staff in '71. That year, many old servants had left terrified. They'd been dealing with mutilated carcasses of small animals tortured to death. In '71, the perpetrator graduated to larger animals such as sheep and goats."

Revulsion squeezed air from Helen's lungs. In 1771, Fairfax would have been anatomically strong enough to subdue sheep and goats.

"Helen, surely you must see that this moment, as in George Town, this is about you finding guidance within yourself." He seized her hands in his. "You must learn to trust yourself. And do not discount the insight of Helen Grey."

***

At six-thirty Tuesday morning, while eating porridge, she reviewed the canvas with its scattered pieces. Badley in league with Prescott to defraud her of Silas's estate: Fairfax's theory ordered a good portion of the chaos. If those two suspected Charles and Jonathan of knowing about their scheme, and if they suspected that Silas's death hadn't been suicide, they might have hired Sims to steal the pistol and kill both men. Use of the dueling pistol hearkened back to the roles of Charles and Jonathan in the duel, framed her for murder, and might have gotten her jailed.

Why had Mrs. Hanley withheld information of such a crucial nature from Helen for so long? Had she been threatened to hold her tongue?

Steam from the porridge thawed Helen's nose, opened her mind to a subtle problem. While managing the turpentine plantation, she'd learned the breadth of her husband's wealth. Had Badley and Prescott defrauded her and split almost all of his wealth between them, they'd be far more wealthy, and to a conspicuous degree. They wouldn't have remained in Wilmington. At the least, they'd have moved to an affluent city such as London to live it up. Badley wouldn't have continued to plod away at a magazine on the edge of the frontier.

They might have disguised the money in investments elsewhere such as the Caribbean to avoid suspicion. Still, nine years was a long time for two avaricious men to delay gratification.

Fairfax paced, unhurried, beyond dragoons who squatted near the fire to eat. Aware of her scrutiny, he awarded her that faint smile. Wood smoke wafted in her face. Smoke. Yes. He'd promoted his theory about Badley at the precise moment when she'd revealed that she understood why he slaughtered Marion's men, steering her curiosity away from the demons that rode him.

Shoulders thrown back in confidence, she carried her cup and mug to Hannah, who scrubbed dishes. "Blasted porridge sticks to everything," Hannah muttered.

Concern panged Helen at tautness on Hannah's face. How ill she'd become after witnessing the gruesome skirmish. Not that Helen hadn't almost puked herself. She gave Hannah's shoulder a pat. "How are you?"

"I shall sort through it soon enough, madam. Please don't worry for me." She eyed Helen. "I'd a memory last night of Papa."

Helen wasn't certain how well Hannah worked through her father's death, but she knew the woman needed a compassionate ear. "Tell me about it, if you wish."

Hannah wiped hands on a towel and faced her. "He used to read *Badley's Review* to us after supper, before he'd secure the house for the night. Mama, my brother, and sister were still alive then. We laughed at stories in the magazine."

She pressed her lips together. "We didn't laugh over your husband's estate settlement. Papa called it unjust, said it wasn't what Mr. Chiswell intended. He spoke of times he'd helped Mr. Chiswell up to bed after he'd drunk too much brandy and gone maudlin. Madam, Mr. Chiswell babbled about people stealing his money, people he trusted. He thanked Papa for being a good servant and said he'd made arrangements for Papa's comfort after he died."

Helen's skin prickled. "Did Charles specify what arrangements, Hannah? A bequest in my husband's will, perhaps?"

She shook her head. "Papa never said. He and Mama decided to keep quiet about it. Papa didn't have proof that he might have been a beneficiary, and you know judges and lawyers. They'd have cast him as a greedy servant trying grab some of his master's wealth, and then they'd likely have laughed him out of the courthouse." Hannah straightened her shoulders. "After that, Papa hired an attorney, had him draw up his own will, gave each of us a copy. He wanted no doubt as to the distribution of his estate and said he'd make sure none of us was left out like him and Mrs. Chiswell."

Nothing in Hannah's story constituted substantive evidence of fraud, yet it was just as suggestive of fraud as Charles's words to David had been. *They'll kill madam if they find it.* Charles may not have told his family all he knew, but he'd suspected wickedness.

If Badley and Prescott had defrauded her and Charles of substantial estate benefits, they'd covered their tracks well. It sure sounded as though some recent event had threatened exposure of a scheme. Widow Hanley was bound up in the mess, and Charles and the widow's messenger had been killed to silence them.

"Mrs. Chiswell, do you think this has anything to do with my father's death?"

"Yes, I do."

The crease of worry across Hannah's brow deepened. With a glance around, she lowered her voice. "That could mean Mr. Badley's involved, being that his magazine was the main beneficiary of the estate. He's one of Wilmington's wealthiest merchants."

And he kept one of Wilmington's smartest lawyers in his pocket. Anxiety tunneled into Helen's chest. If Badley had sent her through the Santee hoping she'd be killed, could she expect a bank draft from him to await her in

Camden, as promised in the contract? Without more funds, she'd be stranded in the backcountry. Depending on where she was stranded, death might be welcome —

No. Fairfax wanted her to panic so he could keep her controlled. She sucked in cold air and whispered, "Hannah, let's walk one step at a time and not try to rush. In truth, all we have are suspicions and no solid evidence. And let us not forget that today, this moment, the assignment with the Legion demands priority."

Hannah's shoulders relaxed, indicating her relief that she wouldn't have to testify in court soon and be discredited and demeaned by attorneys and judges. "Yes, madam."

She returned to the dishes. Helen's gaze flicked over to Jonathan, who helped Roger fold up tent canvas. On occasion, Charles had confided in Jonathan, but had Jonathan possessed more than speculations, she was certain he'd have said something to her, especially after he'd witnessed her economic collapse, especially after all the recent hubbub over "perjury" and Widow Hanley.

Still, it never hurt to approach him from another angle. The thought that Badley and Prescott might have defrauded not only her but also the Landon family nagged her. She resolved to query Jonathan with her theories during the midday break.

Chapter Twenty-Five

THAT MORNING, HELEN battled the urge to head for New Berne and request audience with Widow Hanley. Common sense kept her in the saddle guiding her mare north. Travel to and from the Santee entailed tremendous peril, even with the protection of an armed escort, and the Legionnaires were under orders to return to their unit. Besides, if Badley and Prescott had plundered Silas's estate, the court would take years to recover what it could trace. She and Hannah might never recognize most of it.

Could Badley so desire her death that he'd fake an entire assignment? What would motivate him to finance putting her in harm's way? Fairfax had said there was no Samuel Kerr on the *London Chronicle*. Was Fairfax reliable on that point? Had Badley bought *him* off, paid him to discourage and frighten her?

What if the new magazine didn't exist? Was the Legion assignment pointless?

The party encountered the first demolished farm just up the road, and there were plenty more after it. Although some brick chimneys remained intact, most houses were leveled to their foundations. Burned wagons, plows, and carts stood sentinel over eviscerated gardens and crop fields. Plump buzzards poked with minimal interest among bones. The stench of scorched wood and slaughtered livestock clung to the road and seasoned every breath she took. She had to coax Calliope across the bridge to Jack's Creek. Birdsong sounded tentative, reluctant.

She imagined glassy-eyed women crouched around campfires, embracing babes and children who shivered, while behind them, the wrecks of homes and barns smoldered dull orange beneath the majesty of the Milky Way. How many lives along the Santee Road had been uprooted? Where had the infirm and elderly, women, children, and farm hands gone with their homes destroyed? She thought of war victims in Wilmington, orphans and widows who received the Church's charity. No one ever showed the victims of war as heroes for what they'd endured, yet along the Santee Road, the face of devastation looked the same whether one were Whig, neutral, or Loyal.

She straightened, jolted to the core by the bizarre juxtaposition, and yet compelled to revisit it in her head. Were her thoughts not sedition? Still, her brain persisted in toying with them.

To distract herself off the disturbing tangent, she asked another question of the dragoons while they rode through the devastation: "With what attributes do you describe Colonel Tarleton?"

Compliments poured from them. Valiant, courageous, heroic, brave, just, fearless. She suspected Marion's men would say the same of him. How could the dragoons praise their commander amidst the destruction he'd wrought, destruction they could see, smell, and taste? But then they weren't women: mothers, wives, daughters, sisters. Men seemed to disconnect with more ease from the wound of war.

She asked them, "Is Colonel Tarleton compassionate?"

The dragoons guffawed for a full minute, and Helen felt her face glow with humiliation. "This is war, Mrs. Chiswell. Why does Colonel Tarleton need compassion?" said Davison.

Connor brandished a sour smile. "I've seen him compassionate — when the lady's pretty." The men hooted some more.

Campbell nudged his horse up to pace Helen's, his expression sober. "September, at Fishing Creek, the Colonel came down with malaria. He got delirious and couldn't be moved while he recovered. All around us in the swamps were the rebel dregs who'd butchered Captain Huck in July." The set of his jaw declared resolve. "Not a man in the Legion quit his post."

Helen acknowledged him with a nod. "That's courage and loyalty, not compassion."

"True. One night, a starving brat sneaked past the sentries into camp, said he wanted to join the Legion. Markson took him in, gave him some biscuit and bacon. Remember Markson, lads?"

A somber murmur of assent stirred the men.

"At dawn, Markson was dead, his own knife buried in his throat. The little turd vanished, along with Markson's purse." Campbell spat off to the side of the road. "What use have we for compassion? Bloody lucky we are that he didn't report to the rebels. How they'd love to have caught Colonel Tarleton when he was vulnerable."

"Just as we'd love to find Sumter." Davison beamed.

Campbell moved off, and Fairfax occupied the space beside her. She kept her gaze on the road ahead. Unmistakable, the superciliousness in his voice. "Our conversation early this morning inspired me to ponder your situation further. I shall share my conjectures with you tonight."

"Generous of you, but unnecessary."

He clucked his tongue. "You always have hated it when I'm the correct one, dear sister."

He rode on ahead. Helen inhaled a deep breath of horse sweat and incinerated homestead and coughed.

Noon, the party paused to redistribute weight of baggage in the wagon. Helen snagged Jonathan's elbow and towed him far enough away for privacy. "I suspect that Badley and Prescott committed perjury, misappropriated assets from Silas's will, and swindled Charles and me out of a considerable portion of the estate."

Jonathan studied her, his expression cool, before his gaze flicked over her shoulder to their party at the road. "Interesting. That makes sense of the more puzzling elements of this situation. The scruples of both men are ambiguous enough to render it plausible. Did this angle occur to you unassisted?" He pinned his gaze to hers.

Frost in his eyes startled her. "You dismiss the idea as not credible?"

"I ask that you evaluate the motivations of your source of inspiration. You didn't arrive at your conclusion about my affections unassisted, either. Notice how comfortable you and I are with each other as a result."

Helen felt her expression stiffen and braced her fists on her hips. "I suspect there was another will. Maybe that's what Widow Hanley tried to communicate. Hannah said Charles told his family that Silas intended to provide for them. Really, Jonathan, you're more than envious. You're *jealous*, and I find that unappealing."

"I shall be delighted to discuss your theory at length when we have time and privacy. But do consider the source." With a curt bow, he headed for the horses. She trailed after in annoyance.

The party met no one on the road. The weight of loss mounted upon Helen, and her soul grew more and more restless. Late afternoon, they arrived at what was, until a month earlier, Richardson's plantation. The manor had been fine for those parts, with solid, brick chimneys. She fingered shards of a blue-and-white porcelain tea service, dashed to pieces, probably while Widow Richardson was forced to watch. Remnants of a loom, ladder-back chairs, quilts slashed to pieces, and an oil painting tangled in a mound that had burned in the front lawn and been soaked to mush in a rain shower. Helen strolled in the family cemetery, paused at the grave of General Richardson — who, from the inscription on his stone had been dead but a few months — and wondered if he rested in peace.

She insisted on sketching. Without argument, Fairfax moved her portmanteau and unloaded her campstool and desk. They left her alone for half an hour and waited out on the road.

Two hours farther north in the dark, the bitter stink of destruction behind them, they pitched camp just past the confluence of the Wateree and Congaree Rivers. Exhausted from emotional tumult and lack of sleep, Helen struggled to complete the entry before she forgot nuances of the encounter with Francis Marion, the ambush, and the torched homes. Multiple times, she intercepted intrusion of her own bias. Crossed-out words and sentence fragments blotched pages. Clambering over her mind to distract her was all that she *couldn't* write about: Silas's will, Jonathan, Fairfax, and David.

Roger had refined his movement at musket drills. When Davison showed him a few swings with his saber and placed it in his hand, the locksmith looked so natural with it that Helen pictured him saddled, wearing the green uniform and helmet of brown bear fur. She glanced at Hannah. What did the younger woman think about her husband's dream come to life? But Hannah, who observed Davison and Roger, had her back to Helen.

The nightly chess game proceeded with ill grace. Five minutes into it, she heard the board pushed aside, and when she peered back, Fairfax stood, his glare bored into Jonathan. "I shall have you checkmated in three moves. You are again allowing me to win. I do not enjoy this pandering. Resume the previous position with your piece, and play chess like a man. Otherwise, I shan't engage you in the game again."

Without hesitation, Jonathan slid the chessboard back into place and returned his castle several squares to one side. His expression stony, Fairfax resumed his seat.

Helen continued her journal entry. War waged on the chessboard for almost two hours. During the last half-hour, "Check" traded sides at least three times. Eyes achy with fatigue, she'd sanded the final page of the entry and was in the midst of a stretch and yawn when she heard Jonathan's serene, "Checkmate."

In her peripheral vision, Fairfax rose and bowed to Jonathan, who put up the chess set and strolled off, his shoulders thrown back. She gathered pen and ink and would have risen had Fairfax not sat beside her on the bench facing the fire, elbows supported on his knees. She deposited pragmatism in her tone. "You *did* ask him not to restrain himself this time."

"Hmm." Fairfax stared into the fire, his voice soft to prevent any dragoons from overhearing. "I'm curious who Badley and Prescott hired to assist them in swindling you."

Annoyance swept over her, and she covered a yawn. "*If* they swindled me," she whispered, "why does it matter to you? I'm fairly certain Silas didn't will money to you."

He straightened and swiveled on the bench to regard her. "No upstart frontier merchant or country pettifogger should be allowed to defraud a peer of the realm."

She felt color drain from her face. The class issue again. "This is America, not Britain."

Incredulity loaded his eyes. "Did you dump your peerage overboard during the crossing? Sometimes I wonder."

She trod treacherous ground. "Now who has the overly busy mind? If they swindled my husband's money, it's long gone. However satisfying it might be to see them rot in jail, that wouldn't bring back the money."

"You don't even care to investigate. Someone convinced you that investigation wouldn't help. Perhaps that someone is in the employ of Badley and Prescott even today."

"Badley and Prescott can manage such a scheme by themselves."

"The core mechanics of it, perhaps. But you're an intelligent woman. If I'd been them, I'd have paid a few people to divert your attention elsewhere. Badley may *still* be paying them."

She rotated to the fire, closed her eyes, and sighed. "You think Badley paid a merchant to chase my petticoat all these years. Well, most merchants of Wilmington are idiots, lending the weight of a goose feather to your theory. I'm exhausted."

He gripped her upper arm, leaned closer, and whispered, "Consider those among your *friends* for whom Badley has regard. I heard him defend Mr. St. James when we were in the study."

Helen snapped her head around to glare at him. "Good heavens, what a pathetic attempt."

"I'd be willing to wager with you, madam, that Badley and St. James entered your husband's life at almost exactly the same time. Why? Because they were — are — a team. Now, what do you say? Shall we wager on it?"

Startled, she stared at the fire, and her memory scrambled back eleven years, a fortnight after she and Silas arrived in Wilmington. She'd been in the parlor when the back door whammed open. Silas tottered in jovial, reeking of brandy, shored up by two men she'd never seen before who both looked apologetic and embarrassed. "Helen, my honey! I won at the cockfights tonight! And I brought home two new friends to meet you!

"Gentlemen, I present my wife, the lovely Mrs. Chiswell. Here we have Mr. Phineas Badley, owner of *Badley's Review*. And over here is Mr. David St. James, who travels the colonies playing piquet and one and thirty. What fun, eh?"

Chapter Twenty-Six

"HOLD THE LANTERN closer." Helen winced at the bark in her tone. Hannah didn't deserve it. *A team.* Badley the brains, David the dash. Was that how they worked it? How had Fairfax known? *We have more in common than you're willing to admit.* Helen shuddered.

Hannah lowered the light near Helen's portmanteau. "Tell me what you're looking for. I can help you."

Helen pawed through clothing and slammed her portmanteau shut. Damnation. Must've left the laudanum in Wilmington. Not that she'd used it much, fearing the infamous dependency, but if ever there was a night for drugged sleep, surely this was it.

She sat and stared at the wall of her tent. Her heart felt like a piece of meat tenderized by a butcher's mallet, left all bloody, shapeless, and flaccid on the block afterwards.

Hannah hooked the lantern to the ridgepole, sat beside her, and clasped her hand. "Won't you tell me what's wrong?" she whispered.

Helen's pulse pounded her ears. Drunkenness may have marked Silas as an easy target for a quick purse cutting by "new friends" who'd noticed his win at a cockfight. But for a team to linger another two years, its ultimate goal defrauding him of his estate, required an almost unbelievable amount of dedication, patience, and perseverance — not to mention a degree of skill, foresight, and cunning possessed by less than a thousandth of all criminals.

In 1769, William Tryon was Royal Governor, and Wilmington was quite a town for festivity. At dinner parties, balls, and theater shows, fashion and flirtation flowed. How many times had she danced with David, dined at the same table, smiled greetings across a crowded theater before Silas had left her alone at the house on Second Street and traveled on business?

David's nocturnal visits brought peace to the house. No servant spoke a word of it to the master. Mrs. Chiswell was happy for the first time, treated with tenderness and respect by a fellow who was courteous to them and not so *haut* that he couldn't share humor every once in awhile. David earned their loyalty.

Had it all been an act?

Dragged nine years past by memory, she trembled to relive the bellow of voices in the parlor while she lay abed, her abdomen bruised, her womb cramped with miscarriage.

★★★

"The devil damn you black for abusing her that way!"

"The devil damn you black for fucking my wife! It's your brat she carries!"

"All she's ever been to you is — is livestock to kick around or futter when you're drunk. The woman doesn't matter to you at all. You'd rather poke a sheep or a goat. That's it. She's the first woman you ever emptied your stones into. You're used to livestock!"

"Bastard cur, if we were in England —"

"Well, we aren't in England, you idiot, we're in America."

"Take back those words."

"Kiss my arse."

"We shall settle this, then."

"Yes, we shall. Name your time and location."

★★★

Did David support himself off his skill at gambling, or had he helped Badley and Prescott murder her husband in exchange for a chunk of Chiswell estate? What was that business he'd mentioned during his most recent visit about paying off Prescott a final few pounds?

Hannah released her hand. "I shall fetch the Professor."

"No." Helen snagged her sleeve. More disillusionment and doubt paralyzed her. Jonathan and Badley, cordial. Jonathan, lukewarm over her swindle theory. Jonathan, part of "the team?"

"You're not well, Mrs. Chiswell, I can see it."

"The skirmish with Marion's men. My reaction, delayed." The last thing she wanted was Jonathan's company. "Say nothing to him. Please, I just need sleep. Help me undress."

Conflict nipped Hannah's face, but she complied. After she'd tucked Helen into the cot, she took the lantern with her. Tears seeped from the corners of Helen's eyes, in no way representative of the tidal wave of grief dammed up inside her, and not easing her heartache. She blotted the tears away before they pooled in her ears.

Did David and Jonathan play a charade with her? Not knowing left her in limbo, frozen, indecisive.

In the distance, she heard Fairfax comment to a dragoon about a horseshoe. Anger clenched her gut. The scoundrel, this was his doing. He'd crafted his words to unmoor her and leave her sails stripped of wind, and she dredged up enough self-doubt to muddle her own way. He'd shaken the tree more than she ever could have imagined.

Sleep found her, but in her dreams, both David and Jonathan turned their backs on her and walked away, while she struggled to follow, hampered by wrists tied behind her. That peculiar image of bound wrists again. Metaphor, surely, but deep inside, she felt it meant more. When she woke predawn the next morning to Roger's chipper whistle, she felt as though she'd spent all night bribing the gods to be ferried back from Hades.

***

Next day in the High Hills of Santee, Helen rode forward among dragoons Sullivan, Ross, and Davison and asked them what they enjoyed most about riding with the Legion. Sullivan and Ross commented on their distinctive uniforms and their renowned mobility. Although the Legion went through horses faster than other regiments, Tarleton knew how to divert mounts from other regiments. "Swift, stunning strikes," said Davison, "and the looks of surprise and terror on the face of the foe." He sighed, pleased.

A blend of humor, amazement, and uneasiness wound through Helen at the phrases the men used to describe their commander. "He gives us a sense of purpose." "He's our protector." "He's our champion." In the eyes of his men, Tarleton had assumed the status of a divine warrior from legend, like Achilles or Samson, boundless with stamina and energy.

Divine warriors weren't perfect. They came equipped with a fatal flaw. Odds were that a twenty-six-year-old who was younger than many of his subordinate officers had at least one flaw. But soldiers demanded consistency of their officers.

Esprit de corps didn't arise in a unit whose commander led with his vices — firm one day, lax the next. Were Tarleton cut from that cloth, the dragoons' comments about him would have been disparaging, mocking.

She considered Davison's comment about what he enjoyed the most: *Swift, stunning strikes, and the looks of surprise and terror on the face of the foe.* Characteristic of the Legion was its rattlesnake-like surprise attack. The Legion counted upon chaos created among the enemy with the attack strategy. Uneasiness pricked Helen again. The Legion hadn't always been victorious with its sudden attack.

Assuming her assignment was genuine, could this be the muck Badley's sponsor had hired her to uncover about Tarleton — that he didn't deploy other strategies? Was the Legion, a disproportionately large financial drain of His Majesty's resources in the southern colonies, a disaster waiting to happen? Parliament wasn't hospitable to spendthrifts these days. A feature that Tarleton abused his favored status with Cornwallis and squandered resources would, indeed, be enough to sink a career in Parliament before it ever started.

***

Mid-morning on the ninth of December, the party entered Camden on Broad Street, a packed-dirt thoroughfare running north to south through town. Business from Market Square spilled over into the lower town square. Vendors hawked tobacco, pastries, produce, ribbons, ink, livestock, and anything else they thought they could sell to goodwives, soldiers, frontiersmen, Indians, slaves, artisans, and merchants who wandered among the booths.

Helen couldn't wait to collect Badley's bank draft and post her Santee Road adventures, eat a meal that didn't consist of trail rations or snared rabbit, and spend the night in a decent inn minus bedbugs, where she could rid herself of ten days of Santee swamp slime. She was ready to feel silk against her skin again. And she was worn out on the company of everyone in her party, with the possible exception of Calliope.

Sun and rain had bleached the two-story wooden houses and businesses fronting Broad Street to a uniform gray. Upon closer study, she determined that the bustle and traffic masked early stages of dilapidation in Camden. Shops for a wigmaker and eyeglass seller had closed down. So had a large inn called the Leaping Stag. Paint on the inn's signboard peeled.

The party halted at the office of a purchasing agent for the Legion, located between the courthouse and the Leaping Stag. Fairfax and Campbell dismounted and headed for the front door. A forty-ish, potbellied fellow in a good wig and merchant-class brown wool suit emerged from the office grinning and shook hands with Fairfax. "Mr. Fairfax! Welcome back to Camden. Good to see you again, sir. You look the peak of health, and you, too, Campbell." He and the legionnaire exchanged a handshake. "The Legion's been camped at Woodward's Plantation up the Broad River ever since that business at Blackstock's. You heard of Blackstock's didn't you?"

The man had jammed all that verbiage in two breaths and ten seconds, as if used to wily talk. Something about him was familiar. Recognition oozed into Helen like tar from a broken barrel. Then his Wiltshire accent registered, and horror and disbelief blasted her.

"Good god!" whispered Jonathan. He tugged the brim of his hat lower, seized her upper arm, and spun her around so her back faced the man. "Have you your letters ready to post?"

"Here in my pocket, but Jonathan, that man, he's — he's —"

"Yes, I know! *Don't* turn back around. Roger."

"Yes, sir." Roger moseyed over.

"Inform Mr. Fairfax that his sister and I shall be down the street at the stationer's shop to post her letters, and we shall meet all of you afterwards at the inn on Church Street."

"Very good, sir."

Jonathan hooked her hand inside his elbow and marched her south on Broad Street. Only after they'd passed the defunct Leaping Stag did she dare breathe. Jonathan exhaled relief. "That was close. I don't think he got a good look at either of us."

Helen's teeth chattered. "This is a-a nightmare. What's Tobias Treadaway doing in America?"

Disgust deepened his voice. "His procurement business must have dried up in Wiltshire."

Cold slithered her spine, followed by a wave of heat. "What if he recognizes me? He mustn't see me again!"

"He's the Legion's agent in Camden. You'll encounter him while Tarleton's camped close by. Expect him to dine with us tonight."

"Then I must dine alone, in my room, to prevent his recognition."

"I doubt he'll be able to reconcile your being the gently born sister of an officer and the widow of a gentleman. He'll think his memory is faulty."

"But what if he remembers *you*?"

"A distinct possibility. Let me ponder on it." Still holding her elbow, he paused before the stationer's shop window. "However, I'm certain that if you're to succeed in your deception, you must make your performance with Mr. Fairfax more convincing."

The furrow of concern between his brows tensed her stomach. "How do you mean?"

"Treadaway has spent his life deducing hearts and minds from what's held in the face and body. The 'quarreling siblings' duet between you and Mr. Fairfax may have satisfied the dragoons on the Santee Road. But herein, you must invest more of yourself in the role of Mr. Fairfax's sister to avoid creating doubt in Treadaway. In Colonel Tarleton, as well."

Another groan passed her lips. She'd have to show Fairfax *affection*. Without a doubt, he'd take advantage of her for it.

Chapter Twenty-Seven

HELEN'S ATTENTION DRIFTED off her fellow diners. No bank draft had awaited her at the post office. Rebels and road conditions often delayed riders or prevented posts from arriving. But what if Badley broke the contract and didn't pay her?

Her awareness returned to the private dining room at the inn, and the conversation, not to be missed for its currents of friction. Lieutenant Adam Neville had spoken: Neville, who earned the special attention of Fairfax. And Helen was beginning to understand why.

Neville, the provincial on leave from Thomas Brown's Rangers, who'd introduced Fairfax and Badley, happened to be in Camden to purchase iron for the Legion's blacksmiths. His long face shrewd, he ran the tip of his right forefinger once around the rim of his empty coffee cup before he regarded Fairfax. "Colonel Brown estimates that between a third and a half of the civilian population claims neutrality."

"Neutrals." Campbell pushed aside his empty dessert dish. The ambient warmth of candlelight in a branched, brass holder suspended from the ceiling imparted the hue of fresh-cut grass upon his wool uniform jacket. "What do you expect out of Georgia?" He belted down the Madeira remaining in his wineglass.

At the head of the table, Fairfax steepled his fingers, that chilly smile on his lips, his uniform coat scarlet. "I presume Colonel Brown made his estimation before the rebels besieged him in September."

Neville held Fairfax's gaze. He appeared older than his mid-twenties and still wore his ranger's hunting shirt. "I doubt the siege in September changed his mind." His dark eyes gleamed.

"You doubt hanging thirteen of his captors would change his mind about the intentions of neutrals?"

"He didn't hang neutrals. He hanged rebels."

If such a man existed who could be Fairfax's friend, Neville wasn't that man. Across the multi-course, three-hour supper, the veil over their rivalry thinned to reveal two soldiers of the same rank and competence, one provincial and one regular, who had mistrusted each other for months. From the first moment Helen witnessed interchange between them, they butted heads. The posture of Neville's body belied a capacity for unconventional thought, even when he held his tongue on an issue. His mere presence challenged Fairfax.

If Fairfax's suspicion of Badley was grounded in his suspicion of Neville, his agreement to uphold the cover of Badley's journalist was incomprehensible. Another scheme played out, another agenda advanced. Disquiet snaked over Helen. What was Tarleton's role? Were he and his big dreams of Parliament but sacrifices in their games?

Jonathan had suggested that the assignment might be a plot to discredit Tarleton, but he wasn't there to enjoy the show. To excuse his attendance at supper, where Treadaway might recognize him, he'd feigned a flare-up of an ulcer and taken to his bed. With the Pearsons her silent servants, she'd watched contention unfold during supper.

Treadaway returned his drained wineglass to the table and swiveled to Neville, who sat beside him. "Don't all those neutrals make you nervous? Seems as though a man ought to be able to make up his mind one way or t'other. Someone who cannot or will not do so is a bit dangerous, you know, rather like an alligator lazing in a pond. And I doubt there are neutrals on the *battlefield*." He focused on Campbell. "Have you ever met a neutral on the battlefield, sir?"

The dragoon's lip curled. "Never."

Fairfax spoke as if explaining a simple sum to a child. "There *are* no neutrals. Everyone who claims neutrality is, in fact, a rebel."

Helen studied Neville's tense jaw. Neville being outnumbered interested her. Who else at the table besides Fairfax suspected the breadth of his unconventional opinions? How unfortunate that he didn't debate the issue. She enjoyed watching men fly into a frenzy and guard their opinions as if they were sacrosanct.

Treadaway, inebriated, leaned elbows on the table and ogled her. "Mr. Fairfax, we haven't yet heard your lovely sister's view of neutrals."

Fairfax sounded bored. "She hasn't a view on them."

Helen laughed. "Poppycock, Dunstan, I do have an opinion."

"The gentlemen don't want to hear it, Helen."

Treadaway's eagerness gave him the appearance of a spaniel. "*I* want to hear it."

"Well, then, from Mr. Neville's comments, I should enjoy a chat with Thomas Brown. Not one of the neutrals I've met has ever struck me as being a rebel in disguise." She winked at Fairfax. "They each seemed just as concerned about the disastrous effect of war on the country as Loyalists are. How do you explain that, dear brother?"

"Yes, of course they're concerned, madam!" Treadaway seemed to have forgotten that the moment before, he'd disparaged neutrals. "Surely His Majesty will find a suitable argument to get them to hop off their fence and support the Crown."

Campbell snickered. "That argument is known as a 'bayonet.'"

"Pay that puppy no mind." Treadaway's gaze swept her bosom. "Any *man* can judge your exceptional intelligence. You and I simply must sit down and discuss the philosophy of —"

"Mr. Treadaway."

The steel in Fairfax's voice registered on Helen. He was neither a jealous suitor nor a concerned champion. His motivation for stifling Treadaway's clumsy advance was perfunctory: to maintain their cover as siblings. Still, the interjection relieved her. Treadaway, drunk, possessed the subtlety of a lovesick mooncalf.

"A thousand pardons." Treadaway maintained his enthralled gaze upon her. "Peculiar, Mrs. Chiswell, I could swear that we've met before. Perhaps your late husband and I transacted business years ago, eh? Chiswell. When might he have been in Wiltshire last?"

Oh, hell. Treadaway's memory improved when he was drunk. Helen dropped all pretenses at courtesy and rammed iron into her tone to cover her fear. "We've never met before this night." She concealed a fake yawn and caught Hannah's eye. "Gentlemen, excuse me, but I find myself fatigued after our journey." When she moved to stand, Fairfax pulled her chair out for her. Three other chairs scraped backwards on the floor as the men stood. She curtsied, and the men responded with bows. "Please do stay and help Dunstan finish that last bottle of Madeira." Treadaway, Campbell, and Neville murmured wishes for her pleasant repose.

She escaped with Hannah into the pipe smoke and revelry of the common room. Fairfax overtook them, his expression detached, as usual. "As Mr. Quill is indisposed, I shall escort you to your rooms." Without waiting for Helen's approval, he took her arm and headed upstairs with her. Hannah followed with the candle.

Halfway up, Helen mustered a cool voice. "Don't be rude and leave them to finish the wine by themselves."

"I shan't be long."

Good news. She didn't want his company. They reached the second floor. Hannah walked ahead, opened the door to Helen's room at the end of the hallway, and preceded her inside to light candles and turn down the bed.

Fairfax towed Helen into the dimness of the hallway, where he pitched a soft tone. "You and Mr. Neville share similar opinions."

She kept her tone indifferent. "Do we? I hadn't noticed."

"Of course you noticed that business about neutrals."

She stifled a yawn. "I hope you don't make a mountain from that molehill. It must be terribly disillusioning for you, but I see matters in gray, not in black and white. I'm flawed as a Loyalist."

Light from the room flashed on his smile. "Not disillusioning. A boon. Neville is a valuable resource, but he and I don't seem to communicate."

Helen wished Neville could hear the conversation. He probably wouldn't believe it. She didn't. "The fault isn't on his end."

"Oh, Helen, now you wound me."

"Very little wounds you. You're a bully and proud of it." The plaster wall grazed her back. "So now I suppose you'll attempt to bully me into gaining Neville's confidence so you can manipulate your valuable resource."

"I have no intentions of bullying you."

She glanced to her right, where he'd braced his left hand on the wall in between her and the door. "Ah. I should have paid closer attention. Rather than bully me, you'll attempt to seduce me. No, thank you. I'm for bed. Run along, and develop some skill at communication." He blocked her attempt to head for the door, and she scowled. "After sleeping on a cot for a week and a half, I'm truly looking forward to sleeping on that bed in there — *alone.*"

He smiled again. "You and Treadaway know each other."

"Of course we don't know each other. The effect of wine on satyrs is the same. They recognize every woman they meet as a previous mistress."

"Treadaway *is* a satyr." The warmth of his forefinger traced her jaw line and swept across her lips. "But I think he knows your husband from Wiltshire, and you recognize him." His right arm encircled her waist, and his lips brushed her neck above her tucker.

Gooseflesh rocketed down her side. "Preposterous." When she wedged her hands between their chests and tried to push him away, he reeled her up against him. "Stop that —"

"You never told me your family name, so I suspect you and Chiswell eloped against their wishes, and they disinherited you. Treadaway has repute for dark dealings. Perhaps he and your husband procured young women for Arabian sheikhs. You lured them into the trap by advertising for a lady's companion, and Treadaway peddled them."

Helen stared at him in horror, his salty, musky scent and the solid heat of his chest enhancing the gooseflesh each time she inhaled. She turned her face away, toward the door. "That's — that's absurd —"

"Simple to verify my theory. I ply Treadaway with spirits until his memory returns." He guided her face back around with his left hand. "Care to join me and observe my skill at communication?"

The rasp of her breathing echoed in the corridor.

"Ah, what was I thinking? You're sleepy. Well, off to bed for you."

She anticipated his dive in for a kiss, shoved him out at arms' length at the inception, and grasped for the cohesion of outrage. While outrage took its time arriving, waves of gooseflesh raked her nipples out into hard points. She snarled. "How dare you!"

His deep exhalation subsided into the rumble of a playful panther. "Shall I return in an hour to share Treadaway's memories?" He stepped back, and light from the doorway spilled over magnificence in his face.

Outrage snared her mouth. "Go rot."

His tongue ran over his lips. With a grin, he bowed and sauntered back up the hallway for the stairs.

Chapter Twenty-Eight

AFTER HANNAH LEFT, Helen dropped the bar on the door and took a brass candleholder to bed with her, ears trained on every creak in the inn. Later, she realized that Fairfax never intended to return, but he *had* intended for her to lie awake and think about him.

That bastard. Again, he'd manipulated her.

In disgust, she returned the candleholder to the nightstand and crawled back into bed considering his attempt to maneuver her into a relationship with Neville. He wanted something from the ranger, who'd declined to deliver. Her lips torqued. Before they caught up with the Legion, she'd have plenty of time to acquaint herself with Neville. If she played the piquet with a deft enough hand, she might get to the bottom of the mysterious relationship between him and Badley.

Piquet. David. Humor leaked from her soul. She rolled on her side and hugged a pillow. David — paid to help Badley and Prescott swindle her? Anger at such a revelation made it easy for her to be finished with David, so why couldn't she just cast him off?

Perhaps because such a move justified her not doing penance in that aching, vacant place in her soul. Perhaps because instinct affirmed that David hadn't swindled her.

In a world of scarce love, he'd adored her beyond their shared physical passion. She realized that she'd never been able to return his degree of love, yet she'd selfishly kept him in orbit about her, a desperate attempt to confer wholeness upon herself. David, like an Argonaut ship, beat himself against the treacherous shoreline of Nell Grey. Year after year, he'd returned to her, certain she'd give him the Golden Fleece.

But she had no golden fleece. If her soul weren't frozen, she'd have released him years ago to find his heart's rest in another woman. Maybe Helen deserved to orbit a star just as dark and damaged as she was.

***

"We heard they'd carried Sumter out of Blackstock's on a litter, so we gave chase north. By the twenty-second of November, we tracked them to the Pacolet River." At ease in the saddle beside Helen, Neville shook his head. "Never did catch up with them, but we'd heard reports that Sumter was dead. So Tarleton headed back south, and we reached camp near Brierly's Ferry around the first."

Challenge rode with Neville. The iron-laden wagon, its horse team and driver, and six mounted infantry Legionnaires had joined their party that morning and brought up the rear. "And now you've the responsibility of escorting iron to the Legion." She smiled at the ranger.

His response ghosted hers, the first cheer she'd seen in him. Then it sank into the reclusive look his face often wore. Seconds later, Fairfax trotted his horse by, headed for the rear of the party.

Helen waited a moment. "Colonel Brown interests me. I'd like to hear about your time with him in East Florida."

He lowered his voice. "That's superfluous to your assignment."

She chuckled. "True, but I'm curious about everything, Mr. Neville. Do entertain me with your anecdotes during our next break."

His silence stretched long enough to convey refusal, and she shifted, disappointed, in her saddle. Gaining Neville's confidence would take months, not days. Perhaps Fairfax manipulated her for another purpose. Preoccupied all morning, he'd paid her only the minimum civility. Maybe he sulked because he'd wrung nothing incriminatory from Treadaway.

"I'm a flawed Loyalist, sir. Unable to see in black and white. Makes for interesting writing, don't you agree?"

His expression cryptic, he scrutinized her. "You're a curious choice for the assignment. I wonder why Badley chose you?"

A quick gaze around assured Helen that no one else was close enough to hear. "He thought my cover would be easier to maintain than that of one of his men. How do you know Badley?"

A shrug rolled off Neville's back. "He was a friend of my father's." With a tip of his hat, he trotted on ahead, joining Davison in the lead.

Helen sighed, annoyed. The aloof ranger had told her little, and she doubted she'd left a favorable enough impression on him to stimulate further conversation. Neville, bless him, was stubborn enough to withstand a tornado.

An hour later, the party paused in a clearing for a break. While they stretched, other groups of soldiers and civilians rode by on the busy, well-trod road. Pine barrens, sandy soil, and flat terrain bordered by pockets of swamp surrounded the road southwest of Camden. Hardwoods denuded by winter and a high overcast bleakened a countryside bereft of much wildlife. The view wasn't worth a charcoal sketch.

Side by side, Helen and Hannah watched Roger strut in Sullivan's cavalry jacket, a saber in his hand. Hannah's amusement at the drills had degenerated, and Helen couldn't blame her. She hadn't bargained on trading a locksmith husband for a soldier. "Sullivan's jacket is a perfect fit. It isn't the first time the Legion has recruited from the field."

"Recruit? Hrumph! Not while I have any say in the matter." Hannah's gaze drifted to Neville, who adjusted a horse's bridle, and she lowered her voice. "I've seen him before yesterday."

"Have you? Where?"

"In Wilmington, in Mr. Badley's house. He tried to hide from me both times."

"Hide?" Helen frowned.

"Yes. In September, I helped Papa prepare for a dinner that Mrs. Badley was hosting. Both nights, it was late, past nine o'clock. The first night, we were in Mr. Badley's dining room with the chef when Mr. Neville arrived. That lawyer, Prescott, answered the door as if he'd waited for him all day and hurried him past us into Mr. Badley's study.

"The next night, the door was open to the study, and he paced in there, waiting for Mr. Badley. When he saw me, he ducked out of sight and shut the door."

Intuition zinged Helen. Badley, Neville, and Prescott as a team — and that team aroused suspicion in Fairfax. She considered anew Neville's gaunt appearance and Fairfax's suggestion that she talk with the ranger. Neutrals. Not seeing the war in black and white. Gain the cooperation of a "valuable resource." Bah. Fairfax's true motive wasn't so benign.

What irony. Rather than querying Helen about Neville's association with Badley, Fairfax should have asked Hannah. Helen grasped her upper arm and steered her around so the two of them faced away from Neville and the parading Roger. "Hannah, are you certain it was Mr. Neville? From your account, you but glimpsed him both nights."

"I recognized his voice when I heard it last night. I'd heard him talking in the study with Mr. Prescott."

"What were he and Prescott discussing?"

The younger woman shrugged. "Mr. Prescott said someone named Epsilon would have to make do, even though he didn't have enough supplies, and Mr. Neville responded that Epsilon might be forced to withdraw. Epsilon's a peculiar name, don't you think?"

It was a code name, Helen was sure. Possibilities crowded her head. "Have you mentioned Mr. Neville's September visit to him?" Hannah shook her head. "Does he recognize you from those two nights?"

"He hasn't shown any signs of recognizing me, no."

"Good. Don't mention it to him. Pretend you've never seen him before last night. And don't discuss any of this with Roger."

"Yes, madam."

Skeptical of the team of Badley, Neville, and Prescott, Fairfax didn't trust her, yet he upheld her cover because he needed her to achieve his own ends. He didn't give a damn about winning her trust, and he reveled in any discomfort he caused her. She was his message-runner on a battlefield.

Hannah glanced around, and her shoulders drooped. "At least Roger has given Sullivan back his coat. Here comes Mr. Fairfax. Looks as though he wants a word with you. I shall have Roger ready your saddle."

"Thank you, Hannah."

The younger woman curtsied and left, and with a slight bow of his head, Fairfax stepped into the place she'd vacated, his face impassive. "Let us be off."

Helen declined to take his arm, and they started for the horses. "Your friend Neville is almost as unsociable as you are."

She heard humor in his voice. "Helen, you've read my mind. How did you two get on during your discussion about Blackstock's this morning? You won a smile from him. He never smiles at me."

She exhaled exasperation. "Why should he smile at you? You're spying on him, and you've left him with the impression that you sent me to spy on him, too. I shan't get more than general conversation from him." She strode ahead for her mare.

His amusement trailed after her. "Carry on, dear sister."

Chapter Twenty-Nine

MID-AFTERNOON DECEMBER THIRTEENTH, a Legion sentry chal-
lenged Helen, Fairfax, and Campbell. After they were permitted passage,
Helen drew back on Calliope's reins a moment for her first view of the British
Legion.

The regiment sprawled through bands of wood smoke across several acres
of Woodward's plantation near the Broad River. Triangular white tents and
bells-of-arms gridded avenues of churned mud and straw. Civilians and
green-uniformed soldiers afoot navigated past boggy areas, and dragoons on
horseback rode around them. Above the throb and hum of hundreds of people
crammed together inside garrison lines, axes split timber, farriers' hammers
clanged, and stock lowed and squealed.

Helen scanned the trail behind before she nudged Calliope forward, after
Fairfax and Campbell. The rest of her party lagged an hour or more back,
slowed by two wagons on a road softened by rain. How exposed she felt without the others. But her pulse hopped with thrill to have met up with the Legion
at last.

The swollen sky resumed its drizzle. She drew her hood back over her
head and shivered. In the marketplace, legionnaires haggled with merchants
over ink, drink, and tobacco. Some sutlers, contractors, and merchants had
erected marquee tents against the raw wind. Others huddled within greatcoats
or cloaks to hawk goods spread upon blankets. Odors of old coffee, mold,
unwashed humans, charred pork, and full latrines merged with the smell of
Carolina mud.

Fairfax reined back his gelding and wheeled the horse around to acknowledge the address of an infantryman no older than eighteen years. The young
man caught up and saluted him, informing him that Tarleton could be found
at the manor house.

On the way, they passed the kitchen, where a raggedy woman plunged a
pease-crusted spoon into a cauldron and gave the porridge a stir, and a young

girl fed kindling into the hissing, smoky fire. All the camp women — busy cooking, cleaning, mending — bore a homogeneous bone-weary but resolute expression that furrowed brows and sunk cheekbones, not unlike the battle-blunted look of the husbands, brothers, and sons they'd chosen to accompany. Although several boys with drizzle- and dirt-streaked faces chased a large, wooden hoop parallel to them, that same exhaustion haunted the eyes of the older boys.

Helen, Fairfax, and Campbell dismounted before the brick manor, and Negroes led their horses away. A Legion batman opened the front door in invitation. First into the foyer, Helen glimpsed a silk-gowned, bosomy brunette on the shadowed stair to the manor's second floor. Before she continued her ascent, the woman's sultry gaze lingered on Fairfax.

The batman gestured Helen into the parlor, draped her cloak over the back of a chair, promised hot coffee, and departed. She stripped off gloves that had encased numbness all afternoon and stretched fingers toward the warmth of the parlor's fire, her back to the door.

The stomp of boots on wood floors preceded the boom of another man's voice in the foyer. "At ease. God's foot, I'd about given you up for dead." The word "about" was rendered "a-boat" by a rough Lancashire accent.

Her ears perked. Chilled fingers forgotten, she turned to permit the fire's warmth upon the royal blue wool of her gown's backside. Profiled in the foyer with Fairfax and Campbell was a Legion officer, a red sash about his waist, his uniform's gold lace and buttons glimmery by candlelight and firelight. Fairfax and Campbell, both of medium height, were taller than he by several inches.

Campbell inclined his head. "Sir! The Santee Road grows longer each time I travel it."

Helen started. Good heavens. That short fellow was Banastre Tarleton. Short on the ground only. He probably appeared a giant in the saddle of his charger, drawn saber trapping the sun's gleam, his helmet's black swan feathers bolstering the illusion of height.

"I've noticed the same about the Santee," said Tarleton. "Where are the lads? You didn't lose them to that devil, Marion?"

"They're an hour behind with the wagons, sir. Mr. Neville has iron from Camden. Speaking of Marion —" Campbell's chest swelled. "— we met the old man on the Santee Road about a week and a half ago. Seventeen of his Whig scum backtracked to finish us off. We left them for the buzzards."

Tarleton didn't smile. "Excellent work." From where Helen stood, the gleam in his dark eye and the hook of his nose gave him the appearance of a hawk on a harsh winter day.

Fairfax stood behind Campbell, quiet, in gloom. Allowing Campbell all the attention? Hardly. Fairfax waited his turn to stroke the master: the lap dog with greater rank and discipline. Unnerved, she inched to the fire.

"Thank you, sir," said Campbell. "We marked *your* fine handiwork at Richardson's plantation."

A muscle twitched Tarleton's cheek. Ooh, sore point. He was still rankled over Marion's escape.

"We heard about Blackstock's, sir." Campbell chuckled. "Sumter sure won't be leading any more charges, will he?"

The cheek muscle rippled again. Tarleton wanted that thorn in his side *dead*, for Thomas Sumter the paralytic was still a rallying point for rebels. "Extra rum for you and the lads, Campbell. Send word when they arrive in camp. Dismissed."

Campbell popped a salute, pivoted, and swaggered out the door. He'd sleep well tonight.

"Blackstock's." Tarleton's accent wrung the name into "Blackstoke's." "Ah, Mr. Fairfax. Silent, stealthy Mr. Fairfax. Have you brought me a rebel spy?"

Rebel spy? Helen squinted. To whom did Tarleton refer?

"No, sir." As smooth as Italian red wine, Fairfax's voice.

Tarleton cocked a fist on his hip. "You chased him too hard. He's now hiding beneath Dan Morgan's petticoat. Back off. Woo him out. You'll find a clever way to do it. Let him feel safe enough to emerge, find another press, print his next broadside."

Helen gulped, shocked. The printer protected by the rebel army was David's father, Will.

A raptor smile snagged Tarleton's mouth. "That first edition was a masterpiece, a boon to me. 'Patriots' need a buffoon like Buford every now and then to remind them of their military ineptitude."

"Sir."

Again, Helen shivered. By appealing to the colonel's vanity, Fairfax had sold Tarleton on his personal mission to rout out the St. James family. Tarleton now chased Will St. James.

By then, every publisher in America had seen St. James's first broadside, a crude depiction of a British soldier bayoneting a surrendered militiaman. Its caption, "Tarleton's Quarter," hearkened back to Tarleton's thorough victory over a befuddled Continental Colonel Buford in May, near the Waxhaws, in South Carolina. David's father had intended his production to hang Tarleton's reputation and horrify Loyalists into conversion to the rebel cause.

Instead, the broadside, coupled with the colonel's spectacular string of military victories, had created a Banastre Tarleton who was ruthless, indestructible, and omnipotent. Heady brew for a twenty-six-year-old merchant's son who had only five years earlier purchased his cornet's commission, lowest officer rank in the cavalry. Well Fairfax knew that. He simpered. "And what news from home, sir?"

"Bah." The fist came off the hip, and the hand swept the air in a dismissive motion. "I'm a hero in Liverpool, yet I didn't win support for my candidacy. Explain that, if you will."

Helen's eyebrow lifted. So the meteoric rise had its limitations. Tarleton's celebrity in America hadn't catapulted him into a Parliamentary seat in the recent election.

"Timing, sir. But you don't lack for perseverance."

"The pot calling the kettle black, eh? Fortunately, my brother redeemed the news by sending me a keg of wine for Yule."

"Pardon the interruption." The batman bustled past them into the parlor and set a tray with coffee service on a table. "Coffee for the lady to take the chill off. Gentlemen?"

"Lady? Mr. Fairfax, you've been remiss! Introduce us." Without waiting, Tarleton sauntered into the parlor. The lighting transformed his dark, queued hair to auburn. Full on, he embodied all the sensuous charm of a stocky cupid from a Renaissance painting. Gone was the cold-eyed raptor. A playful boy lifted Helen's fingers to his lips, smile calculated to melt the heart of the most proficient, cynical courtesan. "Madam, I'm at your service."

His switch from chill to charm threw her guard up. Still, it was heady brew for a twenty-nine-year-old widow who had only the previous month been threatened by a Committee of Safety. Well Fairfax knew that, too. His smile became predatory. "Helen, I present Colonel Banastre Tarleton. Colonel, my sister, the Widow Chiswell."

"Your *sister*. Ah." Tarleton released Helen's hand with deference. "To what do I owe the pleasure of your visitation, madam?"

"I thought to share the company of my brother. We've missed each other. Surely you understand. You've a sister, do you not?"

A platonic wistfulness sobered some of his charm. "Indeed." Tarleton held out a chair for her. "Permit me to join you for coffee. Mr. Fairfax?"

"Sir, I should be grateful to have my sister wait here, sheltered, while Campbell and I make certain of the wagons' arrival."

Tarleton nodded. "You are a paragon of duty." The batman positioned a chair for him across the table from Helen, and the colonel sat. "But then you and your lovely sister must join me for supper tonight."

"We shall be honored, sir." Victory stamped Fairfax's lips. He'd been invited to dine with the commander.

Tarleton, divine warrior with a beloved sister, studied the interaction between Helen and Fairfax and waited to be convinced, so Helen lifted her arms. "Dunstan, be careful out there on the road."

Fairfax caught her hands in his and bent over for a kiss on the cheek. In a previous lifetime, perhaps they'd both been actors upon the stage. From Tarleton's sentimental expression, their display of filial affection satisfied him.

How enchanted Londoners would be to learn that the Lion of the Waxhaws had a soft spot. Confidence soared through Helen's soul, the first time in many weeks she'd felt on firm, familiar ground. The batman saw Fairfax out, poured coffee, added another log to the fire, and withdrew. She beamed across the table at Tarleton. "So, Colonel, tell me about your sister."

Chapter Thirty

DRIZZLE PATTERED HELEN'S tent. Her daily journal entry completed, she corked the inkbottle. Camp had quieted after the eight o'clock tattoo on fife and drum. A watchman plodded past on his rounds, boot steps soggy in the grass.

With supper done and the evening's dosage of brash Legion officers and a few chatty officers' wives behind her, insignificant details from the day piqued her interest. The woman who stirred pease soup, the girl with kindling, the washerwomen and seamstresses — who were they? And the sultry-eyed brunette she'd spied on the stairs at the manor — stairs she later learned led to rooms off-limits to all but Tarleton and his retainers. Obviously females associated with the British Legion served His Majesty in various capacities, as they did in regular units.

Her contract hadn't specified a report on civilians. If she fulfilled her assignment literally, those people were invisible, unimportant. Yet she knew they weren't nobodies. Civilians were under Tarleton's command, and her overall report wouldn't be comprehensive without a report of them. On the morrow, she'd ask Jonathan or one of the Pearsons to accompany her for a look at the lower camp, weather permitting.

The candle sputtered and extinguished. She removed her bed gown and burrowed beneath blankets. The rain droned on. In the distance, a dog's bark sounded mournful, miserable.

Fortunately, the Legion wasn't on the move, so if Badley's bank draft arrived in Camden, a postal rider could find them. Again, she wondered if the publisher would renege on funding for the rest of the assignment, but she refused to worry about money yet. She had concerns more immediate.

From the puzzled absorption with which he'd regarded her, Tarleton didn't know what to make of her. Over a supper of beefsteak, rice, collards, pears, cheese, and a good deal of wine, she'd debated with his officers the merits of Vivaldi's concertos, Titian's paintings, and Henry Fielding's literature. She'd discussed Sir Isaac Newton's laws of physics with enthusiasm. Her suggested comparison and contrast of Pascal, Descartes, and Voltaire wasn't greeted with such sanguinity. In over his head, Tarleton had had the prudence to keep his mouth shut through much of the discussion. She suspected he'd have been more loquacious over the topics of horses and rowing.

But Tarleton said enough for her to arrive at an unsettling realization. On the Santee Road, the dragoons had omitted an attribute when they spoke of their leader: one characteristic she suspected must accompany his traits of valor, courage, bravery, and justice.

Vanity.

From what she'd seen of Tarleton's vanity that afternoon and evening, it was a hungry, open maw, sometimes stymied, often titillated, never fully sated.

Wine, women, and gambling may have failed to furnish him with an Achilles Heel, but Tarleton wouldn't be so fortunate with vanity and his mercurial mood swings. Arrogance and impulsiveness laid fine groundwork for manipulation. Helen envisioned Fairfax stepping over Tarleton to secure a post in Parliament. Not quite the hero's journey which Londoners expected.

***

She longed to wring the neck of the rooster that awakened her four hours later. Other cocks soon joined the conversation, and the supplications of a multitude of cows in desperate need of human intervention filled predawn. Where was Private Parker, the Devonshire dairy farm lad, when the Army needed him?

Milk pails clunked. Cows grew less frantic. Helen plugged her ears and rolled deeper into the blankets. But at five-thirty, a drummer rapped reveille out into the mushy South Carolina darkness. Exasperated, she sat up, donned both bedgown and shawl to stave off cold, and groped about for tinderbox and candle. In the Land of the Legion, the best time to write in her journal wasn't bedtime. It was predawn.

She smelled tobacco and wood smoke. Soldiers on their way to a drill sloshed past her tent, the clank of cartridge boxes and muskets dulled by damp. From the Pearsons' tent, Roger broke into a merry whistle, curtailed when Hannah whacked him with some dull, soft object and snapped, "Get up, then, and fetch our coffee."

Two hours later, the cloud phalanx repulsed the sun's valiant charge. Resigned to another day of drizzle, Helen downed three cups of Roger's cheer with her porridge, fleshed out her journal with details of a typical morning in military camp, and mapped out a budget to stretch what money she had left and still allow her to return to Wilmington. With frugal spending, she'd have to head home before Yule. Unacceptable. She must remain on assignment longer.

Accompanied by Hannah, she searched out the quartermaster's assistant, Newman, who handled daily posts. They just missed meeting him at morning parade. Since Roger enjoyed mornings so much, Helen decided that he would attend parade daily, where posts were usually distributed.

She took an embroidery project into the parlor of the house. The journalist in her bemoaned the convention that she was expected to sit with three officers' wives and their maids while Tarleton's gorgeous, brunette mistress read in the company of another courtesan on the other side of the room. How could she wrangle an interview with the woman?

Natter among the wives gravitated to childrearing concerns. Helen absorbed herself in embroidery and silently counted her blessings that she'd miscarried. Having to feed and clothe a child would have overwhelmed her finances.

The wives had no earthly idea of how to prevent pregnancy. Each of them had borne at least four children. They'd never heard of drinking tansy and pennyroyal tonics, or even of the simpler but messier solution of drowning their husbands' seed in honey. She peeked at them, imagined them riding the horn of the moon in the grass at the spring equinox, and covered a snort of humor with a cough.

"Bye the bye, your brother is leading practice this morning, Mrs. Chiswell."

Helen blinked at the bland face of the wife who'd spoken. "I beg your pardon?"

"At nine o'clock. You've time to observe it, if you hurry."

"What is this 'practice?'"

"On horseback, dragoons gallop through lines created by infantrymen lying upon the ground."

"Quite suspenseful to watch," said another wife.

The concept they described required great trust from the infantrymen and skill from the dragoons. Fascinated, Helen resolved to see it demonstrated first-hand. Perhaps Tarleton would provide an impressive, equestrian display to inspire his men. "I believe I shall go. Will any of you ladies accompany me and show me the way?"

All three declined, their excuse the weather. One gave vague directions for locating the north field. Helen signaled Hannah and packed up her embroidery. Outside on the porch, they adjusted cloaks and hoods in preparation for the walk.

The front door opened, and out swayed Tarleton's mistress in a rustle of burgundy-colored silk. Garnets set off with tiny pearls sparkled at her earlobes and throat, and when she draped on her fine, wool cloak, Helen sniffed an expensive floral perfume. "Shall I guide you ladies to the north field?" A receptive smile curved the woman's full lips and extended into her dark, long-lashed eyes.

"We would be grateful of it, madam."

"My name is Margaret." With grace, the courtesan stepped off the porch around a mud puddle and headed north.

Helen caught up with her and walked at her side, Hannah a discreet distance behind. "I'm pleased to meet you, Margaret. My name is Helen." Margaret cocked an eyebrow at her, surprised to hear her bypass convention, and Helen grinned. "Do we not each serve our king in different ways?" Playfulness, not cynicism, flavored Margaret's chuckle, and Helen felt that familiar thrill when an interview subject warmed to her. "The north field must be totally soaked, and I don't see any break in the clouds. Surely this practice won't last long."

"Oh, they'll carry on for hours. Rain doesn't stop them."

Determination among the corps: an excellent morsel for readers.

The three women passed within a strand of oak and dogwood. From leaf-denuded branches, raindrops pelted foliage underfoot and tapped the hoods of their cloaks. "Will the colonel be there?"

"Mmm, I doubt it. He's ever so busy."

Subtle, Margaret's inflection upon the word "busy," but it communicated that she belonged to the sisterhood of women who awaited personal attention from men too engrossed in duty to deliver it. If she didn't expect her lover to show at the practice, why did she slog through a soaked meadow and brave cold and rain?

"I hear you've come from Wilmington. Why trade civilization for an army encampment in the backcountry?"

So now Margaret interviewed Helen. "I haven't seen my brother since late spring. And you wouldn't believe how boring Wilmington's become since the rebels ran out Governor Martin."

"Don't expect much excitement here. Perhaps a dance for Yule, if you stay that long. But you'll never witness a battle. First sign of trouble, Colonel Tarleton sends the ladies home. They're too much of a liability."

To obtain a comprehensive story on the Legion, Helen must somehow get around Tarleton's rule and at least glimpse the regiment mobilized for battle. But how was she to do that?

Her attention lingered on the brunette a moment longer. By daylight, Margaret appeared to be in her early twenties, except for the judiciousness and complexity in her eyes. Helen found it hard to believe that Tarleton sent a mistress so sophisticated and beautiful — one he'd showered with lavish gifts — very far from him. "Where do *you* go when the Legion is on the move?"

"With the camp women in the baggage."

With the nobodies who didn't count.

They emerged from the trees, and the courtesan smiled. "Ah. Here we are, and what luck. You're in time to see your brother demonstrate a charge. Likely no one will be able to equal his skill."

Chapter Thirty-One

NEGRO GROOMS STEADIED six saddled horses. Fairfax pranced his gelding before assembled dragoons and spat out instructions for the exercise. Helen gaped in disbelief past him to a human obstacle course of supine foot soldiers stretched out in parallel lines on a cold, wet field.

Fairfax spotted the trio of women and reined his horse back. Helen waved greetings. He scowled at them. "Tilden, keep those women out of the way!" A dragoon marched back for them.

"Good morning to you, too, lout," Helen muttered, irked at Fairfax's rudeness. Margaret's eyebrows shot up with surprise. Helen winced internally. She'd forgotten her role as Fairfax's sister. "Ah, well, he's never forgiven his older sister for ordering him around while he grew up." Whether that mended her mistake and convinced Margaret, she couldn't tell. She punctuated the end of her comment with a toss of her head.

Herded onto a rise by Tilden, they watched Fairfax, one hand on the rein, an upraised three-foot-long saber in the other fist, spur his mount into a gallop toward the westernmost line of men. The woods resounded with the thunder of the gelding as it hurtled up and down rows. The horsehair crest of Fairfax's helmet bristled, and his uniform blurred scarlet. In less than a minute, he emerged from the course without grazing an infantryman. Approval exploded from the soldiers. A loud huzzah erupted from Tilden, standing nearby.

"God," whispered Hannah, her exhaled breath as pale as her face. Helen eased out her own breath, watched it hang in the air before her. Surely Hannah had recalled, as she had, the night Francis Marion's Whigs had attacked them, a night she'd rather forget.

Fairfax's bellow penetrated the men's praise. "Each of you work the course twice!" He slid the saber into the scabbard, its leather belt diagonal across his chest, and guided the gelding toward the grooms. "Davison!"

"Sir!" One of the dragoons from their party on the Santee Road sprinted forward, caught the reins of a waiting horse, and vaulted into the saddle.

Helen glanced to Margaret, who'd remained silent during the demonstration. Dreaminess filmed the courtesan's eyes, and her lips were parted and moist, as if she'd just emerged from *le petit mort*. Baffled, Helen tracked the object of her gaze, and disbelief twisted her stomach. Tarleton's mistress was infatuated with Fairfax. Small wonder the brunette braved the weather.

On the field, the same grace with which Davison slew Marion's escaping Whig allowed him success on the course. Men chanted his achievement, and he trotted his horse back to the grooms, beaming. At Fairfax's order, another cavalryman bounded for a horse, and it began all over again.

By the time a dozen dragoons had completed the course, Helen's shock had transformed to awe and respect. Each infantryman knew he wouldn't be trampled. The exercise transformed centuries of mistrust between foot soldiers and horsemen and, at least beneath Tarleton's command, bound the two in a mutual pact of reliance and conviction.

Readers in London would devour such a detail. Whose brainchild had the seminal idea for the practice been? Intuition told Helen that Tarleton hadn't created the exercise, but she suspected he'd be credited for it. In yet another way, Fairfax had made himself indispensable to the Legion's commander.

The lieutenant, who had dismounted earlier, strode toward them. His carriage exuded command and victory, and cold, archangelic radiance suffused his expression: the elemental in service to the divine warrior. He eyed Tilden and jerked his head toward the men and horses. "Queue up."

"Sir." The dragoon departed.

Helen clasped her hands and hoped she looked as gushy as she sounded. "Dunstan, that was brilliant!"

"Thank you. Return to camp."

Despite all the moisture, the air crackled with confrontation. Helen compressed her lips and met his stare head-on. "But we're safe out here. It isn't as though we've cannonballs whizzing the air and men dying around us."

Margaret brushed Helen's forearm with her fingertips and murmured, "Let us return."

"Dear sister, I cannot be distracted worrying about your health in such unwholesome weather." Fairfax slithered his stare to Margaret before he returned it to Helen. "How splendid of you to have already made a friend at camp. Do study her example of obedience."

Sickened by a jangle of humiliation in her chest, Helen swallowed a retort and spun around to leave. But Fairfax yanked her back to him and kissed her cheek, his body pulsating with heat and triumph. "*Obedience*," he whispered before he released her.

Hannah and Margaret caught up with her and didn't speak during the walk back — she presumed to allow her time to digest the unpalatable lump of Army protocol rammed down her throat. When they gained the porch of the house, drizzle increased to a steady downpour. Margaret offered a soggy curtsy before she headed upstairs to change. Helen and Hannah found seats near the fireplace, where company in the parlor hadn't changed in their absence.

Helen brooded over the glow of coals while her stockinged feet steamed dry. If Fairfax had Colonel Tarleton trussed up in his tote sack, it stood to reason that he had Tarleton's mistress in there, too. For then not only could he maneuver her to inject a good word for him with Tarleton every now and then, but he could count on her to help him knead Helen Chiswell into submission.

Margaret's price? She wasn't the sort of woman who'd be satisfied with simple rewards, but surely she was shrewd enough to appreciate the advantages of rank and not swap a colonel for a lieutenant. Besides, from the ground he'd gained with Tarleton, Fairfax wouldn't do anything to incur disfavor. No, "silent, stealthy Mr. Fairfax" must be gracing Margaret with manna that Tarleton and his uncomplicated gifts of silk, jewelry, and perfume was too "busy" to provide. Ill-tempered, Helen dallied over dark musings of the form Margaret's manna might take before she caught herself, nonplused.

Where had she come by such base nosiness of a sudden?

A Legionnaire stumped in through the front entrance and shook rain off his greatcoat like water from a bear's fur. To Helen's surprise, the wives, their maids, and the other courtesan rushed the man in a cooing mass of femininity. He protracted the moment, his leer lopsided. "Easy now, ladies, I'm a might damp, and I wouldn't want to drip on your gowns. The roads out there are turning to rivers. No afternoon dispatch. Sorry to disappoint, but you shall just have to wait for parade."

The ladies retreated, dejected. Helen shoved her shoes back on and, while what was obviously the quartermaster's assistant, Newman, conveyed a message to Tarleton's adjutant, she hastened over to the postal carrier. When he'd finished speaking with the adjutant, she introduced herself to him. "And I'm expecting a business letter out of Wilmington. I hoped it would be waiting for me in Camden five days ago, but it wasn't, so I anticipate it will be forwarded to camp."

"Yes, madam. Mail is chaotic out here. Some days we get two posts. Other times, with the Legion on the move, we miss several days. I'm sure Mr. Fairfax will let you know."

Helen frowned at him. "My brother? Why not you?"

"All your party's mail goes through Mr. Fairfax first."

Sluggish to grasp the implications, Helen deepened her frown but kept her voice quiet to not attract undue attention. "Why should my mail and that of my servants go through him first?"

"Policy, madam. Except under special circumstances, officers and men receive posts for themselves and their parties each day at morning parade, around seven in the north field."

At last it hit Helen. As gatekeeper for their mail, Fairfax could cut all four of them off from the outside. Her bank draft from Badley, letters from Enid or attorney Chapman, bank drafts and letters for Jonathan, letters to the Pearsons such as business updates from Roger's apprentice back in Wilmington. No one in the party could post a letter before it met Fairfax's approval. And he could read their incoming and outgoing posts. Her throat clenched, but she steadied herself. "Thank you, Mr. Newman."

Hannah looked up from mending Roger's stockings as Helen resumed her seat before the fire. "Everything under control, madam?"

"Yes." No need to worry Hannah, for everything was under control: Fairfax's control. Control was what the argument in the north field had been about. Those who belonged to the Army — whether they were soldiers or civilians — were subordinate to the Army and either obeyed commands or incurred punishment. The Army was no place for individual voices.

As Helen saw it, since she'd led herself and three other people into a treacherous pit, she was responsible for guiding them out of it. And that meant choosing her battles. She reached for her embroidery. If Fairfax demanded control, well, then, she'd give it to him.

Chapter Thirty-Two

"YOUR SISTER TO see you, sir." At Fairfax's command, the infantryman pulled back the marquee tent flap and motioned Helen and Hannah inside, out of the late afternoon mist.

From behind a foldable table, Fairfax rose and bowed. He looked warm, clean, and dry in his spare uniform, not as though he'd roughed it most of the day with legionnaires in half-frozen mud. "Helen. To what do I owe the honor of this visit?"

An unfinished letter lay on the table. "You're busy. I shall return."

His expression mobilized with curiosity, he covered the distance to her, caught her gloved hand, and led her to a ladder-backed chair. Perhaps he'd expected her to sulk and avoid him after the incident on the north field. "Have you dined yet tonight?"

"No, I —"

"Kennelly." Fairfax dropped her hand and snatched a purse off the table. "Accompany Mrs. Pearson to market and assist her purchase of supper for my sister's party."

Lantern light sparkled on the arc of a coin through the air. Private Kennelly caught it and bowed. "Sir." He stepped to the tent's entrance and awaited Hannah.

Misgiving tweaked Helen. She hadn't planned to be alone with Fairfax. Nevertheless, she nodded approval, and Hannah and Kennelly exited.

Fairfax removed her cloak, hung it in an unlit corner of the tent near his damp coat, and grabbed a folded blanket off his cot. "Sit. Dry your hands." He tossed her a clean handkerchief of fine linen. "Wrap this blanket around you. And take off those shoes. They look soaked." She complied and settled her embroidery basket and gloves beneath the chair. He brought a brazier close and swathed her feet in another blanket.

She allowed herself to sink into the warmth of woolen blankets that smelled of him while he rummaged around in a trunk near his cot. Then he approached and swapped the linen handkerchief for a ceramic cup. "Drink this. You do no one good by freezing to death." Stuffing the handkerchief in his coat pocket, he returned to the table.

The most exquisite brandy she'd ever tasted swirled down her throat and coursed her veins, restored sensation to stiff fingers and toes. For the next quarter hour, she listened to the scratch of pen on paper, coals sighing in the brazier, a scatter of raindrops against the tent, murmurs and laughter from without. Daylight waned, and the interior, lit by only two lanterns, dimmed further. The peculiar utilitarian furnishing of the tent disquieted her, prevented total relaxation. Curiosity over manna slunk back like a shadow from the lengthening day. She set the empty cup down and shut her eyes.

At length, she heard a shuffle across the table: paper folded, a wax seal impressed. When she opened her eyes, she found him motionless in his chair, one elbow propped on the desk, waiting, his stare drilling through her brain.

"I — uh — I came to speak with you about this morning."

Indifferent, he hooked his chair and planted it before her. After adjusting the blanket to cover her neck, he sat.

She fidgeted. "I apologize for arguing with you. Civilians don't understand until they experience it the order that the Army must keep."

He leaned forward, elbows on knees. "By now, Kennelly and Mrs. Pearson will have purchased supper for your party."

"Thank you." She squirmed in the chair. "We — um — need access to our posts."

He smiled and straightened. "Ah, yes."

"Jonathan and the Pearsons have ongoing business and financial concerns that require their interaction." She slid her feet into her shoes. "And I expect bank drafts from Badley, funds for me to continue the assignment. Possibly letters from my attorney."

"Soon as I receive those posts, I shall pass them along to you."

Consternation trickled through her. "You're busy. If you're out for several days on patrol, and an important letter arrives from Roger's apprentice or Jonathan's attorney — oh, why does our mail need to pass through you at all?"

"It's a policy established by the Legion."

"Newman told me there could be exceptions to that policy."

"Darling, you're toying with me again."

When would he cease questioning her loyalty? She exhaled and rolled her gaze away from him. "I understand how important it is for you to capture Will St. James." She gave him a pointed look. "But I don't know where he is." Skepticism curled Fairfax's upper lip. Despair excavated her soul. "You won't be able to find him through me, either. My relationship with his son is over."

"I'm sure you haven't seen the last of him."

She regarded him with disbelief at his implication. "David's no halfwit. He won't approach me while I'm traveling with the Legion."

"You underestimate your own charm. Apparently, so did Silas Chiswell."

She coughed with scorn. "A marriage of convenience. My husband never loved me."

"Well, he certainly couldn't buy love." Fairfax's smile twisted. "Not even when the comely shape of it presented itself so vulnerably during procurement."

The inside of the tent reeled a few times, and Helen's breathing grew ragged before she settled it back down. One second, she debated denial; the next she acknowledged futility. Her voice emerged even. "If you expose my background, your story about Tarleton will never be completed."

"Expose your background? Why should I do that?" He rose and held out a hand to help her up. While sliding the blanket from around her shoulders, he trailed fingers down the length of her arm. "You're a talented writer and artist. And Vivaldi, Isaac Newton, and French philosophers — Helen, you're a delectable piece of work. Granted, your professor helped, but the innate capacity for transformation was yours.

"My stepfather and the vicar debated the sense of my mother's education project. Were they still alive, they'd never recognize you. You transcended expectations she had for those village brats. A most sublime revenge." He caught her hand in his and brushed soft lips over her fingers.

Revenge? The peerage had to mean more to him than that. Surely his plug for Parliament meant he craved acknowledgement and acceptance from the peers. "I presume, then, that it was Treadaway who filled in the missing piece of my identity for you."

"Oh, Treadaway. Bah." He towed her to where their garments hung. Rather than wrap her cloak around her, he took her in his arms. Warm from blankets and brandy, her body heated further wherever he pressed against her. "Treadaway's recall improves dramatically when he's drunk. When he sobers, he jumbles it and misplaces pieces."

It didn't sound as though Treadaway had been of much assistance. "Then you remembered me from Lady Ratchingham's classes."

He stroked her cheek. "Beltane 1767." When she shook her head, he added, "Inappropriate for the wife of an influential Anglican merchant, yes, so you smuggled the gods to America. Why else paint watercolors of the sacred places?"

Fire and ice raced Helen's spine together. She'd done more than smuggle the gods to America. She'd filled her house with them, painting after painting, defying Silas Chiswell. She gawped up at Fairfax and his irreverent, tainted amusement.

Warm and insistent, his lips brushed the side of her mouth. She stiffened, and he whispered, "Remember for a moment. Full moonlight. Drums on the plain. The roaring bonfire."

Then he plunged straight into a wet kiss that tasted of chocolate and coffee, exploring her mouth with the meticulousness of a surveyor who has mapped many frontiers. Bonfire. Bone fire. The scent of salt punched a lightning-shock circuit of her nerves. She resisted a grand total of two seconds before her hips rotated to meet masculine hardness. Through the material of her bodice, heat from his hand penetrated, exacted response from her nipple. Her fingers groped the side of his breeches, squeezed a muscular buttock, and clutched at it.

"Dine with me tonight," he murmured from the mounded upper crescents of her breasts, where her lace tucker opened. He pinned her wrists together and snaked linen around them while his lips traced the line of her jaw. "Divine sister, sibyl of the gods, vision-priestess."

Drums pounded Helen's womb and deafened her ears.

He lifted her hands eye-level, where she stared, her breathing uneven, at her own wrists bound with the handkerchief. "Obedience, darling, yes." His countenance glowed with supernatural light. "Sing for me."

Fascination and fear coiled within her at the sight of her wrists. Bound wrists.

Over his shoulder, the interior of the tent came into focus, its peculiar utilitarian nature registering upon her again: the absence of personality, savage serviceability enforced everywhere, as if Fairfax had filled the marquee with the expected forms of things but bestowed upon them no life. Likewise, the green of his eyes reflected a glacial surface, guarantee of raw futtering without depth. Unnerved, she pushed from his embrace and thrust the handkerchief at him.

Conviction carved his smile. He returned the handkerchief to his pocket. "So many questions in that inquisitive mind of yours. You must learn to trust me."

Ambiguity and more unrest washed over her. Think — no, she couldn't sort it out *there*. She had to get away. She fumbled her tucker closed, hands trembling, and clenched her petticoat. "I've kept three people waiting on supper."

He laughed, impudent again, and spread her cloak open for her. "You know where to find me."

***

The rain held off, and the four sat on campstools outside their tents, supper lit by two lanterns. Hannah plugged the hole in conversation with a spirited account of the dragoons' morning practice.

Divine sister, sibyl of the gods, vision-priestess. Glad for the relative lack of light, Helen stayed quiet. She hated dodging Jonathan's attempts to draw her from reticence.

Her skin felt too tight, her lips too full, her cheeks flushed. Bound wrists. Odd. Eros had visited her dream about Jonathan with an image of bound wrists, and she'd also dreamed of bound wrists on the Santee Road.

Form without content. Sex without unity. At least now, she had an idea of the shape that Margaret's manna took.

Chapter Thirty-Three

NATTER ABOUT RAINFALL buzzed the parlor. Just outside the wives' circle, Helen toed her semi-dry shoes closer to the fire, smoothed a woman's pocket in her lap, and assessed the embroidered, completed cardinal. Her stitches appeared even.

Rain had permitted her scant occupation except writing or embroidering since her arrival. She'd seen little of camp beyond her tent and the manor. At least enough of a lull occurred in the rain most mornings for her to seek the dawn place.

That day, Sunday, she didn't expect mail except emergency posts. But each day she'd sent Roger to query Fairfax, the locksmith had come away empty-handed. Did Fairfax withhold a whole pile of letters from them, contingent upon her gracing his marquee with another intimate visit? Not an opportunity for which she longed. The gods thrust all manner of messengers upon her. Fairfax was by far the most complex and ambiguous.

She'd embroider daisies on a kerchief next.

A familiar, booted tread descended the stairs into wifely griping about the quagmire camp had become. "So this is how the winter of our discontent sounds." A statesman's smile charming his boyish face, Tarleton swaggered between the ladies' chairs. "Shall I move camp to higher ground, just to see each of you smile again? How does upriver suit?"

To hear him talk, feminine approval over the camp location was more important than protecting the garrison at Ninety Six. Helen muffled her laughter at the cloud of silk and satin that engulfed the commander of the Legion. If ladies in Liverpool could vote, Tarleton would have clinched his seat in Parliament the first go-round.

She doused her grin and examined the embroidery. The colonel sweet-talked all the wives and their maids, but, as Hannah had observed the previous day, he singled Helen out for extra flattery every chance he got. Such favoritism could wreak havoc on a journalist's objectivity. Not to be encouraged.

Spurs jingled with his strut over to her chair. "Mrs. Chiswell."

"Sir." She flashed a smile at him and looked at the cardinal, her ears grown hot. If the smolder of admiration in his eyes were quantified in English pounds, she'd be a wealthy woman.

He bowed. "A stunning piece of embroidery. May I see it?"

She handed it to him. His fingers stroked hers in passage. Then he crouched and brought his gaze level with hers, a wistful expression on his face. "Made for a friend, I suppose."

On the verge of admission that she'd just passed the time indoors with it, she caught herself, business sense tingling. "Possibly." She affected disinterest.

"Will you sell it to me?" he whispered, his expression ardent.

She and the wives weren't the only ladies cross over being confined indoors. Margaret must have given him an earful about pitching camp in a massive mud puddle. Just how badly was he smarting? Helen could certainly use some money. She protracted a sigh. "Oh, I don't know if I could part with it. I've grown fond of this particular piece. It did turn out well, didn't it?"

"Very well. Stunning. Magnificent. Four shillings."

He *was* desperate. "Ten."

"Half a pound —? Seven. Seven shillings."

"Sold." She could have wrangled out more, but she had no desire to encourage his leap from admiration to adoration. If he started courting her, her credibility for the assignment would slide right into the vault — foretold by the raised eyebrows she received from the wives while Tarleton counted out payment for the pocket.

Besides, she realized as he tromped up the stairs, he'd done her a favor, made her aware of a market for her embroidery. Sutlers didn't carry much merchandise to delight ladies.

Not long after he jingled back downstairs, Margaret glided into the parlor with a smile of satisfaction. She sat across from Helen and read a book plucked from the pocket displayed on her hip: a pocket embroidered with a stunning cardinal. Ah, domestic peace.

So engrossed was Helen on the daisies a few minutes later that she squeaked out surprise when Fairfax peered over her shoulder at the embroidery. "Oh, how crass of me to startle you. I presumed you'd heard my arrival."

A chill rocketed across that side of her body. For the sake of appearance, she held her tongue, tempered the snappishness common on the first day of her menses. To her dismay, he knelt on one knee before her. Her skin felt too tight again.

"I've missed you, darling," he whispered.

The embroidery needle slipped, jabbed her thumb. She grunted. Oh, gods, he *did* expect another visit to his marquee.

"And I've something for you." He reached inside his coat.

Her first thought was of the handkerchief that he'd twisted around her wrists. Then she wondered whether he'd purchased a gift for her. She glanced at Margaret. The courtesan studied their interaction.

"These arrived late yesterday." He handed over two letters.

One for Jonathan, and the other for Roger. The seal had been broken on both. Jonathan, in particular, wouldn't be pleased that Fairfax had helped himself to his business correspondence — but wait! Panic thrashed her, and she shuffled the letters. Only two.

"Was there nothing for me?" She let inflexibility trickle into her stare. "I expect a bank draft from Badley."

"It hasn't arrived." A softening in his lips didn't reach his eyes. He kept his voice to a whisper. "Do you need a loan?"

Divine sister, sibyl of the gods, vision-priestess.

Thank goodness for Tarleton's seven shillings. "No."

"You believe I'm withholding the draft and lying to you. I said it on the Santee Road, but it bears repeating. Badley wants you dead. He's broken your contract and stranded you out here."

"Thank you for delivering the letters. I've embroidery to finish. You're blocking my light."

He leaned over to kiss her cheek. "The middle of December, and you taste of April strawberries."

A flush stampeded up her neck. Fairfax swaggered out. Across the parlor, Margaret feigned interest in her book, but Helen knew she'd observed the whole exchange.

***

Jonathan handed Helen's desk out of her tent. She set it atop a folded blanket. A respite in the rain permitted everyone to prepare for the morrow's move. Civilians and soldiers were about on errands in the twilight. While Hannah and Roger prepared supper in the camp kitchen, Helen consulted Jonathan.

He emerged from her tent again and brushed hands on his breeches. "All straightened out in there, Lady Helen."

"Thank you. I'm concerned. Badley's draft hasn't been forwarded."

"Everyone talks about the post, my dear, but no one does anything about it. It's seldom on time in Britain. Why should you expect improvement in His Majesty's colonies?"

He had a point there. She sighed, exasperated.

Jonathan sobered. "We know who the villain is here. Stop making excuses for him. Trust your instincts."

"My instincts tell me to trust neither Badley nor Fairfax."

He stepped over beside her, his expression kind. "Your eyes look tired, Helen. How stressful this is for you. Might you rest easier if I loaned you money while you're waiting on Phineas's draft?" When she opened her mouth, he held up his hand. "A loan, not a gift. If you insist, I shall charge you interest."

"If I *insist*?" They laughed, and their gazes found that interlocked sanctuary born of enduring friendship. The clicking and twitching shimmied up Helen's skin again, and she let it happen, certain she was infatuated with Jonathan, but glad for his kindness. How little of his companionship she received. She missed him. "Thank you for your offer, and hmm, I'm not sure I shall ever insist upon interest, but yes, after the move, I shall discuss a loan with you."

"Splendid! Let me arrange everything inside your tent for the night and light a few lanterns."

"Evening, folks." On horseback, Adam Neville rode out of the gathering dusk, reined back his mount near Helen's tent, and touched his hat in greeting.

"Mr. Neville." Helen curtsied. "We've not seen you since Wednesday. How have you been keeping yourself?"

"Busy, madam." He assessed their campsite. "A soldier is never idle." He sounded weary, and night seemed to have taken up residence in his face. "Has Mr. Fairfax apprised you of the morrow's procedure?" He glanced at Jonathan.

"Not yet. He's busy. Do us the honors so we aren't left behind in this bog due to noncompliance with Army regulations."

"Have your horses saddled and wagon loaded before seven. The men will have spread straw toward the road north. Frankly, I don't know how much the straw will help us heave the wagons out, but there you have it."

Helen nodded. "Will you join us for supper?" Perhaps she could coax a story about Thomas Brown out of Neville.

"Thank you, madam, but I've too many duties to tend tonight." He touched his hat again and groped at the rein — far too clumsily, she thought, for a ranger accustomed to the saddle.

The horse danced sideways, a rear hoof clipping Helen's desk. The fatal sound of splintered wood preceded her gasp of disbelief.

Neville stared at the ground below his horse, dismounted, and met Helen as she picked up what remained of her desk. Through the bashed-in top, she saw ink squirted over papers. "My — my desk." Her voice retreated, and she gaped. The desk was kindling.

"Oh, Mrs. Chiswell, I'm so very sorry."

She dropped what was left of the desk and turned to him. "How am I to finish this assignment without a desk, paper, pen, and ink?"

Neville stood staunchly. "Why, I shall replace it for you."

"How? My husband purchased it in *England* twelve years ago. You cannot find another out here in the hinterland." She closed her eyes. The loss started to sink in. No money plus no desk equaled no feature.

"Actually, I saw one this afternoon, in the tent of a merchant. I realize it won't have the sentimental value of the desk from your husband, but I thought it rather handsome, with intricate carvings along the side. At the very least, it will permit you to finish your assignment." He grasped her upper arm. "The merchant may still be open. Please allow me to make amends for my inelegance."

A prickle of queerness crawled through Helen's loss, and she looked from the hand on her arm up into the ranger's face. From what she'd observed of Neville, it was so unlike him to *touch* another person. He was a fortress closed and siege-ready. Perhaps the incident had jolted him out of his defenses. "Very well." She squared her shoulders, and his hand slid away. "But do hurry."

"Yes, madam." He bowed.

She and Jonathan watched Neville canter south for the merchants. "What do you make of him, Jonathan? Contrite?"

"Perhaps. An odd bird, to be sure. And if ever a man didn't fit in the skin he was wearing, it's Mr. Neville."

Chapter Thirty-Four

BY THE TIME camp was pitched at Daniel's plantation the next afternoon, the overcast had broken. The site soon stank of mildewed canvas. Smoke rose from wet wood tossed on fires. Like creeper vines in a forest, lines of clean, wet stockings, underclothes, and towels popped up across camp.

Heavy traffic on the trail churned up more mud. Tempers flared. Accompanied by bodyguards and a brace of sleek foxhounds, Tarleton rode through camp and reminded hundreds of muddy men, women, and children that they were privileged, part of the elite. Grumbles and scowls subsided. Above the plunk of hammer on tent peg and the rumble of carts to and fro, laughter emerged, and music from pennywhistles and fiddles rose in the cool afternoon.

Boots and buttons shined to perfection, the colonel called upon Helen, too. He flirted, informed her of a Yule dance for officers and their ladies, and kissed her hand. Riding with him was Tobias Treadaway, who demonstrated no recognition of Helen, other than as Fairfax's sister. She took care to not draw more attention to herself while they visited her camp, but she wondered what had motivated him to ride out in inhospitable weather and attend the regiment's move. He could have sent a messenger to report on their location.

When Tarleton headed off for the next campsite, she sent Roger after the purchasing agent to query him. Roger reported that Treadaway bragged of knowing where everyone was in the Southern colonies and was proud of his ability to respond to the needs of the Legion and Lord Cornwallis.

Another yappy lap dog in camp. Just what the colonel needed.

Shawl draped round her shoulders, she sat outside and sketched the camp before she settled in to write the day's journal entry and a special letter to Badley querying him about the overdue bank draft. Every so often, she paused to stroke the splendid workmanship of the desk Neville had given her, or sniff the oil finish, or admire grain patterns in the wood. Whorls of flowers and leaves were carved into the dark mahogany along the sides. She felt like a princess every time she opened it. Of Spanish origin, certainly, and at least twice the value of the desk Silas had purchased for her. Which made her curious how such a work of art just happened to be available from a backcountry merchant at the precise moment she needed it, and how Neville had afforded it on the pay of a provincial lieutenant.

Not only had he purchased the desk for her and replaced writing implements destroyed in the accident, he'd agreed to join her for supper that night. At last, here was her opportunity to learn about Thomas Brown, paint for London readers a mini-portrait of another of the king's heroes in the American War — one not so well known, a provincial commander who hadn't received acclaim due him.

Late afternoon, Hannah returned from a foray into market to report that Roger was cooking beefsteaks for supper, but all the spirits in market were bought up. The blonde's mouth made a moue, and she nodded her head toward the lower camp. "They're going to be one happy people tonight, now that the rain's stopped." Helen sent Hannah and Jonathan out to the wagon to pull wine from their stash and reflected that drunkenness and riotousness were punishable offenses. No doubt a certain sub-readership in London would revel in profuse detail of that facet of military life.

Adam Neville arrived at seven and plowed through a full bottle of wine and massive steak like a condemned man issued his final meal. Beneath the stars, the Pearsons and Jonathan waited on Helen and him, and while the celebratory din from the lower camp increased, Neville filled Helen's ears with the glorious tales she'd anticipated. The evening whizzed by like dried leaves on a winter wind.

He left, and while the Pearsons and Jonathan tidied up, Helen strolled out into a meadow beyond their tents, where she recognized dismay. Aside from his mention of joining Brown's Rangers in time for the capture of Fort McIntosh in 1777, the lieutenant had told her nothing about himself. For three hours, he'd drunk her wine, eaten her food, and captivated her attention, and the few times she'd inquired about him, he diverted her to the accomplishments of his commander. After three hours, she didn't know enough about Neville to explain how he'd come by the desk. Quite a sinuous display of dancing from him. He was a wraith. An excellent disposition for a spy. She shivered.

"Rather chilly for a shawl." Jonathan drew up beside her. "Shall I fetch your cloak?"

She smiled in gratitude. "Yes, thank you." When he turned back toward their tents, her hand darted out and caught his upper arm. "A moment, Jonathan. Tell me what you think."

For several seconds, he didn't speak, and the noise from the lower camp became obvious. He grunted. "I think some soldiers will be flogged on the morrow for excessive drunkenness."

She nodded in rueful agreement and released him. "And what of Neville?"

"He speaks a pretty volume, but he doesn't say much."

"I shall endeavor to listen to what he omits. Fairfax thinks he's a spy, and Neville knows that Fairfax thinks he's a spy, and Neville is also convinced that I'm Fairfax's minion."

Jonathan laughed. "Gods, the games these regiments play with each other, just to scramble atop the military sand pile. Do let me run back and inspect the table and Neville's chair for concealed messages before he positions us all to be arrested by Fairfax."

She caught his arm again. "Are you serious?"

"Of course not." When she turned loose his arm, he bowed and walked away. "Spies. Good heavens." His chuckle drifted to her.

The games these regiments play. Helen returned her attention to the night sky, washed of dust and aglow with stars, and mused again. The Army bristled with internal suspicion. Regiments postured for attention from generals, commanders undercut each other's credibility at the slightest provocation, and jealousy simmered. Not that the rebels didn't behave as churlishly within their own army, but backbiting within the Crown forces had, at times, bestowed victory upon a foe when defeat should have been assured. Men did almost anything to gain an edge or divert scarce resources from someone else's regiment. And Tarleton, who could do no wrong in Cornwallis's eyes, excelled at diverting those resources and supplies on numerous occasions — most recently with horses.

Grass rustled behind her. She grinned up at the stars. "You know, Jonathan, I wager Neville wants a piece of Parliament pie, too."

"Fascinating, darling."

She recoiled and glowered at Fairfax's approach. "You've been spying on me!"

"I thought your professor would never leave. Since he won't be gone long, let us proceed to business." He drew up about five feet from her. "You managed to lure the elusive, unsocial Adam Neville into conversation for three hours. Parliament pie, indeed."

"I didn't lure him into anything. I offered supper in exchange for stories about Thomas Brown. I may write a short feature on him. He's performing a great service for His Majesty."

Fairfax waved away her words. "What did Neville confide to make you suspect he has designs on Parliament?"

She propped hands on her hips. "The occasion was social. For the record, I never agreed to spy on him or anyone else for you, so run along, manage your own dirty laundry, and leave me out of it. Preposterous to imagine Mr. Neville confiding in me anyway. Was I supposed to look for ciphers hidden beneath my chair afterwards?"

He took a step toward her, his voice velvety. "You're concealing something from me."

How exasperating. So many men who professed allegiance to the king couldn't trust each other and cooperate. Apparently, the boy who died with the highest rank and most toy soldiers still won. She dumped acid into her voice. "I shall make you a deal. You hand over Badley's bank draft that you've withheld from me, and I'll tell you everything I know about Neville."

"I doubt you'd consider that an equitable arrangement." By starlight, he walked a slow circle around her. "I've no bank draft from Badley, and you decline what I offer as substitute." The delight that unfolded on his face plunged ice through her blood and tightened her stomach. "At some point, you'll realize that you must tell me what you know. On that day, the idea of toying with me won't hold half as much appeal for you as it does right now."

More ice swept her blood at his implication. He anticipated some future event to precipitate her crawling to him to beg for help or forgiveness.

"In the mean time, darling, carry on. Your burgeoning friendship with Mr. Neville is everything I might have hoped."

"Why, it's Mr. Fairfax!" Jonathan's tone matched the blitheness of Fairfax's, and he joined them, Helen's cloak draping his forearm. "Just leaving, are you?"

With a flash of teeth, Fairfax squared off with him. "I've missed our chess games, sir."

Helen cringed and backed away. The encounter felt rotten.

"Have you? You should have spoken up. I'd formed the impression that you quit because you disliked the taste of being checkmated. Well, then, when shall we resume?"

"Eight o'clock on the morrow, after tattoo. Bring your set to my marquee."

"Thank you, Mr. Fairfax. Good night, and rest well."

Chapter Thirty-Five

EARLY TUESDAY MORNING, a rumor reached camp that Brigadier General Daniel Morgan had departed Charlotte Town and crossed to the west side of the Catawba River some eighty miles north. He brought with him seasoned regulars from Delaware and Maryland, plus dragoons commanded by George Washington's cousin, William. Backcountry militia, including many men who had served under Thomas Sumter, rallied to Morgan.

No bugle sounded for saddles, and speculation from the rumor dwindled. Without an order from Cornwallis to pursue and engage Morgan, Tarleton enjoyed his respite after November's hard riding.

After breakfast, Helen headed for the marketplace with her party for a closer look at the rank and file, camp women, and children. Also, the elegance of the new desk continued to intrigue her. She hoped to track down the merchant who'd sold Neville the desk and chat.

Strapped upright to a tree trunk in the lower camp, a legionnaire received lashes from a company musician thirteen or fourteen years old. The boy's arm jerked up, the cat-o'-nine-tails whistled, and another set of bloody streaks sprouted across the soldier's whip-bitten, naked back, accompanied by his writhe and scream. "Drunk and disorderly, first offense" was the explanation volunteered by a fellow legionnaire from among the crowd of onlookers. The man's company mates, required to attend the action, projected the appropriate censure and commiseration needed to bring their wayward fellow back into the fold. "Drunk and disorderly" probably wouldn't happen to one particular legionnaire again for a while.

Helen idled among merchants and sutlers, fewer than those who had camped at Woodward's. She found candles, leather goods, ribbons, tobacco, ink and paper, sewing implements, tin cups and bowls, pewter plates, cauldrons, horn spoons, a few bound books, and a variety of foods. Nowhere did she spot a suitable gift for an officer's wife or mistress, putting into perspective the haste with which Tarleton had pounced upon her embroidered pocket.

Her inquiries over a portable desk resulted in blank stares. What need did the men have for desks while on campaign? Officers brought such luxuries

from home, if they brought them at all. Most of those who maintained the
mile-chewing pace of the Green Horse on the move had little leisure or inclination at the end of the day to write letters.

She continued her stroll. The desk merchant must have been among those
who'd elected not to follow the Legion to Daniel's.

"Madam! Wait up a moment!" A sutler of leather goods bustled toward
her. "I got to thinking about that desk you was asking for." Coffee stains dulled
his teeth. He eyed the Pearsons and Jonathan, and with a gentle nod Helen
encouraged them to walk on ahead. After they'd meandered toward the end
of the row, the tanner said, "Maybe this won't help you none, but two evenings
ago, right before dark, I saw the agent hand over a fancy desk to that ranger,
Mr. Neville. Treadaway's his name, I think. Ask Mr. Neville about the desk.
Maybe he'd sell you his or let Mr. Treadaway know you're looking for one."

"Thank you, sir." More puzzled than ever, Helen curtsied. With a tip of the
hat, the tanner hurried back to his wares.

Ugh, Treadaway. He had money and an interest in her, so he may have
purchased the desk. But why give it to Neville? Why hadn't the agent inquired
after her satisfaction with the gift the previous afternoon? Did he wish his role
in it to remain secret, and Neville to claim full credit for the desk?

The ranger's act of crushing her old desk was deliberate, but why destroy
it, just to replace it? Instinct told her that the easy explanation, that Neville
was enamored of her and sought her favor, was dead wrong. And how was
Treadaway bound up in the incident?

Engaged in the mystery, she took her time rejoining her party and browsed
the commodities. The hornsmith's spoons were lovely. At the stationer's she
fondled a book of poetry but hadn't the money for purchase. Like the tanner,
the other merchants and sutlers deferred to her. The men seldom met her
gaze, the women never. Although she sensed them watching her, as soon as
she looked at them, they glanced elsewhere, and up went the transparent barrier that divided the classes.

How could rebels claim the equality of all men in their Declaration of
Independence while some men would always be more equal than others? No
one escaped the class framework bequeathed by Mother Britain, no matter
how men convoluted the language of bold documents in hopes of bestowing
equality upon themselves. The truth most self-evident for her was that no
signer of the Declaration had begged for food on a regular basis. Nor would he
choose to experience a pauper's life, just to embrace the equality he advocated.
And she, posed as the gentlewoman sister of an officer, would never know what
went on inside the heads of the "nobodies" who, each in a small way, contributed to the well-being of the British Legion.

A half-dozen young boys playing a form of Dare snagged her interest. She
inched toward them, pleased that they weren't aware of her and thus inclined
to expurgate their activities. The leader covered a small bucket with a cloth
and challenged the courage of the younger lads: plunge a hand into whatever
was in the bucket without looking, or play the fool for the next group of soldiers who rode past. From the shock and revulsion on the face of the first "victim," Helen guessed the bucket to contain intestines of livestock slaughtered
that morning. But she was dismayed that the next two boys in line refused the
challenge and chose to play the fool.

A simple lesson in psychology. If you suspected one course of action would yield a more repulsive outcome than another, your imagination worked with the unknown to enhance anticipated unpleasantness, and you avoided the course with the more disagreeable outcome.

Instinct wailed at her that the particulars of the game were very familiar and intimate to her. *Refuse the challenge*, her soul whispered. *Play the fool*.

She and her party returned to their campsite late morning. As soon as Helen entered her tent to fetch the desk, she sensed something amiss and straightened to scrutinize the interior. Without knowing how, she knew someone outside her party had visited her tent. Her gaze swept over her cot and portmanteau to rest on the desk. Disbelief clenched her chest. Oh, no, the journal.

She opened the desk, and much of her tension relaxed. The journal lay intact, its pages ordered the way she'd left them after her last entry. Yet when she'd closed it again and backed off to allow her pulse to stabilize, she clung to alert. Her privacy *had* been violated, and deep in her senses, she'd registered evidence of the intrusion. She couldn't bring it to the surface because the clues were minimal, and the intruder was clever. But she was convinced of it.

Notify the provost marshal? His men would swarm over camp, frightening the intruder. No, if the secret visitor returned, she must find a way to nab him on her own.

***

Just before reveille on Wednesday December twentieth, she jolted awake, her heart slamming her ribcage over a dream in which she'd joined the Dare game. The boy offered her the bucket, her imagination inflated the vileness of the experience into something insufferable, and she backed away. "Play the fool!"

Badley wants you dead. He's broken your contract and stranded you out here. Memory reprised Fairfax's words with startling clarity and vigor. Metaphors and dream wisdom came together at that moment, and she sat, pieced together what she'd lacked perspective to see in Wilmington.

The horror in her bucket was poverty. Prescott knew she was so afraid to touch it that she'd consider the unconventional to escape it. Badley provided her escape in the form of an assignment with the Legion. To accelerate her decision making, Prescott falsified the notice of creditor transferal and lease increase, which explained Chapman's inability to locate whomever had sent her the notice.

No editor named Samuel Kerr had organized the assignment. Badley had no agreement with a new London magazine. Prescott and Badley wanted her gone from Wilmington, dead if possible. To that end, they'd sent her on a hazardous assignment. A land torn by war offered plenty of cover for bank drafts Badley would never send. Cut off her funds while she was in the hinterland, and she couldn't escape to safety. If she died a hero's death on some backwoods battleground, Badley might eulogize her in his *Review*, print letters he'd received from her.

The vehemence with which the two men sought her demise was incomprehensible. They'd tried to run her off for nine years. Silas Chiswell's widow should have followed him to the grave within a year, spirit and health broken from paying his debts, reduced to near poverty. But few people knew about Nell Grey. Helen hadn't always been a lady with servants, fine food, and pretty gowns. For the first seventeen years of her life, she'd lived in a hut, gone without meals, been beaten and detested.

Those first seventeen years had helped her survive the past twelve years like some gnarled root overwintered in the soil. If she expected to survive the hinterlands, she'd have to bring to the surface that tough, scrappy, wounded part of herself, claim it, let it guide her.

Because without a doubt, Badley and Prescott intended to kill her. Adam Neville: their minion? How Neville, Treadaway, and their desk fit as pieces or pawns she'd yet to elucidate. Each action from the two men and everything they said she must regard as suspect — half-truth at best or outright lie.

For all Fairfax's ambiguous and frightening morality, transmitted in no uncertain terms with the first impression he made, he'd lied to her but once, in Badley's parlor, about terminating his search for David. But he possessed a far better tool than mastery of lies for navigating the halls of Parliament. He manipulated truth into shapes that served his purposes. In the murky realm of developing hunches and conjectures into solid evidence, he reigned supreme.

She drew the blanket over her neck to block a wintry draft. Confiding in and trusting Fairfax about the whole conspiracy ran contrary to her logic.

Alas, she could hardly confide in Jonathan when, at every opportunity, he reinforced his belief that Badley wasn't the ogre she believed him to be. She expelled a long breath. No. She could borrow money from Jonathan, but she couldn't yet confide in him. That morning, all she had was hunches and conjectures. Jonathan, a man of science, needed solid evidence.

Either she produced evidence for him, or she trusted Fairfax. An unpalatable choice for breakfast, to be sure.

Outside, the Legion's drummer beat reveille. Hearing the Pearsons move about in the next tent, Helen rose into a stretch and decided her course.

The story about Tarleton was a gem: not to be abandoned. With more gritty detail of the war, she could name her price at any London paper. There were tangential stories to be elucidated from her weeks with the Legion, such as the one about Thomas Brown.

But only a minority of the world's valiant carried swords, spears, or muskets. She revisited her seditious thoughts upon the Santee Road: showing the victims of war as heroes for what they'd endured. They weren't alone in suffering war's hardships.

A story lay obscured among the civilians who followed the army, one without the glitter of braid and gold buttons. Civilians as courageous. People without money or titles as brave.

What a bizarre twist that made for a feature. Why, it was unconventional enough to stir debates in London coffeehouses and taverns for months.

Now that she'd considered it, quitting the Legion and returning to Wilmington wasn't an option after all.

Chapter Thirty-Six

SALLY, A PLUMP woman with brown hair, wrung a man's shirt into a fear-some cylinder and jabbed toward the creek. "Perkins gropes my bum again, I'll shove this bayonet down his gullet."

"You do it," said Jen, up to her elbows in suds. "They pay us for laundry and fancy they got a right to more."

Helen rinsed Roger's shirt in her washtub. In her homespun clothing and Hannah's shawl, she fit right with in the three laundresses at the creek. Her apron had collected grime, her back and arms ached, and her fingers had begun to resemble some queer, dried fruit.

"Watch out for Brady." Liza flogged a stocking with her fist. "He tried to 'pay' me with a lift of my coats — as if I'm not a decent wife with a daughter to raise and a legionnaire husband, as if futtering the likes of *him* is some sort of reward."

"They're going soft. The Colonel needs to run 'em."

"Aye, I'm far more fond of the whole stinking regiment after they've marched for sixteen hours straight and are too tired to eat."

"Jen, since it was your idea to run 'em, we appoint you to stroll to the other end of camp and make the suggestion to Colonel Tarleton." The unified laughter of the three laundresses sliced the cold air with a harpy edge.

Helen grinned with empathy. In the half hour she'd washed her party's underclothes, she'd heard a world different from the chatter of officers' wives. Camp women didn't skirt the pebbles and stones of war, as the officer's wives did. They trudged in the ruts.

Hannah was shocked when Helen proposed her scheme, but she'd kept it secret from the men, accustomed herself to addressing "Nell" instead of Mrs. Chiswell by the time they found the laundresses. *Nell.* Layered in time's dust, odd memories stirred: rum fumes in her face.

Jen, closest to Helen, nudged her arm with a soapy forefinger and returned her to 1780. "Hullo, Nell, not much of a talker, are you? We don't bite."

Helen pointed to her throat and coughed. "Sore throat." Not only did she not want to influence the content and direction of their conversation, but the less said the better to avoid her concocting a colonial accent over what was obviously not American-grown speech.

The laundresses murmured commiseration. Jen scooted a few inches closer to Liza, as if "sore throat" translated to "leprosy" or "smallpox." "Nan's doing poorly."

Liza shoved hair from her face. Soapy water dribbled a channel across soot on her cheek. "Pneumonia, I'm sure of it."

Bitterness chomped Sally's tone. "She won't never get well on a half-pound of pork and rice and a pint of peas each week."

Jen snorted. "And so *we* wash clothing. King George provides the soap, and we each get a shilling and a sixpence per dozen pieces washed, and we buy more to eat. God save the king."

I eat, therefore I must launder, thought Helen, and wrung out the final shirt of her collection with solemnity.

"Nell! Hullo, Nell!" Hannah waved to her up on the trail. "Finished yet?" Helen waved back. "Hurry up." Hannah meandered off toward their campsite, her market basket full.

Helen dragged the washtub apart from where the women labored and overturned it to drain rinse water toward the creek. Then she piled in squeezed-out garments and straightened. A groan escaped her. She kneaded her lower back. When she was seventeen years old, washday hadn't hurt.

Sally, Liza, and Jen chuckled at the groan — the chuckle of sisterhood — and sent wishes for her health. Up the trail, Hannah awaited her and, with a scowl, reached for the tub. "Mrs. Chiswell, give me that heavy thing and take my basket. Look at your hands! You'll need to apply salve on them." They headed for their campsite. "I don't understand why you did this. Who *wants* to launder?"

For Helen's trouble, she hoped she'd gotten everything clean enough. Her hands looked irritated by soap, but she'd no laundering scheduled for the morrow. "It's research."

"What has laundering to do with Colonel Tarleton?"

"The washerwomen are part of the environment created by the Legion."

The blonde frowned into the tub. "Let me launder, please."

Concern wove through Helen. "Did I do a poor job of it?"

"Ye gods, no, madam. I'm amazed that a lady like you could accomplish such a menial task so well. But —" She gnawed her lip. "You're supposed to portray a gentlewoman. What if an officer's wife recognized you out there? How would you explain it?"

Much depended on her ability to call upon Nell Grey, become a woman of the lower class again. At that, she seemed to do well, for the washerwomen had opened up in her company as they never would have with an officer's lady. It had been a matter of undoing Jonathan's teachings on posture and etiquette. Her success also depended upon luck, and she knew she'd have to avoid drawing attention to herself. "I shall have to use caution."

"You don't mean to launder again?"

Helen gave her hands a rueful grin. "All right, perhaps I shall visit the kitchen next time."

"Oh, heaven help us."

Jonathan and Roger had gone to watch another drill that morning and not yet returned, availing Helen of the opportunity to change clothing without their questions. But as she and Hannah approached the tents, she grasped Hannah's arm and slowed her. Before they'd left for the creek, Helen had paused about twenty-five feet from the tents and looked over the campsite. She found her original point of reference and stood in silence, her examination critical.

Hannah whispered, "What is it? Is something wrong?"

The intruder had been back. What piece of evidence, even from that distance, told Helen so? It must be obvious, left in the open, considered inconsequential by most passersby. In her mind, she retraced her steps to leave the tent earlier, walk out to where she stood that very moment, and pass her first critical gaze upon the campsite.

No, wait. She hadn't walked all the way out *immediately*. Her apron had snagged on the lantern just outside her tent door, so she'd angled both the cut branch she used as a stand and the lantern to face away from the door.

Her heart thumped her ribcage again. Someone had moved the branch back around to face the door. In that position, it might snag clothing. Perhaps it was a signal to passersby that her tent — and the desk — had been visited again.

Conscious that Hannah studied her as if she'd lost a few cards from her deck, Helen approached her tent, Fairfax's meticulous investigation of her broken study window in mind. Multiple sets of footprints blended in the rain-softened dirt and grass, far too many sets to separate. At the tent door, she found the flaps tied as if she'd done it herself. Too bad the makeshift lantern stand hadn't grabbed a convenient wad of telltale fibers from the intruder's clothing.

Undaunted by lack of overt evidence, she ordered Hannah to wait outside, let herself into the tent, and allowed her eyes to adjust to a dim interior imposed by the morning's high overcast. The desk sat just where she left it on an open campstool — but had it been moved just off center? To confirm her hunch, she knelt before it and looked for the single hair she'd pasted to the desk and stool with a dab of saliva. Gone: dislodged when the intruder had lifted the desk off the stool.

Just outside, Hannah cleared her throat. "Mrs. Chiswell, are you feeling all right? I'm worried you might have picked up a chill down there at the creek."

Helen had to keep her out of the tent a few minutes longer. "You're right. It *was* cold down there. Before you help me change, might you fetch us some coffee?"

"Oh, yes, madam. Shall I fetch coals for your brazier, too?"

Helen wanted to shuck off the homespun clothes before Jonathan and Roger's return. "Just coffee for now."

"Right away!"

The retreating rustle of footsteps announced Hannah's departure. With a sigh of satisfaction, Helen murmured, "What is it you want with my desk, eh?" She sat on her cot and opened the desk, not surprised to again find nothing from her journal amiss. The intruder wasn't after the journal. That explanation was too obvious.

With the desk closed, she strolled her fingers over handsome patterns along the sides, trellises of roses, stems, and leaves carved into the wood. Spaniards had an eye for magnificence in art that sensible Britons had never claimed. Perhaps David had seen similar desks in Havana. She stroked the mahogany and imagined high romance for the desk's inception...

A nobleman, *un hidalgo*, fell in love with a *Doña* from a family too prestigious to bother with his petitions for marriage. Nevertheless, the couple pledged eternal love to each other. He returned to his humble papaya plantation, too much time on his lovesick hands, and sat beneath palm trees to carve a desk for her as token of his love. With the desk, she would write him every day, and...

The fantasy ground to a halt in her sensible, British head. Any Spanish matron not half-witted would sneak daily peeks into her nubile daughter's desk for love letters to fellows not designated as her betrothed. If the *hidalgo* had been clever, he'd have created a secret compartment in the desk where his *Doña* could hide daily letters to him before she smuggled them to a trusted handmaid —

With a start, Helen regarded the desk anew. Then she bent close to it, scrutiny fresh. Odd, was that panel along the base a trifle offset? She traced it to the rear of the desk, where the offset seemed more definite, wedged fingernails around it, and tugged. Without resistance, a thin panel of wood slid out. Upon it lay an open sheet of paper.

She gasped in astonishment. The body of the letter was scripted in a combination of words and numbers, a cipher. Her gaze darted to the salutation — simply "Epsilon" without title — and scrambled to the closing, which read, "Yrs. In Service, Omega."

Chapter Thirty-Seven

SHE WRESTLED BACK her impulse to heave the desk across the tent as if it contained black widow spiders. Instead, she lowered it to a rug. Throat parched, she poked her head out of the tent. No one in sight. The washtub remained where Hannah had set it.

She withdrew and tied tent flaps with shaky fingers. The drawer dangled like a tongue in a bawdyhouse. Without a cipher key, she'd no way to discern the affiliation of the writer: covetous member of the Crown forces or clever rebel spy. But she reaffirmed her decision to not involve the provost. He'd muddle the situation and never uncover the players. She could ferret out players herself. If Neville was "Omega," others in camp must be involved, for Treadaway had ridden back to Camden that morning.

At some point, you'll realize that you must tell me what you know. On that day, the idea of toying with me won't hold half as much appeal for you as it does right now. Cold penetrated the base of her skull. Fairfax suspected her of conspiracy due to her involvement with the St. James family. He didn't know that Neville destroyed her old desk and messengers swapped notes via a secret compartment in the replacement. If Neville were a rebel spy instead of a lap dog Loyalist, and Fairfax found the cipher in her desk and had a copy of the key —

No. He wasn't going to find the desk, and she had no intention of telling him about it unless she could wield it as leverage. *I offer you this information, and you obtain something I need to complete my project.*

She closed the drawer and replaced the desk. To destroy any messages she found would constitute evidence that she was aware of the secret compartment. Rather, she'd change clothing and stretch her legs at market, allow the messenger to retrieve the cipher. Perhaps she'd double back early one day and spot the messenger in action.

★★★

Outside a wine merchant's marquee that afternoon, Helen noticed Margaret deliberating over red wine. She sent Hannah to the next stall and sidled closer to the courtesan, who then voiced her dilemma. "Which one: Portuguese, Spanish, or Italian?"

Helen felt impish. "Perilous choice. *Any* man from the Mediterranean will steal your heart." Their laughter earned frowns from officers' ladies within the marquee. They subsided into giggles, and Helen gestured to the bottle in Margaret's hands. "A gift for yourself? Try the Portuguese."

"I believe I shall."

Helen leaned in closer, a journalist on duty. "Tell me, how did you and the colonel become acquainted?"

"He took a fancy to me in Camden this summer when my employer went bankrupt."

Few prostitutes were so fortunate. "He treats you well enough."

Mischief quirked the courtesan's full lips, a sensuous invitation. "True, he doesn't beat me or curse me. He provides me a fair allowance and lavishes gifts upon me." After a quick glance around, the brunette's regard of Helen sharpened. "Why refuse him? He takes his time."

Helen scrutinized the other woman, trying to make sense of her words. Fever-bright and famished, Margaret's gaze bored into her. Then comprehension crawled over Helen. Good gods, the courtesan had noticed Tarleton flirting with her and presumed Helen to encroach upon her territory. "Margaret, the colonel flirts with every lady —"

"Not *Tarleton*." Margaret punched out an exhale, as if correcting a dull-witted child. She gripped Helen's upper arm and yanked her in close for a shrewd whisper. "You *ninny*, I know he isn't your brother." Then she released Helen's arm and swayed back into the marquee to purchase wine.

Helen gawped after her. Ninny she was, indeed, and poor at playacting. Panic flipped about her chest like a frog in ferns. If Margaret knew, who else knew? Whom had she told? How much time did Helen have before Tarleton terminated her visit?

She lowered her gaze and breathed reason. If Margaret had told anyone of consequence, Helen would have been booted from camp. Why did Margaret keep the secret? What price did she expect of Helen in return for concealing it?

Price. Margaret seemed willing to *share* Fairfax with her. Helen envisioned the torment and haunting in the brunette's eyes and shuddered. A prostitute's lot in life was lousy sex, multiple times a day, day after day. Fairfax wasn't merely supplying Margaret with intangible manna, such as flattery. He delivered a physical performance that ensnared her like laudanum, beneath Tarleton's nose.

She rubbed her temples. Tarleton wasn't stupid when it came to women. Did she want to be in camp when all that exploded?

Conscious of horses just behind her, she heard Fairfax's dispassionate voice from the saddle. "I suggest that you bypass the Spanish wine. Cortés, Pizarro, and de Soto, fully armored, in every bottle."

Helen exhaled before facing him. "We need to talk."

"Ah, at last." After handing over his horse's reins to Kennelly, Fairfax dismounted and tucked Helen's gloved hand into the crook of his elbow.

She signaled Hannah. The blonde followed between them and Kennelly.

Helen pitched her voice low. "Margaret knows I'm not your sister."
"Don't let it concern you."
The inhumanity of his tone implied that he owned Margaret. Tarleton
wasn't as suggestible as his courtesan. Helen firmed her voice. "What if the
colonel finds out about you and his mistress?"
"Exactly what would he find out?"
Flawless, his blank expression. Neither Fairfax nor Margaret was going to
tell Tarleton about the indiscretion. Helen needed a story about the Legion,
and she wasn't going to tell. She sighed in disgust.
"Mr. Pearson didn't inquire after your mail this morning. Here you go."
Fairfax reached inside his coat, withdrew a letter to Jonathan that had been
opened, and handed it to her. She secured the letter in her basket. "Aren't you
going to inquire where I've hidden Phineas Badley's bank draft?"
"No. Your analysis is correct. Badley stranded me out here and hopes I'll
be killed."
Fairfax's eyebrows shot up. "*Brava*, darling!" He perched her hand upon
his elbow again. "How did you arrive at such conviction?"
"Hackneyed as it may sound, it came to me in a dream."
"I see." He petted her hand. "What are your plans, then?"
"Plenty of magazines will pay for a feature on Tarleton. I've work to
continue."
"Such spirit! The gods reward warriors. You'll see." He craned his neck to
look at a merchant's woodenwares. "And for funding, you brought along your
champion, the many-talented Mr. Quill."
Fairfax envied Jonathan; Jonathan envied Fairfax. That moment, she
wished for a cast-iron skillet and the opportunity to clobber them both in the
head with it. "You're going at your chess matches in much too civilized a manner. Play for parcels of land."
He laughed and tweaked her fingers. When they passed the next merchant,
who also dealt in polished wood, Helen couldn't help but notice Fairfax's scrutiny of the items. He said, "You're at market quite a bit. Might I ask a favor?
Search for a gift for me when you're here. If you find it, have the merchant set
it aside and notify me immediately."
How quaint. He wanted her to shop for Margaret. Helen compressed her
lips and counted to five. She ought to count her blessings while she was at it.
At least he wasn't asking her to spy on Neville. "What is this gift? A book of
poetry?"
"Not at all. I fancy purchasing a portable desk similar to that one you
brought along. The Spaniards make quality desks of mahogany and even go
to great pains to carve birds and flowers into the trim —" He caught her when
she stumbled. "Hullo, watch yourself, there."
Stomach knotted, she swept a frantic gaze over the marketplace. Fairfax
knew about the desk Neville had given her. How much did he know? Her laugh
sounded taut, mocking. "You might find an oaken footstool of American workmanship here, but a mahogany desk imported from Spain? Be reasonable."
"Point well taken. I received a tip that such a desk might make an appearance. What do you say to giving me a bit of help on this?"
An intelligence source had alerted him about the desk, but several days too
late. Now she'd have to sew a canvas carrier to cover it all the time, even when

she left it in her tent.

How to best play out this latest development? Her business sense buzzed. She threw a glance over her shoulder. Kennelly was a discreet distance back. "Hrumph. So I'm your buyer at market, eh?"

"It's just the one item."

She dislodged her arm from his and planted her feet to face him. Kennelly and Hannah halted. "One item becomes several, and my own project languishes while I waste time working for you."

"A bottle of that Italian red wine for you, then."

"Is that an offer or a jest?" Fascination heated in his eyes at her bartering. She almost shrank away. Encouraging his fascination wasn't wise. "Exactly when do you expect this desk to arrive?"

"No definite word."

She exhaled irritation. "I'm a busy woman. I don't have time to dawdle for weeks."

"Not weeks. Within five days."

"Five days." She crossed her arms over her chest and tapped her foot. "Very well, I shall look for your desk. At a rate of two shillings per day, I shall become your agent and comb the marketplace for you."

"*Two shillings?*" His jaw clenched.

"I follow up each day with merchants and sutlers. Your maximum outlay for my services is ten shillings."

"And I suppose you won't find the desk until day five."

Triumph twisted her upper lip. Ten shillings would keep her going awhile longer, push farther into the future the moment she'd have to borrow from Jonathan. "You've already observed that I'm not desperate for your money. Do you want me to help you find that desk or not?"

"One shilling per day."

"Eighteen pence per day." Seven and a half shillings was still a bargain. She stuck out her hand for a business handshake. "Do we have a deal?"

He caught her hand and lifted it to his lips. "Indeed. And I doubt you'll disappoint me."

Her instincts jangling danger, she withdrew her hand and bobbed a curtsy. "Good day, then —"

"Seeing that Portuguese wine back there reminds me of summer. While aboard a ship-of-the-line, I chased a Portuguese brig with a hold full of wine down the East Florida coast. We got so close that, with a spyglass, I could see terror on David St. James's face as he stood on deck."

Jolly. Fairfax was in the mood to swank. "He never told me that story. He must have considered it of little consequence."

"Alas, we lost sight of the brig in a tropical storm."

"Ships wreck against the Florida reefs during tropical storms, just as men dash their brains out holding to senseless beliefs about others. I haven't seen David since the night you ran him from my house. I'm not going to see him again."

"He fancies himself the bravest of knights when his damsel is imperiled." Fairfax grinned. "I assure you, you will see Mr. St. James again."

She sighed, annoyed. "I see where this is leading. You received intelligence that David will arrive in camp within five days carrying a portable Spanish desk made of mahogany."

"I shall be honored to explain it to you over Midwinter supper on the morrow. Roasted duckling, a leek tart, suet pudding, apples, carrots, nuts. Waes hail."

His invitation surprised her. Midwinter on the morrow. She'd almost forgotten. When she'd been eleven years old, Ratchingham had invited his cronies to a Midwinter celebration at Redthorne. For a week when she arrived for lessons in the parlor, the manor smelled of evergreen, roasted pheasant, and drunken gentry and merchants.

A man's blurred visage bobbed up from subterranean memory again. *Ohh, girl.* Rum fumed her face.

What the hell — Was she going mad? From where did this vision come?

"A simple 'yes' or 'no' will suffice."

Propelled to the present by impudence in Fairfax's voice, she blinked. Her imagination furnished a graphic image of Midwinter supper with him: no roasted duckling the centerpiece, but Helen Chiswell, and an accompanying course on obedience. "No. No, thank you."

"Good day, then, dear sister." He took a step back from her, bowed, and swaggered over to his horse.

Chapter Thirty-Eight

BY THE TIME Helen and Hannah returned to their campsite, Helen re-gretted her impulsiveness. Fairfax would *expect* her to turn up a mahogany Spanish desk, and she wasn't about to surrender hers. Now she had to throw him off her trail.

Jonathan and Roger sat outside the tents, the locksmith running his mouth faster than a rabbit with a two-foot lead on a hound in the brush. Both men rose to bow at the women's appearance, and Helen handed Jonathan his letter. She wondered when the argument was coming between the Pearsons. Life in the Legion looked easy, the only apparent prerequisite the enthusiasm Roger already possessed. If Hannah didn't put her foot down soon, Roger might sign himself up.

The lantern was rotated away from Helen's tent door. The messenger had had two hours of everyone's absence to retrieve the cipher. She couldn't wait to check the desk. "Coffee," she whispered to Hannah and shut herself inside.

The secret drawer was empty. She eased it back into concealment. An easy enough delivery schedule to monitor. She'd establish a routine with the Pearsons every morning to encourage regularity. In theory, the four of them could leave the messenger several hours to plant a cipher. She'd pick her point of observation with care. The messenger would never know she watched.

She hid the desk and exited. Jonathan and Roger rose, and she nodded to Jonathan. "Let's walk, shall we?

Halfway to a line of trees in the east, he said, "You don't appear tired today. Phineas's draft came?" She shook her head. Surliness caught his lip. "I doubt it's his fault."

"Come now, Jonathan, this posturing is too polite. You and Mr. Fairfax simply must find a more satisfying metaphor for ripping each other's heads off. I suggested to him that you play chess for parcels of land. *Kingdoms*, if you will."

He smiled. "When did you develop such a waspish tongue?"

"At the same time you eschewed essential points of logic when you formed your conclusions."

"What logic points did I disdain?"

"All our mail goes through Mr. Fairfax before it reaches us. If he intended to make me financially dependent upon him, he wouldn't have allowed your bank drafts through. Far simpler to destroy those pieces of mail and claim they never arrived." And she suspected that Fairfax preferred voluntary surrender, not a thrashing capitulation. It allowed him to claim more of a subject's soul. She leaned toward Jonathan. "Have I made sense?"

His smile had disappeared. "Yes."

"Good. Let us presume that Mr. Fairfax isn't lying to us and thus form hypotheses about the absence of Badley's bank draft. Number one: Badley has posted it in good faith, and it is tangled in the dispatch system somewhere. Number two: Badley has broken his contract and posted me no bank draft. Do you see any other hypotheses?"

"Not immediately. I shall ponder it."

"You do that." She firmed her chin. Fairfax, she felt certain, wouldn't come through with his seven and a half shillings, even if she gave him her desk. "I've run through my money and must transact a loan. Is your offer still available?"

"Of course it is. And don't concern yourself with repaying me right now. Just write your story, and make it the best you possibly can. That's all I ask of you."

The gentle acceptance in his expression carried her to a place where tempests ceased to storm her heart. Jonathan had always believed in her. Why did she forget so easily? She extended her hand. "Thank you."

He clasped her hand and scrutinized her fingers. "What have you been up to, washing dishes?"

Washing your shirts and stockings, she thought with perverse amusement. "My hands got chapped in dry weather a few days ago."

He released her and shook a finger at her. "Salve and gloves." They faced the campsite. His voice softened. "On the morrow is the solstice. I've noticed they don't much celebrate the old ways here. It's even difficult to find a decent bonfire for Guy Fawkes."

She shrugged. "A gloomy lot, the Protestants. From Anglicans to Anabaptists, they barely acknowledge the birth of Jesus. The Jews, they keep to themselves. And the others are far too sensible to find an excuse for revelry. I've always been curious. Does the Enlightened One honor Midwinter Day?"

Empathy fortified his expression of respect. "The Enlightened One honors every day, my dear."

***

Helen and Hannah spent the afternoon in the equine section of camp and talked with farriers who shod horses with iron from Camden. In the heat of the previous May, Tarleton had overtaken and annihilated Buford's command at the cost of dozens of his own horses. When he'd chased Sumter down after Camden and also at Blackstock's, he'd lost more. But she'd never have known it from the geldings and mares in corral. The Legion always got replacement horses.

His expression smug, a farrier volunteered names of commanders whose horses were diverted to the Legion — officers who'd been in the Army twice as long as Tarleton. Not only horses but also supplies and resources like iron were diverted from other units to the Legion.

The consequence of Tarleton's preferential treatment registered anew on Helen. Never mind that he'd recently been denied another rank advancement. He'd risen fast and furious and was far too favored among the generals to be respected by fellow officers.

Without difficulty, she imagined the desk, Neville, and Treadaway as part of some internal movement to equalize that preferential treatment. In Badley's study in September, Hannah had overheard Prescott say that someone named Epsilon would have to make do, even though he didn't have enough supplies. Then Neville said Epsilon might be forced to withdraw. Did Prescott and Badley scheme to divert resources from the Legion to another unit? Perhaps a plot was afoot to pump the Legion with misinformation, make them appear idiots, cost Tarleton his command. The possibilities staggered Helen.

Fairfax would entertain himself by foiling such a cabal before Tarleton ever caught wind of it. Perhaps he'd offer heads on a platter to the Legion's commander with the faux-modesty she'd observed in the foyer at Woodward's Plantation. Elsewhere in the Crown forces, he'd snap military careers off at the base like a tornado on a rampage through a grove of pines.

At times, it amazed her that the British Army possessed enough cohesion to win battles against the rebels.

Half an hour before sunset, Neville caught up with the women en route to their tents. His smile cheery, he dismounted his horse to walk beside Helen. "Lovely weather, eh? No rain in sight, and a good fire tonight will take the chill off. What have you been up to?"

"I've visited the horses. Such well-kept beasts."

"The Legion spares no expense to obtain premium mounts."

"That doesn't sit well with other commanders."

"Bah. Let them ride as hard and fast as the Legion. They'd shut their mouths soon enough." His gaze darted around to ensure that no one except Hannah walked nearby. "How goes your research? I think Mr. Badley made a superlative choice of journalist for this assignment."

"Superlative?" Surprised and a little uneasy, Helen laughed. Neville appeared almost giddy in her presence. Either he wasn't privy to Badley's scheme to dump her in the hinterlands, or he'd just executed some fantastic acting skills.

He seemed to blush a little. "Pardon the warmth of my adjective, but you take this project seriously. You aren't just closeted with the officers' ladies. You're out quite a bit, investigating camp operations." He presented a bold stare. "That desk I found for you — how does it suit your purposes?"

"Very well." She scrutinized his expression. Was this the same Adam Neville who'd resisted speaking to her the morning they left Camden? "It's beautiful." Instinct prodded her to lead with her curiosity. "And Mr. Fairfax wants one just like it."

"I don't doubt it. I fancied it for myself. It's a handsome piece."

"No, you don't understand. He's never seen the desk you gave me, but this morning at market, he asked me to look for one just like it among the merchants. He described it perfectly and said he thought it might make an appearance at market within the next five days."

Winter invaded Neville's eyes. "Well, that's peculiar."

"Which merchant sold you the desk? Perhaps I can point Mr. Fairfax in his direction —"

"I cannot imagine why he expects a desk at market." Neville glanced away and scratched his neck, as if his hunting shirt had grown too tight on him. "I doubt there's another like it out there. Well-crafted pieces just don't show up very often out here. It's probably a good idea to keep your desk out of sight. No point in rubbing Mr. Fairfax's nose in the fact that you got a quality piece before he did. But do continue your search at market. You never know what might turn up there."

Neville was lying. And he was up to something.

He beamed. "Oh, why talk about *him*? Will you dance with me at the Yule celebration?"

Whew, that was quite an about-face. Helen propped her hands on her hips and grinned at him. "How many dances, sir?"

"A half dozen."

Quite a bold request, and she was certain there was method to it beyond the madness he affected in her company. "In London, a mere three dances with the same man is proof of a secret betrothal."

Embarrassment wiped his expression. "Oh, no, madam, I assure you that's not at all my intent."

What *was* his intent? For certain, it wasn't courtship, but he seemed willing to let her think it might be. "Your request is unreasonable. Colonel Tarleton expects to dance with me, and I expect to dance with other officers."

"Five dances, then."

Helen pretended to consider his offer. Neville might want to occupy her with dancing to allow transit of another cipher through her desk. If she wished to outfox him and double back for observation during part of the dance, she'd have to plan ahead. "More than two dances are considered gossip-worthy. I can promise you no more than two."

"This is the Carolina backcountry, not London. Three dances."

She cocked an eyebrow. "Three? I guarantee you that Mr. Fairfax won't get three dances from me that night."

"I'm a better dancer than he."

Great heavens, if Fairfax could only hear what issued from Neville's mouth. Three dances. She'd slip away with Hannah somewhere near the end of the first half for some snooping, and Neville would never miss her because they'd already danced. "Very well, sir. Three dances it is."

Chapter Thirty-Nine

"IT'S JUST FOR six months. Paul can manage business for that time."

"No."

"Hannah, honey, they need me."

"Over my dead body are you joining the Legion."

Helen shivered out a yawn and pulled the homespun jacket on atop her woolen petticoat, shift, and tucker. Twice she pricked herself in the darkness fastening the jacket, but the Pearsons were long overdue for their argument, and she wanted to give them space.

Tugging her cloak across her shoulders, she emerged from her tent. Something snagged at her head and neck. She gasped and identified by touch what draped the top of the tent and dangled before the entrance: holly twined with ivy. Blessed Midwinter.

Dismayed, she dragged the foliage off, flinching over the jab of holly. She resisted her inclination to throw it in a trash pile. Instead, she carried it with her across the field silver and crunchy with tiny jewels of ice. At the dawn place, she looped the holly and ivy, offered the wreath to the frosty ground, and stood in silence, seeking stillness and nourishment from the earth. Sunrise brightened on her face. The hum of life behind her rose, defiant and persistent for another day.

By the time she returned to her campsite, more rumor buzzed, that General Nathanael Greene had left Charlotte Town two days earlier, on the nineteenth, intent on capturing Ninety Six. Considering that he'd have to ram a disparate blend of regulars and militia through the bayonet-lined jaws of the Crown's Southern army, Helen deemed the enterprise unlikely. Greene and his militia counterpart, Daniel Morgan, sounded too intelligent and shrewd. Sure enough, no bugle sounded for saddles.

But she had a hunch about rumors of military movements and ciphers hidden in her desk, so she herded her party away from their tents and out to watch a Legion drill before nine o'clock. Upon their return, she noticed the lantern twisted back to the entrance of her tent. Inside, she found another cipher to Epsilon from Omega.

While the Pearsons bickered more over Roger enlisting, she pondered shadows created by those trees to the east, just outside picket lines: an excellent place to observe who entered her tent. Soon enough, she'd know the identity of the messenger. But she hadn't yet answered a more important question. To whom would she give the information she collected?

***

The tanner with coffee-stained teeth rose from his bench and bowed. "Good to see you again, madam. How may I be of service this afternoon?"

A patron was engrossed in examining hides on a display table. Helen motioned the tanner aside. "I've heard that another desk might appear in market over the next few days, before Christmas, and I should like to purchase it as a gift."

"Did you ask that ranger about the last one?"

"Yes, but I'd rather leave him out of this purchase. Keep your eyes open. When you spot the desk, I shall pay you two pence to secure it for me with the merchant. When I have it in my hands, I shall pay you an additional two pence."

On the chance that a desk appeared in market, she'd have something to show Fairfax. If the tanner found a desk, she'd eat four pence. But if Fairfax paid her, it would offset her outlay to the tanner.

The tanner licked his lips at the mention of money. "Certainly, madam, just tell me where to find you."

She provided directions to her campsite and left the marquee. Hannah, who'd waited outside, caught up with her, and they headed for the food, where Helen supplied enough detail about shopping for supper, along with money, to keep Hannah busy for a while. After pleading weariness, Helen left her and headed back to the tents — but not on the main trail.

She sneaked among trees, picked her spot behind an oak, and settled with a clear view of their tents, some fifty feet distant. She hoped the messenger would arrive before Hannah returned.

Three officers' wives and their maids strolled through the site chatting and paused while one showed something in her basket to the others. In silence, Helen implored them to move along. Next, a slender girl aged ten or eleven skipped past from the lower camp pushing a hoop along with a stick. The hoop bumped and wobbled over the irregular surface of the ground, but the girl commanded its course with precision. Two Legionnaires greeted her and halted between the campsite and trees to monitor the area after she'd gone on her way. Helen held her breath when one walked a circle around the tents, let out her breath in disappointment when both continued on their patrol.

By then, it was almost time for Hannah to return. Maybe the messenger wouldn't arrive until the morrow. Maybe the messenger had spotted her and wouldn't come at all. Maybe she was foolish to believe she could infiltrate a smooth operation.

The girl returned. Her hoop rolled against Helen's tent, and the child skipped over to retrieve it. But after roving a look around her, she untied the bottom of the tent flap and ducked inside Helen's tent. Helen sat straight, her jaw dangling in amazement. The girl emerged within seconds, retied the flaps, twisted the branch around to face outward, and sent her hoop spinning along the trail toward the lower camp.

No time to check the secret drawer. Helen shoved herself up in pursuit. A child couldn't be Epsilon. Who was the next link, the person to whom she delivered the cipher?

Her route wound back among the garrison's tents — an area, she realized after she'd received a few startled stares from legionnaires, that she ought not to wander alone. Pipe smoke and the smells of masculinity, leather, and rum, a fiddle melody, and men's conversation and laughter surrounded her — the military world ladies never visited.

Throats cleared in her wake, verbal leers, but she kept her eyes on the girl and maintained her pace to discourage the impression that she was there to solicit company.

The hoop bounced through open flaps of the quartermaster's tent. His assistant, Newman, emerged with the hoop in his hand and a good-natured smile on his face.

Biting her lower lip, Helen peeked from behind an unoccupied tent to see the girl bob a curtsy of apology. When she extended her hand for the hoop, she palmed him a folded slip of paper: the cipher, no doubt. Newman tucked it into his pocket, patted the girl's head, then popped back inside the tent to retrieve a small sack of flour for her. She curtsied again and went on her way with hoop and flour. On the surface, an innocuous encounter between a girl and a kind-hearted soldier.

Newman the mail carrier. Gods almighty.

"Mrs. Chiswell?"

Helen jumped, then warbled a laugh for Sullivan, one of the dragoons from her escort through the Santee. "Oh, you startled me!"

"I apologize, but — but what are you doing *here*?"

She lowered her eyelashes. "My maid and I became separated. Will you guide me back to the road?"

"Right away, madam." He sounded relieved and extended his elbow. Lieutenant Fairfax's sister strolling among the rank and file: what an interesting tale that would make.

They arrived at the trail just as Hannah was traipsing north on it from market, her basket full. Helen presented him a deep curtsy and received his gallant bow in exchange. Baffled, Hannah looked between Helen and the retreating dragoon. "Mrs. Chiswell, I thought you'd gone back to your tent to rest!"

"Hush." With a glance over her shoulder at Sullivan, out of earshot, she urged Hannah along.

The entire way back, she pondered. Odds were that Newman wasn't Epsilon. However, he had ample opportunity to sneak ciphers away to Epsilon with each outgoing post. Circumstantial evidence pointed to Neville as Omega. How adamant he'd been to dance with her. He must plan a cipher transfer during that time. She'd sneak away from the dance, conceal herself, and take note of those who visited her tent.

Back in her tent, she confirmed the absence of the cipher. A flat-chested, narrow-hipped girl not yet entered adolescence was the last person she'd have expected as a messenger — the last person *anyone* would suspect as a link in a chain of spies. Children and women comprised an invisible segment of the army. How clever of those people with Greek letters for code names.

In all likelihood, Neville or Newman approached the girl with the opportunity to complete a task "in service to King George." She was trying to help her family survive, old enough to have made her own decision. But she wasn't old enough to comprehend all the dangers inherent in that decision. Weakest link in the chain, she made for easy disassembling. Bound wrists...

Queasiness engulfed her. Fragments of old, buried memory clawed up into her consciousness and annealed at last. Her wrists bound in the peaty dimness of a tool shed. A man's hand on the back of her head, her face squashed into the rank hair of his crotch. Her mouth full, her throat gagging. "Ohh, girl," he crooned, his breath sour with rum, "just wait 'til you're a few years older."

Nauseated, Helen squinted into the mist surrounding the memory. Who was this horrid man to force himself on her? His face pierced the mist. *Treadaway.* Tobias Treadaway at Ratchingham's Midwinter celebration, when she was eleven years old, about the same age as the girl with the hoop. Tasting rum, Helen staggered to the little chamber pot in her tent and vomited up the purchasing agent.

While her conscious mind sought to accept and sort the memory as genuine, Hannah untied the flaps of her tent with haste. "Mrs. Chiswell! Are you all right?" The younger woman bent over beside her. "I knew it. This whole journey has been too much for you, and you down there in the damp of the creek yesterday with those washerwomen." The blonde smoothed back Helen's hair and felt her forehead with a frown. "No fever, but you're very clammy. I hope you haven't caught a camp sickness. Let's get you undressed and in bed. No arguments, you hear me?"

No arguments at all from Helen. Hannah helped her into her cot. "I shall fetch you some tea and broth, and coals for the brazier." Off came Helen's shoes. After undressing her, Hannah bustled out to dump the chamber pot, returned it, and closed Helen's tent, on her way to arm herself with potions for an invalid. Her footsteps in the grass receded.

Helen's heaves subsided, replaced with a dull anger that focused, waxed piercing. How dare Treadaway do that to her? When she'd told her parents, they'd yelled at her that it was her fault for being at the manor during Ratchingham's celebration.

Bitterness gouged Nell Grey's soul, wove her stomach with fire. *I hate you! I hate all of you!* Blood hammered in her temples, dizzied her. In her imagination, she seized her parents and Treadaway each by their throats and squeezed until their eyeballs bulged and she'd crushed their windpipes. Any time she desired, she could kill them in her imagination. Gods, how sweet, how divine. A glorious exaltation.

Exaltation. Animals tortured to death. Ratchingham choked over and over. A geyser of blood from the Whig's severed head. *He tried to violate my sister...he shot a friend, someone I've known my entire life, in cold blood...*

Stunned, she stared at the ceiling of her tent, comprehending at last the source of her dual fascination-revulsion over Fairfax. *Divine sister, sibyl of the gods, vision-priestess.* Neither of them doubted his ability to pick up where her parents and Treadaway had left off —manna he'd tailor for her. Then he'd own her the way he owned Margaret.

Without a doubt, she had drawn her "teacher" to her, but why hadn't she learned the lesson? To be sure, her parents and Treadaway had abused her, and her anger was just. But after anger had served its purpose, what did the warrior do with the sword?

If Fairfax found out about the girl with the hoop —

No, he mustn't. A girl on the cusp of womanhood had dreams and hopes, even if many of them were ground underfoot in the advance of a wretched childhood. Nell remembered. Perhaps the girl with the hoop shrugged off as inconsequential the political element of her role in favor of what her involvement gained for her family: extra flour rations, more firewood, a pair of shoes. Did any argument exist to convince her that it wasn't worth it?

Helen stared at the desk, a cadaverous taste in her mouth, and knew that somehow, she must convince the girl to end her role with Epsilon.

Chapter Forty

IN THE WEE hours of the morning on Friday the twenty-second, Helen awakened from a nightmare of Treadaway. Too rattled to return to sleep, she excavated memories from her childhood for similar foul incidents. Beatings and starvings her memory provided in abundance, but as far as she could recall, she'd only been forced that once, in the tool shed.

What a horrific experience to lurk inside the brain, waiting for its moment to pounce. She realized that the degradation of the incident had, from the rear seat of the carriage, steered her opinion of herself for years. *You're not good enough*, it whispered. *You deserve no better.* Anger, fear, and confusion spun her head. How did one undo such a ghastly endowment?

After reveille, the Pearsons resumed arguing. Fuzzy-headed, Helen stood, stretched, and dressed in her homespun clothing, ignoring the stamp of cold in her bones. In a moment of inattention the night before, she'd pinched Hannah's shawl to complete her disguise. The preoccupied Pearsons wouldn't miss her for some time, and neither would Jonathan, always up and away for his ritual before reveille.

From the looks Hannah had been giving her, the blonde thought her health fragile, her sanity questionable. She had no intention of involving Hannah in her research at the kitchen. She'd be back by dawn, before it was fully light, before anyone had missed her or the shawl. Her only regret was skipping a morning of the dawn place.

She slumped her shoulders and adjusted her body into the more casual gait of a lower-class woman. On the trail, she detoured in the icy, wet grass for a group of infantrymen clanking north to drill. "Ohh, Jen, there's my Jenny." A soldier grabbed her buttock in passing and made slurpy, kissing sounds. She whacked his hand away and kept walking in the opposite direction, alarmed. Harsh laughter trailed.

"Brady, wake up," said another man. "She wasn't Jen."

"You imbecile, I've squeezed that cow's arse enough times to recognize it in the dark."

Their banter faded, and Helen stepped back onto the trail, fuming on behalf of the laundresses. They were quite right in their assertion that the soldiers needed more exercise than they were getting.

Green, wet wood made for smoky fires in the kitchen area, where about ten women and as many servants, slaves, and soldiers mingled, a few in murmured conversation. But most just waited, sleepy-eyed, over whatever they cooked: bacon, biscuits, coffee. Liza the laundress bustled over. "Nell, good to see you again! How's the throat?"

Helen coughed. "Better, thanks."

Liza frowned, unconvinced. "Take care of yourself. There's a fever going around." She peered into Helen's basket. "What have you there? Ah, the mistress wants her pot of coffee."

Helen shook her head. "Tea."

"La, now there's a lady with money. I haven't drunk tea in years, thanks to rebel scum. Tuck your pot in beside mine on the coals right here." Liza steered her for one of the fires.

"I need water." Helen coughed again at a cloud of smoke.

"Take some of mine."

Helen dipped water from the proffered bucket, ensconced her pot among coals next to Liza's pot, and crouched to her left. Smoke deposited a layer of grime on her clothing and skin, but how wonderful hot water would feel back at camp, when she washed her face and hands. The previous morning, the distracted Pearsons had brought her coffee but forgot warm water for her morning toilette, so Roger had had to run back and heat water.

To Liza's right, a crouched woman coughed deep and hard, the sound of pneumonia. Helen had seen her stirring pease soup the afternoon she arrived at Woodward's plantation. Even by firelight, the woman looked gaunt.

Liza waved to someone on the other side of the fire circle. "Over here, Rebecca!" She nudged Helen. "Have you met Nan?" Fever glittered in Nan's eyes when she and Helen exchanged a good morning.

A singsong girl-child's voice lifted above the hiss and pop of the fire. "Here's a blanket for Nan, Mama."

"Thank you, Rebecca."

Helen stared at the girl who draped a wool blanket around Nan's shoulders. Then she masked her own expression into neutrality. No mistaking Liza's daughter, the cipher messenger. She'd seen her that first afternoon, too, feeding kindling to the smolder beneath a cauldron of pease soup.

Helen edged closer. "Here with your husband, Nan?"

A grimace puckered the sick woman's mouth. "I buried him at Camden in August."

Helen's heart panged. She soon found out why Nan had stayed with the Legion. Her rebel kin in North Carolina burned their house and barn after her husband joined the Legion. Nan and her thirteen-year-old son barely escaped with their lives. He was the company musician who'd flogged the drunken legionnaire several days earlier.

Helen couldn't linger after her water boiled because others awaited a spot at the fire. She packed the pot, insulated with a towel and old scraps of blanket, in her basket. Her glance returned to Nan. In the widow and her musician son, she'd found focal points for her article on civilians. But as for Liza's daughter Rebecca, transmitter of secret messages, she didn't yet know what to think. To be sure, Rebecca supplemented the family's meager rations, but at what price?

The eastern sky paled, and the trail had grown more trafficked. Near her campsite, she encountered Roger in the company of two legionnaires. Near-panic speared his tone. "Mrs. Chiswell! Where have you been?"

Alarmed that she'd been recognized, Helen closed the shawl around her better to hide her lower-class clothing and straightened her posture. "On a morning stroll."

"Well, you mustn't do that again without at least telling someone where you're going!" Roger flailed his arms around. "Hannah, Mr. Quill, and I had no idea where you were. You weren't even out in the field watching the sunrise as usual!"

The locksmith appeared almost unhinged. Malaise clamped Helen, especially with the presence of the legionnaires. "Roger, there's no cause for alarm. I'm unharmed."

"Tell that to Mr. Fairfax. These lads are ordered to bring you back."

Gods, no, not Fairfax. Arguing with Hannah had cost Roger perspective. In a dither over her absence, the locksmith had sought Fairfax's help. And now she'd gained a jailer.

Obviously, it was time for her to intervene in the Pearsons' domestic squabble. She didn't bother to hide the snap in her voice. "Mr. Fairfax is a busy man. Let's not keep him waiting."

At the campsite, Hannah jumped up from a bench with a cry of relief at the sight of her and rushed forward. "Thank goodness you're well! I'd never have forgiven myself if you'd come to harm." She stared. "That's my shawl!"

"Here. Take it. I must have grabbed it by accident in the dark." Near the bench, Jonathan, who'd been standing, relaxed his shoulders and shot Helen an expression full of perplexity. Guilt surged through her at his look. Maybe she *should* have said something.

Fairfax approached from the picket line. Even from a distance, ice preceded him. She turned her back, knelt, and untied the bottom of her tent flaps enough to slide the basket inside. When she straightened, he was close enough to hear, so she directed a glare at the Pearsons and deepened the snap in her voice. "What's the fuss about? I wanted an early morning walk in solitude. As you can see, I'm unharmed. Did you think I'd been abducted?"

Fairfax's proximity could no longer be ignored, so she shifted her glare to him. Inhumanity seethed in his eyes and wilted her courage. She gulped. Without speaking, he crooked his forefinger at her — *come with me* — and pivoted for the trees.

Jonathan stiffened but didn't interfere. With a ragged exhale, Helen followed the lieutenant. Her fingers had numbed by the time she passed the trees and emerged in the field. Fairfax walked a contemplative circle around the wreath of holly and ivy she'd lain upon the ground Midwinter morning, then studied the eastern sky. She paused about ten feet from him and rubbed her hands.

"What is your business in the lower camp?" He turned and gouged a stare through her.

"I went out for a predawn walk."

"Cease lying to me, Helen. Dressed like a peasant. Reeking of wood smoke. You sneaked away to meet someone in the lower camp and exchange an intelligence report."

"No, not at all. Why do you suspect me of such?" She blinked. He'd positioned her to receive the sunrise full on her face, while he remained backlit by sun, at an advantage for interrogation.

"You evaded Mrs. Pearson yesterday to meet your contact among the rank and file. Did you think Sullivan would say nothing of it to me? The sister of Lieutenant Fairfax dallying among common soldiers. Who is he? To whom are you reporting?"

"No one!" She spread her hands. "I'm not a spy!"

He crossed his arms over his chest. "Perhaps it's time I confined my wayward sister to my marquee for a few days."

Before she could stop herself, she'd backed away a step in horror. "No!" Anger surged through her fear at the smugness on his face, and she lifted her chin. "If you do that, I won't be able to find that desk."

He snorted. "You aren't looking for it."

"But I am. I intend to find it."

"Then stop lying to me and tell me what you're about. You're meeting St. James, aren't you? You're spying for him."

She stamped her foot. "Damn you, I haven't seen him since Wilmington! And I'm not spying. I'm — I'm —" Her shoulders slumped in defeat. "I'm writing another story." She hung her head, knowing he'd mock her. "To show civilians as courageous in this war. One woman in the lower camp was burned out of her home after her husband joined the Legion. She's still here after burying him at Camden because her son now marches on the battlefield —"

"You've allowed personal goals to obscure your priority on this mission: writing about Tarleton and the Legion."

Bitter, disheartened, weary of the confessional, she faced west. Obedience. He wanted obedience. Damn, as long as he didn't imprison her in his marquee. "Whatever you say."

"You shall attire yourself as a lady, clean soot off your face and dirt from beneath your fingernails. Since the clothing you're wearing allows you to mingle in the lower camp, you shall hand both sets of it over to me for safekeeping. Wherever you walk, whenever you walk, you will take at least one attendant with you. I do not expect to hear another report of your dawdling among the rank and file." He walked around and faced her, enjoying every inch of his authority. "And by the bye, it would please me exceedingly if you found my desk."

Chapter Forty-One

FAIRFAX LOITERED IN the campsite until Helen emerged from her tent in a gown, her face and hands scrubbed clean with soap and the warm water she'd obtained on her forbidden excursion. After inspecting her with the enthusiasm he'd grant a barrel of turpentine, the lieutenant left, taking her confiscated clothing and the legionnaires with him.

Embarrassed to meet Helen's eye, Roger set off with Jonathan to make breakfast. Disgusted, she retreated into her tent to capture in her journal as much as she could remember of the trip to the kitchen. Damn Fairfax for being correct. Her priority *was* on the Tarleton feature. But she refused to relinquish the other story.

She became aware of Hannah weeping. After concealing her desk, she exited and sought the Pearsons' tent. "Hannah, what's done is done. Let the events of the morning go, and we shall all move along."

Hannah continued to weep and sounded as though she might be in pain. Concerned, Helen untied the tent flaps and discovered the younger woman curled up on her side among blankets, arms and legs drawn up, head bowed forward, like a baby in a womb. Helen knelt beside her. "What is it? Are you ill?" She pried Hannah's hands from her face. "Talk to me, tell me what's wrong."

The blonde ratcheted up into wild sobs. Confounded, Helen held her. Perhaps Hannah was spending grief, long overdue, on her father. Helen stroked her back and murmured, "I miss him, too, my dear."

A groan trundled from Hannah. "Roger doesn't understand."

The dolt. All he could think about was strutting in a green coat.

"S-Something horrible is g-going to h-happen to the Legion."

"No, the colonel takes care of his men. You've seen how much they trust him." Foreboding sent her memory to Woodward's parlor and the hunger on Tarleton's face: *Mr. Fairfax, have you brought me a rebel spy? You chased him too hard. He's now hiding beneath Daniel Morgan's petticoat.* Vanity and impulsiveness. She winced.

"Ohh, my poor Papa! I m-miss him so. I'm — I'm g-going to have a b-baby."

How c-can I lose Roger, too?" Hannah wailed.

Helen's eyes widened. "Have you told Roger you're with child?"

"Y-Yesss."

Helen fantasized about punching Roger in the nose. Charles would be appalled at his son-in-law. This wasn't about duty to the king. This was about self-indulgence. Vanity and impulsiveness. Cold swept her.

The younger woman's sobs dwindled. After making her more comfortable among the blankets, Helen left the tent to let her rest.

Something horrible is going to happen to the Legion. Smoke from musket fire and cannons, hundreds of legionnaires dead or dying — executed — on a battlefield, horses screaming in fear and agony. In the lovely winter sunshine, Helen shoved the images from her mind.

Back in her tent, she concentrated on her journal. The men returned. She heard Roger gab a rumor that General Greene planned to attack Lord Cornwallis in Winnsborough. Ludicrous. Greene's army was underfed, overworked, and laden with untrained militia. Cornwallis had the seasoned Legion guarding his left flank and reinforcements on the coast, eager to penetrate the interior of South Carolina.

Her mood brusque, she stepped out and draped on her cloak. Roger quieted at the sight of her. "Jonathan, set out breakfast. Roger, this way. I would have a word with you."

They walked about twenty paces, far enough off to not disturb Hannah, and Helen placed the sun in Roger's face. He squinted. "I apologize for what happened this morning, Mrs. Chiswell. I overreacted. I got you in trouble. It won't happen again."

"I'm glad we agree that it won't happen again. Your wife is with child. She also recently lost her father, last of her family. Explain to me why you're so keen on joining the British Legion."

His eyes watered in the light. "I feel strong loyalty to the king."

"Admirable, idealistic. Here's the reality. Hundreds of legionnaires in camp have undergone months of training. You have not. Many are battle-hardened. You are not. If the Legion is attacked, odds are great that you, as a raw recruit, will be one of the first to die.

"How is that more important than giving Hannah the security and love she needs? Bringing a child into this world and helping it thrive and grow is a far greater challenge to a man than stepping out onto a battlefield and pointing his musket at an enemy." Sourness dripped into her tone. "Could it be that's why some men run away and play soldier — because they're not quite grown up, not up to the task of raising a family?"

A snarl rippled over his lips. "Oh, now, see here —"

"Exercise your choice to leap out of my employment into the waiting arms of the Legion, and they'll gladly install you on the front line. But before you do that, think hard on prior promises you made to Charles and Hannah. What does the Legion give you that you lack within yourself? What defines your integrity?"

She returned to the table spread with breakfast. Jonathan bowed. "Porridge and toast with coffee, madam." He pulled a bench over for her.

Shoulders slumped, Roger passed behind Jonathan to his tent. "Keep food warm for the Pearsons, Jonathan," she murmured. She seated herself, and at the smell of the meal, snatched a buttered piece of toast and tore into it with her teeth.

"Yes, madam." Jonathan's electric blue eyes twinkled.

***

Half an hour later, the Pearsons emerged from their tent. When Helen peeped out at them, Roger was serving Hannah breakfast. Helen returned to her writing. Ross, who'd drilled Roger on the Santee Road, showed up to remind the locksmith about a practice. Roger declined to attend. Helen exhaled relief. It felt good to have a united team again.

While the men cleaned up after breakfast, the women combed market for a desk. The tanner caught Helen's eye and shook his head when she passed his stall. He hadn't seen a desk. No desk would appear before Christmas Day, but she'd keep looking.

She overtook a gaggle of officers' wives and bade them good morning, fancying a certain reserve about them. True, she hadn't spent time in their company since Woodward's and had yet to visit the marquee set up at Daniel's for their convenience, so just after noon, she headed there with Hannah to embroider.

Coolness from the ladies met her when she entered. They stopped talking to stare while she settled. When their natter resumed, whispered, she realized they had been gossiping. About her.

In Wilmington, wealthy women had kept a discreet distance from her after her fortune turned, but the Legion's officers weren't from high society. They were wives of middle-class farmers, artisans, and merchants. Helen ignored them.

Margaret sashayed over. "May I see the piece you're embroidering? Daisies, how lovely." She whispered, "Yesterday's incident with the rank and file."

"Why, thank you." Helen pasted on her polite smile. Such stupid, small-minded sows.

Margaret left the marquee, and the buzz among the ladies elevated, availing Helen of snatches of conversation. "Unnatural." "A woman her age still widowed." "No children." "Not with *my* husband." Twice she nudged Hannah to head off a scowl on the younger woman's face. From Hannah's expression, she would have delighted in giving the women a piece of her mind.

One of Tarleton's batmen entered the marquee and glanced around. When he spotted Helen, he strode over and inclined his head. The hens hushed. "Mrs. Chiswell, good afternoon. Colonel Tarleton requests the honor of your company for a ride to hounds at one-thirty."

She heard her own surprise echoed in the silence of the wives and imagined them collecting their jaws off their laps. "One-thirty."

"In about half an hour, madam. My apologies for short notice. I couldn't locate you earlier."

Stares reigned among the wives. Questions crowded Helen's head. She'd wanted the chance to exercise Calliope. Whatever Tarleton's motive for requesting her company, it offered her another excellent opportunity to interview him, even to sketch him, so she'd take her desk in the canvas carrier she'd hastily sewn for it. But she mustn't provide more grist for the gossip mill. "Can suitable mounts be found for my three attendants by one-thirty?"

He inclined his head again. "We shall make it so."

"Very well, I accept." The batman bowed and strode out, and Helen and Hannah scooped up their belongings.

As soon as they left the marquee, conversation exploded from the women inside. One woman's petulance rose above the babble. "He's never asked for *my* company on a ride!"

Helen smirked.

***

Across rolling fields, Tarleton jabbered about London's theater, the political scene, and what Helen suspected was a "ladies'" version of his escapades at Oxford, where he'd studied law. He timed their return for tea, his talk of horses and hounds, held still long enough for her to sketch him, and seemed pleased with the outcome. Then he capped off the afternoon with a gallant kiss upon her hand.

Exceptional fodder for her feature story. Guaranteed, a solid block of writing time. On the walk back to their campsite, she chatted with Jonathan and the Pearsons. However had she managed to obtain an uninterrupted afternoon with busy Colonel Tarleton? What good fortune! Journalists on both sides of the Atlantic would steam with envy.

Fairfax was waiting at their campsite with Kennelly. The Pearsons and Jonathan filed past him. The lieutenant bowed to Helen. Pleased to have the Spanish desk concealed in canvas, she quipped, "Have you been waiting long?" Whatever his business was, she hoped he'd waited quite awhile.

His gaze wandered the length of her, and that faint smile permeated his expression. "How was your ride with Colonel Tarleton?"

"Very informative. He —" Comprehension smacked her. "*You* arranged it." So she'd have no lack of material to write about and not feel inclined to sneak back to the camp women. Plus, her absence had given him ample time to search their tents.

Fairfax shrugged. "He leaped at my suggestion with such enthusiasm that it was obvious he'd been pondering exactly how to initiate the opportunity on his own."

Fairfax studied each of his subjects until he knew the exact chords to strike to make them vibrate and dance. A composer experimenting with harmonics, he'd played her all along the Santee Road. He manipulated Tarleton over her with such finesse that the colonel, a renowned womanizer, wasn't even cognizant of it. How that could possibly bode well for the Legion, she couldn't imagine. Her premonition from the morning resurfaced, climbed into her throat. "Something horrible is going to happen to the Legion," she muttered.

His study of her sharpened. His humor vanished. "What was that?"

Embarrassment flooded her at having thought aloud. "Nothing."

"Colonel Tarleton is Cornwallis's finest cavalry commander. What except good can happen to the Legion?" He gripped her upper arm, expression intense. "You've received intelligence otherwise."

"Bah!" She shook him off and lowered her voice. "You're manipulating Tarleton over me."

He relaxed. "Hardly. Unless you dosed him with aloofness, he'll likely inquire after your company again. As I commented once before, you're a delectable piece of work." His gaze strolled over her, and she remembered the way he and Badley had ogled her in the publisher's study after exercise had brought color to her cheeks and lips. "You're welcome, darling," he whispered. After inclining his head, he walked off, Kennelly following.

Chapter Forty-Two

SATURDAY THE TWENTY-THIRD, no military rumors circulated, no desk appeared in market, and Helen avoided officers' wives. She'd stumbled across a smaller secret compartment in the desk the night before. The entire day she wrestled with the urge to send an anonymous note to Tarleton: "Beware. Fairfax manipulates you." But there were far easier ways to commit suicide.

The morning of the twenty-fourth, day of the Yule celebration, she awoke to the aroma of roasted hog and root vegetables, slow-cooked the night before in pits. Mid-morning, while she was reinforcing stitches on the canvas bag she'd sewn for her desk, Hannah came to the door of her tent. "A message from the lower camp, madam. A tanner says an item you were looking for in market has arrived, and he's secured it for you."

"I'll be right out." Astounded, Helen jammed her sewing kit together and shoved the desk in the bag. Shawls thrown on, they hastened for the lower camp.

Camden and Ninety Six were close enough to receive Neville's express request for a desk, but Helen doubted that Ninety Six commanded a ready stock of pretty, portable desks. Even assuming one could be found in Camden was a stretch. If Treadaway appeared in camp that day, she'd know who had planted the desk for Fairfax to find.

The tanner turned business over to his assistant as soon as he spotted her. All smiles, he led her to the booth of a pewterer where, to their surprise, they were in time to see the pewterer hand a portable mahogany desk over to Fairfax.

"Hullo, what do you think you're doing?" Scowling, the tanner stalked over to the pewterer and shoved him in the chest. "I paid you to hold that desk for *my* customer, not to steal my money and sell the desk to *your* customer, you greedy bastard!"

"Watch your tongue, cheap bugger." The pewterer shoved the tanner back. "I'll tell everyone here about them inferior hides you was passing around beginning of the month."

The tanner lunged for him. Fists swung. Patrons, Helen and Hannah included, rushed from the marquee. The provost's men stormed in and hauled the merchants apart, but they kept threatening each other. Helen peered around the fracas to discover that Fairfax had never left the marquee. Unperturbed, he inspected the desk with the same concentration that he'd lavished on her broken window and journal. She circled the crowd to him.

He didn't pause his inspection. "Darling, look what I found."

"Wrong. I found it. The tanner set it aside for me. You owe me seven and a half shillings."

"Wrong. I owe you nothing." He turned the desk upside down. "Do you suppose it contains a false bottom?"

"You son of a jackal."

He snickered. "So I've been called before. Something tells me that this isn't the desk for me, although I shall purchase it anyway, just to be certain."

She flounced from the marquee, poor pregnant Hannah jogging to keep up with her. Too well, Helen knew what a dancing poppet felt like, and she'd grown weary of it.

Closer to her campsite, Fairfax rode up, dismounted, and handed over the reins to Kennelly so he could walk beside her. "Ire brings such a magnificent flush to your face." She kept walking and looked straight ahead. "I suppose this means you won't dance with me tonight." Not even if he was the only man on the dance ground, which he wouldn't be. She continued to ignore him. "I'm not sure how much you agreed to pay the tanner, but he was delighted over the nine pence I gave him. I never expected such effort on your part to locate the desk. You've redeemed yourself greatly in my sight."

Spoken as if he'd bequeathed a gift of immense value upon her. Fury simmered inside her again. She began counting in silence. One. Two. Three. Four...

"If you'd just tell me when David St. James sneaks into camp — oh, that's right. You're still pretending he won't be here."

David *wasn't* coming. David wasn't an idiot. Five. Six. Seven. Eight... She was running out of numbers.

He sighed. "I hope you won't lack for dance partners. Good day."

★★★

A substantial amount of cooked hog and vegetables, baked apples and pears, and cornbread vanished before dark — largesse from Tarleton, distributed among the rank and file. After nightfall, in a torch-rimmed field north of the manor house, Helen, her garnets at her throat and ears, wandered from a huge bowl of mulled cider to a huge bowl of waes hail to a supply of the best wines from market, avoiding Treadaway. The agent had indeed arrived early that morning, well before the tanner notified her of the desk.

By the time she sat with the officers and their ladies, she'd consumed enough wine to not give a jot whether the overcast sky sprinkled on them. On another section of tables, Treadaway, well into his cups, ogled the cleavage of someone's mistress. She made a mental note to steer clear of him for the remainder of the evening. Thank heaven the agent had never appeared to connect her with the girl in the tool shed.

During the first course of onion soup, she was seated next to Fairfax, but they ignored each other, and the fellow on her other side stayed sober long enough to hold a lucid conversation about deer hunting. How much more pleasant the night would be were she seated with Jonathan. They'd race to identify the herbs and spices in each course, laughing over recipes divine and disastrous. Jonathan danced well, too. But alas, his portrayal of a servant denied them each other's company at both supper table and dance ground.

After the soup was cleared away, a bell rang, and the men scrambled to switch seats, to the laughter and surprise of the ladies. Broiled bass appeared on the tables, and Helen got to hear about horse racing and advantages of various firearms from a cornet and a captain.

The bass vanished, the bell rang again, and Tarleton, ruddy-cheeked, wine goblet in hand, redirected an officer of the militia so he could plant himself next to Helen and scowl at her. Gold and braid on his uniform winked in the candlelight. "You've no idea how I've had to fight my way over here." A plate containing half a chicken manifested on the table before him. She laughed. "Madam, I need your advice on a delicate matter. With whom should I dance the first tune?"

She spotted Margaret in conversation with Fairfax. "Margaret, of course."

"How orthodox. What of the second tune, then?" He wiggled his eyebrows at her.

"With the lady attached to the officer of the highest rank."

"That might be you."

"Mmm, probably not." She shaved a piece of chicken from the plate set before her.

"Exactly when may I presume to dance with you, then? Third?"

"How about the fifth dance?" The soup hadn't quite been hot enough, and the bass was bland, but the chicken was moist and flavorful. She chewed in haste lest someone collect their plates while Tarleton distracted her with flirting, and before she could eat enough.

"The *fifth* dance?" Mock outrage flooded his expression. "Never have I had to wait so many tunes to dance with a woman." He leaned his elbow on the table, pressed his forehead to his palm, and heaved a sigh. "I may languish before then."

"Try the chicken," she whispered. "It will sustain you."

"How cruel." He hacked off a drumstick. "You enjoy chicken while I swoon at your side." He nibbled at the drumstick. "I'm ready to cast my heart at your feet, and — hmm." He chewed off a larger bite and swallowed. "You know, you're right, the chicken is delicious. I'm curious about something."

Beguiling dark eyes beamed playfulness at her. She shivered pleasantly in response. "Do ask."

"When do you expect David St. James to visit you in camp?"

Shock withered her good humor and stiffened her expression. "I'm certain I've no idea what you're talking about, sir."

He barked out a laugh. "Thus spake his mistress." A flush stormed to her face, and he laughed again. "It's his father I'm after. I've hanged a rebel in almost every trade, but never a printer. I don't know whether I'd have forgiven Pat Ferguson if he'd dispatched Will St. James for me. And now, St. James has run to the protection of Daniel Morgan's camp."

Cold spread through Helen's limbs. Although Tarleton made light of it,

David's father had deeply angered him, pricked his pride by printing that broadside. Tarleton wouldn't rest until he'd captured and hanged him.

Somehow Fairfax had tapped into and aggravated the wound. Anxiety claimed Helen. "You don't really want to wade through General Morgan's camp to fetch him, do you? I mean, wouldn't that be ill-advised? Surely there are other rebel printers around, all of them easier to nab."

He grinned. "The more difficulty, the more glory, madam. And for the same reason, I await the fifth dance tonight with infinite patience."

The bell rang a third time. "You will send for me immediately, won't you, if St. James's son pays you a visit in camp?" He bowed and sauntered off with his wine goblet to flatter another woman.

Helen watched him go, her soul tunneled with misgiving. If David were daft enough to sneak into camp and get himself captured, it wouldn't matter whether he knew how to find his father. Tarleton would have him tortured to death. Meanwhile, the Legion's commander crouched with "infinite patience" while Will St. James hid in the mishmash army of Daniel Morgan to the north. Tarleton thirsted to hang St. James. What in the world was he waiting for?

He awaited the blessings of his commander, the Earl Cornwallis, before turning loose the wolves of the Legion upon Morgan — and Will St. James. And Fairfax had convinced him that every bit of it was his own brainchild.

Chapter Forty-Three

NEVILLE, IN HIS hunting shirt, put in an appearance at the main course and tricked a wine-befuddled ensign out of a seat next to Helen. "I apologize for my tardiness. An officer's paperwork must be finished before play."

Especially paperwork that involved scripting another cipher and concealing it in her desk while everyone was busy. And Treadaway was present to retrieve the coded update himself.

She longed to compliment the ranger on the handsome desk his partner had procured to allay Fairfax's suspicions, just to see his reaction. "Your timing is exquisite. I'd saved the first dance for you and was about to relinquish it to someone else."

He speared pork with his knife. "Aren't you dancing the first with Mr. Fairfax?"

She shook her head. "Sibling spat." Amusement relaxed his expression, and she wondered how far she could get Neville to drop his guard, short of a seduction attempt. After all, she wasn't *desperate* to find out which regiments had formed the cabal to discredit Tarleton and redirect Legion resources.

During the fruit and cheese, privates lit the Yule bonfire to one side of the dance ground. Two other privates tuned their fiddles. The more affluent merchants and contractors arrived with their ladies. Except for the fiddlers and men who cleaned up the feast, no rank and file were present. Helen suspected the merchants and contractors had received invitations only to bolster the ranks of women upon the dance ground. The exclusivity amused her. In reality, since the regiment was provincial, negligible social and economic distinction existed between officers and merchants.

Successful at evading Treadaway the entire meal and lining up partners for additional dances, Helen took position on the grounds with Neville for the first tune. As she'd promised him more dances that evening, she was gratified to discover that he could actually dance. However, she wasn't pleased to spot Fairfax observing them from the sidelines.

The fifth tune, couples lined up for a hornpipe, and Tarleton bounded over and claimed her, playacting snaps and growls at men who flocked around her. He paraded her into position with him at the head of the line, eager eyes on her sweat. Clearly he'd transcended his self-imposed proscription over wooing sisters of officers.

Fairfax nodded approval at her, and her stomach tensed with annoyance.

After the sixth tune, danced with Neville, she snagged Hannah and a lantern from where servants gathered beyond the sidelines. During a moment of inattention, Fairfax missed their departure. At least five more tunes would be played before musicians and dancers took a break, so she had a good half hour to snoop back at the tents.

The lantern outside her tent stood in the position she'd left it. Puzzled, she ducked inside with the lit lantern and withdrew the desk from its canvas bag. The drawer was empty. How was that possible? With Treadaway in camp, surely Neville planned for a cipher pickup. Annoyed, she closed the drawer, tucked the desk back in the bag, and grabbed her fan.

Wait. There was a smaller compartment. She returned to the desk and popped open the compartment. Her eyes bugged at a scrap of paper no more than three inches square lodged inside. No cipher, the plain script on it read: *S — F in camp through new year — N.*

"N" had to be Neville, but why did he forgo using both code names and cipher — and why employ the secondary compartment? Who was "S?" She stared at the body of the message. "F." Winter teased her spine. Was "F" Fairfax?

Was Neville working *two* teams, a double agent?

Arctic cold crawled beneath her cloak. Rebecca wasn't coming to the tent that night for a pickup. Nor was Treadaway. The message in the smaller compartment was intended for a different audience than those who plotted to divert Legion resources. The unknown messenger could, that moment, be watching, waiting for her to leave. She must discover who it was.

She closed the compartment and bagged up the desk. Outside her tent, she raised her voice. "I *finally* found that blasted fan, Hannah. Do let's hurry back!" She set out at a brisk pace north, toward the tumult of the dance ground, and Hannah followed.

The trail was deserted. They passed two other campsites. Helen darted a look around, snatched the lantern from Hannah and covered the light, grabbed Hannah's hand, and towed her behind a set of tents. "Hush!" she whispered to the startled blonde. "We're going back there for a look. We must be quiet, or we'll scare them off." Hannah nodded, and Helen could tell she was curious, if confused.

They doubled back and crouched behind an unoccupied tent less than twenty-five feet from Helen's, providing an unobstructed view of their tents as well as the trail. Helen whispered, "We may be here a quarter hour." She didn't expect to wait longer than that. Any messenger would come before the break, before the risk of discovery, when a few dancers might trickle back to tents to fetch personal items like fans.

Minutes passed. Music and crowd-noise from the dance flitted, disembodied, out to them. Damp seeped into Helen's feet and ankles, and dew clasped her cheeks.

Hannah clutched her forearm and pointed. A man of medium height darted across the trail from behind a tree and into their campsite carrying a covered lantern. Helen stared, trying to resolve more of his features before he ducked into her tent. Cocked hat over dark hair, another redcoat — but not of the Seventeenth Light dragoons.

Lantern light blossomed within her tent. Hannah whispered, "He's thieving from you!"

"Be still. Watch."

Soon the light extinguished, and the man emerged. As he retied tent flaps, motion on the trail caught Helen's gaze: a lone woman strolling south. Helen held her breath. Unaware that the woman walked his way, the man shot from the campsite out onto the road. They collided.

The woman squeaked in fright, and he grunted in surprise before grasping her upper arm. "Madam, I do apologize. I didn't see you out here. Are you injured?"

Yorkshire accent, Helen thought.

"No, but you gave me quite a scare." That was Margaret's voice. "I'm looking for a friend of mine. She might have passed this way shortly before me with her maid. Did you see her?"

Helen's eyes widened. Margaret was looking for *her*. Fairfax had sent her after them.

The man released Margaret. "I did not. Excuse me —"

"Say, I know you. Stafford is your name."

"You've mistaken me for someone else, madam." He sounded annoyed. "Good night."

Margaret snapped her fingers. "Camden, in August, at the Leaping Stag. You questioned me about Lieutenants Neville and Fairfax, and that young woman who'd lived in the inn with us." Margaret offered a deep-throated laugh. "Alas, I didn't get *your* kind often enough. Just wanting to talk, you know, Mr. Stafford — no, that's not your name. It's Stoddard. Lieutenant Stoddard."

"You're looking for two women, correct? Now I remember. I saw them walking south not a minute earlier." The dark-haired man twisted and pointed. "If you hurry, I'm sure you'll catch them."

"Thank you, Mr. Stoddard." Satisfaction purred in Margaret's voice. "There's jollification and merriment in the north field. Do join us. I'll dance with you." She curtsied and hurried south.

Lieutenant Stoddard sprinted across the trail and vanished. Helen doubted he'd turn up at the dance. At least now she knew who "S," "F," and "N" were. Why was Neville exchanging secret messages about Fairfax with this Lieutenant Stoddard?

She insisted upon another visit to her tent before they returned and, with Hannah waiting outside, confirmed that the uncoded message was missing from the second compartment. "What did he steal?" muttered Hannah while Helen tied up the tent.

"Nothing, just as I expected. You saw nothing, Hannah, nor did you hear anything, unless I ask you to remember what you witnessed."

The blonde lifted her chin. "Yes, madam. I saw and heard nothing. We returned to your tent to fetch your fan."

Helen popped open the fan. "Precisely."

They reentered the festivities through a cluster of servants and slaves beyond the sidelines who swayed, clapped hands, and stomped feet to the music. Helen waved off Jonathan's "Where have you been?" expression and sneaked around the perimeter, spite curling her lips at the thought of Fairfax sending Margaret after her. A fiddler botched a measure, and sweat beaded foreheads of dancers. The current tune was the final one before the break.

Fairfax's scrutiny of the crowd was so intense that she startled a jump from him when she sidled up next to him. "My goodness, it's warm after you've danced a few tunes." She fanned herself.

He scowled. "Where the devil have you been for half an hour?"

"Half an hour? Poppycock. Hannah and I slipped out for five minutes so I could fetch my fan. Hmm. It looks as though Margaret isn't here. Rotten luck for you."

"Why should I care?"

"Earlier, she rushed past my tent toward the lower camp. My impression was that she knew exactly where to find entertainment there far more appealing than waiting on *your* favor."

The vacuum Fairfax created when he departed sizzled with his wrath. Watching him thread his way south out of the crowd, Helen allowed the wicked smile full sway across her face and murmured, "What a shrew you can be, Helen." Perhaps next time, Margaret would employ discretion before agreeing to spy for Fairfax.

Chapter Forty-Four

THIRTY-SEVEN PEOPLE ATTENDED the chaplain's sermon on drizzly Christmas morning. The faint headache pressing Helen's temples led her to conclude that everyone else was too hung over. She'd rather not have left her tent, except that some Londoners might find coverage of a Christmas service picturesque.

Officers, including Fairfax, comprised much of the congregation. Considering his religious persuasion, Helen wondered how many other officers were just putting in time on the Anglican Church's calendar. How Tarleton managed to drag himself to the sermon after his revelry the night before amazed her. Also, he appeared to be paying more than lip service to the chaplain's message. Remarkable, in light of the rebels' attempts to depict him a godless heathen.

Tuesday morning the twenty-sixth, an express rider galloped in from Winnsborough. Within a quarter hour, intelligence penned by Cornwallis swept camp like fire in a drought-stricken forest, confirming earlier rumors. Six days before, General Greene had marched the bulk of the Continental Army to the Cheraws in South Carolina, about fifty miles northeast of Camden. And General Morgan had already crossed the Broad River with militia and William Washington's cavalry.

The logic of why Greene divided his army, inferior to that of Cornwallis, into two smaller, even more inferior forces, eluded Helen. She and Jonathan spread his map of the Carolinas open upon the table and, with the Pearsons watching, positioned pebbles to mark Crown forces spread in an imposing arc from George Town to Ninety Six, as well as the armies of Greene and Morgan. Jonathan stepped back to study the big picture. "Interesting. Very interesting."

Roger laughed. "We'll grind them to stubble if they push south."

"Perhaps." Jonathan rested the tip of one forefinger on Greene's pebble and the other on Morgan's and dragged them downward at a diagonal to converge on and pinch the Cornwallis pebble in Winnsborough like two halves of a tongs.

Helen's eyebrows rose. "Jonathan, if *you* can see that as an option —"

"Then Cornwallis sees it, too." His eyes twinkled. "You'd hoped to write action into your feature, my dear. You may soon get it."

In the marketplace that morning, more sutlers, peddlers, and merchants had descended upon the camp and opened for business, divining that off-duty legionnaires were willing to splurge. Unmistakable, the bright eyes of legionnaires, their swaggers and rough laughter. After a month of inaction, the men thirsted to be about their business, subduing insurrection and ensuring the safety of their homes.

A milliner was doing brisk business among the officers' ladies, and Helen spotted Margaret posing before a mirror with a stylish hat upon her head. Camp women crowded three peddlers: a paunchy, loquacious fellow who brandished bolts of fabric, a redhead with dried herbs to sell, and a third hawking well-cured deer hides. As fast as they could sell their merchandise, their assistant, a gangly, hunched man with a gray beard and filthy, floppy hat, was there to replace a satchel of herbs or a hide or some fabric.

Entertained by the haggling, Helen's regard returned to the old man. Something about him seemed familiar. His hands. They bothered her. Odd. They weren't the knobby, vein-protruding hands of an old man, but those of a man much younger.

He angled his head up long enough for gray eyes to become visible beyond the brim of the hat, his gaze piercing straight into her. She drew a breath of sheer horror. Hot and cold spun her.

Oh, no, dear gods, no — David St. James.

"Mrs. Chiswell, good morning!"

She jumped what felt like a foot in the air before pivoting to spot Tarleton dismount, swan feathers aflutter, buttons and braid agleam, and strut for her with the playful grin she'd seen a great deal of during Yule. Handsome, handsome. Her back to David, she felt his stare incinerate a hole through her cloak and gown and burrow to her heart. *You will send for me immediately, won't you, if St. James's son pays you a visit in camp?*

Tarleton caught her hand and kissed it. "God's foot, you've lost the color in your face. You aren't going to faint, are you? Whose ghost have you just seen? Not mine, I trust."

"Oh, goodness, no, you — you startled me, sir." David was close enough to hear the exchange. She tried to withdraw her hand, but Tarleton had a good grip on it, so she gestured with the other hand. "Your lady's over there in the milliner's. She's found herself an adorable hat —"

"Splendid. Ride with me again." One eyebrow wiggled.

Half-request, half-command, whole double entendre. Yes, he'd surmounted the sibling issue, or perhaps Fairfax had dispensed with her cover as his sister. Helen worked her mouth but couldn't get a word out. A kind man whose love she'd never been able to return watched them with his heart breaking in two. And Fairfax was dancing *all* his poppets on the stage that moment.

Her hesitation invigorated Tarleton. He jerked his head in the direction of the milliner's stall. "Let's have a look at those hats."

Oh, no, now he was trying to buy her. "Er, what day did you have in mind for the ride?"

Eyes glittering, he closed in. "Day after the morrow. Three o'clock. Supper afterwards, in my marquee." His thumb massaged her fingers.

Was he dismissing Morgan's army, due north? What invincible arrogance. Conquest of any sort must be such fun for him. If there was a wager out as to how soon he'd boot Daniel Morgan in the arse, there was a wager out that he'd bed Helen Chiswell, too.

She reassembled her brains and attempted to pull her hand away, again without success. Maybe she could arrange to fall ill the day after the morrow. Maybe a blizzard would dump a foot of snow on the Carolinas. "Those rebels to the north may decide to attack by then."

"We shall trounce them, and I shall return for our ride."

Agamemnon, Odysseus, Hercules. From his expression, her dithering heightened his interest and increased his stakes in the game. He leaned forward, smiling in anticipation, ready to parry her next objection with ease.

Helen knew with whom Margaret would be occupied during that supper. The only question was whether the four of them would dance a double *pas de deux* in Tarleton's marquee later, but that was too much for her mind to fathom with David privy to the whole earthy mess. "A ride, then. Perhaps supper, but I may be too fatigued by then." That gave her forty-eight hours to concoct an eloquent refusal of the enterprise that would offend no one except Fairfax.

Although she'd agreed to only the ride, Tarleton radiated confidence at obtaining the entire package. He lifted her hand to his lips again before he bowed and took leave of her. Waving to legionnaires in market, he rode off, bodyguards and foxhounds following. Without difficulty, she envisioned him whisking mistresses from beneath the noses of complacent noblemen in Parliament.

Hannah edged up to her. "A fine feast for the eyes, isn't he?"

Flummoxed, Helen realized she was fanning herself and stopped. Then the bottom dropped out of her euphoria. David had watched her make a fool of herself. She spun around, but he'd turned his back on her to fulfill orders for the peddlers. Well, what did she expect?

Not for the world would she have inflicted such a blow on him. She had no idea why he'd risked his life by coming to camp, but by then she doubted he wanted to hear her explanations. For certain, he mustn't linger.

She gripped Hannah by the elbow and drew her away, separating them from the peddlers and David by several merchants' stalls. "Hannah, look at those three peddlers. Do you see their assistant, that old man?" The blonde nodded without recognition. Helen wasn't certain how many times she'd ever met David. "Good. I need you to take a message to him. But you must deliver it to him without it being obvious."

She purchased a bottle of cider. The merchant allowed her use of his stationery and ink to jot a note to David: *Leave camp immediately. F and T will execute you and your father.* She sprinkled fine sand to dry the ink, folded the paper, and gave it to Hannah.

From the merchant's stall, she watched Hannah mosey over to the peddlers, poke around the deer hides, display casual interest in a bolt of fabric and receive an earful from the paunchy peddler about what a deal he'd strike for her, and, without purchasing a thing, brush past David and palm him the note. David slid it into a grimy haversack on his shoulder as he handed a bag of herbs to the red-haired peddler.

On their return to the campsite, Hannah remained quiet until they'd cleared most of the lower camp. Then she said, low, "The old man I gave the note to wasn't old at all."

"Now, Hannah —"

"Yes, madam, I understand. I see and hear nothing unless you ask me to do so."

★★★

Jonathan retired to his tent soon after supper and grew quiet, as did the Pearsons. Helen stayed up past ten writing in her journal. With so much talk of how backcountry militiamen couldn't be relied upon to support the king, Londoners would be delighted to read of the perseverance of the king's provincial soldiers. When the ink had dried on her entry, she closed the journal, blew out the lantern, and crawled into her cot.

Almost as soon as she'd grown comfortable, grass rustled outside the tent, and a familiar whisper floated in through the flaps. "Helen, are you awake? Let me in. We have to talk!"

She bolted up and dangled her feet over the side of the cot, her heart stammering with fear. David, that fool, that utterly crazy fool. Why did he not comprehend *leave camp immediately*?

Chapter Forty-Five

"DON'T PULL THE beard," he whispered. "I'm not sure what paste they used, but I may sacrifice a layer of skin to remove it."

"You stink," she whispered back, cheek pressed to his shoulder, arms wrapped around him.

"Thank you. That's part of the disguise, too."

Her stomach flip-flopped in fear and fury. *Why* hadn't David listened to her? She dislodged herself from his embrace and guided him to the stool, where he sat with a low groan. A blanket wrapped round her shoulders, she slouched upon her cot. "Why are you here?"

"Exactly what I might ask of you."

"Fairfax and Tarleton plan to execute you and your father."

"Harrumph, after what I've been through, what's an execution? Zounds, Helen, you're following the British Legion — and posing as Fairfax's sister! I thought Enid had lost her mind when she told me. Thank Badley and Prescott for finally making sense of it all."

Badley and Prescott? Enid? Pieces connected in Helen's head. "You didn't run away that night. You hid and waited, and you returned to my house on Second Street after I'd left town."

"And it's a good thing I did so. Otherwise, your scummy publisher and his mastiff would have murdered Enid." Helen stiffened on her cot. "Relax. She's unharmed. Middle of the night, they raided your study for Silas's will. I ran them off with my fowler."

Of course the whole black, bloody mess was about Silas's will. She'd realized that for weeks. "I'd a copy filed with my ledgers."

"They weren't after that edition. Isaiah Hanley's widow had the *unaltered* version, which she's put in the care of your attorney. Ten years ago, Silas brought Hanley a copy of his will and asked him to protect it. Unfortunately for most parties involved, Mr. Hanley had a stroke and was unable to communicate where he'd stashed the will. His widow found the will late October, when she was preparing to sell the house."

"Badley and Prescott must have heard rumors that she'd found the will. Charles knew Silas's original will was much different. Hannah told me so. He was a threat to Badley and Prescott."

"'They'll kill Madam if they find it,'" murmured David.

Anger surged through Helen. "Those *dogs*. They hired Arthur Sims to silence Charles and Widow Hanley's messenger. They even tried to kill Jonathan on the chance that he suspected something."

"And they stole Silas's pistol to implicate you in Charles's murder. Badley and Prescott will murder without compunction to avoid being exposed for perjury. It really is too bad they can only be hanged once apiece."

Helen felt weary. "I presume the original will left me a more substantial dower, plus a tidy sum to Charles Landon."

"Ah. So you do know."

"What did Badley and Prescott do with the money?"

"An excellent question. No one knows. Must have been something extraordinary for them to kill to cover their tracks."

She shook her head. "What did they confess?" David cleared his throat, as if uncomfortable. "The Committee of Safety *does* have them in custody?"

"Not exactly. The Committee seized their properties. Badley escaped on a ship to some relative's estate in the Caribbean."

"Bah. He can be fetched back for trial. Where's Prescott?"

"Last reported headed for the North Carolina backcountry." He cut off her hard sigh of incredulity. "See here, you took this assignment because you needed money. Badley lured you out here in the wilderness and hoped you'd get killed, but it's over now. In Wilmington, the properties of Badley and Prescott will provide you with a comfortable dower the rest of your life.

"Prescott is running loose in the hinterland. He wants to kill you. You're asking to die anyway by following the Legion. Two rebel armies are ready to stomp into pulp anyone wearing a green or red uniform in South Carolina. And you're posing as Fairfax's sister! For Christ's sake, that's insane! For no rational reason should you still be here."

In the darkness, she gazed at him a few seconds and processed the reason of his case. "I'm here because there are stories of courageous people that need to be told."

"What are you talking about?"

"The women and children who follow the army, for example."

He groaned again. "That story will never sell. No one cares about them. Don't you understand? The curtain closed on the final act of Badley and Prescott's play. There's no assignment from London, no publisher for whatever story you develop."

A geyser of irritation spouted in her chest. "You don't know that!"

"Helen, be realistic. You're stuck here because Badley's advance ran out." Bitterness wrapped his whisper. "Faced with selling yourself because you cannot leave. It's not worth becoming Banastre Tarleton's mistress. Let me help you. I can get you out!"

He could get her out? Taken aback, she stared at the outline of his form. Logic clamored within her, urging her to listen to him. Did she need to stay? Surely she'd collected enough information about Tarleton by then to create a feature that would dazzle any Loyalist or Crown publisher. David was correct:

the British Legion was a more dangerous regiment to be following than a regular regiment. Furthermore, something nefarious and clandestine was going on beneath the surface with Neville, Treadaway, and the mysterious Lieutenant Stoddard, thus increasing the hazard of her circumstances. One of those rebel generals posturing about to the north was bound to direct aggression upon the Legion soon. Winter was upon them all. Was she so very certain that people cared to hear about the courage of camp women and children? "Get me out — how?"

"Early on the morrow, the peddlers I'm traveling with will leave camp with a rolled rug. We'll hide you inside it."

The logistics felt wrong, and the absurdity of the image claimed her. Hadn't Cleopatra performed that stunt to gain an audience with Julius Caesar? Ice washed over her when she envisioned a legionnaire ramming a bayonet into the rolled rug for a routine inspection. "How did you convince peddlers to engage in such a risky operation?"

"Money. And I know the three of them from last summer."

Three peddlers and David as her bodyguard. She pictured the men who'd sold their wares in market and without difficulty imagined them scampering away from altercations, regardless of how much David had paid them. In a low voice, she said, "What about the Pearsons? They came with me as my attendants."

Obstinacy coated David's tone. "We haven't made provision for them."

"And Jonathan Quill?"

"The Professor will have to find his own way out."

In the darkness, for the first time, she recognized undertones that David's carefree expressions and postures had masked for eleven years. He was jealous of Jonathan, envious of the intimacy the two shared in their imaginations, a unity forged during an Atlantic crossing. David knew that no matter how long he remained her lover, no matter how often their bodies coupled, he would never, ever touch the core of her imagination as Jonathan did.

In horror and betrayal, she covered her mouth with her hands. David was willing to leave his rival behind, consign him to death. Death *was* what the Pearsons and Jonathan would receive if she sneaked from camp — but not before they'd each been tortured.

Had Fairfax, who'd anticipated David's visit, also anticipated her attempt at just such an absurd, harebrained escape as David proposed? She, David, and three peddlers couldn't help but leave a trail easy to follow. Fairfax would hunt them down, drag them back to camp — just as Octavius Caesar might have hauled a chained Cleopatra and her servants through the streets of Rome — and torture them. Hairs stood out along the back of Helen's neck and the length of her arms.

Ferocity and fear fueled David's whisper. "Why dally? We love each other. Let's go!"

She hugged herself and shook her head again, her heart breaking this time, her voice no more than a croak. "No."

"*No?* Bloody hell, can it be that you don't understand the evil with which you've aligned yourself? I'm not speaking of Tarleton and the Legion. I'm talking about Fairfax."

"I can manage Fairfax."

"'Manage' Fairfax? Christ, Helen, don't tell me you've slept with him. No one manages Fairfax. The gods only know how many people he's murdered. He flayed alive a Spaniard in Alton."

Her stomach flipped about again, this time with more fear. "That's the second time you've told me that story about the flayed Spaniard, but I've yet to hear any proof behind it."

"The lieutenant who replaced Fairfax at the garrison in Alton." David's voice held steady. "Astute fellow. He was assigned to solve the murder. We're certain he figured it out, but the redcoats pinned it on another Spaniard. Damn them, protecting their own demon."

In the darkness, she stared at him, intuition clanging. *The lieutenant who replaced Fairfax.* "What was the lieutenant's name?"

"Michael Stoddard. But he's of no consequence here. I have to get you out of camp."

Helen held her breath. Contrary to David's assessment, she suspected Lieutenant Michael Stoddard *was* of consequence. Neville sent secret messages to him about Fairfax's itinerary in a compartment of the desk separate from the Epsilon messages, implying that Stoddard was *not* allied with Neville's schemes with Newman and Treadaway. Rather than trying to protect Fairfax, she'd received the distinct impression that Stoddard was covertly aligned against him.

"Didn't you hear me? Get dressed. Let's be off."

Helen exhaled. "I cannot leave my friends behind. They'll be executed." More realization stunned tears to her eyes. She didn't *desire* David. Had she ever desired him, lusted for him? Yet she'd clutched him to her. Somewhere out there was a woman who was right for him, and she'd waited years for the witch in Wilmington to turn him loose. "David, I-I don't know how to tell you this except just to say it. I've never been able to love you the way you've needed to be loved. I have to let you go."

A noise issued from him as if he'd been punched in the pit of the stomach. He cast himself at her feet and hugged her lower legs. "Helen, sweetheart, you're in so much danger. You cannot realize what you're saying."

She ached to stroke him again, soothe him, but that would only prolong the severing. That moment, she had to break clean from him, or he'd never find the strength to scramble away to safety. "I've had weeks to think about *us*. It's not fair to either of us to continue this way. And — and your family needs you. Your niece Betsy has had a baby." A tear leaked from her right eye and rolled down her cheek. She should have released him years ago, but she didn't have the courage. Her weakness had drawn him into the snare, endangered his life. "If you don't leave camp, if Fairfax catches you — oh, gods, stop trying to be my hero! I don't want to be rescued! I want you to leave, run away!" And live. Yes, David must live, because the elementals she battled cared little for him, but they were willing to dash him to pieces.

She bent over, wrenched his arms from around her legs, and shoved his chest, pushing him backward. He sprawled on his buttocks and hands near the doorway.

The first spear of agony from the terminated love affair whistled out his lungs. *Rhiannon thinks you'll do some singing on this dangerous quest of yours.* Damn all the gods! Was David singing that moment? Was she really expected to sing? She clenched anguish between her teeth. "Leave! Don't come back for me!"

For long moments that wrenched and warped her soul, she feared he wouldn't go, and he'd crawl back to her. She doubted she had the strength to cast him from her a second time. At last, he shuffled to a standing position, his breathing ragged. "I won't *ever* stop loving you." He flung aside the tent flap and staggered out into the night.

Slumped onto her cot, she whispered, "Oh, yes, you will, David." Then she buried her face into her pillow and muffled the release of more than a decade of tears.

Chapter Forty-Six

REVEILLE THE NEXT morning might as well have been metal tent spikes hammered into Helen's temples. From the way her heart ached, the entire camp of legionnaires used it overnight for bayonet practice. Her face felt swollen three times its normal size, her eyes as though sand had scoured them. The whole night, she'd questioned her judgment. She didn't love David — or did she? Her decision benefited all parties in the long run — or did it? She had good reason to remain on assignment — or did she?

David had never been rejected by a woman, but as the interior of her tent brightened with dawn, Helen knew he'd recover. He rolled with life. Some widow would take the sting from his heart, and he would become the folk-tale prince of whom she'd dreamed.

Helen was about as resilient as iron. In a rare display of self-indulgence, she spent the morning abed. No folk-tale hero would ride into camp on a white horse and carry her off to live happily ever after. Camp was, in fact, inhabited by toads bearing officers' ranks. No amount of kissing on them would effect magic. They'd each become more toad-like. Truly, she must not want to be rescued.

But after Hannah had brought her breakfast, replenished coals in her brazier, and pampered her, and Jonathan and Roger had expressed appropriate concern from outside her tent, she found the solitude splendid for speculating, with almost no self-pity thrown in. At some point, she must tell Jonathan and the Pearsons David's news about Badley and Prescott, along with the dark hole of irresolution that trailed it. What had Badley and Prescott done with Silas's money?

Epsilon. Odds were that Neville knew what they'd done with the money. She wondered if she could pry that information from him. She also wondered whether he — or Fairfax — had heard of the demise of the publisher-lord of Wilmington and his attorney. Perhaps it was time to trump players around the table.

Close to noon, Hannah brought in mulled cider and replenished her brazier.

"Right cozy in here, Mrs. Chiswell." Her good-natured expression faded a little. "Er — I've some news that might be a little disappointing."

Helen stiffened and studied her over the rim of her cider mug. Oh, no. She couldn't bear to hear that David had been apprehended.

Hannah lowered her gaze. "I know you looked forward to riding with Colonel Tarleton on the morrow, but Lord Cornwallis requested his attendance in Winnsborough. The colonel expects to be gone the entire day and sends apologies and regards." Hannah fidgeted, curtsied, and let herself out.

Helen exhaled gratitude into her cider mug. Perhaps the gods *did* listen to her. She'd all but forgotten about that riding date and, after the events of the previous night, was in no mood to be seduced by Tarleton. Or Tarleton, Fairfax, and Margaret, as the case may be.

Early afternoon, Fairfax's voice outside her tent yanked her from a snooze. "Helen, I would speak with you. May I come in?"

Her skin prickled at the silk in his tone. She didn't want him in her tent. Thinking about him in conjunction with the charges David had leveled upon him unnerved her. "No." She faked a cough and hoped he wasn't there to gloat over capturing David.

He sounded surly. "Why the devil not?"

"I'm ill."

"You're lying."

In disbelief, she stared at the tent flaps, which he'd begin untying. Panic slammed her, manifested a dry coughing spell that sounded feverish, contagious. At the end of it, her breath wheezed and her eyes watered. "Leave me. Allow me rest."

His hands fell away from the tent, and his tone became more conciliatory. "Very well, my wishes for your speedy recovery. I shall ride to Winnsborough early on the morrow with Colonel Tarleton and return with him Friday the twenty-ninth, mid-morning."

Of course he'd accompany Tarleton. Cornwallis's boots needed buffing, too. Helen doused her smile. It wouldn't do for Fairfax to hear it. She faked a sneeze. "I'm going back to sleep. Good bye."

He grumbled a farewell. She reclaimed her smile and contemplated the ceiling of her tent, feeling better already. Fairfax gone for twenty-four hours: a holiday for everyone except Margaret. Plus she'd earned a box seat for whatever mischief Neville hatched with the mysterious Lieutenant Stoddard while the cat was away.

★★★

Neville looked up in surprise from an examination of his horse's stirrup. "Good morning, Mrs. Chiswell. I heard you'd taken ill."

"I'm well now." She flashed what she hoped was a radiant smile, aware that grooms at the corral watched. "Headed out?"

"In a few minutes, yes."

"Might I speak with you first?" He handed the reins to a groom. She looped her arm through his and steered him from the corral out onto the trail, Hannah following far enough behind to not overhear. "How did you become such an accomplished dancer, living in the East Florida swamps with those rangers?" Behind in the corral, grooms cleared their throats. So much the better if Fairfax returned to camp the next day to hear gossip that she and Neville had become an item.

"I had sisters." He patted her hand, at rest in the crook of his elbow. "But you don't really want to talk about dancing."

His guard was a tough one to break. That grin of his almost always failed to reach his eyes. Helen decided to let him think she'd bought his sincerity and laughed. "Pshaw, you saw straight through me. My, you're in a buoyant mood this morning."

"I might say the same for you."

She slathered snideness into her smile. "Lieutenant Grumpy has gone to Winnsborough."

They shared a chuckle like old warriors, or at least fellow conspirators. "Awhile back, I fancied you'd cultivated a soft spot for him."

Helen sniffed with disdain. "You mistook affection for a certain amount of civility I must maintain because he provides my cover on this assignment — which brings me to a question I have of you." She tilted her head at him and frowned. "I haven't heard from Phineas Badley in a few weeks and was wondering whether you'd any correspondence from him."

Neville shrugged. "It isn't unusual for him to go months between letters." He paused, and concern seeped into his voice. "Peculiar that you haven't heard from him, considering that he's your employer. Rebel unrest must have disrupted your posts."

She could hardly believe her good fortune. Neville had been excluded from Badley's hasty escape plans. He was now stranded in the backcountry without their guidance. "Perhaps you've heard from his attorney, Prescott, then?"

"We don't correspond." He stopped walking and placed her at arms' length, his expression open enough to reveal curiosity.

"Mr. Neville, brace yourself. Badley and Prescott are now fugitives from the law."

"What?" His curiosity transformed to incomprehension.

"Years ago, they altered the will of my wealthy husband and stole almost all my money. The crime was exposed last month in Wilmington, shortly after I left on this assignment, but not before they'd murdered three men to hide the secret. Badley fled to the Caribbean. Prescott remains at-large —"

"Where — from whom did you hear this?" The ranger's confusion appeared genuine and tainted with indignation.

"I cannot reveal my sources to you yet. But perhaps you see that my assignment with Tarleton and the Legion was, on Badley's end, an utter sham, a ploy to drag me out here in the hinterlands in hopes that I'd be killed, preventing exposure of the crime."

"What madness! If this is true, we must get you to safety right away. Camden, perhaps."

"I still do have an assignment, for I'm certain that whatever feature I write about Tarleton and the Legion will sell."

"But you aren't safe out here, and you'll run out of funds."

"I have some financial resources." For the first time since she'd met him, Neville looked distraught, his guard punctured. A little thrill shot through her. She'd managed to accomplish what Fairfax, with his bullying, hadn't yet been able to do. She decided to push Neville harder. "If I were you, I'd watch my back. Your association with Badley and Prescott makes you a suspect for investigators who are searching for anyone who might have been their accomplice." The implication of her statement sunk in, and his eyes widened. She edged closer, levity gone from her voice. "What did they do with my money?"

For half a second, she saw the connection take place in his eyes, stunned acknowledgement that he'd finally realized the mysterious source of Badley and Prescott's wealth. Then his guard resumed. He stepped back from her. "I'm certain I don't know, madam."

"I'm certain you do know."

His eyes glittered, chips of wintry obsidian. "I do appreciate your information, so I shall offer you counsel. Cease prying into the matter. It's too dangerous. If you do indeed possess the financial means, you would be wise to leave today and return to Wilmington."

She produced a smile to match his expression. "What? So Lieutenant Fairfax can hunt me down on the morrow, as soon as he finds me missing from camp?"

"If you go to Camden, I promise you I shall steer him for Ninety Six and give you at least another two days' lead on him."

How generous of him — and the weird thing about it was that she believed the ranger would do it. Two days was just enough time to lose Fairfax from her trail. Did Neville want to get rid of her, or protect her, or both? He was the second person in two days to warn her off the Legion. "Why don't we make a deal, Mr. Neville? You reveal where my money has gone, and I shall inform you of my source of the news about Badley and Prescott."

"That's unfair, madam. As I've already explained, I don't know what happened to your money."

"Anytime you're ready, I'm available to listen."

"Do take my counsel seriously." His head jerked in a bow. "I've a patrol of scouts to command. Good day."

He quit her company and returned to the corral, the morning colder in his passage.

Chapter Forty-Seven

THE CONVERSATION WITH Neville haunted her the rest of the day. She'd *so* longed to discover what Badley and Prescott had done with the money that belonged to her and Hannah that she'd shoved the ranger, much as Fairfax did. As a reward, he'd shut up. He wasn't her friend and didn't owe her any favors. In frustration, she realized she was no closer to learning what had happened to the money.

A horn moon shimmery with frost hovered in the west while Helen and her party ate supper by lantern light. At the conclusion of the meal, she told the Pearsons and Jonathan what Badley and Prescott had done, without revealing David's role.

Roger sprang from his bench. "The devil, you say!"

Hannah wailed, "Oh, my poor Papa!" and burst into tears.

Jonathan rose and began a slow pace. The locksmith, grim-faced, plunked back down beside his wife and tucked her against his shoulder. "Madam, it's dangerous following the Legion this way. Let us return to Wilmington now, before those two rebel armies up yonder attack."

"I agree with Roger." His tone stiff, Jonathan continued to pace.

"My friends, there's another story here that's important to me personally. I'd like to chronicle how courageous some of the civilians have been. You've mingled among them and heard their stories. Do you not think they fight for king and country also?"

Hannah dried her tears on a handkerchief. "So that's why you washed our clothes that morning —" Too late, she slapped a hand over her mouth, eyes wide with guilt.

"You did *what*?" Jonathan peered at Helen with curiosity.

"Oh, no, I'm sorry, Mrs. Chiswell! I promised not to tell, but it slipped out."

"It's all right, Hannah. Yes, I dressed as a camp woman and mingled with laundresses to hear what they had to say. How else does a journalist find the truth? And I'd been down at the kitchen listening to civilians the other morning when all of you panicked for not being able to find me."

"Oh, hell," said Roger after a guilty silence. "Mr. Fairfax took away the disguise that lets you mingle with them. I apologize, madam. But what did Badley and Prescott do with the money? They aren't living as though they're stinking rich with Mr. Chiswell's fortune."

"Good question, Roger. I wish I knew. Perhaps the Committee will coax an answer from them as soon as it can lay hands on one of them. As of right now, all the Committee has in custody is the property of Badley and Prescott."

Roger scowled. "*Committee.* People that inept should never be given the reins of a government. You'd think those Whig dogs would pounce on a couple of Loyalists who'd committed perjury and murder, forget about a fair trial, and string them up. Bah. It's like they made a show of seizing the properties so they could let them get away."

Helen's scalp prickled. "What if the Committee did let them get away, Roger?"

"You mean Badley and Prescott bribed those suckling calves?"

She gazed into the night while the obvious solution crowded her head and heart. Epsilon. Low on resources. Make do. How had she been so blind? "No. Badley and Prescott are *part* of the Committee. They're rebels."

Hannah squealed in disgust and indignation, as if a grass snake had crawled inside her petticoat. "My god! Our money has been donated to the rebel cause!"

"You must be joking," said Jonathan.

"Not at all. The explanation makes perfect sense." Badley, Prescott, Neville, Treadaway, Newman, and little Rebecca — not diverting supplies from the Legion, but spying for the rebels in a long chain of communication that led to where the gods only knew.

What, then, was the role of Lieutenant Stoddard, soldier of the king?

The horn moon had set by the time they finished discussing the new circumstances. Roger and Hannah cleared supper dishes. Jonathan strolled off east toward the line of trees where Helen had hidden to observe Rebecca and her hoop.

She realized that way back in Wilmington, while Badley was positioning her to be killed in the backcountry, Fairfax was setting her up to expose the rebel spy ring. Everyone was using her. Where Fairfax was concerned, it was probably too late to absolve herself of complicity with the rebels.

When the ring of spies was revealed, Rebecca and possibly her mother and legionnaire father would be executed as traitors. If it were possible to spare them, Helen must disrupt Rebecca's activity in the chain before Fairfax returned. But spy rings didn't often release their links. Anything she did to interfere might consign Rebecca to being murdered by Neville or Newman. She wrapped a shiver within her shawl. Perhaps by interfering, she'd position *herself* to be murdered, if she hadn't already done so.

The Pearsons carried dishes back to the kitchen to wash. Helen exchanged her shawl for her cloak, picked her way out to Jonathan, and found him facing east, the week-old holly and ivy wreath at his feet. In silence, they gazed a moment at the sky, where the arm of the Milky Way spun a luminous, dazzling path, seminal radiance of the gods. She stirred. "Might I impose upon you to donate a small sack of flour or cornmeal to a needy family in the lower camp every now and then?"

"Of course, my dear." Melancholy infused his voice. "But charity can only go so far."

"Just for a week or so. The girl's name is Rebecca. I suppose you find my idea of the civilian followers' story absurd. You wouldn't be the first to think so." She laughed to smother the bite of anguish. "For my next lifetime, I shall request to be born several centuries ahead. Perhaps by then, people will be kind to the poor and treat them with respect, rather than fear and loathing."

"I doubt it." His tone softened. "But for what it's worth, I think your idea about showing the courage of followers is innovative enough to stir up controversy after it's in print." There was just enough light from the stars to reveal his smile. "No middle ground on that topic, Helen. You'll be execrated and extolled at the same time. Is that where you want to be, inside a cyclone?"

She grinned, grateful to have found support at last. "Journalists are always inside cyclones, Jonathan. Is that where *you* want to be?"

"I'm here, aren't I?"

"Out of duty."

"No, not out of duty. Are you going to tell me who informed you of Phineas's demise?"

She felt the steady rhythm of her heartbeat. "Two days ago in market, a trio of peddlers appeared with their wares. David St. James was disguised as their assistant."

Jonathan's intake of breath made his shock audible.

"I ordered him to leave camp immediately. He didn't listen. He visited me in my tent that night and told me how he returned to my house after I left town in time to save Enid's life and witness the rest of the story unfold. Yes, Badley and Prescott altered Silas's will. Perjury, Jonathan. They killed Charles, Widow Hanley's messenger, and their own hired man to hide the truth. And if you recall, they tried to kill you.

"I believe they're rebel spies, and my money and Hannah's has been donated to the rebel cause. If we're fortunate, we may recover a tenth of it, but I shan't hold my breath."

Chapter Forty-Eight

THE TENSION AROUND Jonathan eased. "Helen, I failed you. You possessed sound instinct about the matter all along, while I led you astray with poor counsel. I am sorry."

"Don't apologize. Badley and Prescott's operation was so smooth, it even fooled my attorney."

"What of David?"

Sadness tensed her throat, although no longer the wild grief that had kept her awake two nights before. She regarded the sky a few seconds before summarizing David's escape plans and how she'd tossed him from her tent.

"You declined his assistance, and he accepted your answer?" He snorted. "After the years you two have known each other, that's difficult for me to imagine."

His skepticism annoyed her. Again, she felt him shove David at her. "I don't love David. I'm not sure I ever did. He was kind to me when Silas was cruel, but it's long past time for us to have gone our separate ways." She compressed her lips. "And I don't understand why you've championed him as my suitor when you've loved me."

His response was as remote as the stars. "I presumed you and David would marry and have children. You stayed together after Silas's death and your miscarriage."

"I'm grateful for the miscarriage." Regret bled into her voice. "I couldn't support a child on my own, and David wasn't the right man for my husband. And by now the best years of childbearing have flown past me."

"Bah. You're young enough to bear healthy children. So many women do want children. And your lack of dowry is no obstacle. Your talent for unearthing controversial stories may gain you the affections of a number of patrons, bachelors for whom your finances are inconsequential."

Such a peculiar conversation to have with Jonathan. "A woman's finances are never inconsequential."

His tone grew breezy. "My dear, be as cynical as you like, but a woman's lack of dowry *is* inconsequential to certain men. Unless I've grown myopic in my observations, your finances don't matter a jot to Mr. Fairfax."

Fairfax had told her so himself. A flush stormed up her neck into the crown of her head. "Marriage to him would be a disaster."

Jonathan folded his arms over his chest the way he'd done during the Atlantic crossing when she skirted an answer or fed him an answer too simple. Frustrated, she twisted away from him. If she weren't looking at him, perhaps her thoughts would clear, freeing her to speak from her heart.

"Mr. Fairfax's idea of sport resembles that which —" Her stomach knotted. She pressed trembling hands together and pushed on. "— which was forced upon me by Treadaway when I was about eleven years old."

"Tobias Treadaway, the procurer?" Although Jonathan stood behind her, she heard his astonishment.

She nodded. Nausea pressed her gut. Several shaky breaths rattled from her throat. "I tried to be Anglican for Silas. I thought there might be happiness between us if I did so, but I found little comfort in his faith, and he was determined to be unhappy, regardless. After he died, I remembered the Old Ways. But what I practiced in community in Wiltshire I had to modify for secret and solitude in Wilmington."

"Ah, yes," he whispered.

"I initially fancied Mr. Fairfax a colleague, but he has done something with the faith that I'm not certain the gods would approve. His gods are without conscience. So I continue to celebrate in solitude."

"You sound surprised at your accomplishment." Acceptance, certainty, and a bit of humor wrapped his tone. "No one is ever far from the gods, no matter to what ends of the earth she, or he, travels." At a rustling noise, she turned about in curiosity to behold him elevating the holly and ivy wreath to the stars. "Happy Solstice, my dear." Through his amusement, he sounded a little embarrassed, like a boy with a semi-plausible explanation for a load of sweets discovered in his haversack.

"*You* put that on my tent!" For an entire week, she'd presumed it was Fairfax's gift.

He returned the wreath to the ground. In his exhale, humor dwindled. His hand reached for hers, warmth in the winter night, and drew her closer. "Whatever Treadaway did to you, you won't be rid of him until you allow him to go."

Frustrated, she rolled her eyes. "On the surface, doing so seems a menial task, but to ask it of yourself is to reveal a thousand snarls that time has planted from the deed. Each day, you release it, yet it feels as though you never released it the day before. I wonder whether I can achieve peace over it in my lifetime."

"Everyone who desires not to be consumed with revenge asks the same question, performs the same daily quest for peace."

Consumed with revenge. A daily quest for peace. Jonathan sounded as if he spoke from experience. By starlight, her fingers twined with his, she couldn't imagine what might consume a man like Jonathan Quill with revenge. Eerie whispers of Fairfax's voice wended through her memory: *Where are the children and grandchildren?* For eleven years, Jonathan had shoved David at her. Why? She scrutinized his face. "Do you have children?"

In silence, he released her hand and swiveled his gaze to the heavens. Disappointment soured her heart. She'd transgressed into privacy that he would never choose to discuss.

"I haven't told you much about my youth." He searched the night sky, as if inventorying memory for the appropriate genesis. "My family imported silk and porcelain from China to England. We had an alliance with a Chinese family. Like my older brothers, I lived with my father's trading partner, to understand the people with whom we transacted business, just as the sons of my father's partner lived for a time with my family in Wiltshire."

She held very still, almost afraid to inhale. The intensity of her listening magnified each flutter of breeze or hoot of an owl.

"At twenty-two, I fell in love with a Chinese widow who had two young sons. There was friction over the topic of marriage. So I purchased her as my concubine and settled with her in China, for her sake willing to be expatriated and act as a permanent agent for the business. After we'd been together but one year, she was murdered by a nephew of my father's trading partner."

Shock punched the breath from Helen.

"The nephew's execution did not ease my grief and anger. Dead, he continued to taunt me until I thought I would go mad. Tensions between our families rose. The alliance, strong for four generations, verged on collapse. My father ordered my return to England. But I did not obey him."

He fell silent again, and she visualized the Chinese concubine and her glorious fan of dark hair. This wasn't the end of his story. Something profound had happened to him after that. "Where did you go? To a monastery?"

"No. We of the West are forbidden in the Temple. But there are mountains in China — green and scented with trees, cool with the tumble of clouds, lush with streams that cascade hundreds of feet into rainbowed mists — where masters seek solitude. And sometimes, a master will draw a student to him in his seclusion. An unworthy young man eaten with despair helps him tend garden beds, and sleeps on a woven mat, and absorbs what the masters — the human as well as the mountain — have to say. After awhile, he begins each day in gratitude, with a sincere desire to be released from his anguish. And it happens, little by little."

Helen felt humbled. "How long were you on that mountain?"

"Six years. Oh, my heart was mended well before then, but I stayed on to continue learning." He chuckled. "I had grown to enjoy peace. I no longer cared about the business. My father didn't grudge me the choice I'd made during those years. Then I received word of his failing health. Time for me to leave the mountain. I arrived in Wiltshire three days before he died. My eldest brother never made it home. His ship went down in the Channel. And a few months later, my other brother took a fever and died."

"You inherited the business." Helen eyed him with awe.

"I sold it, set up trusts for my brothers' children with their shares, made investments, traveled the world on my earnings."

Envy stomped her when she thought of Jonathan's massive library. What a life he'd lived. Was there anything he lacked? But with her next pulse, she realized, and turned him to face her. "You had no children with your concubine."

"A Chinese doctor placed the fault with me."

"After only one year of trying?" Incredulity filled her voice.

"She hasn't been the only woman to share my bed. No children."

He'd pushed David at her all those years because he knew David could give her children, and he presumed she wanted children. Just as he'd presumed the doctor's analysis was correct, and none of his ladies had tinkered with the likes of tansy and pennyroyal.

No. Jonathan was too sophisticated for that. Her gaze on him became shrewd, and she thought of his huge, empty house. "Children frighten you, don't they?

He turned away from her again. "Helen, leave it."

"Vulnerable, volatile, one moment full of energy, the next lying in your arms aflame with fever." She embraced him from behind, crossed her arms over his torso, and inhaled the scents of sandalwood, frankincense, and myrrh. The warmth of his back penetrated her chest, and her skin clicked and twitched. "I frighten you, too." His hands caught hers, and his thumbs stroked her palms. "Vulnerable and volatile, but not a child, not like that girl in Ratchingham's parlor."

He faced her, years of hunger engorging his expression. One of his hands seized her waist and rocked her pelvis forward, propped her upon the horn of the moon. The other hand cupped her face. Fire followed the track of his lips over her earlobe and across her neck, and the heat of his mouth sought hers.

Later, in the darkness of her tent, his fingertips painted splendorous spirals in her sweat. Across her lips and throat, around her shoulders and breasts, over her ribcage, winding to and from her navel, he drew the gods' emblem of eternity, traced whorls on the damp inner thigh of the great earth before probing her slippery, swollen warmth. She arched into the sacrament again and again, the poem and poet.

The second time, they coupled much more slowly, immersed in the euphoria of arousal without release. Her flesh and bones became translucent, and her exhale became his inhale, the rhythm of earth and heaven.

Before reveille, she awakened to find him tugging on his shirt. "Time to dance with the Enlightened One, eh?"

"A charming metaphor." Wool sighed as he pulled on his stockings. "In more than a quarter century, this is the first morning ever that I've debated sleeping in."

"Cease debating. I've a visit to the kitchens to make in Hannah's spare clothing."

"Camp woman." His tone grew merry. "A little soot on you in no way reduces your appeal. I do hope you let me bathe it off you."

"You *enjoy* portraying my servant."

With a snicker, he slid on his breeches. Then he straddled her above the blanket and leaned close. "*You* enjoy laundering my shirts." His lips caressed her chin before following the line of her jaw to her earlobe, where he whispered tenderly, "Despite what you believe, I don't think you've ever been infatuated with me."

Unexpected tears sprang to her eyes. "Ah, Jonathan." She stroked beard stubble on his jaw and knew he could hear her smile. "The Enlightened One awaits. Go give gratitude."

Chapter Forty-Nine

JOY SNEAKED TO Helen's mouth while she greeted the dawn. She surrendered and laughed at the sky. Her spirits sobered. A grave task lay ahead of her for the day, one for which she required full focus. She must cut Rebecca free of the spy ring.

When she returned to the campsite, the Pearsons awaited her before the tents. "Top of the morning, madam." Roger sounded more chipper than usual and rattled the lit lantern.

"It's a lovely day, madam." Pre-coffee perkiness from Hannah was about as common as tulips in December.

Happiness blossomed across Helen's mouth again, and she looked away from the knowing smile on the blonde's face. Obviously she and Jonathan hadn't been quiet enough.

The trio headed south lugging buckets and breakfast gear, Roger's lantern a bob of light on the trail. Per Helen's instruction, the Pearsons separated from her company at the kitchen to allow her a more solitary appearance. Liza and Sally descended upon her, curious over her absence. Within a minute, submerged in their stream of gossip, she'd rejoined the camp women.

Her visit to the creek to fill her bucket coincided with Rebecca's visit. The girl clambered up the bank and spilled her water. Helen set down her own bucket. "Let me help."

Rebecca yawned and didn't protest. Helen toddled back up the bank and placed the girl's full bucket at her feet.

Curious, Rebecca peered up at her. "Thank you. You're kind."

"My name's Nell."

"Pleased to meet you, Nell. Rebecca." The girl dropped a clumsy curtsy.

Helen returned the curtsy with more grace. A darted glance around assured her that she and Rebecca wouldn't be overheard. "Do you and your family have enough food?"

The girl grimaced. "No one has enough food."

"I can get you flour or cornmeal because I know you need it." The girl tensed with suspicion and reached for her bucket, and Helen whispered, "Listen to me. Those men for whom you're delivering messages — no, don't lie about it. I watched you enter my mistress's tent one day. Then I followed you to the postmaster's tent, and I saw Newman give you flour in exchange for a message."

"In service to His Majesty." Rebecca squared her shoulders.

"Why would His Majesty need secrecy among his own? Those men aren't in service to the king, but they *are* eager to take advantage of your family's poverty."

Rebecca looked ready to bolt. "How do you know?"

"Do servants not have ears? My mistress is loyal to the king. She's being used, set up for a traitor, just as you are. No one would believe the word of a servant against Army officers. I have to find another way to stop it."

"What do you want of me?"

"Don't deliver more messages for those men. If you need flour, come to Mrs. Chiswell's campsite discretely. Tell Mr. Quill your name. He'll give you flour without asking anything of you."

Her lower lip quivered. "They might look for me."

Irritation flared through Helen. What valiant men, Neville and Newman, terrorizing girls. "They might. But you know how to make yourself busy and invisible."

"Yes." She stared up at Helen. "Are you from England?"

Helen pursed her lips, annoyed at her own garrulity. "There's your bucket. I must run. Don't tell anyone we had this conversation." Without waiting for the girl's response, she lugged her own bucket back to the kitchen.

It felt wrong, intuition told her while she waited for water to heat. During the trudge back to the campsite with the Pearsons, she played out the conversation with Rebecca in her head. Although she couldn't find fault in it, it still felt wrong.

What felt right was the sight of Jonathan in his greatcoat rising from a bench where he'd watched the sunrise, his smile illuminated to rival the dawn. "Let me help you with that water, Roger. Hannah, get Mrs. Chiswell's clothing changed —"

"I thought you wouldn't mind doing those honors this morning, Professor, seeing as how my husband and I are occupied with the meal." Hannah twitched her nose at Jonathan. "I've apples and a cheese to cut up before these biscuits and coffee get cold."

Roger placed a bucket at the entrance to Helen's tent. "Yes, hurry, Professor, don't let the water chill, or the lady might have you flogged."

Stifling laughter, Helen sashayed past Jonathan and ducked inside her tent. He followed her, transferred the bucket inside, and straightened with a grin. "No point in trying to be quiet tonight." He fastened the tent flaps.

She dropped her tucker and apron on the cot. "Alas, we've no time to tarry in here this morning. Colonel Tarleton and Mr. Fairfax are due back from Winnsborough. And I'm starved." She paused while opening the front of her jacket, and a wicked smile captured her lips. "Will this end your nightly chess games?"

"Of course not." He kissed her naked collarbone. "It's merely incentive to achieve checkmate in one-quarter the time. I'd much rather spend the night with you."

***

The men strolled down to market, and Helen and Hannah took advantage of winter sunshine to embroider and mend. At ten, Tarleton and his party thundered back into camp trailing a cloud of dust. Helen added more daisies to her embroidery project.

Close to noon, Fairfax's aide, Kennelly, strolled into their campsite and bowed to her. "I've come to inform you that your brother didn't return with Colonel Tarleton. He's still in Winnsborough."

She frowned. "For how long?"

"I'm not privy to that information, madam. You might request an audience with the colonel to obtain more details."

An audience with Tarleton meant his opportunity to reschedule their riding excursion. But all posts to her party were being held for Fairfax's screening. She, Jonathan, and the Pearsons must have access to their mail. Flummoxed, she saw no option but to obtain Tarleton's intercession.

"Kennelly, will you take a note to the colonel for me?"

"Certainly, madam, if you write it quickly. I'm due to help strike Mr. Fairfax's marquee at noon and send his trunk to Winnsborough."

"His trunk?" She regarded the legionnaire. This felt ominous. "It sounds as thought he's not expected back here for quite awhile."

Kennelly shrugged. "Again, madam, you might ask —"

"— ask Colonel Tarleton, yes." Confounded, she set aside her embroidery and entered her tent to compose the note to Tarleton. When she handed over the note, she remembered that her "camp woman" clothing was among Fairfax's belongings. "My brother has some of my clothing. I will appreciate the opportunity to retrieve it before you break everything down."

"Your clothing?" He appeared perplexed. "I've not seen a woman's clothing in his marquee."

"He probably stored it in his trunk."

"His trunk is locked, and I haven't a key."

She nodded. "One of my attendants is a locksmith." Dubiousness crossed the legionnaire's face. "I assure you that Roger won't damage the trunk or lock. Come now, please allow me to fetch my clothing. Or must I first obtain Colonel Tarleton's approval for it?"

He threw up his hands. "Meet me at his marquee at noon."

"Thank you, Kennelly."

He took off at a trot to deliver her note. Noon. That didn't give her much time. She signaled Hannah. "Fetch Roger and Jonathan, and all of you meet me at Mr. Fairfax's marquee at noon. Have Roger bring his picks. And have Jonathan bring his conversation skills."

"Yes, madam." The blonde paused long enough only to deposit her sewing basket in her tent. Then she hurried south on the trail.

For a moment, Helen considered stashing a note to Fairfax in his trunk, a letter in which she owned up to the petty theft of her own clothing. Then she muttered, "Bugger him, forget it."

Overnight, she'd realized that, in his mind, the moment to completely exonerate herself from espionage had been that night in Wilmington, when Fairfax and George Gaynes barged into her house looking for David. Only by exposing David would she have attained exoneration. In essence, she'd started off as suspect, and each subsequent action had dug her in deeper.

Fairfax was on a mission to expose as many spies as possible, bolster his image as an indispensable guardian of His Majesty's empire. Never mind that his net pulled in some who weren't guilty. For weeks, he'd been expecting her to pop open the Epsilon pustule. But what would have been her reward for doing so?

At some point, you'll realize that you must tell me what you know. On that day, the idea of toying with me won't hold half as much appeal for you as it does right now. She doubted Fairfax would let her go. He excelled at twisting circumstantial evidence. With that evidence, even she could make a superficial case that she was a spy.

So his trunk must travel to Winnsborough minus her clothing and minus a note of explanation from her. No point in giving him more fodder with a written confession.

Chapter Fifty

JONATHAN HAD DISTRACTED Kennelly with small talk, but Helen didn't know for how long. "Hurry, Roger," she muttered, crouched beside the locksmith.

Click. Roger withdrew his pick from the lock on the trunk. "Have at it, madam." He slid the opened lock off and scooted aside.

The scent of cedar wafted out to greet Helen, along with the darker scent she associated with Fairfax. Her clothing lay atop several men's shirts of silk and fine linen. She retrieved the garments, fancying a rubbery tug-of-war with residual energy in the trunk, as if Fairfax had cast a spell to prevent her taking anything.

Below the shirts were the civilian suits he'd worn in Wilmington as Special Agent Black, and stockings of silk and wool. All the clothing, even hers, was folded to a uniform shape that sent the hairs on her arms standing out. Without trouble, she imagined Fairfax's hands pressing fabric, forcing every article of clothing into submission. Absurd, she told herself.

*The gods only know how many people he's murdered...*She peered deeper into the trunk, half-expecting evidence to substantiate David's claims of torture. No favorite instruments of barbarism presented themselves — no knives, needles, chains, whips, saws, axes, brands.

Lower down, two books caught her attention, a dictionary and an almanac. How ordinary. Her gaze detoured to the bottle of superlative brandy she'd sampled and a small phial beside it. The phial looked familiar. Puzzled, she reached for it.

"Found your garments, Mrs. Chiswell?"

She jumped at Kennelly's voice, unable to believe what her hand grasped: the bottle of laudanum that she had, on the Santee Road, convinced herself she'd left behind in Wilmington. "Yes." She rose, slid the phial in her pocket, turned to the legionnaire, and wrapped both arms around her folded clothing. "Thank you."

"You're welcome." Kennelly retrieved the lock from Roger.

Outside in the sunlight, Fairfax's scent haunted Helen. She shoved her clothing off on Hannah. "Wash it this afternoon." She strode ahead to their campsite, her skin crawling.

The phial in her pocket banged against her thigh. When had Fairfax stolen her laudanum? *Why?* Surely the company surgeon had laudanum, at least for ill or injured officers. Even had Fairfax acquired a dependency on the poppy, he had the money to afford his own supply. She'd met enough opium dwellers to recognize signs of dependency, none of which she'd ever observed in him.

For Fairfax, the otherworldly experience — contact with the gods — wasn't attained with a drug. She shuddered to recall Francis Marion's dead henchmen.

Tarleton's batman awaited her at the campsite and informed her that Tarleton would see her, briefly, at one o'clock in his marquee. She agreed to the appointed time and thanked him.

In the privacy of her tent, she examined the phial of laudanum. None of it appeared to have been consumed. She secured it in her portmanteau and sat on her cot, baffled.

At times, Fairfax seemed obsessed with her to the point of surreptitiousness. Yet if a man had a fetish for a woman, surely he'd sneak off something more personal from her: a hair ribbon, an embroidered kerchief, a fan, a comb. True, he'd confiscated two sets of her clothing, but she'd had full knowledge of it. If he were skillful enough to steal her laudanum, might there be other personal items of hers locked in his trunk?

She recalled Kennelly's words: *I've not seen a woman's clothing in his marquee.* It wasn't so much that a woman's touch was absent. Trunk and marquee: *all* of it lacked character. A dictionary and almanac: nondescript. No works of Shakespeare, philosophers, scientists, or popular authors like Fielding. No portraits of family members or stack of letters. Fairfax's property might belong to any man with money.

As if he had grafted the trappings of humanity about him like a shell, and those trappings served no purpose except to give shape to mist, to bestow upon a phantasm a handsome exterior that passed for human. Form without content. She shuddered.

***

The smells of boot polish, wine, coffee, and ink surrounded Helen as the batman guided her and Hannah past Tarleton and three officers in discussion over a map-cluttered table. She sat on a camp chair near the cot in the marquee, Hannah hovering nearby. A whiff of Margaret's perfume teased her nostrils, and the silken sleeve of a bedgown peeked from beneath a blanket folded in haste upon the cot. If the courtesan were distressed over Fairfax's absence, she was making the best of the situation.

Cheeks flushed from exercise, Tarleton strode over, caught her hand in his, and kissed her knuckles. "How are you? I heard you were ill." He straightened, the spark of eagerness in his eyes.

"Much improved, thank you. The ride from Winnsborough has agreed with you. You're the picture of health." With discretion, she tried to pull her hand from his, but just as that morning at market, he captured it with his other hand and stroked it, so she gave up.

"Being in the saddle will never disagree with me. And I apologize for canceling our ride. I'd reschedule straight away, but for matters heating up with Morgan. We've reports that he fancies capturing Ninety Six with his rag-tag army. Impudent, eh?"

She averted her gaze from the battle lust boiling in his eyes. Even his hands resonated with pent-up energy. He ached for Morgan to head south so he could make another Buford of him. He coveted the sight of Will St. James dancing in a noose. And he chafed against the strategy of watching and waiting that Cornwallis had imposed upon him in Winnsborough.

Fairfax's whispers into the ear of the Legion's commander had become a holy directive.

She glanced from the officers awaiting their commander's return, to the maps on the table between them and the pieces that marked where players banged shields and rattled swords, and she heard Hannah's plaintive cry from days ago: *Something horrible is going to happen to the Legion.* Resignation poured through her soul.

"I shan't keep you, sir." She squared her shoulders. "I came to inquire when I might expect my brother's return."

Disappointment skirted Tarleton's dark eyes, as if he'd hoped her visit had a more personal basis. "Your brother. Yes, of course. He's in Winnsborough a few days at my Lord Cornwallis's request."

What would Fairfax whisper in *Cornwallis's* ear about the rebel spy ring around which his net was closing, the net in which she was entangled? To mask her own unease, Helen puckered her brow with what she hoped looked like sisterly concern. "Kennelly is sending Dunstan's trunk on to Winnsborough and striking his marquee, as if my brother will be gone for more than a few days."

"You wonder whether you should move on to Winnsborough to be with him, eh?" Tarleton stroked her hand again, his appraisal earthy. "Don't rush off just yet. Those rebels to the north have blustered before, trying to startle a reaction out of us. If the Legion is called to move out, I shall send you and the ladies to safety." His thumb massaged her palm. "But if not, I shall likely find time to reschedule our ride."

Not even Tarleton had definite word of Fairfax's return. Soon, she could find herself either riding to Winnsborough to rejoin her "brother" or remaining with the Legion to field Tarleton's advances. Neither prospect boded well for a journalist who needed an objective story. She doubted Jonathan would warm to either option.

"In the mean time, Mrs. Chiswell, if there's anything I can do for you, don't hesitate to ask." He planted another kiss on her hand.

"As a matter of fact, sir, there is something you can do for me." Anticipation loaded his expression. "My brother receives mail for my party. With him gone, I've no idea what important correspondences the postmaster might be withholding."

Tarleton granted her a generous smile. "I see no reason why your party shouldn't receive mail directly in his absence. I shall send word to the postmaster."

"Thank you, sir." Relieved, she stood.

Her reeled her in a few inches, close enough for her to smell his masculine warmth, and kissed her hand one more time. "You're most welcome, madam."

***

Late that afternoon, Newman arrived at Helen's campsite with a letter for her that appeared untouched. A good thing that was, for it had been scrawled in Enid's own rough hand. "I wrot this letter in case Mr. David was not able to git threw to ye." It corroborated everything David had told Helen three nights earlier. The housekeeper's postscript tightened her throat with emotion: "I give Mr. David back his hat, mistress, seeing that you won't be needing it."

Indeed, what use had she for the hat of a man she no longer desired? Enid's sagacity earned Helen's silent thanks. David had brought color into her ghastly world, and for that she was grateful. In the absence of word to the contrary, he must be long gone from the area, beyond the clutch of Fairfax and Tarleton. She praised the heavens for his safe departure.

She slipped Jonathan the letter and allowed him to read it. Then, while he and Roger prepared supper at the kitchen, and Hannah, whose stomach disagreed with her, rested in her tent, she burned Enid's letter.

In the wee hours of the morning, Saturday the thirtieth of December, she started awake on the pallet she and Jonathan shared in her tent and gaped into the darkness. Not even the tranquil warmth of Jonathan asleep against her left side banished the portent of her dream.

In a courtroom devoid of witnesses, spectators, and most officials of the law, she faced her judge from the box of the accused. "How does the accused plead?" intoned a bewigged, black-robed Fairfax, his expression devoid of humanity.

She scowled. "Not guilty."

"Not guilty, *your honor*."

"You aren't 'my honor.' I'm not guilty. Show me my accuser."

The bang of the judge's mallet echoed around the polished, somber wood in the courtroom. "Silence! We find the accused guilty of violation of the inner sanctum and sentence her to punishment."

Her scowl transforming to a snarl, Helen leaned forward. "Punishment? What is this 'punishment?'"

He towered over her and smiled, and she shrank from the wraith-white face, the eyes of green frost. "Violation of the inner sanctum."

Chapter Fifty-One

WHILE HELEN LOOKED at hatpins in the milliner's marquee Saturday morning, her gaze happened to track Adam Neville strolling past, his companion a dark-haired redcoat of medium height. Braid on his shoulder: was he the mysterious Lieutenant Stoddard?

A ribbon-trimmed hat had captivated Hannah's attention. Helen slipped from the marquee without her to tail Neville and the young officer. At first the marketplace throng concealed her, and alacrity rewarded her with a snatch from their conversation.

"Winnsborough?" Impatience scratched at the redcoat's tone.

"I expected his return with Colonel Tarleton yesterday."

Her pulse quickened. They were talking about Fairfax.

The redcoat's voice iced. "He's twenty miles away." His was the same voice and Yorkshire accent she'd heard the night of the Yule feast.

"Nothing I can do about it. Did you expect me to tie him down?"

S — F in camp through new year — N. Neville and Stoddard were indeed plotting against Fairfax.

Neville seized Stoddard's upper arm and spun them around to confront Helen. Heart whamming, she pasted a smile to her lips. "Mr. Neville! I apologize for startling you." *Think quickly*, she told herself. "You mustn't have seen me wave to you."

He released Stoddard's arm. "I'm indisposed." The stare he thrust at her held as much warmth as frost-rimed onyx.

"Oh. Of course." She smiled at Stoddard, received a stare no warmer, and looked back at the ranger. "Stop by my campsite later? I'd like to hear more of Colonel Brown's relationship with Governor Tonyn." Confusion clouded the cold of Neville's expression. She breathed easier. Her request lent credence to her awkward appearance behind them. "I'm curious about those pivotal months when the colonel earned the respect of Florida's governor."

Some of the harshness in Neville's expression thawed. "I won't have the leisure to talk with you for several days."

She hoped her sigh of dejection sounded authentic. "As soon as you find the chance —"

"Yes, yes, I shall sit down with you."

"Splendid. Thank you." She transferred her smile to Stoddard, allowing herself a good second look at him. Tense and alert in her presence, mid-twenties, a few pimples on his chin, an even-featured face. He studied her with just as much attention to detail, and his dark, determined eyes invited to mind David's description of him: *astute*. Yes, this Stoddard fellow was astute.

"Good day, Mrs. Chiswell." Neville and Stoddard stomped off, their postures bespeaking adversaries united for the sole purpose of achieving a single outcome. Helen exhaled apprehension. Behind her, Hannah called her name. She waited for the younger woman.

Back at the campsite, the lantern stand was twisted around to signify the presence of a message in the Epsilon drawer. As expected, the secondary compartment was empty of a message.

She made sure her party stayed away from their site that afternoon and was relieved later to find that Rebecca hadn't played messenger. The cipher remained in the Epsilon compartment. By then, she had no doubt that Neville was a double agent. Did the Army sanction what he plotted with Michael Stoddard?

Rebecca sneaked into their midst after supper and asked for Mr. Quill. Helen ducked into her tent, unwilling to trust a crooked flicker of lantern light and an elegant gown to conceal Nell. The girl left soon, a bag of cornmeal in her hand and, Helen hoped, none the wiser about the mistress of the campsite.

The final day of 1780, she awakened before reveille to the sound of Hannah vomiting with morning sickness. Jonathan had already left for his routine. Helen pulled on her shift, stockings, shoes, and cloak and sent Roger to the kitchen for a crust of dry, stale bread. A cloth soaked in ice water in one hand and a lit lantern in the other, she entered the Pearsons' tent, knelt beside Hannah, and swabbed her face. "Roger will bring you dry bread. Don't rush eating it, and don't rise or move around much until you've finished it. A breeding woman creates foul humors in her stomach for several weeks. Give the bread time to absorb it. Tonight, prepare your dry bread for the morrow."

"I've never felt less like eating."

"You must eat the bread nevertheless. Otherwise, you'll feel wretched the entire day."

When Roger returned, Helen repeated instructions for him. Then, because her confiscated clothing was still damp from its launder the previous afternoon, she borrowed Hannah's petticoat and jacket again and walked out to greet the dawn.

Afterwards, she contemplated babies and the solstice wreath and reprimanded herself for her blithe behavior with Jonathan. She'd left her herbs behind in Wilmington and hadn't purchased more. The decades-old diagnosis of a Chinese doctor hardly assured her. She might already be pregnant. They had to be more cautious.

Except that she didn't want to be cautious. When she and Jonathan made love, she lost time and found the rhythm of the universe. Even thinking of their amorous play stimulated the slippery twitch between her thighs. She drew a deep breath of cold air, bemused to realize that lust wasn't confined to eighteen-year-olds. But for Jonathan and her, it wasn't just about lust. It was about life: life in the midst of death and destruction.

***

While they were out that morning, the lantern stand regained a neutral position, and the cipher vanished from the desk. Rebecca hadn't picked up the cipher. Helen had spotted the girl in the kitchen with her mother. "Omega" had lost his messenger.

Expectation filled the camp New Year's Eve and New Year's Day, prompted by messengers on horseback. At five o'clock Tuesday morning, January second, at least two horses galloped past in the direction of Tarleton's marquee. Helen, who'd drowsed while Jonathan finished dressing, bolted upright in the pallet.

Men's shouts followed the horses, and a moment of silence, as if every human and creature held its breath, and the sun paused in its climb for the horizon. Then she heard what she'd been expecting for weeks: the bugle for saddles.

One tent over, Hannah retched, too jarred to ease herself into the morning. Jonathan rushed Helen into her stays and gown, while around them, horses whinnied, metal clanged, tents were struck, and people shouted and ran about. The two dashed out to the trailside to learn that Daniel Morgan was reported en route to Ninety Six, and Cornwallis had ordered Tarleton west over the Broad River to drive the rebels back. At Brierly's Ferry, before crossing the Broad, the Legion would collect the first battalion of the 71st Regiment of Foot and its artillery piece, stationed there under Major McArthur.

Meanwhile, the trailside filled with family members, servants, and slaves, all come to bid adieu to the infantry, cavalry, artillerymen, militia, and scouts assembled on the trail by torchlight. Among the civilians were a number of merchants, officers' wives, Margaret, washerwomen Jen, Sally, Liza, and Rebecca — all stoic. Among the corps, Helen also recognized faces. Campbell, Connor, Davison, Ross, and Sullivan, the dragoons who'd escorted her safely through the Santee and told her so much of themselves. Kennelly, the infantry private who'd served Fairfax. And Neville, his expression impenetrable as befitted a ranger and scout, a two-faced Janus to Helen now. Although she searched, nowhere did she see Lieutenant Stoddard.

Tarleton trotted his charger along the column for a final inspection, his buttons and braid glittery in torchlight, the swan feathers atop his helmet taunting the stars. Harsh as the scrape of a rake in brown leaves, his voice leaped out to the men. "The rebel scum are at it again, lads! Killing, burning, and looting a path to Ninety Six through *your* homes, *your* lands, *your* kin! We're all that stands between Morgan and anarchy! What are we going to do about it?"

The roar of five hundred feral wolves surged from the men. "Kill 'em! Send 'em back! Stomp 'em! Grind 'em underfoot!"

Helen gaped at the commander of the Legion. The flicker of torches rendered his expression electrified, determined, headstrong. At home in the sweep of bloodlust, chosen of the gods, he pranced his horse back and forth, and the cheer of five hundred disciples engulfed his passage. The foyer at Woodward's, the afternoon ride, the Yule feast: all were occasions when she'd encountered

Camp Follower

the magnetism of his leadership. With a single message from Cornwallis, she experienced it anew.

Tarleton waited for the men to settle down a bit before he bellowed again. "The rebels are diseased, starved, disorganized! What match are they for the finest unit in His Majesty's Southern Army?"

"Huzzah!" Legion-thunder reverberated earth and heaven.

"The finest unit in the *whole* Army!"

"Huzzah!"

"Ninety Six, lads, where the rum and wine flow, and the loyal lassies will thank the Legion! Are we ready?"

"Huzzah!"

"Let's give that whoreson Morgan a reception from hell! For king and country!"

"For king and country! Huzzah!"

Chapter Fifty-Two

THE STOMP OF hooves and boots, clank of weapons, and creak of wheels beneath the small cannon faded before sunrise had washed away the stars. The Legion left behind the rank odor of predators gone a-hunting, and a skeleton force to guard the heavy baggage.

Back in her tent, a lantern lit, Helen captured every impression in her journal, almost oblivious when Jonathan left to perform his morning ritual. When the Pearsons returned from the kitchen, they delivered a report on the exodus of people from camp.

Daylight revealed that tents of the rank and file had been packed away. Some officers' slaves and servants were also striking tents, and a few merchants and sutlers prepared for departure. Depending on the exigency of the battle situation and how well they foraged, the Legion might fly for several weeks without the heavy baggage. They might just as easily trounce Morgan and return within a few days. Therefore, most of the civilians remained. However, everyone moved close to the hub of activity for protection.

Of Fairfax, Helen received no word. Description of the Legion's victorious return would make an excellent end to the feature on Tarleton, so she decided to linger another day or so.

At noon, highlanders from Major McArthur's 71st arrived escorting the battalion's heavy baggage, on order from Cornwallis to leave it in the Legion's encampment. They brought news that boosted the rush of recent events. George Washington's cousin had sent forty of his dragoons to attack a nearby fort manned by Loyalist militia. Learning of the dragoons' advance, the commander and his men had abandoned the fort three nights earlier and fled for the safety of Ninety Six. William Washington's dragoons had taken possession of the fort.

Helen recognized that the Loyalists' flight represented another chapter in the Crown forces struggle: maintaining an effective militia. Neither side could depend upon militia, but most Londoners didn't grasp the fact that the rebels always seemed to have a larger pool of militia to pull from. Helen suspected that her feature on Tarleton and the Legion could show those across the Atlantic just how crucial His Majesty's provincial units had become in a war that dragged on and drained optimism from everyone. Her resolve to remain on assignment deepened.

Tuesday night, she and her party dined on beefsteak, purchased from a butcher who was closing shop. Hannah picked at her meal. For the first time, Helen listened to her inner concerns about the younger woman's condition. Hannah hadn't found a respite to her morning sickness. If Tarleton ordered the heavy baggage to relocate, would she be able to keep the pace?

The absence of communication from Fairfax for almost a week both relieved and concerned Helen. Surely he'd received his trunk and realized what she'd confiscated. And what was Neville up to while riding with the Legion, in service to the rebels, his cover intact?

In her tent that night, she only half-responded to Jonathan's spiral of caresses and kisses. He soon gave it up, rolled over, and fell asleep. She listened to his soft, even breathing long into the night, agitated by conspiracies: the rebels, Neville, and, in particular, Fairfax. Had she felt him motivated by justice, she'd have trusted him with her knowledge of the spies' activities. But justice wasn't a priority for him.

***

Too pukish to leave her tent, Hannah remained abed Wednesday morning. Roger headed alone to the kitchen for coffee and hot water. Later that day, communications flew. Tarleton, bivouacked six miles west of the Broad River, had found no trace of Morgan and pressed farther west to sniff around for the rebel commander. He requested that Cornwallis have the Seventh Regiment of Foot standing by at Brierly's Ferry with the rest of the 71st.

News came from Cornwallis, too: doubt that the story of Morgan's movement against Ninety Six was accurate. The Earl promised the Seventh to Brierly's. But there was no mention of the Seventeenth Light Dragoons in the day's messages, and Helen heard nothing from Fairfax.

The sky clouded over. Drizzle accompanied supper. Winds shifted to the northwest, cold and dreary. Early afternoon on Thursday the fourth, a courier hastened to Winnsborough with Tarleton's request that both the Seventh and the Seventeenth Light escort his baggage to him. Since he expected to move quickly, he specified that "no women" come along to slow his progress.

The officers' ladies packed up, prepared to head home in the morning. Disappointment and relief cascaded inside Helen. Disappointment that her assignment had come to an end, and she'd miss the heart of Tarleton's story, witnessing him in action against a foe. Relief that she could return to civilization and need no longer put up with reveille, latrines, inferior hygiene, lukewarm food, and a tent's damp interior. Relief also that she wouldn't have to deal with Fairfax anymore.

Despite drizzle, she strolled in the lower camp to observe departure preparations of the women. Nan, the woman with pneumonia, had left on the second, too ill to remain. But to Helen's surprise, she discovered Margaret, Sally, Jen, Liza, and Rebecca packing up with the intention of accompanying the baggage into whatever purgatory Tarleton ordered the Legion through. How they intended to defy the Legion's commander mystified her. They must be resolved to make themselves no burden, deny their own femininity if necessary, put the needs of the unit far above their own. A harsh existence, one that demanded courage.

With a jolt, she comprehended that if she obeyed Tarleton, not only would she miss the heart of his story, she'd miss the heart of the story about the followers and why they were resolved to deprivation and self-sacrifice. Rain, icy wind, inadequate food and shelter, assault from rebels — what was their reward for enduring?

She'd never know. She wasn't traveling into purgatory with them. The more she stewed over it, the more disquieted she became.

She might face appalling danger by continuing with the camp women. But she'd settle for unfinished stories if she didn't do so.

Mid-afternoon, she signaled Jonathan for a conference in her tent and lowered her voice, so the Pearsons wouldn't hear. "I haven't seen the Legion in action against a foe. Nor have I seen camp civilians united in action with them."

He studied her without response for several seconds, his gaze flicking over her face. "You're considering remaining with the Legion on the morrow."

"I am."

"Hannah is unable to carry on."

All-day "morning" sickness, a burden borne by some pregnant women, could debilitate or kill those who were unable to slow down. Frustration and concern spilled into her exhale. "I realize that. If you lend me financial support, I shall send the Pearsons to Camden to wait for me for a month."

Perhaps the set of her jaw or shoulders or the firmness in her eyes indicated her resolve and lack of romance over what lay before her. He leaned forward on his campstool, elbows on his knees. "A month?"

"Well, can you imagine Tarleton taking more than two weeks to find Morgan?"

"No." He nodded once with conviction. "I shall come with you."

She fancied faint amusement about his eyes, and some of her resolve faltered. He'd volunteered for a journey to the interior of Hades. "Jonathan, I cannot compel you to go."

"You'll go regardless of whether I join you. If David hadn't put that ball through Silas's head, your husband would have died of apoplexy over your doggedness."

She leaned toward him, curious. "You aren't the apoplectic type. What does my 'doggedness' do for you? Does it make you want to rescue me?"

He snorted. "You are the most un-rescue-able woman on the face of the earth."

She reached for his hands, and her gaze lingered on his fingers twined with hers. Years ago, the two of them had moved beyond teacher and student. Jonathan now meant more to her than friendship and imagination. "Thank you."

★★★

During a lull in the rain, she summoned the Pearsons and informed them of their next steps. Hannah wailed about failing Helen, emotions snarled in the strange brew that flowed through the veins of a mother-to-be. Roger, at first blustery and indignant, subsided with morose resignation. If he wanted a healthy wife and baby, he had to get Hannah to safety and comfort and help her manage her debilitation. Travelers from the Legion's camp at Daniel's Plantation would assist them to Camden with the wagon and horse team.

While daylight remained, the four prepared for departure. Helen packed most of her belongings with the Pearsons. She debated sending Calliope with them, too, for the Legion might appropriate the mare to replace horses killed on campaign. But she and Jonathan needed Calliope as long as possible to carry the canvas and blankets they'd use in place of a tent, as well as their own emergency trail rations.

That night, she lay with Jonathan, rain drumming the top of her tent, and for the second night in a row, found herself too distracted to relax in his arms and enjoy him. Her mind went over and over what they'd packed until Jonathan again fell asleep without making love to her. She dozed, her brain a haze of lists.

In the dark before reveille on January fifth, she awakened. The Seventh Regiment of Foot would arrive at Daniel's Plantation in a few hours. Late the previous evening, confirmation had arrived that Cornwallis promised the Seventeenth Light to Tarleton also. The infantry and dragoons would escort civilians and heavy baggage to Brierly's Ferry and proceed west across the Broad River to rendezvous with Tarleton.

She expected to encounter Fairfax. She felt it in the ether, the energy of trillions of spiky particles that herald a tornado, and knew in her blood that he'd marked what she'd removed from his trunk and denied her any communication or acknowledgement. She'd incensed Ares, god of war.

Jonathan might be traveling with her, but if she wanted the final chapters on her features, the ordeal — the *appeasement* — was hers to undertake, alone.

Chapter Fifty-Three

MORE THAN ONE hundred sixty infantrymen of the Seventh Regiment descended upon Daniel's Plantation on the morning of Friday, January fifth, the scarlet of their uniforms dulled and their footsteps and clank of gear muffled by misty drizzle. Around the foot soldiers rode a hornet swarm of red-coated cavalrymen upon steaming horses: fifty dragoons of the Seventeenth Light. After Tarleton received the baggage, the Seventh would march to Ninety Six and help guard the town. The Seventeenth was ordered to accompany Tarleton down the very throat of hell, if necessary.

Base camp was fully struck by then, the baggage ready on a road grown muddy from the departure of non-essential personnel. Officers discussed strategy and postured. Infantry from the Seventh and 71st assumed position in the train. Cavalrymen from the Seventeenth ranged back and forth inspecting wagons and securing the route.

Helen huddled in the train with Jonathan and Calliope and talked herself past Hannah's anguish at their farewell that morning, substituting it with the sagacity on Enid's face. *I had a word with Rhiannon last night, and she assures me you'll be back in good time.* The gods rewarded warriors. Several times, Fairfax trotted past her upon his gelding. If he recognized her, he didn't acknowledge her. Ample time later for their reunion. Huzzah.

Flatboats conveyed baggage, infantry, civilians, and some horses across the Broad River, and cavalry splashed across at the ford. On the opposite bank, the army drove westward through winter-dreary Carolina forest, following a trail gouged by the Legion three days earlier. Fallen branches popped beneath the crush of wheel and hoof, horses whinnied, wagon wheels creaked, and men called out to each other. The wet wind smelled of splintered pine, tobacco smoke, churned mud, and horse turds. Dragoons of the Seventeenth faded into the forest around the baggage train to act as vanguard, rear guard, and shield during the march. Messengers came and went on horseback.

No one said a word about the females who remained with the army. Helen's sense of paradox and black humor swelled. They weren't invisible. In a few days' time, Sally, Liza, Jen, and Margaret would provide a woman's secret softness to their men: touches of humanity in the vast, grim game they played.

By late afternoon, when they halted for the night, Helen was tired and dirty, having thrice lent her strength to freeing wagons from mud, but the soul of two stories hummed in her blood. As soon as she and Jonathan set up their own site, he ambled off to make supper. Beneath a canvas slope, she used remaining daylight to pen an account of her first day on march.

They crawled north and west during the following days, rain and cold such a frequent companion that Helen's enthusiasm at going where no woman reporter had gone before deflated under the weight of reality. Despite her oiled leather boots and heavy woolen gloves, chill seldom left her hands and feet. While she wrote in her journal, she stored her bottle of ink inside her bodice to keep it fluid enough for the quill. Dried peas, johnnycakes, coffee, and an occasional nip of rum formed the monotonous sustenance for the army, once or twice supplemented with beef jerky. She dreamed of bathing in warm, lavender-scented water, and eating peaches in the sunshine. She awakened to omnipresent drizzle, to smoky, moldy, dampness that snaked beneath her clothing and smeared a residue of foulness on her bones.

Late on Monday the eighth, the army and baggage arrived at Tarleton's bivouac on Duggin's Plantation, south of the rain-swollen Enoree River. Tents emerged from wagons, along with celebratory victuals, for although rain pursued them, the colonel had received word that Morgan had scampered back north, and the Earl Cornwallis had reportedly marched his mighty army north from Winnsborough that day. Cornwallis on the move just on the other side of the Broad River provided reassurance to the Legion and a serious threat to Greene, stationary near Camden, and Morgan. However, the rain hampered everyone, so there was nothing for it but to hunker down and wait for skies to clear and treacherous rivers to subside.

Deep in the night, when camp quieted, Helen awakened, restless, and stared overhead at the slope of canvas shielding her and Jonathan from rain. A familiar scent invaded her nostrils. Comprehension and fear knifed her gut. She shifted to gaze over Jonathan at a silhouette in the open entrance.

He crouched facing them, as if he'd studied their repose many minutes — although surely no human's eyesight could discern details back as far as she and Jonathan lay. Shadowed in greatcoat and night, he rose and slipped away with the stealth of a nocturnal predator.

She sank back, resolve repairing the tatters panic made of her nerves. On the morrow, she and her brother must be reunited. Perhaps he'd let her keep the desk afterward. But there were certain to be unpleasantries traversed before Fairfax did her any more favors.

***

Moisture-swollen clouds smothered sunrise the ninth of January. Each breeze stung exposed skin as if laden with ice. Harsh greenwood smoke hazed the encampment. Eyes watered. People coughed. Off-duty soldiers milled around the fires and stamped to stay warm.

Word spread that sentries had nabbed a couple of backwoodsmen loitering at the perimeter and brought them straight to Tarleton. The colonel's charm didn't extend to the business of interrogation, for the men wasted no time confessing their mission from rebel chieftain Andrew Pickens. The domestic pound and bang of wheelwrights and blacksmiths almost obliterated the fuss the duo made when the Legion dispensed the standard treatment for spies caught behind enemy lines. Major John André would have appreciated it.

After the spies had grown silent, Jonathan stepped out to stretch his legs, and Helen wrote in her journal. Finding her light blocked, she looked up at the three washerwomen. "Why, good morning." She noticed their sober expressions and corked her inkbottle.

Liza flicked a glance to the desk. "What are you writing?"

Unease spread through Helen at the remoteness hollowing their expressions. She shut the journal in the desk and started to rise. "Sit down," said Liza. All three women ducked beneath the tarp and surrounded her. "Hand the desk over to Sally, Nell."

Her heart pounding, Helen complied. Sally squatted, opened the desk, searched through it, and perused journal entries in silence. Helen studied them, guessing the purpose for their visit. They needed to reconcile why "Nell" had remained with the Legion after her mistress had departed camp. Perhaps they suspected her of spying.

Liza made a vague motion with her chin to indicate somewhere outside the tarp. "Mr. Quill is a family servant. We understand him staying with Mr. Fairfax. But women don't march with the Legion unless they got a good reason."

Sally scanned a page. "You write real pretty, Nell. Better than men who write for them magazines. Why don't publishers let women write more than silly society news?"

Jen snorted. "Because they think we don't have brains."

Liza tapped her foot. "Maybe they're afraid of what we'd say."

Sally peered at Helen. "My Grandpa taught me letters and ciphering, but you write like a fancy book writer. And you talk like an English lady. Where'd you learn to write and talk so well?"

Helen let out a slow breath. "I was born in England. The lady of the manor amused herself by bringing in the local vicar and having him teach village children reading, writing, and arithmetic."

"Whoo-wee." Jen laughed and slapped her thigh. "While you're washing laundry, I wager Mrs. Chiswell has some dolt of a man balancing her ledger. But you haven't yet explained why you're here, why you didn't go home with the other two servants."

Helen shrugged. "Mr. Fairfax wants a record of his campaign. Mr. Quill doesn't write as well as I do."

Sally extended the papers to Liza. "Nothing here to make her look like a spy."

Helen felt the pressure of dull anger. Why did women combat each other? Liza, her cool gaze unwavering, motioned for Sally to return the desk.

Sally added, "Peculiar thing is that she doesn't just write about soldiers. She writes a good bit about the rest of us. Servants, mistresses, washerwomen, merchants, artisans."

Liza cocked her eyebrow. "Why waste your ink on us? We just follow our men."

Helen shrugged again. "But we've just as much courage as our men, haven't we?"

The three seemed taken aback for a moment, as if the thought had never occurred to them. Then Liza chuckled. "Say, that's a fine idea. I wish I could rub those words in randy Brady's face the next time he grabs my arse."

"Rub it in several faces." Sally scowled. "Do 'em good. Nell's right. We aren't cowards."

Jen grabbed Liza's wrist for a second. "Glory, I just had a sweet fancy. After Tarleton whips the breeches off Morgan, the Legion's puts *us* on the payroll!" The humor of three harpies pierced the woods.

Liza wiped her eyes. "Carry on, Nell." She signaled Sally and Jen, and they backed from the tarp to leave Helen to her writing.

At noon, the watch tromped past to replace morning sentries. Frowning, Helen walked out, peered around, and fanned away wood smoke. Where had Jonathan gone for so long? Perhaps she'd best stretch her legs and look for him. Beneath the tarp, she settled her cloak around her shoulders, knelt, and fished in a sack for her gloves.

Boot steps squished through mud, and daylight dimmed again. "Mrs. Chiswell." Three Legion infantrymen stood before the tarp. "Step out here with us. Keep your hands where we can see them."

Puzzled, she complied, noticing that the men carried muskets. "What's this about, gentlemen?"

The first infantryman glowered at her. "Mr. Fairfax has ordered an immediate audience with you. We're to convey you there. He commands us to bring your desk and associated paperwork."

Trepidation blasted through her, and the day grew colder in a second. She pulled her cloak closer about her. "The desk is in that canvas bag, back there. I shall fetch it, as well as my gloves."

The lead infantryman gripped her upper arm, hauling her outside with him. Before she could protest, one of the other two pushed her cloak aside. "No weapons on her that I can see." The third soldier grabbed the bag, leaving her gloves behind.

Appalled at their treatment, she adjusted the cloak when they released her and fell into step with them, mud sucking her boot soles. An audience with Fairfax. Anger and fear dizzied her. Jonathan would be so worried when he returned.

Incidentally, where on earth was he?

Only a couple steps farther, she stumbled, apprehension impaling her. Had Fairfax something to do with Jonathan's absence?

Chapter Fifty-Four

THEY MARCHED HELEN to the opposite end of camp, where two corpses of Pickens's spies swayed in the wind, battered faces and smashed noses purple, trousers reeking with human waste. A legionnaire shoved aside the flap of a marquee. "Wait in there."

One man strode off with her desk. The other two, on guard outside, tied the tent closed after she entered.

In the vacant interior, she exhaled a frigid cloud into gloom. Dark fluid stained turf that had been torn and gouged near the middle of the marquee. She envisioned the hanged spies just outside the tent. Anxiety crawled up her back. Right there, they'd been questioned and tortured. The marquee had been set aside for interrogation.

She paced, as much to keep warm as to occupy her nerves. She'd withheld everything from Fairfax, broken into his trunk, and removed her clothing. *Violation of the inner sanctum.* And her laudanum bottle. Laudanum — she didn't understand it. Tears blurred her vision. She dabbed them with her handkerchief, impatient, angry with herself: her feeble attempt to cram back terror.

One o'clock passed, demarked by the calling of the watch. She imagined Fairfax exploring the desk's secrets, fascinated by them. He'd also read her entire journal. If he spared her, perhaps he'd spare the journal. She'd invested so much time in it.

Jonathan. Guilt and grief clenched her throat. She'd betrayed him, hidden the intrigue surrounding the desk. That his body didn't already sway beside those of the spies provided scant comfort.

The urge to use the latrine awoke in her bladder. Her stomach growled. She kept pacing. The tent was the temperature of a crypt.

Close to three o'clock, the flaps were untied. She ceased pacing and backed from the entrance, away from bloodied ground. Two legionnaires hung lanterns on the ridgepole, opened a couple of campstools on either side of a small table, and dropped two canvas bags near a stool. From one bag protruded a corner of her desk. The other covered some smallish rounded object. The men swept out.

Fairfax slapped the entrance open, horsehair on his helmet bristling, and tied the flaps closed from the inside. Then he regarded her, his face devoid of expression, his eyes reptilian, his scarlet uniform a wash of blood across the marquee's entrance.

She said nothing, even when he strolled around her. At the furniture, he removed his helmet and placed it on the table. Hair eluded his queue, creating a russet halo by lantern light. His back to her, he said, "The heroics of rebels never cease to amuse me. Pickens and his rabble are providing a shield between us and General Morgan."

Helen suspected that he'd helped interrogate the spies. Her gulp was audible.

"Three spies visited us last night. One escaped." He swiveled to her, voice silky. "Imagine Colonel Tarleton's vexation when he learned that the escaped man was Will St. James."

Unavoidable, the shock that she felt flood her face.

He assessed her reaction. "When was the last time you saw David St. James?"

"In Wilmington, in my bedroom." Aware of his icy skepticism, she regarded the tent entrance.

"How is it you came by the desk for which I'd been searching?"

"I received it as a gift from Lieutenant Neville."

Fairfax laughed. "That desk costs more than a year's pay for him. The truth this time, as well as where you put your original desk, and why you concealed the Spanish desk from me."

She drew a shaky breath. "The final night at Woodward's, Mr. Neville backed his horse onto my original desk and crushed it. Naturally I was distressed. He told me he'd seen a desk in market, and he purchased it as replacement. I did wonder how a ranger could afford it. After you asked about the desk, I inquired among sutlers and merchants. The tanner to whom you gave nine pence told me he saw Mr. Treadaway pass the desk to Mr. Neville."

"Treadaway, the Legion's agent. That's encouraging news."

Helen darted a glance at him and shuddered at the predatorial twist to his lip. "Mr. Treadaway has the financial means to acquire such a desk. I assumed it was his attempt to win my favor. But giving you the desk would have left me without the means to conduct my work." She eased out another breath. Surely the explanation possessed the ring of veracity. After all, it was about ninety-nine percent true.

He sat on a stool. "Were it not for a few details, I'd believe you. For example, the five secret compartments built into the desk —"

"— Five secret compartments?" She felt her eyes bug. *Five.* Damn! She'd only found two.

"And each of them crafted to hold a slip of paper such as a ciphered message."

Time for a bluff. "I don't believe you. I've used that desk daily for weeks and never noticed any secret compartments." She mustered her best sneer. "*You're* lying. How dare you pin espionage on me, just because you cannot catch the real spies."

He extracted the desk from the canvas bag and sat it on his lap. "One." He exposed the first compartment. "Two. Three. Four. And here's our fifth little piggy who went to market." He allowed her a long stare at the drawers before sliding them back into place and bagging up the desk. "It's your move, darling. Shall we call it checkmate?"

Oh, the tent was cold. She rubbed her hands together. "Several times, I suspected someone went in my tent while we were out, but nothing was ever stolen. Now, I see. They used my desk as a drop off."

"*They?*"

Uh oh, eager to feed Fairfax's game, she'd slipped him too much. "The day that Sullivan found me in the men's camp, I'd been tailing a boy who emerged from my tent." No way would she implicate Rebecca.

Fairfax's eyes narrowed. "Is he here now with the Legion?"

"I haven't seen him."

"Whom did he visit in the lower camp that day?"

"The postmaster's assistant, Newman."

Preternatural radiance sparked in Fairfax's eyes. "Newman! Splendid! You're so close to redeeming yourself that I shall reward you with news out of Wilmington. Your publisher and his attorney defrauded you and Mrs. Pearson of Mr. Chiswell's estate and redirected your money to the rebel cause."

"My god!" She whirled away from him, hoping he'd read shock in her posture. Fairfax possessed quite an impressive network of his own spies. For a minute or so, he swanked through details about the altered will and the murders. She blotted her eyes with her handkerchief and sniffled because he expected tears. At length, he ceased his prattle. Handkerchief back in her pocket, she squared her shoulders to face him with, she hoped, forbearance.

Victory swelled in his expression. "Wouldn't you agree that it was considerate of Enid to return Mr. St. James's hat to him?"

Horror slammed the breath from her. Fairfax *had* read Enid's letter. A shudder rocked her composure. *I wrot this letter in case Mr. David was not able to git threw to ye.* Oh no, oh dear gods, no. She'd lied, and he'd caught her in the lie.

Why hadn't she the sense to return to Camden with Hannah and Roger?

Fairfax clicked his tongue. "Clearly, Mr. St. James loves you very much. When a man loves a woman to that degree, he doesn't stop at exposing villains who impoverish and endanger her. He rides to her rescue. When was the last time you saw David St. James?"

"In Wilmington." How much less definite she sounded than just minutes earlier.

"Your cloak. Give it to me."

Worn and agonized, she handed her cloak to him. Her nerves jangled. Cold rushed to penetrate her tucker, jacket, and petticoat.

His fingers worked along seams and hems in her cloak. "Your tucker." He rose and dropped her cloak upon the other campstool.

Flushing, she tugged her tucker from her jacket and tossed it to him. "Neville, Newman, and Treadaway are spies. Execute them."

He held her tucker up to lantern light for an examination and dropped it atop the cloak. "Newman and Treadaway are disposable at this point.

However, I must play Neville along farther." A smile flitted over his mouth. "I do enjoy playing him along. Your boots and stockings."

She scowled. "Are you daft? It's freezing in here. Give me back my cloak and tucker."

Inhumanity churned in his eyes. He took a step toward her. "Hand them over."

His order finally connected in her tired brain, and she gaped at him. "You think I'm hiding secret messages in my boots like a spy!"

"I think you're capable of many things."

She yanked off her boots and pitched them at him, dismayed when he caught both without being struck. After she'd thrown her stockings and garters at him, the soles of her feet registered the ground's frigidity, and her teeth began chattering. "Get on with it."

Again, he perched upon the stool, this time to conduct a meticulous examination of her stockings and boots. Her nose ran. She honked into her handkerchief, jammed it back into her pocket, and rubbed icy hands together. At length, Fairfax rested elbows upon his knees. "Your choice what to give me next: your petticoat or your jacket."

"I shall give you neither." Cold, anger, and fear shook her voice. "Find a woman to complete the search."

"Alas, we're short on women. Margaret and those laundresses like you, so I doubt they'd be objective. But fear not. I'm your brother." The smile he'd worn at the mention of toying with Neville scooted over his mouth.

"No. I won't remove my clothing for you like a whore. You must rip it off me. And I shall let the entire camp know about it."

His eyebrows arched, and he chuckled. "Helen, darling, such theatrics. Since you insist, I shall contribute some theatrics, too."

He pushed up from the stool. She balled her fists and braced herself, teeth clenched, heart whamming her throat. Maybe she'd bloody his nose before he overpowered her. But Fairfax merely extended the second canvas bag to her. She said, "What's that?"

His smile transformed into the appalling angelic radiance that overcame him when he killed someone. "Take a look inside."

Limbs singing with adrenaline, she snatched it from him and withdrew a fashionable man's hat. David, no, not David! With her next breath, however, she realized it wasn't David's hat, for she detected the scent of frankincense and myrrh. Agony excavated depths she'd never imagined in her soul and heaved up a groan as bruised and battered as the dead spies' faces. Tears filled her eyes. "M-my god, what h-have you done to Jonathan?"

Contentment settled over Fairfax's countenance. He plucked the hat and bag from her stiff fingers and chucked them atop the bag containing her desk. After reseating himself, he grinned. "When last I saw your professor, he was enjoying a spot of tea, surrounded by armed legionnaires. I'd never dismiss the aptitude of his hands and feet. So, what shall it be next, the petticoat or the jacket?"

She groped her pocket for her handkerchief again, blotted her tears, and blew her nose. Her fingers wobbly with cold and ebbed adrenaline, she unfastened her jacket and tossed it to him. While he examined the seams, she removed and wadded up her petticoat and pockets and threw those at him.

The skin over her entire body transformed into gooseflesh, and the thin wool of her shift enhanced nearly every delicate detail of her breasts.

He took his time inspecting her clothing. Her teeth at a constant chatter, fingers and toes as white as frost, she hugged herself in a futile attempt at seeking warmth. He added her garments to the pile and sauntered over. She fixed her stare upon the entrance and tried to shut out the feel of his leer lapping her, over and over, like the tongue of a jubilant dog.

"Hands at your sides," he hissed. She obeyed. From behind, his breath caressed her neck. "For more than a decade, you and Mr. Quill carried on a platonic relationship that even the Pope would approve. But off I go to Winnsborough, and *pffft*, you begin competing with Tom Jones and Fanny Hill for endurance upon the mattress."

He breathed down the other side of her neck. Her nipples contracted further. "Mmm. At first, I postulated that my presence in camp dampened your lust for each other. Then I realized some constant that warded off your romance with him had changed and ceased to be. Yes?

"What a grand resolution for the new year. Out with the old, in with the new. You wasted no time seeking solace with Mr. Quill afterwards. When was the last time you saw David St. James?"

"W-W-Wilmington," she whispered.

"I don't imagine you shall much favor me in a moment, after I've ordered you to remove your shift. The covert areas of a woman's body supply delectable alcoves for hidden messages."

Violation of the inner sanctum. The tent contracted, darkened, and became the inside of a tool shed in Wiltshire. She gagged.

"But before that, I shall transact implied business with your professor. Pity. He's an invigorating chess opponent."

"D-David in camp t-two days after the Y-Yule feast."

"December the twenty-sixth. Colonel Tarleton and I were in camp then. How did Mr. St. James manage it beneath our noses?"

"D-disguised as a p-peddler. My t-tent that night."

"Unimaginative. You learned of the Badley-Prescott cabal from him. Enid's letter arrived a few days later, confirmed that he'd visit you. He offered protection in Pickens's Brigade?"

Helen tried to laugh with black humor, but her stomach lurched instead. "P-Pickens? No. P-protection w-with the p-peddlers."

Fairfax walked around and faced her. "Peddlers? He's a halfwit. When will you see him again?"

She shook her head. "T-told him I d-didn't love him. F-final."

"Aha!" He snapped his fingers. "That's why you pretended illness the next day. Licking your wounds." He strutted away, no longer fascinated with her half-frozen, three-quarters naked condition. "Inconvenient of you to spurn him. He could lead us to his father, Pickens, or Morgan. I wonder, how might you entice him back?"

Lure David back to betray him? No. "W-wouldn't work. I d-don't want him. He knows it."

"Damn." He clasped his hands behind him, paced, paused with his back to her. "Two nights after the Yule feast. Bah, I'd have wagered good money that you met Mr. St. James in your tent the night of the Yule feast, when you and your maid sneaked off."

She managed the ghost of a laugh. Time to play the one trump she possessed. Steadying her quivering jaw as best she could, she said, "Not David in my t-tent that night. Someone named Stoddard."

As if spun in a whirlwind, he whipped around, his jaw slack. "Stoddard? *Lieutenant* Stoddard, an officer of His Majesty?"

Her chattering teeth had carried her beyond intelligible speech. She nodded and sniffed, her nose dripping.

Fairfax strode to her and slammed the campstool loaded with her clothing at her feet. "Dress. Expect my return in ten minutes." En route to the tent flaps, he snatched up his helmet and the sack containing Jonathan's hat. By the time he let himself out, she'd already dove into the pile and retrieved her stockings.

Chapter Fifty-Five

HELEN ALMOST SCALDED her throat in effort to down the tea. Halfway into the second cup, she realized she'd drunk it black, no milk or sugar.

Fairfax slathered blackberry preserves on two cornmeal biscuits and slid the wooden plate across the table to her. While she gobbled biscuits, he handed the teapot out of the marquee and ordered it refilled. By the time she finished eating, the terrible ache of cold up her legs into her backbone had retreated, she'd ceased to shiver, and her thoughts had assumed cohesion.

More tea arrived. He poured her another cup. Surely he was bursting to question her about Stoddard, but he didn't rush her along. So this was how Tarleton felt when Fairfax buffed his arse. She fought the urge to shrink from him and allowed steam from her tea to penetrate her nose instead.

He sat on the other stool. "I presume you've thawed out, darling. I queried into the whereabouts of Badley and Prescott. Unlike the frontier justice to which you've grown accustomed, I've a capable network of informants. They tell me, for example, that your precious David St. James was recently spotted playing piquet in Camden — for the moment, out of my grasp."

Fairfax was swanking yet again. Why hadn't David run farther? Determined to steer conversation off him, she set her tea down and eyed the lieutenant. "Badley and Prescott donated almost everything to the rebel cause. Realistically, much of the property Hannah and I recover will be consumed for legal hogwash."

"Would it surprise you to learn that Mr. Prescott was reported heading for the backcountry?"

She waved her hand in dismissal. "It's the place to go when you've a price on your head."

"He's been spotted near Camden. Mr. St. James was in Camden. Coincidence?"

She rolled her eyes. If she heard of the Badley-Prescott-St. James conspiracy from Fairfax again, she'd shriek.

"I'm not certain that losing pursuit is Mr. Prescott's primary goal. He may be trying to intercept the Legion."

"Yes, seek the solace of his partners after the shock of losing so vast a fortune."

"What if he plans to visit you?"

Laughter seized her belly for about half a minute. Wiping her eyes with her handkerchief, she said, "I haven't laughed like that in so long. You've quite a sense of humor."

He didn't crack a smile. "Why does the suggestion amuse you?"

"Prescott would never bother looking for me. He's hated me for years. As far as he's concerned, I'm as good as dead out here."

Fairfax's eyes glittered with curiosity. "Why does he hate you?"

"I suspect he's angry because the money he squeezed from me didn't sate his avarice. Men like him don't know when to stop."

"Have you more money somewhere?"

Sarcasm overrode her aversion and fear of him. "Is this leading to a marriage proposal? You don't strike me as the type who'd marry for money unless there's power attached to it. A seat in Parliament, for example." Her teeth bared.

He bathed her with a frigid glare. "Answer my question."

"Oh, for god's sake! If I'd money, do you think I'd have taken on this wretched assignment?"

"Yes, I do."

Her snarl ebbed. Fairfax knew her too well, and his question *Have you more money somewhere?* nagged her. "Surely Silas's will accounted for all the money —"

"Don't be naïve, Helen."

For months, Fairfax had been wooing Neville for Epsilon's identity, but Neville was tough. Prescott was softer than Neville and had a motive for seeking out the Legion. She thought of Pickens's dead spies just outside the marquee. If Prescott knew the right information, and Fairfax laid hands on him, oh, yes, the lieutenant would get his answers.

"I'm unaware of more money." She flicked a biscuit crumb off her sleeve. "You haven't gone through the effort of placating me after interrogation so we can chat about my finances. Let's stop beating around the bush. This Stoddard fellow interests me. I never saw you quite so amazed as when I mentioned his name. Tell me about him."

Fairfax sat back and scrutinized her several seconds. "Describe him."

"A redcoat with a Yorkshire accent, dark hair, about your height."

"You said he entered your tent the night of the Yule feast."

"I'd hidden a short distance away, expecting to catch that boy. But Stoddard showed up instead, in such a hurry when he left that he collided with Margaret. And I heard her say that she knew him from last summer in Camden."

Fairfax growled. "Stoddard hasn't the competence for more than training his master's falcons and sweeping out the mews. But a Yorkshire baronet without issue waxed sentimental years ago and purchased his falcon-boy an ensign's commission."

"The class into which a boy is born doesn't necessarily predestine his character in manhood. Tarleton is the son of a merchant. More than Stoddard's common background must aggravate you."

"Last June, I'd begun investigating a murder in Georgia when I was transferred to the Seventeenth Light. Stoddard was assigned to complete the investigation, so I courteously turned over my notes to him. Within days, he'd botched the investigation."

Through contempt in Fairfax's voice, Helen heard a point he'd glossed over. Michael Stoddard hadn't remained an ensign. He'd been promoted. For that to happen, he must have demonstrated more than a nominal amount of competency. She reconsidered her brief meeting with him more than a week earlier. He didn't seem incompetent that morning.

David's words whispered through her memory: *Astute fellow...We're certain he figured it out, but the redcoats blamed another Spaniard. Damn them, protecting their own demon.* If David was correct, Fairfax murdered a man and concealed it. Stoddard solved the murder but was silenced by superiors frantic to prevent word from leaking out about their fellow officer. Her skin crawled. "I trust an innocent colonist wasn't blamed for the crime."

"No, just a stupid Spaniard."

The snatch of overheard conversation between Stoddard and Neville returned to her. A dark explanation began to shape itself in her imagination, a tarry, black blob of scaffold that allowed macabre pieces to drop into place. She pushed it aside for the time, not quite ready to believe it.

"Stoddard was transferred to Charles Town in September." By lantern light, a feral gleam rose to Fairfax's eyes. "Why was he out here for Yule? Running a dispatch? Did he retrieve a secret message from the desk? Bloody long way to travel, just for a message from Neville." With a grin, he refocused attention on her. "I was in Winnsborough more than a week. While I was away, did you see Stoddard in camp?"

She held his gaze and said, "No," with more conviction than she believed herself capable, unsure why she lied. It wasn't to protect Neville. "If you've finished your interrogation, do allow me on my way." She wondered where the nearest latrine was.

He held up his hand to stay her rising, his grin vanished. "If it's your intention to remain on assignment, I must warn you that conditions could deteriorate."

"Ah, well, what's a bit more rain and filth to trudge through?"

"Weather is only part of the equation." He rested his hands on his knees. "We're headed through land stripped of provision by rebels. Colonel Tarleton laid in a supply of flour. After floodwaters recede and we march, we must catch Morgan within four days or go hungry."

How many times had her parents starved her? How many nights had she and Enid gone to bed with their bellies growling? She lifted her chin. "I've known hunger before."

The gleam of triumph in his eyes unnerved her. "The gods reward warriors." He stood and extended his hand to her.

She accepted his assistance rising and found herself pulled against him, the thumb of his hand stroking her palm, the flat of his other hand caressing her back the way farmers fondle prize stock. Her attempt at breaking free brought their bodies into more solid contact, and the earthy scent of his skin and hair filled her head. She averted her face, fear clenching her throat. "After being cooped up in this tent for hours, I've an urgent need to visit the latrines. Good day."

He resisted her second attempt to draw away, lifted her palm to his lips, and kissed it. "The battlefield," he whispered, "is no place for those who don't trust themselves."

"How arrogant of you to conclude that I resist your advances because I don't trust myself."

"If so, answer this question. Is Mr. Quill all you'd dreamed he'd be, or have you thought of me while lying in his arms?"

Two nights, she'd done so. She inhaled rum fumes from her memory, coughed, and gritted her teeth. "Damn you!" Obviously she had unfinished business with her memories of Treadaway.

"I'm flattered. Consider exploring that with me before we engage the rebels. Although the battlefield does create a canvas for the painting of one's own demons —" He kissed her palm again. "— oftentimes it's a most unforgiving canvas." He released her, scooped up the sack containing her desk, and presented it to her with a bow.

***

Between the latrine and her tarp, memory visited Helen with an instance of her father drawing a knife on her. She recalled the grip of his hand on her wrist and glee in his eyes when he stroked her throat with the knifepoint. She'd seen that satisfaction in the eyes of Treadaway, Silas, and Fairfax. What compelled her to walk the same path over and over? It became more nightmarish each time she did.

The Chinese believe that everyone who enters your life is your teacher with a lesson for you. Should you fail to learn the lesson the first time, the universe will provide you a more potent teacher the next time, and stronger and stronger teachers, until you've finally learned the lesson. Crows cawed, raspy and ominous. Helen peered through the tangle of drippy, witch-fingered trees and heard the hoarse squeal of gray squirrels. How did she stop attracting these "teachers?"

By chance, she intercepted the return of Neville among a mounted party of scouts. She waved down the ranger. "Good afternoon. Spotted any more of Pickens's spies?"

"No, but they leave us no doubt that they're watching us."

"By the bye, I thought your friend quite a gentleman. You know, the officer back at Daniel's Plantation." Neville slammed neutrality over a flash of irritation. "Is he stationed in these parts?"

"That I cannot say." He tipped his hat. "Pardon me. My superior awaits a report." He rode off, shoulders stiff. Each syllable had sounded clipped. Neville didn't like Stoddard any more than Fairfax and was determined to not release information about him.

Stoddard on the coast, Neville in the interior: whatever they'd plotted in December, it hadn't come together. She wondered whether they'd try again.

Her heart leapt at the sight of Jonathan waiting before their tarp unscathed, still and quiet, although from the vigor of his embrace and tenderness of his kiss, she realized how difficult calm had been for him to attain. He passed a critical eye over her, looking for signs of abuse. She shook her head. "I'm unharmed." She held up the desk. "But I owe you an explanation."

With what daylight remained, she showed him secret compartments and discussed the involvement of Rebecca. But for the time, she withheld information about meeting Lieutenant Stoddard in the marketplace. Stoddard was out of the picture. If Fairfax interrogated Jonathan and pried the detail of that meeting from him, she didn't want to consider the mercy Fairfax would extend to her for holding out on him again.

After supper, anyone not on watch retreated to tents or tarps. Hours later, when Jonathan finally allowed her to doze off, she wished for the opportunity to make love to him in broad daylight, to see his ecstasy instead of just feeling and hearing it.

The wee hours of the morning nudged her awake: drizzle on tarp, the routine call of a guard, a whiff of smoke. The nasty scaffold came together in her head. She stopped shoving back the incredulity borne on her conclusions. Jonathan rolled over. "Awake?"

"Just thinking. Curious about the Army. Officers. Protocol." The sleepy nonchalance in her voice was the opposite of what she felt. "Jonathan, what would happen if two officers hated each other, and one plotted the murder of the other but was found out?"

"Oh." Jonathan yawned. "He'd be executed."

"Yes, I thought so. Thanks. Good night."

He kissed her cheek and snuggled against her backside, warm and comfortable, soon sound asleep. But Helen stared at the canvas a long time before regaining sleep. She surmised that Stoddard had uncovered Neville's operations as a double agent and held that over him to force his compliance with his own scheme. The ranger was in an ideal position to carry out the murder of Fairfax. But Neville was a chameleon: not at all the sort of man upon whose fidelity one should hang a career and life. Michael Stoddard must be desperate.

Chapter Fifty-Six

BITTER COLD FOLLOWED a cessation of rain on January tenth. By then, it had been more than a week since the Legion had seen sunshine. That afternoon, Helen eavesdropped on an exchange between Tarleton and soldiers camped near her. "Aye, lads, we've seen better weather, but it won't be long now. Between us and Lord Cornwallis, we'll crush Morgan's pathetic army. Hallo, Simpson, you like that picture, eh, lad?" The colonel's easy grin mirrored the legionnaire's amusement, and he slapped the soldier's shoulder with camaraderie. "You fellows are the finest in the army. Never forget that. It's an honor to serve His Majesty with you."

Each man stood taller as his commander swaggered for the next group of soldiers. Minus his lithe foxhounds while the unit was on the move, the Legion's commander didn't lack for presence in his swan feather helmet and spotless uniform.

She smiled over Tarleton's heartfelt pride and penned her observations. The dragoons in the Santee had verbalized their leader's regard for his troops, but had she not tromped through mud and ice with them, she'd never have seen it for herself. What a glorious story for Londoners. She ignored Hannah's protest in her memory: *Something horrible is going to happen to the Legion.* That moment, she didn't believe it. The colonel cared for his men. He wouldn't let it happen.

Thursday the eleventh of January, Tarleton received Cornwallis's permission, rain-delayed, to march the Seventh Regiment north with him instead of sending them to Ninety Six. The Legion departed Duggin's Plantation and camped south of the petulant Indian Creek. Before dawn next morning, guards escorted a Loyalist scout through picket lines. About forty-five miles north, Morgan had parked his army on the scout's property at Grindal Shoals, a crossing on the Pacolet River. While Pickens's Brigade offered Morgan a buffer and early warning to the south, the general gouged the land of provision.

Confident in Cornwallis's support to the east, even though weather perforated communications, the colonel roused the Legion. The churning water of Indian Creek had subsided enough to permit their crossing, as had that of Dunkens Creek farther to the north, but with the ground soaked, a scant six or seven miles was all they could manage for Friday. Their mileage fared little better the following day, the second of Tarleton's four days of flour, although the entire unit pulled together with amazing teamwork at freeing bogged down wagons. Helen remembered Fairfax's warning about going hungry.

Sunday, day three of the flour supply, the Legion crossed the Enoree River, thirty miles from Grindal Shoals. Tarleton pushed northwest to cut off retreat by Morgan and threaten Wofford's ironworks, where farriers serviced the horses of Morgan's dragoons.

Exhaustion lined faces around campfires that night. Those on foot had forded creeks knee-deep in water the temperature of glaciers. When cooked rations became available, Helen, her appetite gone, forced herself to eat, unsure how conditions would deteriorate in subsequent days. She also forced out a journal entry, her script jittery with chill, even after Jonathan tucked a blanket around her. Morgan wasn't far ahead of them, and his scouts orbited the Legion.

Monday dawned gray and bitter and delivered two surprises colder than the air for Helen. The first came around five in the morning, when sentries found Newman the postal carrier just outside picket lines, his throat slit. No one questioned what Newman, not on patrol, had been doing out there. The consensus was that Pickens's scouts had murdered him. Helen, jittery, wondered whether Fairfax had lured him out and delivered his version of Crown justice.

The second surprise arrived in the personage of Tobias Treadaway, who found his way to them as they were breaking camp. The gabby agent had ridden from Cornwallis's encampment on the fourteenth; that moment, His Lordship was making ready to cross the Broad River. To Tarleton, who had received no correspondence for several days from his superior, the news was welcome. It positioned Cornwallis and his army but thirty miles east of them.

Helen was bothered that Treadaway, integral to the Epsilon spy ring, didn't bear correspondence from the Earl. The agent could be lying about Cornwallis's position, encouraging Tarleton into a trap without adequate reinforcements. What was Fairfax doing about it? Nothing that Helen could see.

She debated going directly to Tarleton and telling him everything she knew — but then militia scouts, Neville among them, netted another spy. The man revealed that Morgan was headed for Burr's Mills on Thicketty Creek and that he'd heard reports of Cornwallis crossing the Broad River that day, southeast of them. When the intensity of the interrogation ramped up, the spy diverted the soldiers long enough to swallow a poison he'd concealed, thus depriving his captors of watching him thrash in the noose. Fanatics, the rebels. The Legion hanged his body anyway.

Helen, shivering, saw it as the army marched out in pursuit of Morgan, who'd sounded retreat from Grindal Shoals. To her, the incident stank worse than five hundred Legionnaires on campaign without any soap among them. Her weary journalist's brain trotted out the lurid scheme of a rebel spy who'd committed suicide, rather than confess to supplying misinformation about Cornwallis's position. Fairfax hadn't been present during the interrogation.

Otherwise, she suspected the spy might have confessed far more.

The fatigued, hungry Legion arrived at the Pacolet River late afternoon. Scouts reported fords guarded a good distance in either direction along the opposite bank. Across the roiling river, Morgan's militiamen gathered to jeer and offer obscene gestures. A dozen lined up to synchronize dropping their breeches and wagging bare buttocks at the Crown forces. "Shit," muttered a legionnaire near Helen.

Noisy as the river was, it transmitted an Ulster Scot's accent —"Tory sons of whores!"— along with regional accents. "Come and get it, pigs!" and "Kiss my arse, Ban!" A breeze also wafted over the aromas of fried pork and johnny-cakes. The rebels didn't lack for food. The inside of Helen's mouth tasted of the same disgust, hunger, and muddy exhaustion borne by every soldier who marched with Tarleton.

One of Morgan's sharpshooters picked off a pine branch above a Legion dragoon, dumping cones and needles atop him and spooking his horse. Soldiers growled, and at least twenty muskets cocked.

"Hold your fire!" bellowed an officer. His command carried to the rebels, who hooted and guffawed at the Legion's restraint. Or more appropriately, its impotence.

The angry army withdrew into the evergreen screen. Pickets were set, scouts were redeployed. Tarleton ordered fires lit for meal preparation — the final day of the flour supply — but specified that the army not encamp. He and senior officers sequestered themselves to strategize.

Bone-tired and grimy, Helen refused to think about marching farther or even rising from the blanket where she'd eaten supper. Little conversation passed around the fires. Men stood or crouched in silence, Highlanders from the 71st twitchy with the need to fight, others dazed with exhaustion. A volatile mix.

One cookfire over, Treadaway squatted in a stupor. Fairfax ambled to him, whipped out the superlative brandy he'd served her, and nudged the agent in the shoulder with the flask. Treadaway revitalized and thrust out his tin mug. Fairfax obliged with a liberal slosh. A waste of brandy, considering Treadaway's "disposable" nature. Maybe one of Newman's final acts had been to sample Fairfax's brandy.

With a sigh of weariness, Jonathan laid the desk on the blanket at her side and scooted around to face her, blocking her view of the pair. "The colonel must be a fencer." He began massaging her hands. "I recognize a feint in the making."

She groaned. "The army is worn out. Every ford is guarded. How can we fool Morgan? Best to set up camp here and rest overnight. Deal with Morgan on the morrow."

"A good tactician understands that night is his friend."

She groaned again. "Damn. We're going to march in the dark."

"You've another journal entry to complete by then."

"I can hardly put one foot before the other."

"This moment, only writing is required of you."

His humor and sagacity encouraged her smile. Not for the first time, she felt the support and focus he gave her. Gratitude warmed her heart. Before she took up her quill, she stroked his cheek.

The march started at nine, illuminated by plenty of torches so Morgan couldn't miss the offensive toward the vulnerable Wofford's ironworks. Rebel scouts hallooed alarm. Torchlight blossomed, and the camp across the river, complacent for the night, awakened.

For three hours, Tarleton marched along the river before he signaled bivouac and ordered everyone except guards to rest — no fires except a token display near the bank. The rebels took up position and camped, although Helen felt certain they weren't as smug as before. Morgan had taken the bait, but for what did Tarleton bait him?

At two in the morning, Jonathan coaxed her awake. Around her, soldiers softly rolled up their blankets. "Hush, my dear. We're countermarching. Tarleton's gambling that Morgan pulled in his guard from a ford downriver, and we can cross there."

Dew-sodden and stiff with cold, she shook out a yawn and helped him roll blankets. Her legs felt lined with lead, her eyes as if they'd been blasted by grit. She fell in line behind a wagon, Jonathan leading Calliope beside her, and concentrated on placing one foot before the other without tripping. The night smelled of river, pine, and wet Piedmont soil.

Bridles and wheel-creak muffled, the Legion left a guard to maintain fires awhile and keep rebel watchmen believing they were still camped opposite the Pacolet. The guard caught up with Tarleton's main army less than an hour before dawn.

Advance scouts reported Morgan's guard about six miles downriver had drawn in. Helen's hazed brain grasped at Tarleton's cleverness and also at the reality. She'd seen Jonathan's map of the area: woodlands and cattle ranges. Morgan couldn't run far north before the Broad River cut off his escape. Later that day, Tuesday the sixteenth of January, the two armies could do battle.

She must stay awake for it — no, she had to snatch sleep before then. She couldn't ever remember being so tired, even when she was settling Silas's final debts. Must be a combination of physical labor, sleep deprivation, inclement weather, and scant rations, like a drug, yes, almost like laudanum, and *why* had Fairfax stolen her laudanum?

She stumbled mid-stride. Jonathan steadied her. An ensign hissed for silence. "Helen," Jonathan whispered, "do you want to ride Calliope?"

"No." She sucked in several deep breaths that hurt her lungs and stung her eyes. Soldiers around her trudged along. They felt just as wretched. The rebels had food and slept, dry and warm, hours away from the Legion. Did Tarleton expect his hungry, exhausted troops to prevail over that? *Something horrible is going to happen to the Legion.* She shuddered and shook off Hannah's words.

At dawn, they crossed the Pacolet River at Easterwood Shoals, another opportunity to experience frigid, knee-deep water. On Morgan's side of the river at last, Tarleton surveyed his dripping, shivering army, his back straight in the saddle despite his own damp uniform. Triumph and perseverance glowed in his eyes. "*Now* we have them." A snarl tore over his face. "He won't fight. He's a coward. Are you with me, lads?"

Muskets and sabers rose to greet the dawn overcast, and a roar ripped from the wolves. "Huzzah!"

Chapter Fifty-Seven

CAVALRYMAN CAMPBELL TROTTED his gelding over to a cluster of dismounted dragoons. "They scampered like rabbits!"

"Huzzah!" erupted in unison from the dragoons.

Wind and cold had chapped color to the cheeks of the next man who spoke.
"The colonel was right. Morgan won't stand up to us."

"Not to *us*. Not even to his own mother."

Rowdy laughter rolled over Helen, bundled nearby in her cloak and burrowed against Jonathan for warmth. She longed to record her impressions of
the mid-morning bravado, but she anticipated a march soon. Her gaze tracked
the escorted arrival of another captured rebel scout. Surely by then, the reconnaissance team had determined the location of ambushes.

Campbell, dismounted, fired up again. "If Morgan weren't such an idiot,
he'd remember how we overtook that addle-pate, Buford."

Helen mused that General Morgan certainly did seem to be foolish of late.
He'd been duped for his lack of vigilance the previous night and was allowing
himself to be cornered into a region where cattle farmers grazed their stock. A
battleground full of cow turds: la, what a ripe bunch the Legion would be when
it was over. Still, the rebels were rested, and Morgan was certain to seize cattle
farther north to ensure that his men stayed well-fed.

Her mouth watered at the mental image of a sizzling beefsteak on a plate
before her, medium rare and tender, and a glass of red wine, and buttered
rice and turnips and beans and cheese and an apple tart and — Her stomach
clenched with hunger and spasmed her body.

Jonathan caressed her shoulder, and she heard his stomach growl. They
had emergency rations of dried fruit and meat hidden away in Calliope's pack,
but she suspected that Jonathan would grow a good deal hungrier before he
partook of them. Besides, eating from their stores without sharing among the
empty-bellied soldiers was poor form.

Treadaway plodded past, intent on Campbell. "My friend, sell me a ration, eh?" He jingled coins in his purse.

The dragoons laughed, and Campbell looped an arm over the agent's shoulder. "Would that I had a ration to sell. I could command a pretty price for it. Maybe you should have stayed with his Lordship's army. He's plenty of food." Campbell thumped his shoulder. "Chin up, old boy. I fancy we'll dine on beefsteak soon."

A murmur of agreement and resolve swept the soldiers, and a long-faced Treadaway stumped off. The agent stuck out like a thumb whacked by a hammerhead. Why was he there among them? And why was the "disposable" agent still alive? Had Fairfax not yet found a tight enough cover for slitting his throat?

Another thought seized her. Newman's murder coincided with the arrival of Treadaway, his fellow spy. What if it had been the agent, not Fairfax, who murdered the postal carrier? Was Treadaway the leader of the branch of Epsilon spies planted within the Legion, empowered to take the lives of members who'd slipped up? Or had a leader from the Epsilon ring contacted Treadaway in Camden, ordered him to seek out the Legion and purge Newman from the group?

Camden. Fairfax said something about Camden the afternoon he interrogated her. David in Camden, yes. Someone else there, too. Exhaustion and cold kept her mind from seizing the detail.

Besides, the army was on the move again. She and Jonathan steered clear of Highlanders, who jostled each other and those around them with ill-concealed fatigue and battle lust. Overnight, fuses had shortened on men from other units as well. *Sleep and food*, she thought. If Tarleton couldn't find that combination for his men soon, rebels might well hold the field, despite their foolish moves.

Scouts reported that Morgan's rear guard had quit its post to join the main army. The Legion's cheer thundered through the forest.

"Scotland the Brave" yowled with abandon from bagpipes, and Tarleton astride his charger paraded up and down the line. "Sing! We have them on the run! Sing, lads!" Men's voices belted verse after verse to the overcast sky, daring it to rain on them again. And the rain held off.

***

Late afternoon, they occupied the site Morgan abandoned that morning. A half-cooked meal awaited them: pork, cheese, hominy, johnnycakes, and coffee. Some was inedible, burned or ruined with dirt, but fires were built up to cook what was salvageable, and the chaplain blessed the meal as a portent for Tarleton's victory.

Their most recent meal was twenty-four hours earlier. Even with civilians receiving one-quarter rations, soldiers couldn't eat their fill. Men first tried to buy or trade for food. Then they scuffled. From a safe vantage point, Jonathan and Calliope at her side, Helen watched the rank and file teeter on anarchy with mingled horror and fascination before junior officers restored order. Could it be true that civilization was a myth, and without food, humans were but a day or so from becoming animals?

The march resumed by torchlight along the rebels' wide, sloppy trail, testament of their panic, but the condition of the route impeded baggage wagons, forced the army to a crawl. Helen staggered over churned ground and tree branches. Hunger wrung her insides with ferocity. A dull ache crept into her skull.

Her ankle snagged on a sapling. Down she sprawled into wet, moldy leaves less than a foot from a horse turd. Jonathan hoisted her to her feet and pulled the mare out of traffic. "Ride Calliope."

A groan echoed in her stomach. She whispered, "I need to eat."

He glanced at soldiers and civilians milling past them and held his voice low for her. "Then I shall provide a diversion."

While he faced away from the traffic, unbuttoned his breeches, and relieved himself, Helen fumbled the pack open enough to locate their food, sneaked a piece of beef jerky, and shoved more jerky and dried apples into her pockets. They rejoined the march, and over the next few minutes, under cover of darkness, she passed rations to Jonathan and fed herself. To her relief, her stomach quieted and the headache receded, but her limbs still ached. Sating her need for rest wouldn't come so easy.

The march paralleled Thicketty Creek. Dampness penetrated to her feet as if she wore no boots. Numerous scouts, Neville among them, overtook and intercepted the army. On a stretch of high ground, Tarleton halted his advance to receive reports and question more captured rebels. After the order for rest came, exhausted soldiers not on duty rolled up in their blankets and sought sleep on the hard ground around smoky campfires. Many shivered or trembled in their sleep, cold and hunger a barrier to the deep rest they craved.

The lit candle Jonathan held over Helen's shoulder allowed her to pen a journal entry: one paragraph, her script rickety like that of an old woman. She sanded the entry and reflected a moment upon the final sentence: *Rebel army awaits Legion where cows are penned.* Cowpens. Good gods, what a bloody boring name for a battle site. Londoners would hate it. She'd have to research a more colorful name after Tarleton beat the pulp out of Morgan. Many of those imbeciles who'd jeered and cursed the Legion just a day earlier would beg for mercy on the morrow. With a sigh, she closed the desk.

She slept the same shivery sleep of soldiers. Furies with skull heads haunted her dreams. Two swept near her, bony faces leering. She shuddered, not sure whether she'd half-awakened and was pinned a witness to their banter by her fatigue.

"Damned excellent brandy. I say, old boy, spare me more. It's quite taken the chill off."

"In a moment. But first, look closely at her, Mr. Treadaway. Are you certain you don't recognize her?"

"Forgive me for saying this, but your sister looks like a wench I sold back in Wiltshire. I could swear I sported with her a few years before that."

"She isn't my sister."

"She isn't? Who the hell is she, then?"

"The wench you sold."

"The devil you say! By god, that's rich. What a talented little mouth she had. I wager her mouth's even more talented now."

"I shan't dispute you on that point. Who purchased her?"

"Merchant named Silas Chiswell."

"Is he the man with her now?"

"Nah. Looks like one of Chiswell's advisors. Quill is his name."

"Your recall astounds me. Let's see to some brandy for you."

Helen clawed her way awake, coughed in the raw, smoky night, and struggled to a sitting position, her gaze swinging around the campsite. Jonathan blinked up at her in question.

Sentries picked their way around snoring blankets. Campfires had burned down, more coals and less smoke. Neither Fairfax nor Treadaway was in sight.

Jonathan's arm encircled her waist. "Bad dream, eh?"

"What a nightmare."

"I haven't slept so well tonight, either." He stroked her. "Unless I've read the signs wrong, we've an early start on the morrow. You'd best crawl inside this blanket with me and take what sleep we have remaining."

She obeyed and snuggled against him. "Jonathan, you're the best friend I've ever had." His hand clasped hers, and she regained sleep.

***

The bugle shattered what little rest she claimed and flung her into the chaos of men forming up to march. She studied the overcast. No sign of dawn, and it didn't feel as though she'd slept much. She helped Jonathan fold their blankets. "What time is it?"

"Around two. Reports are in. Morgan has reinforcements on the way. Tarleton decided to intercept him first."

In dismay, she swept her gaze north, where the terrain roughened. She spotted Liza, Jen, Sally, Rebecca, and Margaret. "The route grows more impassable. We'll be another full day traveling this byway." Another day without food. Her stomach rumbled.

Jonathan indicated the 71st light infantry, in position to march. "They're heading out first to clear the way." By firelight, he fixed her with a sober expression. "My guess is that Tarleton will leave the baggage behind for this final leg of the march."

Her dismay converted to alarm. "We're vulnerable without soldiers!" Disappointment's barb lodged in her heart. Not only would those left behind be vulnerable, they wouldn't be present for the battle. In one instant, she drew a breath to protest all the miles and weeks she'd traveled and toughed it out with the Legion, only to be denied a first-hand observation of her story's climax. In the next instant, she sagged her shoulders. Even were she permitted to mount Calliope and ride out with the Legion, she was too worn to do so. In truth, she had by then woven such a tapestry of detail about the courage of Tarleton and the Legion that she didn't need to see the actual battle to dazzle readers with their victory. She had enough for her story.

Jonathan sniffed. "Do you think Tarleton would come this far, just to leave his baggage guarded by *civilians*? I've peeked into it. Quite a few bottles of wine cached away, a victory celebration planned for his officers, no doubt. Soldiers need to guard it."

A laugh gusted through her. As usual, Jonathan had the wisdom of it. The baggage wouldn't be left defenseless. She also realized that she'd omitted plenty of points from her journal out of fatigue and haste. Here at last was her opportunity to catch up, while she could still remember that information.

Chapter Fifty-Eight

HELEN CRANED HER neck for a yawn at the sky, its leaden color paling, and acknowledged the clarity of a soldier's features when he walked past on patrol. If the rain held off, opposing forces north of them would be able to distinguish each other well enough to know friend from foe. She shivered.

At three o'clock in the morning, the remainder of the army had set out. Tarleton ordered the civilians and guard detachment to remain upon their ground until full daybreak. She fought the urge to stand and pace, instead regarding Liza, Jen, Sally, Rebecca, and Margaret, who sat upon another blanket not far from her. How could they exchange recipes and mend stockings when those they loved were miles away, assuming position for battle?

Their quiet, feminine unity touched her. She swallowed at poignancy in her throat. They'd left her undisturbed to write in her journal, but she knew they'd welcome her. For centuries, women snared in the savagery of war had kept each other's company and formed citadels of calm and courage because it was the way of women.

The ether around Helen vibrated and convulsed, as if from a thunderclap. Conversations hushed. Everyone paused. A spider of ice crawled over Helen's skull and dragged her gaze north. In her bones, she understood: a shock wave from a huge volley, the battle underway.

Jonathan secured her desk on Calliope. Baggage guards, representative from each corps that marched with Tarleton, continued patrols, dawn's light marking their steadfastness. Artisans and slaves checked wagons and draft horses to ensure the baggage was ready to roll. Jen recited a molasses cake recipe for the women on the blanket. Treadaway wove between them all gnawing his lip, useless.

Rebecca left the women and knelt at the edge of Helen's blanket. Surely the girl was anxious for her father and frightened for her own well-being, yet she didn't display those concerns. Try as she might, Helen couldn't summon a smile of encouragement for her. Rebecca didn't want her encouragement.

With a stab of empathy and horror, she recognized childhood terminated by war in Rebecca's face, not unlike her own terminated childhood.

Rebecca waited to be certain Treadaway was out of earshot. Then she moistened her lips. "Thank you." Her child's voice was the whisper of fallen autumn leaves. "For helping me."

Helen nodded. Rebecca returned to the blanket of women, and Helen considered Newman, now dead, and Neville and Fairfax, fighting miles to the north with Tarleton, and she hoped Rebecca truly *was* out of the Epsilon ring. She deserved that much.

Distorted sounds drifted to her, a distant cacophony of cannon fire and discharged muskets. She struggled to picture Morgan's militia flinging down their muskets in terror, scattering before the deafening charge of dragoons from the Legion and Seventeenth Light, but the images refused to bind. All she could envision was hollow-eyed exhaustion and hunger on the faces of the soldiers headed north, swallowed by night several hours before.

In charge of the baggage, Ensign Fraser of the 71st ordered their departure. Thirty-five wagons creaked into motion, preceded by two batmen and Negroes, their horses laden with portmanteaus, including that of the paymaster.

The high ground degenerated into swamp. Tremors gripped Helen's muscles before she'd marched five minutes. Travel grime plastered her face and hands, and her brain phased in and out of a fantasy where she was clean, dry, and warm, well-fed, and rested. Even by daylight, the terrain tripped her, fought her advance north. The saber of winter wind sliced through wool and rasped in the trees. *Go. Go.* Trickster crows swooped down nearby, cocked their heads, and mocked the procession with beady eyes. *Haw-haw!* Helen's gut rippled with hunger, her constant companion for at least three days. How had Tarleton and his men prevailed?

She almost tottered into the rear of a wagon before realizing the train had stopped, the road beneath them high ground again, fringed by copses of oaks, dogwoods, and pines. Battle sounds from the north had dwindled. Her gaze tracked on Fraser, who trotted ahead.

The advance guard had detained three civilians on horseback: clean, middle-class men who didn't look to have fought their way through a battle. One man waved an arm. "Halloo, you folks with Tarleton? If I were you, I'd scatter. Your commander just lost a battle up yonder!"

Disbelief shimmied up Helen's back like a hundred ants of ice. Consternation erupted along the line —"Who is he?" "What's he talking about?" "Tarleton *lost*?"— before Fraser reached the three civilians. "Who are you?"

"We were visiting kinfolk, cattle farmers. We saw a battle." The man's voice quavered with shock. "Tarleton's officers are dead. His infantry collapsed. Morgan's men aren't far behind. For god's sake, save yourselves while you can!" He slapped his horse's flank. "Heigh, get up!" No one tried to stop the civilians from bolting.

Soldiers shoved people aside and began dumping Tarleton's hoarded delicacies upon the ground to prevent rebels from confiscating them. Hungry artisans bellowed with rage. Two slammed Helen as they leaped to pull soldiers off the baggage. Jonathan dragged her and Calliope out of the fray.

Head spinning, she watched soldiers wrench themselves free, cut loose draft horses nearest them, and flee south upon the road, Ensign Fraser in their lead. Becoming a rebel prisoner of war was not an option for a man who'd served with Banastre Tarleton.

Sally wailed. Men rushed to unhitch remaining draft horses and escape, or dive into the baggage for food. Margaret pushed a man away from a horse, her brusqueness so shocking him that he backed off and allowed her to claim it for her own flight. Jonathan yanked Helen's arm. "We're getting out. Now."

Two-dozen whooping militiamen on horseback thundered in from the north and discharged firearms into the group of civilians. Four men and Jen sprawled on the ground, bloody and screaming. Swords whooshed the air, artisans' muskets fired, and Helen dove for cover beneath a wagon. When she scuttled around to look for Jonathan, she saw Calliope's legs. Where was Jonathan?

"Yee-aww, *women!*" hollered a rebel. Liza and Sally shrieked. A man seized Helen's forearm and tried to drag her from beneath the wagon. "Got me one right here!" She gripped the underside of the wagon with her other hand. Unbalanced, he sprawled belly down. Expression screwed into a snarl, he started to crawl beneath the wagon. She gouged one of his eyes with her fingers. He bellowed and wiggled away. Gooey blood from his eyeball clung to her hand. She shrieked, her heart pounding with horror, and smeared her gory fingers through the mud.

Dozens more horses thundered onto the scene. The song of sabers unsheathed rang through the site. Rebels, as one, howled with terror. Blades slammed together, men cursed, horses whinnied — Calliope, where was Calliope? Heart whamming her throat, Helen rotated her head toward the outer edge of the wagon. Again, she spotted Calliope's legs, dancing around. But where was *Jonathan?* She had to find Jonathan.

Certain that Tarleton's cavalry had engaged the Whigs, she scuttled toward the inner edge of her cover, hoping for a glimpse of dragoons. She froze at the sound of a moist, heavy impact. A severed head hit the ground inches from her nose, blood spraying away from the wagon. The man's eyes blinked twice before glazing over. His lips, twisted in a grimace, revealed space where a front tooth was missing. Parker, from Devonshire, Parker — no, it couldn't be Parker, because Parker wasn't a rebel.

Her stomach heaved and brought up nothing, not even bile. Fancying she smelled rum on the dead rebel, she gagged, squeezed her eyes shut, and rolled to the other side of the wagon. Horror tossed her gut, dizzied her mind. Flee, yes, flee. Calliope's reins trailed the ground. She seized them, dragged herself from beneath the wagon. The mare whickered at the sight of her.

Smeared with mud, Helen crouched behind the wagon, waiting for her stomach to quiet. She finally poked her head up when, above the moans of the wounded, she heard Tarleton's grief-thickened voice: "God save the king, but I cannot stay! None of us can!"

Sweat and dirt streaked his face. Grime dulled the gold buttons and braid, and the swan feathers drooped. The horse beneath him wasn't even the magnificent charger he'd ridden out on five hours earlier, but a tired old gelding. "How valiantly each of you has served His Majesty and me. I'm unable to repay your loyalty. Morgan, that whoreson with no decency, he shot *officers!* The infantry lies dead or grievously wounded!"

Helen darted a glance around at the uniformed men on horseback — Legion cavalry with some dragoons from the Seventeenth Light — and reality finally speared her. Daniel Morgan and his militia rabble had obliterated Tarleton's infantry in less than half an hour. All Tarleton had left of an army of a thousand was fewer than two hundred dragoons.

Her gaze shot to the colonel again. The streaks of moisture on his face. Not sweat, no. Despair and grief lumped in her throat. Tarleton would never forgive himself this defeat. He'd been as devoted to those men as they'd been to him.

"Heed me. More rebels are on the way. We must ride to my Lord Cornwallis. Leave the baggage. Save yourselves!" He wheeled the gelding about south. Cavalrymen steadied horses bearing bound prisoners who'd survived the attack upon the baggage.

Betrayal and more horror climbed through Helen's despair. What was Tarleton doing? Was he leaving them to Daniel Morgan, and the settling of old scores? Tarleton's Quarter — no, no, surely not!

Margaret, in just as much muddy disarray as Helen but somehow still sultry and beautiful mounted upon a draft horse, thrust her way through the crowd to Tarleton. Then they were off southbound on the road, Tarleton, Margaret, perhaps one hundred fifty cavalrymen, and their prisoners. Helen and the others gawped at their retreat in stunned silence and disbelief.

"God damn you to hell!" A wainwright shook his fist at the retreating horses. "You bloody bastards, you left us to die!" A roar of panicked agreement swelled from the artisans.

A hand jiggled Helen's shoulder. With a gasp, she faced a grimy, rumpled Treadaway. "Come quickly, madam." His breath was short, as if he'd been running. "Your friend, he's hurt badly!"

Confusion and fear snared her reason. "Jonathan!" Still gripping Calliope's reins, she stumbled off-road after the agent, into the brush. Dead briars snagged at her petticoat and cloak.

"Hurry!" Treadaway paused, his expression twisted with concern, and waved for her to follow him into a copse of trees.

Brambles and brush detained her. "Mr. Treadaway, wait up! Jonathan, I'm coming!" She finally cleared underbrush and glimpsed the agent ahead in the gloom. "Mr. Treadaway!" She trotted ahead, peering around tree trunks. "Jonathan?"

Calliope snorted and shook her head, as if she'd smelled something foul. Helen halted, of a sudden aware of her isolation and how far she'd traveled from the road. A primordial chill not of winter's making chiseled her spine. A crow cawed. Her heart pulsed in her ears.

Treadaway emerged from behind trees and strolled toward her. A smile crawled across his mouth that she hadn't seen him wear in twelve years: the satisfaction of a procurer who'd made a premium sale. She spun around to run for the road and drew up short, retreat blocked by a pistol held in the hand of a red-eyed, stubble-jawed Maximus Prescott, not ten feet before her.

"Excellent work, Treadaway. At least one of you men can follow orders. As for you, you bloody whore, they're going to give you my property." A muscle in the attorney's cheek twitched. "I should have killed you years ago." He cocked the pistol. "Guess who betrayed you to us? Your very own 'brother,' Lieutenant Fairfax. Now that's justice."

Chapter Fifty-Nine

A DUN-COLORED BLUR pounced upon Prescott with a wink of steel and a child's warrior scream. He howled in pain, Rebecca's knife embedded in his thigh, and flung her off him into the leaves. "Rebecca!" Helen's desolation echoed through the wood. Prescott yanked out the knife, flung it down near Rebecca, and took aim at her. Helen's denial drowned in the report of the pistol. The girl shrieked and convulsed, chest bloody.

Her mind blank with survival, Helen dropped Calliope's reins and sprinted for the road. The men overtook her. She kneed Treadaway in the groin, doubling him over, and swung for Prescott's face. His nose popped blood. Rage roared from him. He seized her hair and dragged her deep into the copse. "Treadaway, on your feet!"

She chomped into Prescott's hand. Bone crunched. He released her hair and slapped her face, sending a dazzle of stars through her vision. She sprawled near the twitching, moaning Rebecca, and through the demon's twirl of forest, saw a bloody-nosed Prescott descend for her, teeth bared. His second slap split her lip. She clawed his face. He punched the pit of her stomach, and agony danced her around. Then the lion's maw of earth swallowed her whole.

★★★

The first time she came around, her face and stomach were afire, so she didn't fight the slide back into oblivion. But the second time, perplexity drove her past the throbbing in stomach and face. That queer noise behind her, an animal in pain, mewling, bleating.

On her side among dead leaves, cold numbing face, shoulder, and hip, she tried to roll over, alarmed when her limbs didn't respond. She was bound, ankles and wrists, her wrists behind her back. Pain in her bruised stomach checked her attempt to right herself. She coughed at dust and mold. The forest spun again. She collapsed. Rebecca lay still about fifteen feet away. Helen shuddered.

The mewling noise revived. Elemental horror blasted her. A human was in pain. Teeth chattering, she struggled to peer behind. All she saw was trees. The forest gyrated, an arm clothed in scarlet caught in the spin. She sank into the leaves again to allow pain and dizziness to abate.

A man's moans ratcheted up into full-scale sobbing, his voice distorted with agony. Horror raked Helen. That was Maximus Prescott suffering. Memory flashed the image of the arm clothed in scarlet, and more cold than she could ever imagine impaled her bones. *Guess who betrayed you to us? Your very own brother...*

Gods, no. Now she remembered the significance of Camden. Fairfax's informants had spotted Prescott near Camden. How stupid could the attorney and Treadaway have been? Fairfax hadn't just betrayed her to them. He'd used her as bait for them. Now he was indulging himself with two spies from Epsilon.

Her "brother" had bound her, and she awaited his pleasure. "Epsilon, Mr. Prescott." She heard no impatience in Fairfax. Rather, his voice coaxed, soothed. Then he did something to elicit another scream from the attorney. The urge for self-preservation and flight smothered her rational mind. She thrashed against her bonds, raising more dust, catapulting herself into coughing.

Afterward, she lay recovering her breath, her stomach and face hurting more than ever. Leaves rustled. Hair on the back of her neck rose. A glance over her shoulder rewarded her with the sight of Fairfax watching her, his face radiant, angelic, while he cleaned the blade of his knife on a piece of cloth. Even bound, she leapt several inches in terror. "Damn you, don't touch me!"

Puzzlement trickled into his expression, and he ambled to her. She screamed; Prescott mewled. She never believed that she and the attorney could agree on something.

Knife sheathed, Fairfax crouched and hoisted her into a sitting position. She tried to find her footing. The world twisted. He picked leaves from her hair and jacket and settled her mobcap back on her head. "You've looked better, darling, but it's nothing a bath and rest cannot mend." He caressed her face, the metallic stench of blood on his hand.

She shrank from him. Horror and revulsion beat through her, demanding that she flee. She glared at him with as much hatred as she could summon. "You used me to bait Prescott and Treadaway!"

"You don't recognize the brilliance of the scheme?"

"You lout, they almost killed me!"

"Nonsense. You disabled Treadaway to unconsciousness and worked over Prescott's face magnificently. Double gouges down one cheek, his nose crooked at the oddest angle —"

"Kill him."

"I shall."

"He's a rebel spy. Execute him. Shoot him. Treadaway, too."

"You wouldn't be so quick to dispense mercy if you'd heard what Prescott confessed a few moments ago." He paused for effect. "Agatha Chiswell was your mother-in-law, yes?"

Helen started, picturing Silas's mother in Boston, even though she'd been dead for several years. "Surely you aren't going to tell me she was a rebel spy!"

"She circumvented inheritance laws and set some land aside for you. A thousand acres just outside Boston, from what Prescott tells me. Prime location, quite valuable."

She gaped. "Why haven't I heard about it?"

"Badley and Prescott intercepted every one of her letters inviting you to visit her and claim your gift. For years, they've been trying to figure out how to swindle you out of the land so they can contribute it to the rebel cause. Their obstacle has been that the dowager Chiswell stipulated you must claim it in person. No matter how well they forged your signature, neither of them resembles you in person. Ironic. You needn't have lived like a pauper. You've a bit of wealth."

Disbelief punctured Helen's revulsion. "But I don't have it. Agatha Chiswell is dead."

"The land is still available, but you must claim it in person."

She knew that the rise of her anger mobilized her expression, fed Fairfax's elation. For years, she and Enid had scraped by, suffered in winter from too little firewood — but far worse, she'd missed a relationship with her mother-in-law. Not that she'd felt great warmth for the old lady the one time they'd met, but Badley and Prescott had stolen that opportunity from her forever.

"Badley and Prescott decided to kill you when Widow Hanley's copy of the will exposed their crimes." Angelic beauty recaptured Fairfax's face. "Prescott deserves what I have planned for him, wouldn't you agree?"

Her stomach burned. Prescott had stolen and squandered her husband's estate, murdered three men, and tried to kill her and Jonathan. She wanted him dead — but tortured to death? She firmed her voice. "Execute him. Torturing him is pointless. I've served my purpose as bait. Let me be on my way."

"Don't be absurd. Rebel patrols are sweeping the road. I could never forgive myself if I allowed you to fall into their hands. Your only way out of here is with me, and I promise I shall get you safely out as soon as I've finished with Prescott and Treadaway. Besides, when an oracle appears in a man's life, it's a message from the gods of his pending greatness, so he'd best take care of her, pamper her."

Oracle? What was Fairfax talking about? Perplexity tugged at the corners of her mouth. "I'm an oracle? How do you figure that?"

He traced her lower lip with his forefinger. "Laudanum and wine. Visions."

Exactly what she'd told him after their encounter with Marion's men. So that was why he'd stolen her laudanum. Stunned, she opened her mouth to clarify what she'd meant by visions.

"'Something horrible is going to happen to the Legion.' You said that before Yule. Morgan has decimated the Legion, making your journalist's story worthless in London. As a prophetess, you're far too reserved with your gift. Why waste yourself at journalism?"

She shut her mouth and lowered her gaze. If she rectified his misconceptions, he'd have no use for her except brief carnal dalliance. She was witness to his torture of Prescott. He couldn't afford to release her when his goal to attain a seat in Parliament hinged upon his performance in the colonies.

For the time, let him believe she could prophesy. Before he plied her with that first glass of laudanum-dosed wine, she must escape, or the extent of her ability as an "oracle" would be obvious.

He tilted her chin, scrutinized her face, and leaned forward as if to kiss her but stopped just a few inches from her mouth. She felt sweat pop out on her forehead. For a second, it wasn't Fairfax leaning over her but Treadaway. Appalled, nauseated, she blinked and shook her head, dislodged the vision.

He steadied her head in his hands and brushed his lips to the uninjured side of her mouth. Revulsion hammered away at her. *Play his game. Give him what he wants.* She prayed that pretense wouldn't demand that she sleep with the hate-filled seven-year-old.

Agony looked like acquiescence to Fairfax. When he drew back to study tears on her cheeks, base victory sparked his eyes. "You've greatness ahead of you, Helen. Trust me to help you develop it. I shall be your teacher." A reptilian smile wrung his lips. "Your new *professor*."

Another blast of horror stranded breath in her throat. What had happened to Jonathan? "No, no, you didn't."

Bored, he pushed up to his feet. "Mr. Quill was likely separated from you in the skirmish and thought you'd headed south without him. Forget him. It's time you moved on to better things."

A man's scream penetrated the copse, followed by Treadaway's voice, shrill with horror. "Ah, god, Prescott — barbarians! Halloo! Help! Help! Untie us!"

Fairfax's lips twisted wryly. "Treadaway has regained consciousness and lost his gag." He shook out Helen's cloak and nestled it over her shoulders. "I know how hungry you are. Prescott has food stashed in his horse's saddlebags." He jutted his chin to indicate a location past her right shoulder. "Soon as I'm finished, I shall fetch us a meal." After straightening, he gloated down at her, a tundra pervading his eyes. "Such a talented mouth, oh, yes." Then, swaggering back the way he'd come, he whipped out his knife. "Mr. Treadaway, you should have waited your turn."

Chapter Sixty

WHILE HELEN EXPLORED with frantic fingers the rope that bound her hands, a performance she never wished to witness unfolded on the other side of the brush. "*You* did that to Prescott?" Treadaway's voice leaped an octave. "You bleedin' monster! Help!"

A series of humid thuds followed, reminiscent of the sounds grain and seed bags made when plopped upon each other at the wharf in Wilmington. When the impacts ceased, Helen knew that Treadaway was no longer of a humor to holler for help, just as she knew she wouldn't be able to untie her bonds blindly. Nevertheless, she must free herself before Fairfax finished with the two men, or the pendulum of power between them would shift to favor him at the physical level. She could not defeat him there.

Morgan's men would search the area for those who'd marched with Tarleton, but the wine-filled baggage train posed a serious distraction in the immediate vicinity, and Fairfax did seem to have located his sport far enough off the road that his guests' screams weren't easily heard. Add the chaos of battle aftermath, and she admitted a distinct possibility that Fairfax wouldn't be discovered. Thus far, only Rebecca had found her way to Helen. Now the girl was dead. As for Jonathan, the two of them had somehow become separated in that horrid skirmish. Since she and Calliope had disappeared together, Jonathan must have concluded that she fled south with others to avoid capture.

No one was going to rescue her. Alone, she must escape.

"Monster? Treadaway, I'm miffed. You've quite a touch with throat slitting. Newman never put up a fight. Who's really the monster here?"

The agent said something unintelligible. He sounded sluggish, as if his brain were swollen.

"Thus far, Prescott has failed to provide me with intelligence about Epsilon, but I haven't given up on him yet. I agree that he looks a bit worse for the wear. Why don't you give your fellow spy a break? Epsilon's identity, if you please." Treadaway whimpered pieces of words. "You don't know? Hmm. Tell me what you know about Lieutenant Michael Stoddard."

Helen blinked in disbelief. Fairfax thought Stoddard was a spy for the rebels. "D-don't know anyone named Stoddard."

"You rebels always insist upon eating your loaves with stones." The pummeling resumed.

She smelled vomit and human waste. Horror swamped her again. *Run away! Run away!* Fright and flight drove her hands into another fruitless struggle with her bonds. Her soul wailed in helplessness. Nothing she was doing advanced her escape, but she *must* escape.

She inhaled, tried to calm herself with deep breaths, as Jonathan had taught her. Her nose detected the smell of horse. She twisted her neck for a look over her right shoulder, in the direction Fairfax had indicated for Prescott's horse, but saw only brush and trees. The horse must be tethered. Were other horses back there?

Hoping that Treadaway's loud sobbing would act as a cover, she whistled once past her shoulder and heard Calliope's snort of recognition. Although she was bound and the mare was tethered, gratitude welled in her eyes. She wasn't totally alone.

She visualized Calliope laden with blankets, food, and the desk. Her desk with the story of Banastre Tarleton — bane of Thomas Sumter and Francis Marion, and Lord Cornwallis's favorite — tromped by Daniel Morgan at a place with the dull name of Cowpens. What London paper would buy *that* story? Fairfax was right. Tarleton's defeat had made her efforts worthless.

Worthless? Her thoughts performed an about face. Worthless to *Londoners*, but the colonies harbored rebel presses aplenty. She'd witnessed what would surely be reckoned a pivotal battle, and she could disguise her bias. Ah, she couldn't imagine a more fitting poetic justice than convincing rebels to pay for the story.

Memory drifted to her last sight of Tarleton. He'd no intention of helping his civilians escape Morgan. She imagined artisans overtaken by Washington's men, slaughtered like Marion's Whigs in the Santee — despite their courage and dedication, no match for seasoned dragoons. Anger stung her gut. So Tarleton wanted to hang a rebel printer, eh? Poetic justice, indeed, if a rebel printed her story and metaphorically hanged Tarleton.

Treadaway's scream of suffering hauled her back to reality. Not until she'd escaped Fairfax could she make plans for her work. She'd written a story no other journalist would be able to obtain. One of Fairfax's first acts would be to destroy it. Not only did he deem the story worthless, but its existence blocked her total capitulation. Her writing was pointless to him. He needed his "oracle" subsumed to him, as Margaret had been back in December. He had no use for another person's independence.

Margaret had chosen to ride off with a defeated Tarleton, rather than wait for Fairfax. But now, Fairfax had Helen Chiswell, and oh, the manna he planned to feed her...such a talented mouth, yes, indeed...just like Treadaway...

Treadaway no longer sounded human. Helen closed her eyes and focused on each breath to evict the panic that shredded her logic. When she reopened her eyes, panic still hovered at the periphery of her soul, but it no longer choked her. Instinct's delicate voice whispered something she hadn't heard before: that in the dissonance of terror, she'd overlooked a clue to her escape. She must calm down enough to recognize it.

For the first time, she swept her gaze over Rebecca's body, face and hands already the pallor of death. Sadness trickled through her. A life over so soon — yes, there was another story. All the camp women deserved a voice for their courage, but especially Rebecca, who had given her life for Helen. Prescott's pistol had been aimed at her face. He was so close she could see the muscles in his trigger finger contract. But Rebecca had flown from the brush and stabbed him in the leg, taken the pistol ball in Helen's place, given Helen a chance to escape.

Rebecca had had a *knife*. Prescott threw it into the leaves after he decked the girl, near where she collapsed.

No knife showed through the brown leaf carpet that separated Helen from the girl. Considering how thorough Fairfax was, he must have removed it while she was insensible — no, she mustn't assume. She shrugged off her cloak. She had to check for the knife.

Unavoidable, unmistakable, the rustle of leaves that announced her scoot-hop toward Rebecca. Almost all the way there, hair on her neck stood out again. She bowed her head and quivered her shoulders to deepen her deception. "Poor child." She sniffed. "She was so young."

"Forget about her, darling." Fairfax strolled closer. "She was nothing."

Resentment simmered in Helen. Nothing. A nobody. And that nobody had saved her life. Helen's knee pressed something hard beneath the leaves. Without moving her head, she rolled her eyes downward and glimpsed steel. She jutted her right hip to allow her petticoat to cover some of the blade. "So young, and now her life is over. Please go away. Allow me time alone with her."

He vented exasperation through his nostrils. "As you wish." His footsteps receded in the leaves, and he said in a chipper tone, "Hullo, Prescott. Thought I'd forgotten about you, eh?" The attorney, who had been quiet too long, bleated again.

Helen blinked at tears. "Thank you, Rebecca. The gods grant you peace."

Shimmying around, she grasped the knife hilt and tried to manipulate the blade upon rope. Her wrists chafed, and she nicked herself twice before she paused, sweating, to reconsider. What she needed was a way to brace the knife while she sawed the ropes with the blade.

She glanced upward, felt mist upon her face, and licked her lips. Several feet away, a small tree had been snapped at the base.

Prescott and Treadaway were sobbing. "Neither of you knows Epsilon's identity? Come now. It's nearly noon, and it's raining."

She dragged herself over and examined the jagged wood of the stump, not yet too decayed, before wedging the hilt of the knife into the stump, blade angled up, and backing against it. If she could avoid toppling over onto it and stabbing herself, the action might succeed.

Muscles in her neck and shoulders bucked at overextension while she sawed rope. Twice the knife popped loose, but after a few minutes, she felt the rope loosen. She shook her arms and rolled her shoulders back. Seizing the knife, she freed her ankles.

Pure terror clobbered her at the wink of red uniform in the brush. Heart pounding, she had just enough warning to reposition rope over her ankles and jerk her arms behind her back in pretense, the knife clenched in her hand.

Fairfax emerged from his sport and frowned at her. She yanked her gaze to the girl's body, hoped she stared at it vacuously, and rocked back and forth. "Rebecca, Rebecca," she murmured, in silence imploring the gods to send Fairfax away.

"We mustn't have you taking a chill." He retrieved her cloak.

More terror electrified her. He'd spot the loosened ropes on her ankles when he replaced the cloak over her shoulders. If she wanted to escape, she had no choice but to knife him. "The gods reward warriors," she whispered.

"I didn't hear that, darling." He draped the cloak over her. At the same time, his gaze registered the ropes on her ankles.

With a screech, she stabbed upward for his groin. Quick reflexes jerked his body. The knife caught his inner thigh instead. She shoved herself away from his fury and agony and rolled to a crouch, the knife still gripped in her hand.

He fell short in a lunge, hobbled, blood spreading across this thigh. "Damn you!"

She slashed air near his fist, stumbled to her feet, tripped on her cloak, snatched it up. Balance regained, she fled from torture and murder toward the horses. Her face and gut ached, and she shuddered with cold, shock, and fatigue.

"Damn you, you witch!" The woods reverberated with the god of war, foiled and in pain.

A backward glance confirmed that he offered no immediate pursuit. Calliope snorted with pleasure at her approach, and she hugged the mare's neck. Two geldings were tethered nearby, probably Prescott and Treadaway's mounts. Neither was Fairfax's battle horse.

He could well have tethered his own mount elsewhere. That meant the possibility of his pursuit on horseback later, even though he hadn't yet come after her.

Calliope was burdened as a packhorse. No leisure to redistribute supplies. Helen adjusted stirrups on the smaller gelding, stowed the knife in a saddlebag, and made certain the canteen and supply of trail bread and dried venison were where she could reach them. With the other horses roped in tow behind, she climbed into the saddle, her petticoat hitched, her stockings muddy. To hell with propriety.

Maybe the knife had nicked Fairfax's femoral artery. No elation penetrated her shocked numbness at the speculation of him bleeding to death in the woods. All her attention was bent on flight, especially when she imagined hearing him holler her name once more. Or was that wind and fatigue playing with her?

After circling well around the site of his recreation, she marked with apprehension her approach to the road from the laughter and cheers at the abandoned baggage train — rebels celebrating with Tarleton's supplies. Oh, how they'd love to get hold of three horses and a woman. Terrified, she walked the horses parallel to the road south and kept hidden. The voices faded. She guided the mounts up onto the road. Then she clicked her tongue and sent them into a trot.

A steady drizzle lowered upon her, and her breath and that of the horses plumed frigid clouds before them. She ate trail rations and drank from the canteen and couldn't quite remember when she'd last slept. But she was *free*. And tears of raw relief mingled with the rain on her face.

Chapter Sixty-One

THE APPROACHING RUMBLE of horses alerted Helen in time for her to steer the team into the brush. Morgan's men galloped past with captives. By the fifth such incident, she realized that panic no longer twitched her hands.

Fairfax didn't overtake her. Maybe he'd bled to death. Maybe he'd been captured. How lucky she was to have escaped him and the patrols, a woman alone. She thanked the gods over and over. But only in folk tales did gods manifest a sanctuary for travelers. Night came early in January, in the hinterland. Exhaustion pounded her. She had to find shelter.

Where was Jonathan? Anguish and uncertainty badgered her to return to the baggage train and look for him among the victims, but she hadn't seen him injured after the skirmish that morning. *Trust me to guard my own back*, he'd said in Wilmington. She imagined him telling her, "Your obligation is to your own safety."

While she continued to push south, her heart ached beyond the worry of what had happened to him, and tears dampened her face. She smeared them off with the back of her hand, but they kept misting the road ahead, just as confusion and exhaustion obscured her future. Camden. Roger and Hannah Pearson. Rebel publishers. Wilmington. Badley and Prescott's property. Chiswell land in Boston. The road ran on and on. None of it made sense to her: blindfolded, spun around, turned loose to stagger about.

Distant rifle fire east of the road jolted her from a daze. She walked the horses and advanced with caution, wishing Prescott or Treadaway had left her a firearm. She pulled out the riding crop and readied the knife, its blade still stained with Fairfax's blood. Ugh.

Just around a curve, a dark-haired man shambled from the foliage and flopped belly-down upon the road about thirty feet ahead of her. She gasped with fright and reined back. He was dressed in the hunting shirt of a backwoodsman, and his right lower leg was bloody, and there was something far too familiar about him.

From the east came faint shouts of pursuit. The man propped himself up and scanned the road south, still unaware of her. She sucked in a breath of shock. Lieutenant Adam Neville.

He struggled to his feet, almost collapsed, and groaned. Then he swiveled about and spotted her. Recognition exploded across his face. He took a step forward in entreaty and crumpled to his left knee, face blanched with pain.

Neville wasn't going anywhere afoot. His rifle was missing. He must have lost his horse and gear in that altercation to the east.

She walked the horses closer, misgivings piled up in her soul. He'd used her to transmit messages to rebels. On the other hand, she was fairly certain he'd no part of Badley and Prescott's scheme to cut off her funding and strand her in the backcountry. A scout familiar with the land, he might know where she could shelter for the night.

"Well met, Mr. Neville." She brandished the crop. "Pursuit will be upon you before long."

His gaze tracked the riding crop as if it were an old enemy. "Mrs. Chiswell, allow me to ride one of your horses a few miles. I shall tell you anything else you wish to learn about Colonel Thomas Brown."

She barked a laugh. "Who's chasing you this time — Whigs or Loyalists?"

He scowled. "Stinking, bloody Presbyterians, shooting anything that moves, mistaking me for a clan enemy."

Whatever Neville had been up to deep in feral Whig territory, it had misfired. She didn't want to encounter any Presbyterians. She pointed the crop at his leg. "You need medical attention."

"I know where to find it." He gestured south. "About five miles that way, an apothecary. Where's Mr. Quill?"

Her lips firmed, but she wasn't sure whether he spotted the tremble just before she'd tightened them. "I don't know."

"You need protection. The apothecary operates a safe house. I cannot believe you've gotten this far alone." He scanned her face. "And mostly unharmed."

"Let me be certain we understand each other. You need safety and medical help, know where to find it, but lack transportation. I have transportation and need safety but lack knowledge of where to find it."

"I think we understand each other, Mrs. Chiswell."

Her inner thighs throbbed from riding. She dismounted without grace, towed the horses forward a few more feet, and flaunted the crop. "Then we have an agreement."

"My thanks." He regarded the crop with respect.

"Toss all your knives out on the road." She collected three and stashed them in the lead gelding's saddlebags. "Climb aboard that gelding back there. Hang on, and don't pass out before telling me where to turn off to the apothecary's land."

"Madam." He limped back to the gelding, and with what must have been superhuman effort, climbed into the saddle.

Sounds of pursuit neared. Helen, remounted, sent the horses into a trot. Ten minutes later, when they'd left the Presbyterians behind to wonder over their quarry's escape, she spared a glance at the ranger, both pleased and disappointed that he remained in the saddle and hadn't galloped away.

He managed a weak salute. "Have you any food?"

Awakened again to hunger, she scooped two-thirds of the beef into a handkerchief for herself and tossed the satchel of remaining jerky to the scout. "That's all that's left."

"Thank you. With any luck, we'll eat beefsteak tonight."

She chuckled to recall her fantasy just a day earlier. Beefsteak for supper: sheer fancy.

***

Palmer the apothecary scratched at his stubbly chin. Candlelight drove haggard lines across his skinny face. "A wagonload of grain and five hogs. Pickens didn't compensate us for any of it. He just told us to be glad he wasn't burning our buildings." He propped elbows on the rough-hewn table and his head in his hands. "All this he said in front of my wife. He's no gentleman, that's for sure."

Mrs. Palmer set a covered pot on the table and rested her hands upon her very pregnant belly. "We're fortunate they didn't harm us." In the loft overhead, the healthy squeals of children wrestling attested to the truth of her statement. "More stew for our guests?"

Neville declined, his injured leg bandaged beneath trousers and stretched out. Helen felt guilty when she eyed the pot. Beef stew with carrots, turnips, and onions: the first substantial meal she'd eaten in a week. Mrs. Palmer read her hesitation and ladled a third bowl of stew for her. "Thank you," she murmured. Eyes shining, Palmer's wife carried the pot back over to the hearth.

Helen listened to conversation and wondered whether the family would offer Neville hospitality if they knew he'd betrayed people just like them. She could understand neutrals in the war, but she didn't understand those who deceived both sides. Where did Neville hang his hat? What riled him? Did he honor allegiance anywhere?

In the distance, dogs barked, frenzied. The apothecary's brother burst in through the front door nearly out of breath, a rifle in his hand. "A party on horseback riding up the road toward the house."

Stew bowl and spoon were whisked away from Helen. The brothers slid the table six feet to the side and shoved back a rug beneath it. Two wooden planks lifted to reveal a ladder angled down into darkness. Palmer handed Neville a lit lantern and gestured for Helen to follow the ranger down.

The hiding-hole, its packed dirt walls reinforced with wood beams, was large enough for two or three adults to stand in and led to a low tunnel: a fugitive's egress from the house. Mrs. Palmer passed down Helen's cloak and desk, and the men shut the planks over them. Shuffling and scraping overhead told Helen the rug and table had been repositioned. She sighed. Gods, she didn't want to run back out into the cold night. She'd washed her face and hands for the first time in over a week and had near to a full belly, and all she wanted to do was sleep in relative warmth.

The barking dogs neared the house. Someone whammed at the front door. It creaked open, and a man's voice boomed. "Evening, folks. We're with Major Triplett's battalion out of Virginia, checking to make sure everyone's safe. We've orders to apprehend and detain anyone who traveled with Tarleton's army this morning."

The apothecary's brother quieted the dogs. Palmer struck up such a cordial conversation with the rebel that Helen was certain she'd have to remain in the hole until dawn. Neville was near the bottom of her list of people with whom she'd want to be stuck in a hiding-hole.

The ranger said, low, "I presume you'll return to Wilmington."

She faced him and inclined her head in acknowledgement. Cognizant of the rebels' proximity, she kept her voice soft. "I presume you'll return to spying." Neville wouldn't have it any other way.

His expression didn't change. "The horse you were riding looks like Tobias Treadaway's horse." She nodded. "What happened to him?"

"Lieutenant Fairfax happened to Treadaway." Neville's lips tightened. "Mr. Fairfax also happened to Maximus Prescott. You rode *his* horse."

"How did you get the horses away from him? How did *you* get away?"

In the confined space there was no way to hide the clench of horror on her face, the memory that would stay with her a lifetime of being forced to witness the torture of two men.

Neville's whisper savaged the damp, still air. "Did he injure you?"

Above her head, Palmer and the rebel from Virginia were laughing over some jest. She glowered. "Does it matter to you, Mr. Neville? Does anything matter except your amusement over playing both sides in this war against each other?"

"I don't owe you an explanation for what I do."

"You're just as evil as he."

"I'm nothing like Lieutenant Fairfax."

Conversation above had quieted. She waited for it to resume, then whispered, "Prove it, even if nothing else on this earth matters to you. He's a fiend, a parasite." She flinched, recognizing David's exact words, and steadied her breathing. "You and Mr. Stoddard must bury the hatchet and find a way to rid us of him."

"How did you —?" A snarl exploded through his expression. With self-control, he maintained a low voice. "How much about Stoddard does Fairfax know?"

"I don't have an answer for you, but I cannot imagine him idling while you and Mr. Stoddard resolve your differences." Especially since Fairfax now suspected Stoddard of being a member of the Epsilon ring. She sighed and braced fists on her hips. "At the point I'd managed to leave Mr. Fairfax's company, it didn't sound as though he was going to obtain the intelligence he sought about Epsilon from Prescott or Treadaway. Fate could easily have allowed you to encounter him upon the road today in your injured condition."

Lantern light threw inhuman sparks in Neville's dark eyes, but he said nothing. She faced away from him again, arms crossed beneath her cloak. Silence between them yawned. It was just as well. She had nothing further to say to a man who was a ranger in every sense of the word.

Chapter Sixty-Two

THE PALMERS LODGED Neville in the stable with horses and Helen in the loft with squirmy, whispery children aged four through twelve. While the night was far from quiet, it was warm.

Memory persisted in replaying Tarleton's panic, agonized screams of Prescott and Treadaway, and supernatural radiance in Fairfax's face. Outside the cabin, in the wilderness between the Pacolet River and Thicketty Creek about fifteen miles south of the Cowpens, wind whistled through trees, owls hooted, and dogs sounded an occasional warning to a wayward possum or raccoon. All of it hummed Helen awake long after the house had settled down.

The proximity of other warm bodies reminded her that Jonathan had slept beside her every night for several weeks. His absence echoed in her heart. The feel of her desk safe and nestled beside her in the loft, its story intact, only emphasized the absence.

Trails of slow tears stained the side of her face. Across twelve years, she reached out and embraced Nell Grey, restored her into her heart, bestowed upon her long overdue gratitude. Nell — tough, scrappy, and common born — had saved her life.

She slept through cockcrow, through children rising to tend morning chores, and awakened after dawn to the aromas of flapjacks, frying bacon, and fresh-brewed coffee, the obstinate mahogany of the desk pressed into her ribcage. After draping Mrs. Palmer's extra shawl over her shift, she descended from the loft, shoved on her boots, and paid a morning visit to the vault.

The rain had stopped, and the overcast appeared to be lifting. She saw no one except Mrs. Palmer, so she drew on her filthy clothing and helped her cook breakfast at the hearth, even though she felt more like crawling back up into the loft and sleeping.

The lady handed her a crock of butter and a plate heaped with flapjacks. "Weather's clearing today. We'll be able to launder. I'll help you with that bath you were wanting last night."

Helen sneaked a flapjack before slathering the rest with butter. "I thank you for your hospitality and courage last night, but for your family's protection, we must leave today."

"Mmm. Here's cane syrup to go with those flapjacks. For *your* protection, you'll have to stay with us a few days. We heard Tarleton and his cavalry safely forded the Broad River late yesterday, but rebels are still searching the area. You don't want to become their prisoner."

Helen tried to count days in her head, assess whether she had time to reach Camden before the Pearsons left. Reuniting with them was critical. "I must meet friends in Camden before the ninth of February so they can escort me home. And I'm worried about another friend. I lost him in a skirmish yesterday. I suspect he may be trying to reach Camden also —"

"Look here, honey." Mrs. Palmer gestured with her spatula. "You can't go off roaming the countryside. It's too dangerous. Let the rebels quit strutting their victory. We'll find a way to get you to Camden. We aren't the only safe house in these parts. Maybe your friend found his way to one of the others, and folks are telling him what I'm telling you. Relax. Rest. Eat." She wrinkled her nose. "Bathe."

Despite concern over Jonathan, the corners of Helen's mouth crept upward. She had to admit that she stank. "You'll have to tie down Mr. Neville to get his cooperation."

"Hah." The other woman turned to the hearth and stirred bacon sizzling in the skillet. "Too late. He left out of here before dawn on the same horse he rode in on yesterday."

Shock and anger belted through Helen, and she gave herself a mental kick. She should have realized that Neville would steal a horse and hasten back to the business of spying. Then acceptance settled over her. Good riddance to Neville. Good riddance to Prescott's gelding, too, reminder of her recent nightmare.

Mrs. Palmer extended a plate of greasy, sizzling bacon. "What's in that desk of yours?"

Helen set the bacon on the table. "It's a story."

"So you're a writer."

She squared her shoulders. "I'm a journalist."

Keen perception filtered through the other woman's expression. "If what happened up there at the Cowpens is your story, seems to me you need time to finish it."

★★★

Helen's lips crooked slyly, and she slid the last page of her story about the Legion atop the other papers of her journal before closing them into the desk. Rebels would be appalled and outraged when they read Tarleton's final moments with his civilians, just before he and his dragoons rode off: "We may have lost the Cowpens, but we aren't beaten. We shall never suffer the rebel curs to count their victories. We are the might of His Majesty! God save the king!" Uncowed, cocky, and lethal as ever — and after a supposed defeat. With elevated fear and loathing, the cry of "Tarleton's Quarter!" would spread faster than lice in summer among the rank and file. Children of rebels would be terrified to sleep lest the demon in green lurking beneath their beds rise in the middle of the night and slay them. Will St. James might even print another broadside in the colonel's honor.

She envisioned Tarleton reading the account of the defense of the baggage train and setting the magazine aside, puzzled. It was, after all, what he desired: to be a source of terror in every rebel household and a source of grim pride among the Loyalists. But, how odd, had he spoken those exact words?

Everyone, she decided, would get just what he or she needed from the feature on the Legion. And as for the story about the courage of civilian followers, she could already hear hot debate in taverns and coffeehouses.

The apothecary slipped in through the front door and closed night without for a moment. "Ready to leave, madam?"

Two days of sleeping with squirmy children had more than readied her to leave. "Yes, Mr. Palmer." She fastened her cloak.

"Luck to you, honey," said his wife. Helen curtsied to her, picked up the bag with her desk, and followed the man out.

Inside the stable, doors closed, Palmer's eldest son uncovered a lantern, enabling Helen to secure her desk upon the remaining gelding, now her packhorse and roped behind Calliope. She scratched the base of the mare's ears. "What a pleasure to ride *you*."

Palmer led their horses for the exit and paused. "Here's our plan again, madam. Five miles to cover before we reach Abbott's house. Loyalists from two other safe houses will meet us there. Mr. Abbott will guide you across the Pacolet River to the Cherokee road. Then you're on your own."

"Thank you for everything, sir." They shook hands. "God save the King." The apothecary's son covered the light and opened doors.

Palmer guided her south-southeast over rolling meadows and through pine copses. As much as possible, they kept the horses to a trot. In the bitter, breezy night, clouds sallied past the waning crescent moon. Cold stripped the breath from Helen and hurt her teeth.

Her menses had arrived a full week late and gifted her with backache. She'd greeted its arrival with a peculiar blend of disappointment and relief. During her ride to Mr. Abbott's house, however, she glimpsed the wisdom of the universe and allowed herself to accept what was. Pregnancy would have heaped a multitude of complications upon her life.

In Abbott's barn an hour later, she met two Loyalists who'd found their way there from the baggage train. While they waited for arrivals from the other safe houses, she learned that both men were headed to the homes of relatives in Camden. Both swore to help reunite her with the Pearsons after they reached the town.

Axle squeak and snorts from horses announced an arrival. The two men cracked open the barn door for a look. Her pulse jumpy, Helen peeked out at a wagon, six men aboard. Abbott slipped from his house to greet the driver, his tone friendly. When he aimed the passengers for the barn, the men with Helen opened the barn door in silent welcome, and she relaxed a bit.

One refugee received a bundle of clothing from Abbott, and as he drew nearer, Helen realized he was a uniformed dragoon from the Seventeenth Light. Those first seconds, her breath froze at his stature, so similar to Fairfax's by moonlight, and her brain fumbled with escape actions — mount Calliope, kick her into a gallop, and fly past everyone. But as the arrivals neared them and she discerned more of his features, she leaned against the barn door and heaved a sigh of relief. Not Fairfax, but a cavalryman unhorsed, his saber lost, his life endangered.

"Helen?"

A cloud had blocked the moon. Her stare pegged on another refugee. He dislodged himself from the others and trotted ahead for her. Her heart leaped a mile, and she sprang for him, ecstasy unleashed and singing in her blood-stream. She needed no moonlight to know him.

Jonathan caught her up in his arms, and a moan of union soared from them. "Hsssst!" said an irate voice from the barn. "Get in here and quiet down!"

Inside, Calliope snorted a greeting for Jonathan, who roughed her neck with affection before he drew Helen away from the nervous men at the door. They embraced again. He kissed her with the searching tenderness of a first love, his lips tasting tears at the corners of her eyes. Forehead to forehead, they swayed. He whispered, "I lost you in the skirmish. When I searched, you and Calliope had gone. I presumed you'd fled south ahead of me."

"Let's discuss details later. What matters is that we're uninjured, and we've found each other."

"Yes." He paused. "But your story about the Legion —?"

"I finished it last night in Palmer's safe house." She laughed softly. "I shall sell it to the rebels."

For a second, he stiffened. Then he whooped with laughter, and she joined him to the consternation of those holed up in the barn with them. "For god's sake," snapped another man, "keep it down, or Pickens's lackeys will be all over us."

They subsided. Jonathan pecked her nose. "Ah, Helen, the rebels deserve that story, and you deserve their money. I take it you'll write publishers before we leave Camden?"

"Exactly, and — well, there's a matter I must investigate in Boston, too. I've heard that Agatha Chiswell left me land up there."

"Good heavens." Intrigue and amusement laced his tone. "I smell another adventure."

She peered up at him in the darkness, suddenly shy. "*This* adventure turned out to be far more than you ever bargained for. I don't blame you if you want to rest. I'm sure Enid will be delighted to accompany me in your stead."

"Hah. The former Helen Grey descends upon the Chiswells of Boston for the second time in the century." He groped for her hand, raised it to kiss her wrist, and sighed with merriment. "My dear, I wouldn't miss that party for anything in the world."

Chapter Sixty-Three

MORE THAN A week after the Battle of the Cowpens, Helen and Jonathan arrived at a modest inn near the Camden courthouse and were reunited with the Pearsons, who awaited them there. Hannah was much improved from having a roof over her head and rest, and she, Roger, and Helen wept at the reunion.

Helen learned that Cornwallis had ordered his army north after General Greene. Camden's residents expressed a palpable apprehension at the departure of several thousand British troops from South Carolina. What army would occupy the void next?

The trickle of battle refugees into town didn't ease any nerves, especially when refugees brought tales of atrocities committed by Morgan's men. One fellow visited taverns with a horrific tale of finding three bodies in a wood: a young girl, shot to death, and two men, bound and tortured. Those rebels, he insisted, were demons.

His story drew a shudder from Helen. If she'd been more dexterous with the knife, there'd have been a fourth body in that wood. Fairfax had left the site of his recreation alive. Regardless of whether he'd become Morgan's prisoner or rejoined Crown forces, she mustn't linger in Camden, where he had informants.

Jonathan made the acquaintance of a scholar who prepared to leave town with his party, bound for Cross Creek, North Carolina through the Cheraws — a northeast route that veered away from any impending conflict between Cornwallis and Greene. From Cross Creek, Wilmington was but a few days' travel southeast. The gentleman was delighted at the prospect of Jonathan's company on the road. Helen dashed off letters to rebel publishers.

Shortly after dawn on the twenty-ninth, while Jonathan and Roger readied horses and wagon outside the inn, she passed more letters to the inn's proprietor. "Glad to send this batch off for you with the ten o'clock post." Mr. Booten winked. "What a great day for your departure. No rain in sight, and not too cold."

She transferred her basket to Hannah and counted out postage money. Jonathan hadn't disclosed how much he'd tipped Booten for services such as delivering breakfast in bed, but the fellow did look disappointed that they hadn't stayed longer.

He handed her a sealed note. "This arrived by special courier."

Mystified, she studied the address: *Helen Chiswell, Booten's Inn, Camden, South Carolina.* Who knew she was in Camden?

"And just before you came downstairs, a gentleman inquired after you. I told him you and your party were leaving today."

Fear pumped her blood. Damnation, Fairfax had tracked her to Camden. "What did he look like? Mid-twenties? Reddish hair?"

"Closer to thirty, I'd say, dark-haired and well-dressed."

She eased out relief. That didn't sound like Fairfax.

"He asked to wait in the common room. I wasn't sure whether you wanted a visitor. You want me to get rid of him?"

Curious now, she looked toward the common room, its doors ajar. Dark-haired. Was the mystery man Neville? Likely not. Booten had said *well-dressed.* "Please do attend me."

He led the way, and she followed, the unopened note in her hand, Hannah behind. Booten pushed the doors of the common room open further. Chair legs scraped the wooden floor, and David St. James rose from a seat near the fireplace. Relief, wonder, regret, and sadness twined together within Helen's heart. Stone-faced, he bowed to her. She said to Hannah and Booten, "A friend. Wait for me outside, please."

Out of courtesy, Booten had lit a fire. New tongues of flame quested among logs in the fireplace, adding light to the room but no heat yet. Helen and David regarded each other across the ten feet and eleven years that separated them, and he said, "I couldn't just leave matters the way we left them that night at Daniel's Plantation, but I wasn't sure whether you'd see me again." His jaw clenched. "One last time, that is. I'll seek out my sister and niece now."

A lump built in her throat. Was she so sure she didn't love him?

He held up his hand to stop her from speaking. "I should have spared you what you went through in your tent after I left. Yes, I heard you weep. And spared you this moment, too. I've been a selfish cad, enjoying you for short, stolen seasons but ever too much of a boy to accept the responsibility of a life-time commitment."

"No, I'm at fault here. I selfishly kept you in orbit around me."

He waved his hands to dispel her words. "I've known all along that Jonathan's the fellow for you. Perhaps if I'd cleared out years ago, you might have recognized it sooner, and this — this disaster, this peril to your life might never have happened."

"Now, see here. It was my decision to follow the Legion."

"Yes, but I had a hand in it. Are you headed back to Wilmington now? Good. Please, stay out of harm's way. If there's anything I can do for you, a last favor, I'd be glad to help."

She was on the verge of shaking her head in negation when a wild idea hit her. David would probably think her daft to suggest it, but she didn't care.

"Does your father have access to a press?"

He stared hard at her a few seconds, as if he'd expected a different request. Then he skittered his gaze away in affirmation.

"I knew it." She lowered her voice. "And you also know how to find him?" His gaze shied off in the opposite direction, and she stamped her foot. "I've a story to sell a lucky rebel publisher. The eyewitness account of Banastre Tarleton's defeat at the hands of Daniel Morgan. Tell your father that. You know where to find *me*."

He gaped. "Helen, you dare not publish that story. The redcoats would jail you for sedition. Besides, no woman journalist has ever followed the Legion — or any unit, for that matter. No one would believe it."

"Correct. Therefore, the author's name shall be Henry Clancy, not Helen Chiswell." She almost laughed aloud at the play on initials, as well as her own joke.

"Henry Clancy — Lord Ratchingham?" Some of the disapproval left his expression, replaced with a glint of humor in his eye.

"Yes. Does the thought amuse you?"

"In a black sort of way. Ratchingham, speaking from the grave."

"Then you'll ask your father?" At his nod of approval, she laughed, short. "Don't take too long. Mr. Clancy has posted query letters to other rebel publishers. One of them is bound to bite."

His sudden playful smile took her back to a summer night when they'd danced beneath the stars at one of Governor Martin's parties. Again she wondered if she'd never loved him. Then she realized that although he was no longer as impulsive as he'd been the summer of 1770, he'd pegged the problem himself. *Ever too much of a boy.*

His smile faded. He bowed. "Godspeed back home, Helen."

"A safe journey for you as well." She curtsied.

He walked from the room, to her relief without expecting an embrace, and left the doors open behind him. She remained rooted a moment, listened to the quiet, and watched dust motes dance upon early morning sunlight. A tear slid down her cheek. When she blotted it, she spied the note, still in her hand. *Helen Chiswell, Booten's Inn, Camden, South Carolina.*

As she broke the seal, a dark earthy scent lunged for her. On a base level, she recoiled. Her eyes widened over the scripted message: *Divine sister, for the Moment, I'm indisposed in Service to Cornwallis, but rest assured that I shall find a Way to express my Gratitude over your Gift. D.*

Dread clenched her hand, crumpling the note, and she flung it into the fire. Then she swept from the room to rejoin her party. Long past time to be leaving Camden — and its network of informants.

Finis

Historical Afterword

History texts and fiction minimize the importance of the southern colonies during the American War of Independence. Many scholars now believe that more Revolutionary War battles were fought in South Carolina than in any other colony, even New York. Of the wars North Americans have fought, the death toll from this war exceeds all except the Civil War in terms of percentage of the population. And yet our "revolution" was but one conflict in a ravenous world war.

The Battle of Cowpens occurred on 17 January 1781 in South Carolina. Brigadier General Daniel Morgan's army was at a disadvantage for battle training, and British Lt. Colonel Banastre Tarleton caught Morgan in retreat. However, the price for cornering Morgan was that Tarleton and his seasoned soldiers suffered sleep deprivation, exhaustion, hunger, and winter weather extremes. Almost immediately after Crown forces engaged Morgan's army, battle fatigue and panic set in, resulting in a swift, shocking victory for Morgan. The British Army never recovered from the collapse and loss of Tarleton's infantry at Cowpens.

A controversial figure from the Southern Theater of the war, Banastre Tarleton was one of Lord Cornwallis's subordinates and commanded Loyalists in the mobile British Legion. The "villain" mythology shrouding Tarleton is difficult to pierce, sustained by a body of folklore created about him for decades after he left America, perpetuated even in modern times through such vehicles as the evil Colonel Tavington in "The Patriot." For certain, he practiced the Total War Cornwallis was reluctant to administer himself. Although Tarleton was undeniably intimidating, ruthless, and hotheaded as well as a gambler, a drinker, and a ladies' man, his counterparts among the Patriots, such as Henry ("Light Horse Harry") Lee, were no less intimidating and ruthless. For the war in the South was a *civil* war, fueled by hatred. Certain incidents attributed to Tarleton — for example, disinterring corpses and butchering pregnant women — simply don't fit with his personality and are more the realm of horror fiction and sensationalism. Reliable evidence for his having committed these sorts of acts doesn't exist.

The impact of women during the American War, especially those on the frontier, has been minimized. Women during this time enjoyed freedoms denied them the previous two centuries and the following century. They educated themselves and ran businesses and plantations. They worked the fields and hunted. They defended their homes. They ministered their folk religion at gatherings. They fought on the battlefield. Although unable to vote, women did just about everything men did.

Although the term "camp follower" did not come into use until the early 19th century, civilians have followed armies throughout history. Contrary to popular belief, most camp followers during the War of Independence were not prostitutes. They were contractors, merchants, sutlers, and craftsmen, and the slaves, servants, friends, and kinfolk of soldiers. Women and children followed an army to preserve the fragile family unit, but they also derived protection from the army. When a man enlisted, those of his family who remained at home risked death or abuse from vindictive parties on the other side of the fence.

War correspondents as we know them today didn't exist during the American War. A journalist's motivation for following an army was almost always to report on the army as a good investment for political entities such as the Spanish government that had a stake in the outcome of the conflict. Women operated printing presses, contributed society news to papers and magazines, and were involved in other aspects of printing in 1781, but not until the following century did they find solid, professional ground as journalists.

Selected Bibliography

Dozens of websites, interviews with subject-matter experts, the following books and more:

Babits, Lawrence E. *A Devil of a Whipping: The Battle of Cowpens.* Chapel Hill, North Carolina: The University of North Carolina Press, 1998.

Barefoot, Daniel W. *Touring South Carolina's Revolutionary War Sites.* Winston-Salem, North Carolina: John F. Blair Publisher, 1999.

Bass, Robert D. *The Green Dragoon.* Columbia, South Carolina: Sandlapper Press, Inc., 1973.

Boatner, Mark M. III. *Encyclopedia of the American Revolution.* Mechanicsburg, Pennsylvania: Stackpole Books, 1994.

Butler, Lindley S. *North Carolina and the Coming of the Revolution, 1763-1776.* Zebulon, North Carolina: Theo. Davis Sons, Inc., 1976.

Butler, Lindley S. and Alan D. Watson, eds. *The North Carolina Experience.* Chapel Hill, North Carolina: The University of North Carolina Press, 1984.

Gilgun, Beth. *Tidings from the Eighteenth Century.* Texarkana, Texas: Scurlock Publishing Co., Inc., 1993.

Mayer, Holly A. *Belonging to the Army: Camp Followers and Community During the American Revolution.* Columbia, South Carolina: University of South Carolina Press, 1996.

Morrill, Dan L. *Southern Campaigns of the American Revolution.* Mount Pleasant, South Carolina: The Nautical & Aviation Publishing Company of America, Inc., 1993.

Peckham, Howard H. *The Toll of Independence: Engagements and Battle Casualties of the American Revolution.* Chicago: The University of Chicago Press, 1974.

Scotti, Anthony J. *Brutal Virtue: the Myth and Reality of Banastre Tarleton.* Bowie, Maryland: Heritage Books, Inc., 2002.

Schaw, Janet. *Journal of a Lady of Quality: Being the Narrative of a Journey from Scotland to the West Indies, North Carolina, and Portugal in the Years 1774 to 1776.* eds. Evangeline W. Andrews and Charles M. Andrews. New Haven: Yale University Press, 1921.

Tunis, Edwin. *Colonial Craftsmen and the Beginnings of American Industry.* Baltimore: The Johns Hopkins University Press, 1999.

Watson, Alan D. *Society in Colonial North Carolina.* Raleigh, North Carolina: North Carolina Division of Archives and History, 1996.

Watson, Alan D. *Wilmington, North Carolina, to 1861.* Jefferson, North Carolina: McFarland & Company, Inc., Publishers, 2003.

Watson, Alan D. *Wilmington: Port of North Carolina.* Columbia, South Carolina: University of South Carolina Press, 1992.

Regulated for Murder

A Michael Stoddard
American Revolution Thriller

by Suzanne Adair

For ten years, an execution hid murder. Then Michael Stoddard came to town.

Bearing a dispatch from his commander in coastal Wilmington, North Carolina, redcoat Lieutenant Michael Stoddard arrives in Hillsborough in February 1781 in civilian garb. He expects to hand a letter to a courier working for Lord Cornwallis, then ride back to Wilmington the next day. Instead, Michael is greeted by the courier's freshly murdered corpse, a chilling trail of clues leading back to an execution ten years earlier, and a sheriff with a fondness for framing innocents—and plans to deliver Michael up to his nemesis, a psychopathic British officer.

Please turn the page to follow Lieutenant Michael Stoddard's journey as an investigator in Book 1 of an exciting new series.

Chapter One

A MESSAGE SCRIPTED on paper and tacked to the padlocked front door of the office on Second Street explained how the patriot had come to miss his own arrest:

Office closed due to Family Emergency.

Family emergency? Horse shit! Lieutenant Michael Stoddard hammered the door several times with his fist. No one answered. He moved to the nearest window and shoved the sash.

Two privates from the Eighty-Second Regiment on the porch with him pushed the other window sash. It was also latched from within. One man squinted at the note. "What does it say, sir?"

Michael peered between gaps in curtains. Nothing moved in the office. Breath hissed from him. "It says that the macaroni who conducted business here sold two clients the same piece of property and skipped town with their money under pretense of family emergency."

"A lout like that wants arresting." The other soldier's grin revealed a chipped front tooth.

"Indeed. Wait here, both of you." Michael pivoted. His boot heels tapped down the steps.

Afternoon overcast the hue of a saber blade released icy sprinkle on him. He ignored it. Ignored Wilmington's ubiquitous reek of fish, wood smoke, and tar, too, and trotted through the side yard. At the rear of the wooden building, two additional soldiers came to attention at the sight of him. The red wool of their uniform coats blazed like beacons in the winter-drab of the back yard.

He yanked on the back door and found it secured from the inside, rather than by padlock. The young privates had no luck opening a window. Michael looked inside, where curtains hadn't quite covered a pane, and confirmed the stillness of the building's interior.

A plume of white fog exited his mouth. He straightened. Ever since Horatio Bowater had grudgingly dropped assault charges against Michael and his assistant days earlier, Major Craig had bided his time and waited for the land agent to supply him with an excuse to take another rebel into custody. A disreputable business transaction presented the ideal pretext for arrest.

And when James Henry Craig ordered someone arrested, it had damn well better happen.

Michael squared his shoulders. By god, he'd nab that bugger, throw his dandy arse in the stockade, where the premium on real estate that past week had risen in direct proportion to the number of guests incarcerated.

Surely Bowater had left evidence in his office. Business records or a schedule. Without facing his men, Michael regarded the back door anew, attention drawn to the crack between door and jamb. "The men sent to Mr. Bowater's residence should be reporting shortly. However, I suspect our subject has departed town." He half-turned toward his soldiers. "Henshaw."

"Sir."

"Fetch a locksmith from the garrison, quickly. Tell him we've a padlock on the front door."

"Sir." Henshaw jogged for the dirt street, the clank of his musket and cartridge box fading.

The other soldier, Ferguson, remained quiet, awaiting orders. A wind gust buffeted them. Glacial sprinkle spattered Michael's cheek. Another gust sucked at his narrow-brimmed hat. He jammed it back atop his dark hair. He and the men would be drenched if they didn't complete their duties soon and seek shelter.

He shrugged off February's breach beneath his neck stock and ran fingertips along the door crack. The wood was warped enough to reveal the metal bolt of the interior lock. He wedged the blade of his knife into the crack and prodded the bolt with the tip. Wood groaned and squeaked. Splinters shaved from the jamb. In another second, he felt the bolt tremble. He coaxed it, one sixteenth of an inch at a time, from its keeper until he found the edge and retracted the bolt.

He jiggled the door by its handle and felt it quiver. At the edge of his senses, he registered an odd, soft groan from inside, somewhere above the door.

But the warmth of enthusiasm buoyed him past it. There was no bar across the door on the inside. The latch was free.

Satisfaction peeled his lips from his teeth. Horatio Bowater was such a careless fool. Had the agent replaced the door and jamb with fresh wood, an officer of His Majesty would never have been able to break in like a common thief.

He stepped back from his handiwork and sheathed his knife. Ferguson moved forward, enthusiastic. Michael's memory played that weird impression again, almost like the grate of metal upon metal. Careless fool indeed, whispered his battlefield instincts. He snagged Ferguson's upper arm. "Wait." He wiggled the latch again. Skin on the back of his neck shivered. Something was odd here. "Kick that door open first, lad."

Ferguson slammed the sole of his shoe against the door. Then he and Michael sprang back from a crashing cascade of scrap metal that clattered over the entrance and onto the floor and step.

When the dust settled and the cacophony dwindled, Michael lowered the arm he'd used to shield his face. Foot-long iron stalagmites protruded from the wood floor. Small cannonballs rolled to rest amidst scrap lumber.

The largest pile of debris teetered, shifted. Michael started, his pulse erratic as a cornered hare. With no difficulty, he imagined his crushed corpse at the bottom of the debris pile.

Bowater wasn't such a fool after all.

Ferguson toed an iron skillet aside. His foot trembled. "Thank you, sir," he whispered.

Words hung up in Michael's throat for a second, then emerged subdued. "Indeed. Don't mention it." With a curt nod, he signaled the private to proceed.

Ferguson rammed the barrel of his musket through the open doorway and waved it around, as if to spring triggers on more traps. Nothing else fell or pounced. Michael poked his head in the doorway and rotated his torso to look up.

A crude cage stretched toward the ceiling, a wooden web tangled in gloom, now clear of lethal debris spiders. Bowater hadn't cobbled together the device overnight. Perhaps he'd even demonstrated it for clientele interested in adding unique security features to homes or businesses.

Michael ordered the private on a search of the stable and kitchen building, then stepped around jagged metal and moved with stealth, alone, past the rear foyer. The rhythm of his breathing eased. He worked his way forward, alert, past an expensive walnut desk and dozens of books on shelves in the study. Past costly couches, chairs, tables, brandy in a crystal decanter, and a tea service in the parlor. He verified the chilly office vacant of people and overt traps, and he opened curtains as he went.

In the front reception area, he homed for the counter. The previous week, he'd seen the agent shove a voluminous book of records onto a lower shelf. No book awaited Michael that afternoon, hardly a surprise. Bowater was devious enough to hide it. And since the book was heavy and bulky, he'd likely left it behind in the building.

Wariness supplanted the self-satisfaction fueling Michael. A suspect conniving enough to assemble one trap as a threshold guardian could easily arm another to preside over business records. Michael advanced to the window beside the front door. When he unlatched it and slid it open, astonishment perked the expressions of the redcoats on the front porch. "I've sent for a locksmith to remove the padlock." He waved the men inside. "Assist me."

While they climbed through and closed the window, Michael's gaze swept the room and paused at the south window. Through it, the tobacco shop next door was visible. The owners of the shop kept their eyes on everything. In contrast to Bowater, Mr. and Mrs. Farrell hadn't griped about the Eighty-Second's occupation of Wilmington on the twenty-ninth of January, eight days earlier. If they'd happened to notice atypical activity in Bowater's office over the past day or so, he wagered they'd be forthcoming with information.

How he wished Private Nick Spry weren't fidgeting, restless and useless, in the infirmary, while his leg healed. But for the time, Michael must make do without his assistant. He signaled his men to the counter, where Ferguson joined them. "Lads, I think Mr. Bowater left his records book in this building. I want the entire place searched for it."

Michael's hands sketched dimensions in the air. "The book is about yea high and wide. Medium brown leather. Heavy and large. Pick any room to begin your search." He checked the time on a watch drawn from his waistcoat pocket. "Going on three o'clock." He rapped the surface of the counter with his knuckles. "Help yourselves to candles here if you need some light." He replaced his watch and turned to Ferguson to receive the private's report.

"Sir. The stable was swept clean. From the looks of it, months ago. No straw, no dung, just reins and a broken old harness hanging on the side, gathering dust. Dust in the kitchen, too. I found an old broom and bucket and some cracked bowls. That's all."

Flesh along Michael's spine pricked. "My orders, lads. If you believe you've located the records book, don't touch it. Fetch me first."

★★★

The privates dispersed to search the office. Henshaw returned with the locksmith, a slight fellow about three inches shorter than Michael. Pick in hand, the civilian contractor squatted before the padlock. Michael directed Henshaw to the tobacconist's shop to learn whether the Farrells or their apprentices had witnessed recent unusual activity associated with Bowater.

As Henshaw clanked down the front steps, the locksmith stood and brandished the freed padlock like a severed head. Michael sent him to the back door to assess how to secure it. Then he lit a candle and strode to Bowater's study. One of the privates was already inspecting books and shelves, his examination meticulous, cautious.

Moments later, the scuff of shoes in the doorway interrupted Michael's scrutiny of bills and letters he'd spread open before him on Bowater's big desk. "Sir," he heard Ferguson say, "I believe I found the records book."

Michael swiveled and spotted the bleak press of Ferguson's lips. His tone snapped at the air. "You didn't touch it, did you?"

"No, sir, not after what happened out there. I did as you ordered. Told the others to stand back."

Thank god his men weren't rash. Michael relaxed his jaw. "Good." He caught the eye of the soldier in the study with him and jutted his jaw at the door. "Let's have a look."

In the parlor, soldiers and the locksmith had withdrawn a prudent distance from where a plush rug had been rolled away and three floorboards pulled up. Michael regarded the floor, then Ferguson. "However did you find this hidden compartment?"

"The floor sounded peculiar when I walked over it, so I pulled away the rug and realized that the boards weren't quite flush with the rest of the floor."

"Excellent work." Michael knelt beside the hole in the floor and gazed into gloom.

"Here you are, sir." One of the men handed him a lit candle.

The faint glow enabled him to resolve the shape of a book lying flat about three feet down in the hole. Something lay atop it: an open, dark circle that appeared to contain a smaller, closed circle in its center. Without sunlight, he doubted that even a torch would provide him with enough illumination to identify what lay atop the book.

The gap in the floor howled at him of the cage above the back door, loaded with projectiles. Foulness wafted up from the hole. Like feces. Like death.

No way in hell was he was sticking his arm down there. He rocked back on his heels, stood, and gave the candle back to the soldier. "Ferguson, fetch the broom from the kitchen."

"Sir." He sprinted out and returned with the broom in less than a minute.

Michael inverted the broom, handle first, straight into the hole. As soon as the end of the broom made contact below, he heard a loud clap. The broom vibrated, gained weight. His arm jerked, and he tightened his grip. Men in the room recoiled.

He brought the broom up. Metal clinked, a chain rattled. Affixed to the handle, approximately where a man's wrist would have been, was a metal leg trap used by hunters to snag wolves and bobcats. Its teeth, smeared with dried dung, had almost bisected the broom handle.

A murmur of shock frosted the air. "Damnation," someone whispered.

Revulsion transfixed Michael. His stomach burned when he thought of anyone catching his wrist in the trap. Almost certainly, the victim's hand would need amputation, and the filth on the metallic jaws would encourage the spread of general infection, resulting in slow, agonizing death.

The locksmith coughed. "Mr. Stoddard, sir, I've a question of you."

Michael blinked, broom and trap still in his grasp, and pivoted to the locksmith. The wiry man held a metal chunk that he must have pried off the floor while inspecting the rear door. Hair jumped along Michael's neck when he recognized the metal as a bayonet, its tip broken off.

A muscle leaped beneath the locksmith's eye. "Who designed that trap at the back door?"

"The owner, Mr. Bowater, I presume."

"Sir, with all the valuable property in this building, there's no reason Mr. Bowater shouldn't have secured the rear as well as he did the front, except that he..." The locksmith trailed off. His lips pinched, as if to seal in disgust.

Michael leaned into his hesitation. "Except that he what?"

"Inferior workmanship, warped wood on the door. I believe Mr. Bowater intended to lure someone in with the promise of an easy entrance, then kill him horribly in a rain of debris. You've a madman on your hands." The artisan glanced over the redcoats. His empty palm circled air twice, fingers open. "Battle places its own gruesome demands on you fellows. But outside of battle, have you tried to lure a man into a trap and kill him?" He caught Michael's eye.

Michael's expression and body stilled. He held the man's gaze. Winter crawled over his scalp and down his neck. The artisan didn't know, Michael told himself. How could he know?

"You see my meaning." The locksmith raised the bayonet for emphasis. "A decent man like yourself would never set up such a snare."

End of Chapter One

Made in the USA
Lexington, KY
29 October 2014